The Haunting of Jeremiah Scrooge
The Haunting of Ebenezer Scrooge

The Haunting of Jeremiah Scrooge

The Haunting of Ebenezer Scrooge

A MAGICAL, MYSTICAL, MUSICAL CHRISTMAS MADRIGAL DINNER

IN PROSE BEING

A Complete Christmas Carol

Complete with Christmas Carols

ORIGINAL BY

CHARLES DICKENS

NOVELLAS & LYRICS

ROBERT DWIGHT

BROWN

MUSIC BY

BETTE

LUNN

LONDON

ALLONYMOUS BOOKS

ALLONYMOUS BOOKS
A Division of Chi Xi Stigma Publishing Company, LLC

Christmas Caroling Edition — ISBN 13: 978-1-931608-63-3

Copyright©2004-2023 Robert Dwight Brown

Based on the musical *The Haunting of Jeremiah & Ebenezer Scrooge*, an adaptation and expansion of Charles Dickens' *A Christmas Carol*, with book and lyrics by Robert Dwight Brown and music by Bette Lunn.

THE HAUNTING OF JEREMIAH & EBENEZER SCROOGE was first presented by the Damon Runyon Repertory Theater Company in December, 2015. It was directed by Martha Page and Jedidiah Edward Duarte, with musical direction by Bette Lunn, with orchestrations by Jim Lunn; the set design was by Bill "Bro" Setzer, the costume design by Melissa Ritter, the production stage manger was Jedidiah Edward Duarte.

The cast was as follows:

JEREMIAH Scrooge	Jeremy Nickell
EBENEZER Scrooge	Robert Dwight Brown
BOB CRATCHIT/PETITIONER	Chris Oswald
YOUNG MARLEY/MARLEY'S GHOST	Matthew Coats
LITTLE FAN	Kiara Lehermeier
FIRST SPIRIT	Kiera Roberts
SECOND SPIRIT	Tony Oswald
THIRD SPIRIT	James Page
YOUNG EBENEZER	Brenden Dewar
ELIZABETH SCROOGE	Alyssa Frazier
FRED'S NURSE/CHARWOMAN	Bryanna Dewar
FRED	Brett Hund
UNDERTAKER'S MAN	Zach Edgerton
OLD JOE	Jedidiah Edward Duarte
FUNDRAISER	Andrew VanDeGrift
MR. FIZZIWIG	Mike Reininger
TOPPER	Matt Anderson
SCROOGE'S NIECE/CAROLINE	Kimberlyn Reinhardt
CAROLINE'S HUSBAND	Chris Corey
MRS. CRATCHIT	Lacy Keyser
MARTHA CRATCHIT/FRED'S MAID	Lacey Hunter
LAUNDRESS	Kiera Roberts
CHILD EBENEZER/TINY TIM	Bernard Hund
BOY WHO HIDES	Lily Coats-Freeman
YOUNG GIRL	Keeley Miles
Adult FAN	Linda Haylett
"Ignorance" and "Want"	Fiona Freeman & Johanna Aparicio

Introduction

—**Author's Note:** As with any creative work, the inception of *The Haunting of Jeremiah and Ebenezer Scrooge* began with a strange convergence of seemingly unrelated events. Many of you may ask, where does this extended prologue to Dickens' classic work come from? In the early aughts, my best friend wanted to star in a one-man version of *A Christmas Carol* (*ala* Patrick Stewart). I was chosen by our theatre company to direct. In my research, I discovered that Charles Dickens himself performed readings of his *Christmas Carol*. He had found that even his slender volume was too long for a reading, so the author himself edited his novel into a reader's script.

During rehearsals, one line struck out at me. Little Fan visits a young Ebenezer at school and says, "Father is so much kinder than he used to be, that home's like Heaven!" One line. A single, solitary line from the entire novel put the spark of an idea into my head. "What if the Spirits of Christmas visited Ebenezer's father?" And from there was born Jeremiah Scrooge, who wasn't so kind, and Elizabeth Scrooge, the kind and warmhearted soul that helps the poor. The prologue fleshes out other characters as well. I hope Charles Dickens takes no offense at this: *A Christmas Carol: Episode 1 "The Haunting of Jeremiah Scrooge"* (my apologies to George Lucas, too).

The second event was a year or two later, I was hired to run lights and sound on a Madrigal dinner at a prestigious restaurant. I fell in love with the format. Singers sang Christmas carols, actors acted in short scenes, then another carol, another scene, then a dinner, more carols, more scenes, a dessert, more carols, and more scenes, until the night ended. I wondered if *A Christmas Carol* could be told, not as a musical, but as a Christmas madrigal dinner.

I began writing *A Christmas Carol* madrigal dinner, but Fan's line about her father continued to echo in my brain all those years later and I decided to pull a George Lucas and write a prequel to *A Christmas Carol*. I would weave Jeremiah Scrooge's haunting by the Three Spirits into and out of the story of Ebenezer's own haunting. I christened this new play/musical/madrigal: *The Hauntings of Jeremiah and Ebenezer Scrooge*. The title at first glance seems more suited for Halloween than Christmas, just as Tim Burton's *A Nightmare Before Christmas* is in itself a Halloween movie more suited to Christmas.

And as the years turned into a decade, I always desired to take my musical/madrigal and return it to its roots as prose, a Christmas carol in prose, as Dickens promoted the original novel as. But the project was far too intimidating. My musical blended in and out of the Dickensian rather well I might add, but could I accomplish the same in the larger scale of a novel? During the Christmas season of the year of our Lord two thousand-and-seventeen, I hunkered down out of the cold winter chill to achieve the no mean feat.

—Note On the Madrigal Dinner: Instead of acts and scenes, the musical version of *The Hauntings* is organized with the singing of carols and the acting of scenes. Unlike traditional Madrigal dinners, *The Hauntings* tells a unified and (mostly) linear story. During Fezziwig's own traditional madrigal celebration, while the carol "The Boar's Head Carol" is sung, dinner would be served to the audience. The play itself would pause for an "intermission" while dinner is consumed. Once dinner is finished, *The Hauntings* would continue into its second "act". During the singing of the carol "The Cratchits Wish You a Merry Christmas", dessert should be served. After a brief(er) intermission for the dessert, *The Hauntings* would then continue until the curtain.

—Note on Structure: Charles Dickens conceived of *A Christmas Carol* being a Christmas carol in prose. This was illustrated on the title page of the very first edition in 1843. He wrote a rather slim novel with five chapters, yet chose to call each of the chapters "staves", after the music term for a group of lines forming the basic recurring music for various verses within the entire structure of a song. Dickens believed in the musical quality of his prose. In my adapting, adding to, and rearranging of *A Christmas Carol* into my own composition, *The Hauntings of Jeremiah & Ebenezer Scrooge*, I sought to add to my prose novel elements of the composition of concertos and symphonies.

When characters appear in operas and musicals, there is often a "little motif" unique to the character that repeats with sometimes slight variations throughout the work. To the modern ear, the dramatic music, "The Imperial March", accompanying Darth Vader's appearances on screen throughout the *Star Wars* movies, continue to send harrowing shivers up the spines of many a Gen-Xer. The motifs in my *Haunting* include, but are certainly not limited to, repeating dialogue and descriptions by directly quoting them, paraphrasing them, or shifting their points-of-view throughout the new work. Using often the exact same words is intentional on my part. There is a familiarity to the repeating of music throughout a song and I desired to capture this familiarity in prose, a Christmas carol in prose.

In keeping with this concept, there are many movements within the larger stanzas or chapters, some prose, some authentic Christmas carols, and others are original Christmas carol or Dickensian paraphrased Christmas carols. Having been reared in my theatrical career on musicals, I am delighted to have fashioned a "musical" novel or an madrigal in prose.

To the novice of Classical music or to the outsider, the conductor of a symphony or orchestra is merely waving his hands about like a lunatic. First, the conductor is the time-keeper for musicians, but must be more than "just a time-beater" (as Wilhelm Furtwängler once sneered) Second, the conductor has a unique interpretation of the work. This at first seems strange because Mozart should sound like Mozart and Beethoven's 9th should sound like Beethoven's 9th, but each conductor brings their own personality, intensity and the "waggling [of] his fingers in character with the music". The musicians have possession of the notes, and presumably could complete the piece without the need of a conductor, but the conductor must be a leader, reigning in the individualism of the singular musicians into a collective whole. This is less a democracy and more a military action. The audience has to believe that, although they have heard the piece, perhaps dozens of times, that they hear it completely anew for the very first time. This is why the conductor is cheered, applauded, and revered.

My goal with *The Hauntings of Jeremiah & Ebenezer Scrooge* is to take a 175 year-old novella, a classic of the English language, and the inspiration for the modern Christmas season, and create something completely anew, all while keeping the Dickensian style, spirit, and speech as accurately as humanely possible. Some critics will snide that I "copy and pasted" by way through this work, but to my mind, I am a conductor, preserving the individual notes of a great composer while interpreting the piece as a whole. This is Dickens, but it is more than Dickens. This novel is Brownian. I bring my own personality, intensity, and the waggling of my own fingers on keyboard of a modern computer to the work.

> *One of the surest of tests is the way in which a poet borrows. Immature poets imitate; mature poets steal; bad poets deface what they take, and good poets make it into something better, or at least something different. The good poet welds his theft into a whole of feeling which is unique, utterly different from that from which it was torn; the bad poet throws it into something which has no cohesion. A good poet will usually borrow from authors remote in time, or alien in language, or diverse in interest.*
> —T.S. Eliot

—Note on First Person versus Third Person: One of the beautiful aspects of *A Christmas Carol* is the way Dickens breaks the "fourth wall" by occasionally speaking to the reader directly. Everywhere else in the book, he speaks in third-person omniscient, but when his Dickensian wit is at its sharpest is when he is directly communicating to the reader, which he often did during readings of his *Christmas Carol* at parties. The first Stave features a dinner party and Ebenezer asks his father, Jeremiah Scrooge, to do a recitation of the father's Haunting for all of the assembled guests, just as Charles Dickens would be repeatedly invited to read *A Christmas Carol* at similar parties. Near the tail end of writing *The Hauntings*, I got a wild hair. I decided to rewrite Jeremiah's haunting into the first person, so that he was telling the Ghost of an Idea to assembled guests at Henry and Fan Bishops' Christmas party. I loved the shift in person so much, that I decided to rewrite Ebenezer's Haunting into the first person as well. The shift helps, at least partially, to make the nearly verbatim *A Christmas Carol* a little bit more Brownian.

The second aspect of this shift into first person was inspired by Anne Rice's *Interview with The Vampire*. The novel is literally an interview between Louis, the titular vampire, and an unnamed boy. For the bulk of the novel, while Louis is reciting the story to be recorded on cassette tapes, each paragraph of his first person narration begins with a quotation mark. This is consistent throughout the work, only breaking when the narration shifts from Louis' first-person to the third person, when the boy interjects. I thought that maybe I could use this editorial technique to show how the Haunting of Jeremiah is being told to the guests of the Bishops' party. I liked it so much, that the Haunting of Ebenezer follows with the same technique.

To further this technique, I began each first person paragraph with the British inverted commas, instead of the more common (for Americans) double quotation marks. Why novels written by British authors often need to be "translated" into American English is beyond me *(cough- Philosopher's Stone-cough)*. My adaptation and expansion of the esteemed 19th century British class needed to feel both 19th centurial and British in more than just spelling.

—Note on Self-Publishing *A Christmas Carol*: One of the historical curiosities of Charles Dickens' *A Christmas Carol* was that it was, essentially, self-published. Dickens was a world-famous author of *Oliver Twist*, yet three commercial and critical flops, including his most recent novel, *Martin Chauzzlewit* made his publisher, Chapman and Hall, wary of publishing something as odd and noncommercial as a Christmas novel. Britain of 1843 was a different creature during the Christmas season than what it would become in the aftermath of the publication of *A Christmas Carol*. Christmas was seen as a minor holiday, something of a queer Catholic feast day. Dickens was able to get Chapman and Hall to publish the novella by paying the costs of publishing himself, or in today's parlance, he self-published. He also paid for an illustrator, John Leech, and its binding in rich red Moroccan leather. Dickens was being overwhelmed in debt, and the threat of debtor's prison, no doubt, hung over him like a sword of Damocles. The risk he was taking by assuming all of the costs of printing was palpable. He only had six weeks to write the book and get it to the printers in time to be published on December 19, 1843. The 6,000 copies that were printed sold out by Christmas Eve. Charles Dickens' *A Christmas Carol* not only saved the life of his most famous character Ebenezer Scrooge, but his own life as well.

—On Self-Publishing *The Hauntings of Jeremiah & Ebenezer Scrooge*:
In the early decades of the 21st century, self-publishing is rapidly evolving.
In the later half of the 1900's, self-publishing has been an albatross around
the neck of any author who dared subvert the publishing industry to publish their book themselves. Few distributors would distribute the books to
bookstores and few bookstores would put the books on their bookshelves.
Many great books were first self-published. *The Joy of Cooking* was self-published by its author Irma S. Rombauer in 1931. James Redfield sold copies
of his *The Celestine Prophecy* out of the trunk of his Honda, to the tune of
100,000 sold. Because of the advancements of printing techniques, namely
print-on-demand publishing, the availability of self-publishing has opened
a flood-gate to a new breed of independent author, one who not only writes,
but oversees the editing, cover and interior design, marketing, publicity,
etc. The popularity of eBook readers opens up an entire world-wide-web
of digital design and distribution. I have, since 2010, independently published a number of books including a Passion play in Shakespearean verse[1],
a partial Study-Bible from the Devil's point-of-view[2], an erotic adaptation
of *A Midsummer Night's Dream*[3], a "hoax" screenplay purporting to be a lost
Orson Welles' *War of the Worlds* script[4], and, most remarkably, a sequel to
the Holy Bible, the Next Testament[5]. With the publication of each book,
I thought my ship would finally come in. That fame (perhaps infamy, due
to some of the more controversial works) and fortune were assured. The
days of slaving away in my mother's basement writing, designing, and publishing each work as I finished it, would soon be over. Yet, the difficulty of
marketing and publicity would soon overwhelm me, and each work would
be abandoned to the bottomless depths of the Amazon.com catalogue and
shelved on my own bookcases. Then I would invariably turn to the next
book. Always the writer and never the marketer. I dream of escaping my
own debtor's prison, my mother's basement, due to the thousands of dollars
invested in his books with nary a sale to be seen. I devoted the 2017 Christmas season to the writing of the book and planned to devote the entirety of
2018 to the editing, publishing, marketing, publicity, release, and promo-
tion of *The Hauntings of Jeremiah & Ebenezer Scrooge* to get the book you
hold in your hands, actually, for once, in your hands. But once again, the
book rested on the shelves forgotten, until the germ of an idea to create a
"Christmas Caroling Edition" purred me to action once again -*sigh*- **again!**

---

1 *The Gospel According to Shakespeare: The Passion* (ISBN: 978-1-931608-30-5)

2 *Satan's Study Bible: The Gospel of Mark* (ISBN: 978-1-931608-25-1)

3 *Marquis de Sade's* A Midsummer Night's Wet Dream (ISBN: 978-1-931608-36-7)

4 *Orson Welles' Lost* War of the Worlds *Screenplay* (ISBN: 978-1-931608-23-7)

5 *The Holy Bible Trilogy: The Old, New & Next Testaments* (ISBN: 978-1-931608-49-7)
   The Holy Bible Trilogy: The Crusadic Testament (ISBN: 978-1-931608-50-3)

Libretto

In Novel / *Sheet Music*

Stave 1 - Intro - The Ghost of an Idea   3

Wonderful Party, Wonderful Unanimity {1813}   3

A MERRY CHRISTMAS, EBBIE (GOD SAVE YOU) {1813} 5, *98*

GOOD KING WENCESLAS {1813}   8, *102*

The Haunting of Jeremiah Scrooge

Stave 2 - The First of the Three Spirits   13

The Blessed Star {1795}   13

JOY TO THE WORLD {1795}   15, *104*

A CHRISTMAS CAROL {1795}   17, *106*

A Scrooge (To a Poor Home) Is Led {1790}   19

THE FIRST NOWELL {1790}   19, *110*

IMMACULATE WASSAIL {1790}   23, *112*

Such a Delicate Creature {1786}   25

Hath a Demon and is Mad {1775}   31

O COME O COME, EMMANUEL {1775}   33, *119*

A Solitary Child (Neglected) {1792}   38

ADESTE FIDELES {1792}   39, *121*

Robin Crusoe {1793}   40

Stave 3 - The Second of the Three Spirits   42

The Treadmill and Poor Law in Full Vigour {1795}   44

Thin Veil Between Life and Death {1795}   50

BIRTH OF A CHRISTMAS SOUL {1795}   51, *123*

THE GLORIA (THE GLORY TO GOD) {1795}   55, *128*

Stave 4 - The Last of the Spirits   62

Scrooge & Marley {1808}   62

"Linger Here Too Long" {1808}   71

THE COVENTRY CAROL {1808}   72, *130*

Stave 5 - The Last of the Spirits - Part the Second   76

Marley was Dead (To Begin With) {1836}   76

A SQUEEZING, WRENCHING, GRASPING, CLUTCHING, COVETOUS OLD SINNER {1836}   78, *131*

A MERRY CHRISTMAS (GOD SAVE YOU) {1843}   81, *135*

IN WANT OF COMMON COMFORTS {1843}   83, *139*

GOD REST YOU MERRY, GENTLEMAN {1843}   86, *141*

CORNHILL CAROL {1843}   89, *144*

A FATHER'S CHRISTMAS CAROL {1843}   91, *148*

Stave 6 - Bridge - A Ghastly Interlude   93

❧ THE BETHLEHEM HOSPITAL CAROL {1813}   94, *152*

The Haunting of Ebenezer Scrooge

Stave 1 - The Ghost of Jacob Marley   183

Stave 2 - The First of the Three Spirits - Reprise   194

❧ Ebenezer Home From School {1795}   197

❧ HOME'S LIKE HEAVEN (SUSSEX CAROL) {1795}   200, *154*

❧ FEZZIWIG'S WASSAIL {1802}   202, *156*

❧ THE BOAR'S HEAD CAROL {1802}   204, *160*

❧ A Golden Idol {1809}   206

❧ Hath a Demon and is Mad (Reprise) {1814}   208

Stave 3 - The Second of the Three Spirits - Reprise   220

❧ Where's Martha? {1843}   226

❧ THE CRATCHITS WISH YOU
     A MERRY CHRISTMAS {1843}   230, *161*

❧ SILENT NIGHT {1843}   233, *163*

❧ Comical Old Fellow {1843}   238

❧ A Drink to His Health {1843}   243

❧ Ignorance and Want {1843}   245

Stave 4 - The Last of the Spirits - Reprise   246

❧ Upon 'Change {1844}   247

❧ The Pawnbrokers {1844}   250

❧ Christmas Mourning {1844}   254

❧ How Green A Place {1844}   255

❧ SILENT NIGHT (Reprise) {1844}   257, *163*

❧ The Churchyard {1844}   259

Stave 5 - Coda - The Spirit of Christmas Cheer   261

❧ (Hark) It's Christmas Day {1843}   262

❧ HARK! THE HERALD ANGELS SING {1843}   265, *165*

❧ O COME, ALL YE FAITHFUL {1843}   269, *167*

❧ THE BEGGAR'S PETITION {1843}   270, *169*

❧ A CHRISTMAS CAROL (PRAYERS ANSWERED) {1843}   273, *171*

❧ GOD BLESS YOU MERRY, GENTLEMAN (REPRISE) {1843}   275, *176*

❧ Back At the Counting-House {1843}   275

❧ GOD BLESS US, EVERY ONE! {1852}   276, *178*

The Haunting of Jeremiah Scrooge

Stave I
"Intro - The Ghost of an Idea"

Ebenezer Scrooge, a most respectably-dressed young gentlemen, had established 'Scrooge and Marley' as a most profitable business exactly five years previous. He proved his businesses profitable by being a tight-fisted hand at the grind-stone; a squeezing, wrenching, grasping, scraping, clutching, covetous sinner, still in the prime of life! Hard and sharp as flint, from which no steel had ever struck out generous fire; secret, and self-contained, and solitary as an oyster. The cold within him had slowly begun to freeze his features, nip his pointed nose, shrivel his cheek, stiffen his gait; and make his eyes red, his thin lips blue and speak out shrewdly in his grating voice. A frosty rime was on his head, and on his eyebrows, and his wiry chin. He carried his own low temperature always about with him; he iced his office in the dogdays; and didn't thaw it one degree at Christmas.

A particular family member, now little more than a stranger cried in a cheerful voice. "A merry Christmas, Ebbie! God save you!" It was the voice of Ebenezer's sister, who came upon him so quickly that this was the first intimation he had of her approach. Nor did he

3

notice her swollen belly, hidden quite well behind his high-desk, its ledgers, and stacks of receipts.

'Bah!' said Ebenezer, 'Humbug!'

She had so heated herself with rapid walking in the fog and frost, this sister of Ebenezer, that she was all in a glow; her face was ruddy and handsome; her eyes sparkled, and her breath smoked again.

'Christmas a humbug, Ebbie!' said his sister. 'You don't mean that, I am sure.'

'I do,' said the brother. 'Merry Christmas! What right have you to be merry? What reason have you to be merry? You're poor enough.'

'Come, then,' returned the sister gaily. 'What right have you to be dismal? What reason have you to be morose? You're rich enough.'

Scrooge having no better answer ready on the spur of the moment, said 'Bah!' again; and followed it up with 'Humbug.'

'Don't be cross, Ebbie!' said the sister.

'What else can I be,' returned the brother, 'when I live in such a world of fools as this? Merry Christmas! Out upon merry Christmas! What's Christmas time to you but a time for paying bills without money; a time for finding yourself a year older, but not an hour richer; a time for balancing your books and having every item in 'em through a round dozen of months presented dead against you? If I could work my will,' said Ebenezer indignantly, 'every idiot who goes about with 'Merry Christmas' on his lips, should be boiled with his own pudding, and buried with a stake of holly through his heart. He should!'

'Ebbie!' pleaded the sister.

'Fan!' returned the brother, sternly, 'keep Christmas in your own way, and let me keep it in mine.'

'Keep it!' repeated the sister. 'But you don't keep it.'

'Let me leave it alone, then,' said the brother. 'Much good may it do you! Much good it has ever done you!'

'There are many things from which I might have derived good, by which I have not profited, I dare say,' returned the sister. 'Christmas among the rest. But I am sure I have always thought of Christmas time, when it has come round -- apart from the veneration due to its sacred name and origin, if anything belonging to it can be apart from that -- as a good time: a kind, forgiving, charitable, pleasant time:

Christmas time is the only time I know of,
In the long calendar of the year.
When men and women seem by one consent
To open their shut-up hearts without fear.

Christmas time, apart from the veneration
Due to its sacred name and origin.
Is a kind, forgiving, pleasant time,
The only time where charity is genuine.

To think of people below them as if
They are fellow-passengers to the grave.
And not another race of creatures
Bound on other journeys like a slave.

And therefore, Ebbie, though it has never
Put a scrap of gold in my pocket.
I believe that it has done me good.
And will do me good; and I say, "God bless it"

Dick Wilkins, the clerk in the tank involuntarily applauded: becoming immediately sensible of the impropriety, he poked the fire, and extinguished the last frail spark for ever.

'Let me hear another sound from you,' said the employer, 'and you'll keep your Christmas by losing your situation. You're quite a powerful speaker, miss,' he added, turning to his sister. 'I wonder you don't fall Father into Parliament.'

'Don't be angry, Ebbie. Come! Dine with us tomorrow.'

Her brother said that he would see her -- yes, indeed he did. He went the whole length of the expression, and said that he would see her in that extremity first.

Jacob Marley, sitting in his own office, at his own high-desk, tending to his own ledgers and receipts, he turned the collar of his jacket up as if to protect himself from the wintry winds of familial squabble. His own meagre fire in his own hearth was a blaze of hellfire compared to that of his partner. Neither he nor his partner walked abroad among their fellowmen, and traveled far and wide.

Mankind was not their business. The common welfare was not their business; charity, mercy, forbearance, and benevolence, were, all, not their business. The dealings of their trade are but a drop of water in the comprehensive ocean of their business. 'Scrooge and Marley' was their business. Their only business. But Scrooge and Marley both have begun to make a strong length of coil link by link, and yard by yard; they girded it on of their own free will, and of their own free will they wore it.

'But why?' cried the sister. 'Why?'

'Why did you get married?' said the brother.

'Because I fell in love.'

'Because you fell in love!' growled the brother, as if that were the only one thing in the world more ridiculous than a merry Christmas.

'Good afternoon!'

'I want nothing from you; I ask nothing of you; why cannot we be friends?'

'Good afternoon,' said the brother.

'I am sorry, with all my heart, to find you so resolute. We have never had any quarrel, to which I have been a party. But I have made the trial in homage to Christmas, and I'll keep my Christmas humour to the last. So A Merry Christmas, Ebbie!'

'Good afternoon,' said the brother.

'And A Happy New Year!'

'Good afternoon!' said the brother.

His sister left the room without an angry word, notwithstanding. She stopped at the outer door to bestow the greetings of the season on the clerk, who cold as he was, was warmer than Ebenezer; for he returned them cordially.

'There's another fellow,' muttered Ebenezer; who overheard him: 'my clerk, with fifteen shillings a week, and a wife and family, talking about a merry Christmas. I'll retire to Bedlam.'

The next day, on a Christmas day, with his counting-house untimely closed, and having docked his clerk half-a-crown for it, Ebenezer passed a particular door, an unfamiliar door, but an inviting door, a dozen times, not to be particular, before he had the courage to go up and knock. But he made a dash, and did it:

'Is your mistress at home, my dear?' said Ebenezer to the girl. Nice girl. Very.

'Yes, sir.'

'Where is she, my love?' said Ebenezer.

'She's in the dining-room, sir, along with the master-of-the-house. I'll show you up-stairs, if you please.'

'Thank you. She knows me,' said Ebenezer, with his hand already on the dining-room lock. 'I'll go in here, my dear.'

He turned it gently, and sidled his face in, round the door. They were looking at the table (which was spread out in great array); for these young housekeepers are always nervous on such points, and like to see that everything is right.

'Little Fan!' said Ebenezer.

Dear heart alive, how his brother-by-marriage started.

'Why bless my soul!' cried Little Fan, 'who's that?'

'It is I. Your brother Ebenezer. I have come to dinner. Will you let me in, Fan?'

'Let you in? Let you in?' She said and it was a mercy she didn't shake his arm off, or dislodge her child from her womb. 'Let you in!'

'My dear, I hope you'll forgive a stubborn man,' Ebenezer apologized. Then he glanced down at her amble life-giving belly. For a man of learning, a man of business, he was a dunderheaded simpleton when it came to the affairs of the fairer sex. At first blush, he thought her plump because of too many plum puddings, cheesecakes, fruit pies, curds and whey, trifles, pound cakes, gingerbreads, or apple jellies. So slowly, his eyes widened with the realization that she– his little, Little Fan– was swollen with child.

Little Fan could not not see the gaze of her brother upon her belly. She rubbed her belly like a beggar would rub a heathen Happy Fat Buddha just for a lucky wish. 'Would you like the feel the baby's kick,' Little Fan asked her brother. He would not have, if not for the compulsion of his sister's hand on his wrist. The belly was not like anything he imagined it to be. It surely wasn't like a sack of wet laundry, was it, Ebenezer? Then the baby kicked, perhaps he too knew of Ebenezer's wretched reputation; the child flinched at the touch as if his Uncle Ebenezer had seized a ruler with such energy of action that sent him fleeing in terror, burying himself up behind his mother's liver. Little Fan buckled slightly at her child's aerobatics. Then said—

'Ebbie, this is my husband, Henry— Henry Bishop. The father. My husband.'

'Scrooge, Ebenezer Scrooge. You may call me Ebenezer if you wish.'

'It would be an honour, sir.'

'Ebenezer,' he said, correcting his brother-by-marriage.

'I stand corrected. Ebenezer.'

Ebenezer knew his sister, and had in that quick moment knew his brother-by-marriage and their unborn child, and there was a miscellany of Henry's family and dear friends and mild acquaintances assembled together in their home. And Ebenezer would be at home in five minutes and nothing would be heartier, if there was any-one-thing that Little Fan dared say about it.

And their father stood up from his chair dressed in the finest vestments of a proud Anglican Parson of the Church of England, the rusty black shirt and jacket, with stark white tie, rusty black trousers, and polished black buckled shoes. So, Ebenezer thought, the doddering old man had finally done it, there was no doubt in his mind. He knew their Father had gone to seminary because he footed the bill every single penny. Father was, albeit, unaware he was picking his son's pocket the first of every month, but even Ebenezer was not yet so cold as flint as to reveal himself as his father's true benefactor. Whether Jeremiah Scrooge was at the seminary or an asylum, as long as his father was nary seen and never heard, just he himself had been instructed as a boy.

'Father has come to dine with us this Christmas Day, Ebbie. When was it you were together last?'

Ebenezer did not know the answer. It must have been many years. The bills from the seminary had either dried up due to his taking his Orders or lost in the post, either solution to the constant drain on his pocket was acceptable.

'Little Fan, I beg your pardon, but I have brought along a friend, an acquaintance, whom would too be alone on a Christmas Day.'

'Of course, but of course, Ebbie. Any friend of your's is a friend of our family's.'

'Permit me, assembled guests, to introduce you to Dr. Chattlesworth.' The good doctor was impeccably dressed for the occasion, for despite his profession was not immune to glad-tidings, comfort, and joy. He absent-mindedly fingered the object in his watch pocket.

After tea they had some music. For they were a musical family, and knew what they were about, when they sung as commanded by the Spirit of Christmas Cheer:

Good King Wenceslas looked out, on the Feast of Stephen,
When the snow lay round about, deep and crisp and even;
Brightly shone the moon that night, tho' the frost was cruel,
When a poor man came in sight, gath'ring winter fuel.

'Hither, page, and stand by me, if thou know'st it, telling,
Yonder peasant, who is he? Where and what his dwelling?'
'Sire, he lives a good league hence, underneath the mountain;
Right against the forest fence, by Saint Agnes' fountain.'

'Bring me flesh, and bring me wine, bring me pine logs hither:
Thou and I shall see him dine, when we bear them thither.'
Page and monarch, forth they went, forth they went together;
Through the rude wind's wild lament and the bitter weather.

'Sire, the night is darker now, and the wind blows stronger;
Fails my heart, I know not how; I can go no longer.'
'Mark my footsteps, good my page. Tread thou in them boldly
Thou shalt find the winter's rage freeze thy blood less coldly.'

In his master's steps he trod, where the snow lay dinted;
Heat was in the very sod which the saint had printed.
Therefore, Christian men, be sure, wealth or rank possessing,
Ye who now will bless the poor, shall yourselves find blessing.

But they didn't devote the whole evening to music. Henry inquired which games they must play: 'Shall we play at forfeits, for it is good to be children sometimes, and never better than at Christmas, when its mighty Founder was a child himself.'

This is something fair, even-handed, noble adjustment of things, that while there is infection in disease and sorrow, there is nothing in the world so irresistibly contagious as laughter and good-humour. When Little Fan's husband laughed in this way: holding his sides, rolling his head, and twisting his face into the most extravagant contortions: Ebenezer's sister, though laden with child, laughed as heartily as he. And their assembled friends being not a bit behindhand, roared out lustily.

There would, in the telling of this tale, being only one man more blest to laugh than Ebenezer's brother-by-marriage, and that man would be Little Fan's unborn child, Fred Bishop, whom resting comfortably in his mother's womb, no doubt laughed as heartily as his own father. We shall all get to know him, too, for he will be introduced in due course and we can all cultivate his acquaintance.

The shyness was his guests did not put an extinguisher cap upon the flame of his Christmas spirit, Henry continued to inquire which game should be next and with each denial, he roared with peals of laughter. Yes or no, a wild goose chase, Blind-man's bluff?

'I shall no more believe any man playing here was really blind than I believe he had eyes in his boots,' Ebenezer scowled– jesting, of course. Of course, he was jesting. Wasn't he? I will go to my grave believing it was all in jest. But the guests knew him by his ugly reputation in the district and the cold temperature he kept about him even now, with such a fire blazing in the hearth, they would be most willing to swear an oath upon the Holy Bible that his breath was still frozen, visible in the air. Little Fan laid her hands on her swollen belly in order to shield her unborn child from the frosty wintry winds blowing from Ebenezer's feeble attempt at a jest. But the flame of Christmas Spirit in her husband warmed the entire room when he suddenly burst into a fresh roar of laughter; and was so inexpressibly tickled, that he was obliged to get up off the sofa and stamp. And soon the rest caught the infectious disease and all manner of laughter prevailed: chuckling, giggling, howls, belly laughs, neighing, snickers, twitters and a sow-like snort that reddened one particularly plump particular face.

Surely, Henry inquired, there was some manner of entertainment that would please them all.

'I have a request,' Ebenezer said, shyly raising his hand as if he were still at the school in the country before Little Fan had been sent in a coach to bring him home. And he was to be a man! And a man he became. Yet, a shy and awkward man away from his books and ledgers who said, 'If I may be permitted.'

'Yes, yes!' his sister squealed with glee. 'Anything your heart desires mine desires as well.'

'Years and years ago, though Little Fan had never taken a coach to visit the school in the country-side, never once. She went in, across the hall, to a door at the back of the house. She opened it before her, and it disclosed a long, bare, melancholy room, made barer still by lines of plain deal forms and desks. She possessed no knowledge, no memory, that the room had become a little darker and more dirty. The panels had shrunk, the windows had cracked; fragments of plaster had fallen out of the ceiling, and the naked laths had been shown instead. And a little girl, much younger than the lonely boy reading near a feeble fire, came darting in, and putting her arms about my neck, and often kissing me, addressed me as her "Dear, dear brother."

' "I have come to bring you home, dear brother!"' she said, clapping her tiny hands, and bending down to laugh. "To bring you home, home, home!"

' "Home, little Fan?" I couldn't believe in own senses, were they playing cheats, she could have been an undigested bit of beef, a blot of mustard, a crumb of cheese, a fragment of an underdone potato.'

The guests at the Bishop home laughed, though uncomfortably.

' "Yes" your wonderful host said as a small girl, brimful of glee. "Home, for good and all. Home, for ever and ever. Father is so much kinder than he used to be, that home's like Heaven! He spoke so gently to me one dear night when I was going to bed, that I was not afraid to ask him once more if you might come home; and he said Yes, you should; and sent me in a coach to bring you. And you're to be a man! And are never to come back here; but first, we're to be together all the Christmas long, and have the merriest time in all the world."'

Little Fan clapped her hands at the telling of the story and laughed, and tried to touch his head; but being too short, laughed again, and stood on tiptoe to embrace him. Then she began to drag him, in her childlike eagerness, towards the centre of the room; and he, nothing loth to go, accompanied her.

'And I couldn't help exclaim as a poor boy, "You are quite a woman, little Fan!" And now she is quite the woman, isn't she?'

'Go on, Ebbie, go on! Please, Ebenezer!'

'When I got home to Father, he told the most interesting of stories. As a boy, I could not comprehend the change in our father. Once as hard and cold as flint, he now became as good a father, as good a friend, and as good a man, as the good old city knew, or any other good old city, town, or borough, in the good old world. Some people laughed to see the alteration in him, but he let them laugh, and little heeded them; for he was wise enough to know that nothing ever happened on this globe, for good, at which some people did not have their fill of laughter in the outset; and knowing that such as these would be blind anyway, he thought it quite as well that they should wrinkle up their eyes in grins, as have the malady in less attractive forms. His own heart laughed: and that was quite enough for him.

'That Christmas evening, he told us, his two wide eyed children a wondrous little ghost story of three Spirits of Christmases Past, Present, and Yet to Come haunting him, our father, Jeremiah Scrooge with phantasmical journeys through his past, his present, and his future. Father, I would like to hear the story once again, for I believe its purpose is to do me good, and as I hope to live to be another man from what I am, I am prepared to listen well, and do it with a thankful heart.'

'Lord bless me!' cried his Father, as if his breath were taken away. 'My son, are you serious?'

'Will you not tell us the ghost story, Father?'

'I shall endeavour in this Ghostly little tale,' Jeremiah said taking the centre stage, 'to raise the Ghost of an Idea, which shall not put my listeners out of humour with themselves, with each other, with the season, or with me. May it haunt this home pleasantly, and no one wish to lay it.'

Stave II
"The First of the Three Spirits"

‘ "Bah! Humbug!" I said it once. I said it often. To me, it was a warm phrase. A comforting phrase. A phrase that protected me from the cold wintry winds of Christmas glad-tidings, comfort, and joy like it was a warm woollen great-coat.

‘ "Merry Christmas, Father."

‘This was Little Fan, who had hurried into her father's bedchamber, dressed in a simple dressing gown. Her bare feet padded silently across the floor with a gaily bounce to her gate. She laid her head upon my leg. Her light brown curls were a low London fog billowing over the lap of my dressing-gown. She heeled to me like a shy little puppy.

‘ "Bah..." I said, lightly, with a little reservation, "Humbug."

‘ "But it's Christmas Eve, Father," said Fan, her child-eyes gazing up at her father, shining with the bright light of the Blessed Star, a star I failed to perceive. I never looked to the North Star for guidance on any journeys to this place or that place, nor at Orion or the Dippers in both awe and wonderment. The astrolabe was a foreign instrument to me. Yet, the learned man I was believed I may have

13

encountered the knowledge of this star in passing. Why couldn't I identity the light of this star?

'The papers and ledgers of my memory were organized and filed with an efficiency that would make any man's clerk proud. Yet, knowledge of this star was locked away in a dusty, musty trunk hidden in the dank and stank, cobweb-festooned cellar of my thick head. The Holiest of All Scriptures could not be found amongst the piles of papers nor the stacks of ledgers, nor in the trunks locked in the cellar of my memory. What was there was a book-sized hole on the shelves of the bookcases of my mind; there was also a opened-book-sized ring of dust on a high-desk; there was a pile of ash in an waste bin beside a high-desk.

'I had never once heard the joyful crack of sacred leather being opened. Surely, the son of a Parson had heard such sweet sounds since my earliest days. Surely, the Holiest of All Scriptures did not collect dust in the Scrooge home, for the surest way to dust your Bible is to open it quite regularly. No, in actuality, I had heard the crack of sacred leather with regularity, but it was not a joyful sound to me, much to the chagrin of my draconian father.

'I was no longer aware that in the days of Herod the king, behold, there came wise men from the east to Jerusalem, Saying, Where is he that is born King of the Jews? for we have seen His star in the east, and are come to worship Him. When Herod the king had heard these things, he was troubled, and then he privily called the wise men, inquiring of them diligently what time the star appeared. And he sent them to Bethlehem, for thus it is written by the prophet: And thou Bethlehem, in the land of Juda, art not the least among the princes of Juda: for out of thee shall come a Governor, that shall rule my people Israel. Herod said, Go and search diligently for the young child; and when ye have found Him, bring me word again, that I may come and worship Him also. When they had heard the king, they departed; and, lo! the Blessed Star, which the wise men saw in the east, went before them, till the Blessed Star came and stood over where the young child was. When they saw the Blessed Star, they rejoiced with exceeding great joy. And when they were come into the house, they saw the young child with Mary His mother, and fell down, and worshipped Him: and when they had opened their treasures, they presented unto Him gifts; gold, and frankincense, and myrrh.

'Nor could my daughter's quiet humming of a Christmas carol dislodge my memories as to the sacred origins of the Blessed Star dancing in her eyes. The words to this carol, sung by carollers on the corners of the streets of Cornhill and the steps of St. Paul's Cathedral, and heard on the cold wintry breezes from the slums of Devil's Acre and Whitechapel to the heights of Parliament and Westminster Abbey, was unknowable to me:

Joy to the world! The Lord is come:
Let earth receive her King!
Let every heart prepare him room,
And heaven and nature sing,
And heaven and nature sing.

Joy to the earth! the Saviour reigns:
Let men their songs employ;
While fields and floods rocks hills and plains
Repeat the sounding joy,
Repeat the sounding joy.

No more let sins and sorrows grow
Nor thorns infest the ground;
He comes to make his blessings flow
Far as the curse is found.
Far as the curse is found.

He rules the world with truth and grace,
And makes the nation prove
The glories of His righteousness,
And wonders of His love,
And wonders of His love,
And wonders, wonders of his love.

' "Bah," I said more pronounced. I wished to be busily tending to my papers piled in heaps upon my desk, not tending to the wishes and whims of a foolish little girl.

‘ "And to-morrow is Christmas Day!"

‘ "Humbug!"

‘ "And what of Brother? May I take the carriage and bring him home. It has been so long—"

'From the papers and ledgers of my memory, an illustration was dislodged and fell upon my desk. I could see myself in my horse and carriage, recognising nary a gate, nor post, nor tree; until a little market-town appeared in the distance, with its bridge, its church, and winding river. Some shaggy ponies now were seen trotting towards me with boys upon their backs, who called to other boys in country gigs and carts, driven by farmers. All these boys were in great spirits, and shouted to each other, until the broad fields were so full of merry music, that the crisp air laughed to hear it.

'I left the high-road, by a poorly-remembered lane, and soon approached a mansion of dull red brick, with a little weathercock-surmounted cupola, on the roof, and a bell hanging in it. It was a large house, but one of broken fortunes; for the spacious offices were little used, their walls were damp and mossy, their windows broken, and their gates decayed. Fowls clucked and strutted in the stables; and the coach-houses and sheds were over-run with grass. Nor was it more retentive of its ancient state, within; for entering the dreary hall, and glancing through the open doors of many rooms, I found them poorly furnished, cold, and vast. There was an earthy savour in the air, a chilly bareness in the place, which associated itself somehow with too much getting up by candle-light, and not too much to eat. I drew the carriage to a halt at a door at the back of the house. It opened before me, and disclosed a long, bare, melancholy room, made barer still by lines of plain deal forms and desks. At one of these a lonely boy was reading near a feeble fire, all the lonelier due to the season of the year.

'Not a latent echo in the house, not a squeak and scuffle from the mice behind the paneling, not a drip from the half-thawed water-spout in the dull yard behind, not a sigh among the leafless boughs of one despondent poplar, not the idle swinging of an empty store-house door, no, not a clicking in the fire, but fell upon the heart of my son with a softening influence, and gave a freer passage to my tears.

'I brushed the illustration off of my deck and from my memory. I then pushed Little Fan aside out of irritation, not anger, "Ebenezer's place is at school, not at home making himself idle with merry Christmas! Be gone foolish girl!"

' "But father?"

' "Fan—"

'I seized a ruler with such energy of action, that the girl fled so quickly her shadow for the moment forgot to flee. Fan padded down the hallway, her footfalls thunderous in the quiet dark of evening. The wind of her dressing-gown flickered the flames of the candles.

'She passed along the hallway the empty and dusty bedchamber of her brother. The hearth hungered for the satiating coal that the coal-scuttle was barren of. How the hearth yearned to breathe both flame and heat to beat back the wintry chill into a hasty retreat. The wicks of the candles were as cold as the North Pole. The bedsheets had forgotten cool spring breezes when hung upon the line in the garden. His pillow no longer recalled the warm embrace of its owner's head nor the tickle of his mop of brown hair. His chair no longer wore his jacket upon its back. How it longed to pretend once again to be a fearsome monster hiding in the shadows cast by the passing ghostly galleon of a full, full moon. This masquerading phantasm often quite frightened the young boy into burying his face into the warm and prickly down of his pillow.

'Little Fan threw open the sash of her window and gazed up upon the Blessed Star, shining through window, casting what would be called limelight upon the stage of her bedchamber. With her hands clasped, she fell onto her knees in supplication and prayed:

I pray to the Christmas Spirits Three.
Listen to this child, hear her cry.
Please visit my Father this Christmas Eve,
Without your help his love will die.

Father has forgotten what is of the Past.
Father is blind to what shall be,
Please haunt my father I pray this night,
Please haunt him on this Christmas Eve.

Aah-aah-aah-aah-aah-aah-aah-aah (sang a choir of angels)
Please visit my Father in this time of Yule,
Aah-aah-aah-aah-aah-aah-aah (sang the choir)
And bring my brother home from school.

Father has forgotten who his family is,
Father is deaf to the cries of love.
Please visit my Father this Christmas Eve,
I pray to Spirits up above.

'The Christmas Spirits Three appeared phantasmically out of the clear night walking down a staircase from the Heavens, the very light cast by the Blessed Star. Each tread they stepped on was a verse of scripture until they reached their landing before the girl and the entire Word was told with the grace of our Lord Jesus Christ be with you all, most certainly including this little girl.

'Little Fan's eyes were closed in supplication as she prayed and observed not the appearances of these three. Her eyes peaked open just enough to see two brightly lit feet float past, the lower trim of a great robe walk by, and a darkness, a shadow so dark, so very, very dark. All three forms processed three times around her. Then the shadow receded, and a hearty chuckle of a great bellied man could be heard as the strangest Chinese fire-works sparkled over her head and down about her dressing-gown. And the bright light of that strangest of candles disappeared in the very direction of her bedchamber door.

'The strange figure walked– did it, in fact, walk?– walked down the hallway and through the door into her father's bedchamber. Distracted by the extraordinary brightening of light in my bedchamber, I proceeded to snuff out one of the candles sitting upon its stick on my desk. Not only did the light in my room not diminish, it increased in its luminosity. Bewildered, I looked about and saw–

'It was a strange figure -- like a child: yet not so like a child as like an old man, viewed through some supernatural medium, which gave him the appearance of having receded from the view, and being diminished to a child's proportions. Its hair, which hung about its neck and down its back, was white as if with age; and yet the face had not a wrinkle in it, and the tenderest bloom was on the skin. The arms were very long and muscular; the hands the same, as if its hold were of uncommon strength. Its legs and feet, most delicately formed, were, like those upper members, bare. It wore a tunic of the purest white, and round its waist was bound a lustrous belt, the sheen of which was beautiful. It held a branch of fresh green holly in its hand; and, in singular contradiction of that wintry emblem, had its dress trimmed with summer flowers. Its hair was parted down the middle with the oddest little boyish cow-lick– no, it was a wick, a candle's wick– that held a flame that from the crown of its head there sprung a bright clear jet of light, by which all this was visible; and which was doubtless the occasion of its using, in its duller moments, a great extinguisher for a cap, which it now held under its arm.

' "Rise, Jeremiah Scrooge," bade the Spirit.

' "Who?–" I asked. "Who trespasses in my chamber?"

' "I am the Ghost of Christmas Past."

' "A ghost? Bah–"

' "Yes, a Humbug, quite," the Spirit said with a smirk. "Rise! And walk with me!"

' "By whose consent gives you the right to speak to me? And in my own home. Speak to me plain, or I'll call for a constable."

' "The infant Christ has heard a Child's prayer this night and a Child's prayer cannot be denied nor forgotten. It rides on the wings of the wind; from the north to the south and from the east to the west; from the beginning of time until the end. Rise! And walk with me!"

' "You are nothing but a foolish dream. I will walk with you, Dream."

'Elizabeth Scrooge was putting on her greatcoat, hat, and gloves. For the night was cold and dark and only the warmth of glad-tidings, comfort, and joy would accompany her. There was a small wooden box, adorned with holly that contained a porcelain figure of the in-fant Christ. The Spirit of Christmas Cheer put a carol upon her lips as she prepared to walk out of the door.

The First Noel, the Angels did say
Was to certain poor shepherds in fields as they lay
In fields where they lay keeping their sheep
On a cold winter's night that was so deep.

Noel, Noel, Noel, Noel
Born is the King of Israel!

They looked up and saw a star
Shining in the East beyond them far
And to the earth it gave great light
And so it continued both day and night.
Noel, Noel, Noel, Noel
Born is the King of Israel!

And by the light of that same star
Three Wise men came from country far
To seek for a King was their intent
And to follow the star wherever it went.
Noel, Noel, Noel, Noel
Born is the King of Israel!

This star drew nigh to the northwest
O'er Bethlehem it took its rest
And there it did both Pause and stay
Right o'er the place where Jesus lay.
Noel, Noel, Noel, Noel
Born is the King of Israel!

Then entered in those Wise men three
Full reverently upon their knee
And offered there in His presence
Their gold and myrrh and frankincense.
Noel, Noel, Noel, Noel
Born is the King of Israel!

Then let us all with one accord
Sing praises to our heavenly Lord
That hath made Heaven and earth of nought
And with his blood mankind has bought.
Noel, Noel, Noel, Noel
Born is the King of Israel!

' "What is this? Spirit" I asked. "A vision? A hallucination? Spirit, what affliction have you set upon my eyes to see what cannot be."

' "This is but the first step towards your reclamation."

' "Elizabeth! Not, again. I cannot permit this to happen– again." I broke from the Spirit and lept down the staircase taking the steps two at a time.

' "These are but shadows of what was!" He warned me, I did not heed him. And to himself, he said, "Poor fool, he can only repeat his mistakes."

'I seized the arm of my wife, Elizabeth, rather too forcibly.

' "Jeremiah, release my arm this instant," Elizabeth pleaded, the pain quick and quite unexpected.

' "I will not allow you your foolish fancies, Elizabeth. You will not waste your time or charity upon the paupers and the idle."

' "Lo! the Blessed Star—"

'Again with this blasted Blessed Star. What was the concerns of stars to me? Was I a Gypsy fortune teller swindling tuppance from dunderheaded fools? What were the superstitions of ancient agnostic astrologers to the modern materialistic world? Were their pagan laws debated in Parliament? I thought not.

' "—that once led the wise men now stands over the poor homes, the slums, the debtors' prisons, the hospitals, and the asylums. When I see the Blessed Star, my large heart rejoices with exceeding great joy. The Devil's Acre? Joy! Whitechapel? Joy! Marshalsea prison? Joy! Middlsex Infirmary? Joy! Bethlehem hospital? Joy!"

' "Elizabeth!"

' "Jeremiah! And when I come unto their houses, I see the aged, the sick, and the infant poor, and I worship them, opening the treasures of my heart: the common welfare, charity, mercy, forbearance, and benevolence, and mankind are my business."

' "Would you expose your frail nature to filth and disease? All of those places are foul and narrow; the shops and houses wretched; the people half-naked, drunken, slipshod, ugly. Alleys and archways, like so many cesspools, disgorged their offences of smell, and dirt, and life, upon the straggling streets; and the whole quarter reeks with crime, with filth, and misery.

' "As for the debtor's prisons? When the miserable wretches have worn out the charity of their friends, and consumed the money which he has raised from his cloths and bedding, and has eaten his last allowance of provisions, he must then grow weak from want of food, with the symptoms of a fever, and when he is no longer able to stand, if he can raise to pay the fee of the common nurse of the prison, he can obtain the liberty of being carried into the sick ward. But he can linger for a month or two, by the assistance of the afore-mentioned prison portion of provision, and then they must die. And decrease the surplus population!"

' "Jeremiah! The horrors of your words are a pain on my heart!"

' "You expose your husband, your son, and your daughter to the plagues of the poor."

' "Expose you? You are never at home. Always at Parliament; al-ways on travels. And expose Ebenezer? You sent that poor boy away to school when he was still toddling around your writing desk. And you have never once sent for him to return to his home and to his bed, on holiday or at Christmas time."

' "His place is at school not making himself–"

' "Making himself merry at Christmas? And as for little Fan? Her heart is so filled with love for her fellow man that she would gladly, with beaming smiles, join me in my labors of love and compassion. And if she or I or any man die with the love of a single life in our large hearts then ours was a life well lived."

'Elizabeth twisted her arm, releasing herself from my firm and impulsive grip.

' "I forbid you to step across the threshold of that door."

'Elizabeth turned to her husband and smiled at me with sadness.

' "I love you, Jeremiah, with all my heart. And I shall return in a few hours time. Good-bye."

'My dear sweet Elizabeth picked up her wooden box and walked out the door, leaving her husband alone in the doorway. At the street, she was met by her fellow wassail wenches, those English women who go door-to-door at Christmas carolling and calling blessings on the homes they visit. They carried wassails bowls filled with stream-ing drink.

' "Elizabeth, I forbid you to beg like a pauper for alms."

'But she was gone.

' "Elizabeth! You shame your family by offering our neighbours a cup of that slabby stuff, begging for monies! Elizabeth! Don't go," I pleaded. I then addressed the Spirit as it I were at Parliament. "By what cruel torture, Spirit, do you come before me to torment me with the Past? Her sickness came not long after, and her suffering -- watching her wasting away -- it haunts me daily."

' "It is not enough of a payment to simply bare witness to the Past," answered the Spirit. "The payment that Time demands of you— of every man, is to relive those moments whose course brought you to the Time and Place that is the Present."

' "I cannot affect change on this scene any more than an actor can change what the playwright has writ. Therefore I will repeat, Spirit: This is a cruel torture."

'And a spirit came upon the women, and not just any spirit, the Spirit of Christmas Cheer, a barrel-chested woman, with a most amble-bosom that strained her costume breast-plate to the limits of its leather strapping. Her blonde hair was pleated into two pony-tails as intricate as any Christmas Celtic knot. And upon her head sat a shining winged silver helmet. Her character, Brünnhilde, would not stand upon the German stage in Wagner's *Die Walküre* for nearly a century, thus was the confirmation of the immortal timelessness of Christmas Spirits. The soul of her spirit was that of a silent soprano, for no note ever escaped her thin lips. Yet, when she desired to sing, she opened her mouth, and took a deep breathe, and out of the mouths of others, the mortals, the men, the women, the children came her song.

'As the wassail wenches went from stoop to stoop, door to door, offering their steaming drink to each and every neighbour, they sang their wassail,

> *Wassial, wasssail, all over the town.*
> *We wassail Mary and her virgin crown.*
> *We are not paupers, who beg door to door.*
> *We are known to you, we are your neighbours.*
>
> *The first joy of Mary was the Annunciation.*
> *When an angel proclaimed "It has begun!"*

The second joy of Mary was the Visiting Angel.
A child in her womb. Joseph, she could not tell.

   Wassial, wasssail, all over the town.
   We wassail Mary and her virgin crown.
   We are not paupers, who beg door to door.
   We are known to you, we are your neighbours.

The third joy of Mary was the Nativity.
Mary gave birth to her child, full of glee..
The fourth joy of Mary was the Epiphany.
The Magi came to adore the child divinity.

   Wassial, wasssail, all over the town.
   We wassail Mary and her virgin crown.
   We are not paupers, who beg door to door.
   We are known to you, we are your neighbours.

The fifth joy of Mary was Jesus in Temple.
And astonished the rabbis by what he could tell.
The sixth joy of Mary was Jesus Resurrected.
Jesus was alive after being crucified and bled.

   Wassial, wasssail, all over the town.
   We wassail Mary and her virgin crown.
   We are not paupers, who beg door to door.
   We are known to you, we are your neighbours.

The seventh of Mary was ascending into Heaven.
Those are the joys of Mary that number seven.
We have wassailed the seven joys of Mary.
Please, a tuppence or a shilling for Charity.

   Wassial, wasssail, all over the town.
   We wassail Mary and her virgin crown.
   We are not paupers, who beg door to door.
   We are known to you, we are your neighbours.

'The screams of Elizabeth Scrooge pierced the walls of her bed-chamber as if they were as immaterial as the gossamer bed-curtains of a bridal suite and descended down the staircase like a quick moving London fog, flowing out into the night.

' "Elizabeth?" I cried out. "What insanity is this? The order of these visions you oblige me to witness are askew. Moments ago she walked out of our door to beg for alms and now? She is crying out in child-birth? "

' "You remember this scene?"

' "It was only a few Christmases before she wassailed with those wretched wenches," I said, when there was a knock upon the door, which I opened, revealing the doctor whom Elizabeth desired at her child's birth in lieu of a midwife. We were nothing if not a modern couple. The doctor proceeded up the stairs towards the bedchamber of Elizabeth, with each step became more and more immaterial until he vanished into what appeared to be an invisible shroud of fog.

'Then a hand rested on my shoulder and when I turned there stood my father, whom had come by coach upon word that his daughter-by-marriage was in labour. Instead of offering comforting words, Ezekiel Scrooge chose ones that would invariably lead to conflict between father and son, "Why did you get married?"

' "Because I fell in love," I said.

' "Because you fell in love!" growled my father. "You married so far beneath your station in life."

' "Why? Am I changed in nature; in an altered spirit; in another atmosphere of life; another Hope as its great end? Why is everything that made her love of any worth, valueless in your sight? You would that I would not seek her out and try to win her even now, Father! Our contract was an old one. It was made when we were both poor and remained content to be so, until, in good season, we improved our worldly fortune by our patient industry."

' "And now, as latterly elected to the House of Commons as Member of Parliament," Ezekiel said, "you are chided for being 'new' money, and your house, the furniture in it, the paper on the walls, the paintings on their hooks, the chandeliers from the ceiling, are beyond your means. When your debts are one day called upon, it shall be the prison for you and the workhouses for your son. You come from old money, my son; our family name and my endorsement on the pulpit alone won you election. Why live in the squalor of the poor for so long?"

' "I will not beg for alms from my own father. I may have lowered myself to the station of my wife in your eyes, but by our patient industry I have raised my worldly fortune. The contract I made with Elizabeth has been a fortuitous one."

' Ezekiel then quoted Scripture from what he held to be the Holiest, "You shall not let your cattle breed with a different kind."

' "I beg your pardon, Father. Why should I not marry for the love of a woman?"

' "Bah!"

' "Just because another idol has displaced your God, and since it can cheer and comfort you–"

' "What Idol has displaced my Lord and Saviour Jesus Christ?"

' "A golden one."

' "This is the even-handed dealing of the world!" my father said. "There is nothing on which it is so hard as poverty; and there is nothing it professes to condemn with such severity as the pursuit of wealth! Bring ye all the tithes into the storehouse, that there may be meat in mine house, and prove me now herewith, saith the LORD of hosts, if I will not open you the windows of heaven, and pour you out a blessing, that there shall not be room enough to receive it."

' "You fear the world too much," I answered, matter-of-factly. "All your other hopes have merged into the hope of being beyond the chance of its sordid reproach. I have seen your nobler aspirations fall off one by one, Father, until the master-passion, Gain, engrosses you. Have I not?"

'Ezekiel said,"If you were free to-day, to-morrow, yesterday, can even I believe that you would choose again a dowerless girl against the wishes and desires of your father?"

' "Through her have I learned a Truth like this, again and again, I can assure you that I would choose her time and time again, never by an altered life. Why should I not marry a dowerless girl -- in my very confidence with her, weigh nothing by Gain: and, choosing her, not for a moment am I false enough to my one guiding principle to do so, do I know that happiness and contentment would surely follow?"

' "Honour thy father and thy mother, as the LORD thy God hath commanded thee," Ezekiel said quoting his Holy Scriptures, "that thy days may be prolonged, and that it may go well with thee, in the land which the LORD thy God giveth thee. Children shall obey their parents in everything, for this is pleasing to the Lord."

'And I then quoted my own, "For this cause shall a man leave his father and mother, and shall be joined unto his wife, and they two shall be one flesh. This is a great mystery: but I speak concerning Christ and the church. Nevertheless let every one of you in particular so love his wife even as himself; and the wife see that she reverence her husband."

' "Bah!" Ezekiel growled, "The devil can cite Scripture for his purpose. An evil soul producing holy witness is like a villain with a smiling cheek, a goodly apple rotten at the heart."

'The continued and continuous screams of Elizabeth Scrooge harrowed my soul, knowing I could not alleviate her pain in giving birth to our child, our first-born son, Ebenezer.

'Ezekiel Scrooge offered his own ill-timed advice, "Unto the woman the LORD said, I will greatly multiply thy sorrow and thy conception; in sorrow thou shalt bring forth children; and thy desire shall be to thy husband, and he shall rule over thee. Remember a woman when she is in travail hath sorrow, because her hour is come: but as soon as she is delivered of the child, she remembereth no more the anguish, for joy that a man is born into the world."

' "How dare you quote scripture at this time," I said. "Nothing good can come from it."

' "All of the time is the correct time to quote scripture. How could I have reared such an agnostic child? This revolution into industrialization has not yet torn our fine nation from the firm and loving grip of the Church of England and our Lord and Saviour Jesus Christ."

' "What sign is there of your Christ? Why live so far in the past, Father, can you not discern the signs of the times?"

' "A wicked and adulterous generation seeketh after a sign; and there shall no sign be given unto it, but the sign of the prophet Jonas! Whereunto shall I liken this generation? It is like unto children sitting in the markets, and calling unto their fellows, And saying,

We have piped unto you, and ye have not danced; we have mourned unto you, and ye have not lamented. Be not like your agnostic brothers, a stubborn and rebellious generation; a generation that set not their heart aright, and whose spirit was not stedfast with God. You have been rebellious against the LORD from the day I knew you.

‘ "I shall comfort you whether you wish it or not, my son. It would be improper of me to do anything other than this," Ezekiel said as comfortingly as possible for a man as cold and hard as flint. And despite, or in spite of, his son's wishes, he sermonized his daughter-by-marriage's travails, "The woman, for her sin, is condemned to a state of sorrow, and of subjection; proper punishments of that sin, in which she had sought to gratify the desire of her eye, and of the flesh, and her pride. Sin brought sorrow into the world; that made the world a vale of tears. No wonder our sorrows are multiplied, when our sins are so. He shall rule over thee, is but God's command, Wives, be subject to your own husbands. If man had not sinned, he would always have ruled with wisdom and love; if the woman had not sinned, she would always have obeyed with humility and meekness. Adam laid the blame on his wife; but though it was her fault to persuade him to eat the forbidden fruit, it was his fault to hearken to her. Thus men's frivolous pleas will, in the day of God's judgment, be turned against them."

‘Ezekiel so intent on his sermon, the recollection failed to observe a nurse fetch his son up the staircase to the bedchamber. He heard not the cries of his newborn grandson, nor the torturous and tumultuous silence suddenly issued from his daughter-by-marriage. Her travails in child-birth were of no consequence to such a vainglorious man, this Man of God, as Ezekiel Scrooge– if man he be in heart,

‘ "Did travailing pains come with sin?" he continued without any concern, "We read of the travail of Christ's soul, Isa 53:11; and the pains of death he was held by, are so called, Ac 2:24. Did subjection came in with sin? Christ was made under the law, Ga 4:4. Did the curse come in with sin? Christ was made a curse for us, he died a cursed death, Ga 3:13. Did thorns come in with sin? He was crowned with thorns for us. Did sweat come in with sin? He sweat for us, as it had been great drops of blood. Did sorrow come in with sin? He was a man of sorrows; his soul was, in his agony, exceeding sorrowful. Did death come in with sin? He became obedient unto death. Thus is the plaster as wide as the wound. Blessed be God for his Son our Lord Jesus Christ," the ill-timed sermon soon faded into the unseen fog of the Past."

'The Spirit had followed me up the stairs, its own bright jet of light piercing the darkness of the forgetfulness and regretfulness of the Past. At the door to Elizabeth's bedchamber, I hesitated, unsure of how to proceed or whether I should proceed. The nurse vanished into an unseen fog in the room, while a wet-nurse stepped forth from the gloom ladening the room. She cradled a babe in swaddling clothes, crying for the milk only her amble-bosom, burdened with life-sustaining milk, could provide at that particular moment. "Where is my wife, the mother of this child?" I implored.

'The wet-nurse pointed into the gloom, without saying a word, yet her silence screamed so agonizing my soul was sent into its own silent screaming. The light issued from the Spirit illuminated the bedchamber of my wife and I was met with a ghastly sight. The floor was wet with a colour so crimson, so distressing, that I briefly could not comprehend its source. Did the rapid advancements of modern medicine require the painting of the floor with a red lacquer for the disinfection and sterilization of the bedchamber for child-birth? Then the realization of the true nature of the stain brought forth a torrent of tears. My knees buckled.

'The doctor tried to bar me from the room, but the immaterial memory could not manhandle the grief-stricken man, whom dropped on my knees beside my wife's bed, blood soaking into my dressing-gown. I cried out for my Elizabeth, whom had died in child-birth. I wept and wailed like a woman in the eyes of my father, whom now stood in the jamb of the door.

'Then the glimmer of hope began to shine into the room by the moonlight when she breathed. The breath was laboured and wet, but defiant. It was still a breathe, I reasoned seeking any denial of my wife's death. She lived! Life giving breaths issued and persisted, for at the very least that moment. My wife, the mother of my child, was alive, if but scarcely.

' "She lived," the Spirit said.

' "But she lingered on the door to Death for months as she regained her strength. She was weakened from loss of blood and the tearing of her womb."

' "She lived and she bore another child, your daughter Little Fan, quite ably."

' "She was such a lively, spirited woman, now after the birth of our son, Ebenezer, she became such a delicate creature, whom a breath might have withered."

' "But the Blessed Star that led the Wise Men to that poor abode so long ago, would lead her to poor homes, to the aged, the sick, and the infant poor. Her heart became so filled with love for her fellow man that she gladly laboured with love and compassion. And if she or any man die with the love of a single life in their large hearts then their was a life well lived," said the Spirit with the words of Elizabeth Scrooge upon his own lips.

' "Her laboured birth of our son weakened her. Her sickness came not long after shaming her family by offering our neighbours cups of that slabby stuff, begging for monies! and visiting the inmates of the poor homes, the debtors' prisons, the hospitals, and the asylums -- her suffering -- watching her waste away -- it haunts me daily."

' "And you place the weight of this blame upon the your son?"

' "His place is at school," I said, not answering the question in the slightest.

'As the words were spoken, we passed through the wall, and stood upon an open country road, with fields on either hand. The city had entirely vanished. Not a vestige of it was to be seen. The darkness and the mist had vanished with it, for it was a clear, cold, winter day, with snow upon the ground.

' "Good Heaven!" I said, clasping my hands together, as I looked about me. "I was bred in this place. I was a boy here."

'The Spirit gazed upon me mildly. Its gentle touch, though it had been light and instantaneous, appeared still present to the old man's sense of feeling. I was conscious of a thousand odours floating in the air, each one connected with a thousand thoughts, and hopes, and joys, and cares long, long, forgotten.

' "Your lip is trembling," said the Ghost. "And what is that upon your cheek?"

'I muttered, with an unusual catching in my voice, that it was a pimple; and begged the Ghost to lead me where he would.

' "You recollect the way?" inquired the Spirit.

' "Remember it!" I cried with fervour -- "I could walk it blind-fold."

' "Strange to have forgotten it for so many years," observed the Ghost. "Let us go on."

'We walked along the road, I recognised every gate, and post, and tree; until a little market-town appeared in the distance, with its bridge, its church, and winding river. Some shaggy ponies now were seen trotting towards us with boys upon their backs, who called to other boys in country gigs and carts, driven by farmers. All these boys were in great spirits, and shouted to each other, until the broad fields were so full of merry music, that the crisp air laughed to hear it.

'Where had I encountered similar visions?

'The jocund travellers came on; and as they came, I knew and named them every one. Why was I rejoiced beyond all bounds to see them? Why did my cold eye glisten, and my heart leap up as they went past? Why was I filled with gladness when I heard them give each other Merry Christmas, as they parted at cross-roads and-bye ways, for their several homes?

'We left the high-road, by a well-remembered lane, and soon approached a mansion of bright red brick, with a little weathercock-sur-mounted cupola, on the roof, and a bell hanging in it. It was a large house, blustered by great fortunes; the spacious offices were in full use, their walls were dry and clean, their windows intact and washed, and their gates latched securely. Fowls clucked and strutted in the stables; and the coach-houses and sheds were cleaned regularly and free of grass. For entering the merry hall, and glancing through the open doors of many rooms, we found them fully furnished, warm, and vast. There was an perfumed savour in the air, a warm fullness in the place, which associated itself getting too much to eat and giving too much charity. The students housed within were to be educated in the ways and means of the church and to be her Parson, so named because such a one, Sir Edward Coke once observed and he only, was said *vicem seu personam ecclesiae gerere* ("to carry out the business of the church in person"). The students were to be by their person the church, which is an invisible body, was to be represented; and he was in himself a body corporate, in order to protect and defend the rights of the church (which he personates) by a perpetual succession. This was and is the most legal, most beneficial, and most honourable title that a parish priest could then and now enjoy.

'We went, the Ghost and I, across the hall, to a door at the back of the house. It opened before us, and a terrible voice in the hall cried. "Bring down Master Scrooge's box, there!" And in the hall appeared the schoolmaster himself, who glared on Master Scrooge with a ferocious condescension, and threw him into a dreadful state of mind by shaking hands with him; shaking a boy's hands bruised and scabbed by his repeated rapping of a ruler. The headmaster then conveyed this shade of myself and my father into the veriest old well of a shivering best-parlour that ever was seen, where the maps upon the wall, and the celestial and terrestrial globes in the windows, were waxy with cold. Here he produced a decanter of curiously light wine, and a block of curiously heavy cake, and administered installments of those dainties to a father, whom had journeyed all the inconvenient distance by carriage from London to observe the punishment and expulsion of the boy, more man now than child.

'And it came to pass, Ezekiel Scrooge returned, with his son, to his parish and his congregation for it was also a Sunday. The impressive service of the Church of England was spoken—not merely read—by the grey-headed Parson Scrooge, and the responses delivered by his auditors, with an air of sincere devotion as far removed from affectation or display, as from coldness or indifference. The psalms were accompanied by a few instrumental performers, who were stationed in a small gallery extending across the church at the lower end, over the door: and the voices were led by the clerk, who, it was evident, derived no slight pride and gratification from this portion of the service. The discourse was plain, unpretending, and well adapted to the comprehension of the hearers.

' "He hath a Demon and is Mad," glared Parson Scrooge, a coarse, hard-faced man of forbidding aspect, clad in rusty black, and often bearing in his hand a small plain Bible from which he selected some passage for his text, while the hymn was being sung,

O come, O come, Emmanuel
And ransom captive Israel
That mourns in lonely exile here
Until the Son of God appear
Rejoice! Rejoice! Emmanuel
Shall come to thee, O Israel.

O come, Thou Rod of Jesse, free
Thine own from Satan's tyranny
From depths of Hell Thy people save
And give them victory o'er the grave
Rejoice! Rejoice! Emmanuel
Shall come to thee, O Israel.

O come, Thou Day-Spring, come and cheer
Our spirits by Thine advent here
Disperse the gloomy clouds of night
And death's dark shadows put to flight.
Rejoice! Rejoice! Emmanuel
Shall come to thee, O Israel.

O come, Thou Key of David, come,
And open wide our heavenly home;
Make safe the way that leads on high,
And close the path to misery.
Rejoice! Rejoice! Emmanuel
Shall come to thee, O Israel.

O come, O come, Thou Lord of might,
Who to Thy tribes, on Sinai's height,
In ancient times did'st give the Law,
In cloud, and majesty and awe.
Rejoice! Rejoice! Emmanuel
Shall come to thee, O Israel.

'When the hymn concluded, my younger self was then brought before the congregation of our father for our trial. The congregation had invariably fallen upon their knees, and were hushed into profound stillness as Parson Scrooge delivered an extempore prayer, in which he called upon the Sacred Founder of the Christian faith to bless his ministry, in terms of disgusting and impious familiarity not to be described. He began his oration in a drawling tone, and his hearers listened with silent attention. He grew warmer as he proceeded with the trial of his son.

' "His essays at the seminary preach the most ungodly heresies you have ever dared read with pious eyes. He venerates the most unholy blasphemies against our Lord and Saviour: Jesus the Christ," Parson Scrooge howled, his gesticulation became proportionately violent. He clenched his fists, beat the book upon the desk before him, and swung his arms wildly about his head. A low moaning could be heard, the women rocked their bodies to and fro, and wrung their hands; the preacher's fervour increased, the perspiration started upon his brow, his face was flushed, and he clenched his hands convulsively, as he drew a hideous and appalling picture of the horrors preparing for the wicked in a future state.

' "I offer my son the opportunity to defend himself," Parson Scrooge said.

' "Offer or demand, Father?" my young self said.

' "Demand! you agnostic wretch."

' "First, the prophet Isaiah, seven centuries before the birth of Jesus in a manger in the city of Bethlehem, prophesied, Therefore the Lord himself shall give you a sign; Behold, a virgin shall conceive, and bear a son, and shall call His name IMMANUEL, which being interpreted is, God with us. Now the birth of Jesus Christ was on this wise: When as His mother Mary was espoused to Joseph, before they came together, she was found with child of the Holy Ghost. Then Joseph her husband, being a just man, and not willing to make her a public example, was minded to put her away privily. But while he thought on these things, behold, the angel of the Lord appeared unto him in a dream, saying, Joseph, thou son of David, fear not to take unto thee Mary thy wife: for that which is conceived in her is of the Holy Ghost. And she shall bring forth a son, and thou shalt call His name JESUS: for He shall save His people from their sins.

' "But was Isaiah's prophesy truly fulfilled? I learnt my Greek at seminary. I learnt by Hebrew as well. Jesus is but the Latin form of *Iēsous*, which in turn is the rendition of the Hebrew *Yeshua*, or the name Joshua. Should not the angel of the Lord have instructed Joseph, the son of David, to name his son Immanuel? Is Matthew, also called Levi, attempting to shoe-horn Jesus of Nazareth, His historical name recorded by the Roman-Jewish historian Josephus, into Isaiah's prophecy?"

' "Blasphemy!" Parson Scrooge bemoaned. "Let us look to the circumstances under which the Son of God entered into this lower world, till we learn to despise the vain honours of this world, when compared with piety and holiness. The mystery of Christ's becoming man is to be adored, not curiously inquired into. It was so ordered that Christ should partake of our nature, yet that he should be pure from the defilement of original sin, which has been communicated to all the race of Adam. Observe, it is the thoughtful, not the unthinking, whom God will guide. God's time to come with instruction to His people, is when they are at a loss. Divine comforts most delight the soul when under the pressure of perplexed thoughts. Joseph is told that Mary should bring forth the Saviour of the world. He was to call His name Jesus, a Saviour. Yes! Jesus is the same name with Joshua. Of this my son is correct. But where he errs is Joshua means the Saviour, the Deliverer. And the reason of that name is clear, for those whom Christ saves, he saves from their sins; from the guilt of sin by the merit of His death, and from the power of sin by the Spirit of His grace. In saving them from sin, he saves them from wrath and the curse, and all misery, here and hereafter. Christ came to save His people, not in their sins, but from their sins; and so to redeem them from among men, to himself, who is separate from sinners. Joseph did as the angel of the Lord had bidden him, speedily, without delay, and cheerfully, without dispute. By applying the general rules of the written word, we should in all the steps of our lives, particularly the great turns of them, take direction from God, and we shall find this safe and comfortable."

'The congregation murmured their acquiescence in his doctrines: and a short groan, occasionally bore testimony to the moving nature of his eloquence.

' "But, Father," my younger self protested, debating scripture like a barrister, "This does not take into account the *sola scriptura*, Scripture alone, you hold so dear to your heart. A sensible modern man does not look towards the French lunatic Nostradamus, whose quatrains are vague to the extreme of ridiculousness, for the fulfilment of prophecy. The Messianic prophecies of the Old Testament are by the very nature incomprehensibly specific. Only Jesus of Nazareth, a Galilean Jew, could have fulfilled them all by the revelations of the New Testament. The foundation of Christianity depends on this truth. Demands this truth! The prophet Micah foretold, But thou, Bethlehem Ephratah, though thou be little among the thousands of Judah, yet out of thee shall he come forth unto me that is to be ruler in Israel; whose goings forth have been from of old, from everlasting. If this prophecy, also seven hundred years in the making, is fulfilled by the birth of our Lord so accurately, how could Isaiah's prophecy have been so inaccurately fulfilled. I acknowledge the name Immanuel means 'God with us' and the name Joshua means 'a saviour'. And I stipulate without controversy great is the mystery of godliness: God was manifest in the flesh. Howbeit, I will repeat, emphatically repeat, the 'name' given to our Lord and Saviour is not Immanuel, but Jesus of Nazareth."

‘ "He hath a Demon and is Mad," Parson Scrooge prayed unable to stomach the heresies. A great excitement was visible among his hearers, a scream was heard, and some young girl fell senseless on the floor. There was a momentary rustle, but it was only for a moment -- all eyes were turned towards the preacher. He paused, passed his handkerchief across his face, and looked complacently round. His voice momentarily resumed its natural tone, as with mock humility he offered up a thanksgiving for having been successful in his efforts, and having been permitted to rescue one sinner from the path of evil and the girl was removed. Then suddenly encouraged by these symptoms of approval, and working himself up to a pitch of enthusiasm amounting almost to frenzy, he continued to denounce his own son, Jeremiah Scrooge.

‘Parson Scrooge was a weak man of faith, whom withered under the breath of any challenge to his faith, accepting the teachings of his Church as a faithful, albeit blind sheep that any heretical wolf waited to consume with the agnostic bite of apostasy. Howbeit, he believed he stood having his loins girt about with truth, and having on the breastplate of righteousness; And his feet shod with the preparation of the gospel of peace; Above all, had taken the shield of faith, wherewith he shall be able to quench all the fiery darts of the wicked. And had taken the helmet of salvation, and the sword of the Spirit, which is the word of God, "Verily, I say unto you, Jeremiah, All sins shall be forgiven unto the sons of men, and blasphemies wherewith soever they shall blaspheme: But he that shall blaspheme against the Holy Ghost hath never forgiveness, but is in danger of eternal damnation."

' "Any of the great Men of Faith do not kowtow blindly," I argued, Would we have the glory of the Reformation if not for Martin Luther in Germany and Thomas Cromwell in our own? We would still be genuflecting to the Pope in Rome. I thought you wanted me to learn, not only the Holiest of the Scriptures, but to find some truth to the Word of God that can only be found in the mind of a modern man, Father. Not the ancient Church Fathers nor centuries old thought, but from the mind of a modern man with a deep sense of his great responsibility always upon him when he exercises his art, one of his most constant and most earnest endeavours has been to exhibit in all my good people some faint reflections of our great Master, and unostentatiously to lead the reader up to those teachings as the great source of all moral goodness. All my strongest illustrations drawn from the New Testament; all my social abuses are shown as departures from its spirit; all his good people are humble, charitable, faithful, and forgiving. Over and over again, I claim them in express words as disciples of the Founder of our religion; but I shall admit that to a man (or a woman) they all arise and wash their faces, and do not appear unto men to fast."

' "In their case the god of this world, Satan! has blinded the minds of the unbelievers, to keep them from seeing the light of the gospel of the glory of Christ, who is the image of God," Parson Scrooge said, parroting greater men of faith than he.

' "You, my son, shall be likened unto a foolish man, which built his house upon the sand: And the rain descended, and the floods came, and the winds blew, and beat upon that house; and it fell: and great was the fall of it. I am the wise man, which built his house upon a rock: And the rain descended, and the floods came, and the winds blew, and beat upon that house; and it fell not: for it was founded upon a rock."

' "Father, you are blind!" my younger self protested, "What difference can be found between a man buries his nose his banker's book or the man who does the same of the Good Book?" I said, "The miser may believe that every idiot who goes about with 'Merry Christmas' on his lips, should be boiled with his own pudding, and buried with a stake of holly through his heart. But my father considers Christmas a queer little Catholic feast day and yet at this festive season of the year, turns the poor away from the stoop of his parish to the miseries of the poor houses, the treadmill, the union workhouses. I believe that a laymen may yet affect more change of the spirit of Christmas than a thousand clergymen!"

' "Begone! Begone! Forever begone from my sight!" Ezekiel sank back into his seat, exhausted with the violence of his ravings."Be gone!"

'And suddenly, the Ghost and I were gone. I found myself in my horse and carriage, and drew the carriage to a halt at a door at the back of a house. It opened before me, and disclosed a long, bare, melancholy room, made barer still by lines of plain deal forms and desks. At one of these a lonely boy was reading near a feeble fire, all the lonelier due to the season of the year.

' "The school is not quite deserted," said the Ghost. "A solitary child, neglected by his friends, is left there still. Do you remember this scene."

'I said I knew it, of course I did.

'The boy held the hymnal with a veneration that would have made him a foreigner in his own family home. He looked down upon the Latin, and recited the words, not rote like his lessons, but with a reverence. His heart was lifted by the Spirit of Christmas Cheer to the highest heights of Heaven, despite the alienation of his schoolmates, his family, and his father:

Adeste fideles læti triumphantes,
Venite, venite in Bethlehem.
Natum videte
Regem angelorum:

Venite adoremus
  Venite adoremus
    Venite adoremus
    Dominum.

Deum de Deo, lumen de lumine
Gestant puellæ viscera
Deum verum, genitum non factum.
Venite adoremus
  Venite adoremus
    Venite adoremus
    Dominum.

Cantet nunc io, chorus angelorum;
Cantet nunc aula cælestium,
Gloria, gloria in excelsis Deo,
Venite adoremus
  Venite adoremus
    Venite adoremus
    Dominum.

Ergo qui natus die hodierna.
Jesu, tibi sit gloria,
Patris æterni Verbum caro factum.
Venite adoremus
  Venite adoremus
    Venite adoremus
    Dominum.

' "At the very least he has learnt his Latin. Is this not why I invest such sums into his schooling, Spirit?"

'The Ghost smiled thoughtfully, and waved its hand: saying as it did so, "Let us see another Christmas!"

'Ebenezer's younger self grew larger at the words, and the room became a little darker and more dirty. The panels shrunk, the windows cracked; fragments of plaster fell out of the ceiling, and the naked laths were shown instead; but how all this was brought about, I knew no more than you do. I only knew that it was quite correct; that everything had happened so; that there he was, alone again, when all the other boys had gone home for the jolly holidays. Any father feels that his children grow up before his very eyes, but never in the recorded history of the world has the feeling been so utterly literal.

' "Then step forward. I offer you the chance to speak again what you spoke then."

' "You offer a chance or demand one?" I said, always the politician.

' "The choice is yours."

' "What are you reading, Son?" I said stepping into the scene.

' "Father, have you come to take me home for Christmas?"

'After a pregnant pause, "Not this year, Ebenezer. I was nearby on business and I just came to–"

' "To what, Father?"

' "What are you reading there?"

'Suddenly a man, in foreign garments: wonderfully real and distinct to look at: stood outside the window, with an axe stuck in his belt, and leading by the bridle an ass laden with wood.

' "Why, it's Ali Baba!" Ebenezer exclaimed in ecstasy. "It's dear old honest Ali Baba. Yes, yes, I know. And Valentine," said Ebenezer, "and his wild brother, Orson; there they go. And what's his name, who was put down in his drawers, asleep, at the Gate of Damascus; don't you see him? And the Sultan's Groom turned upside down by the Genii; there he is upon his head. Serve him right. I'm glad of it. What business had he to be married to the Princess."

' "There's the Parrot." cried Ebenezer. "Green body and yellow tail, with a thing like a lettuce growing out of the top of his head; there he is! Poor Robin Crusoe, he called him, when he came home again after sailing round the island. 'Poor Robin Crusoe, where have you been, Robin Crusoe?' The man thought he was dreaming, but he wasn't. It was the Parrot, you know. There goes Friday, running for his life to the little creek! Halloa! Hoop! Hallo!"

'I, beside myself with genuine concern for the sanity of my child, shook young Ebenezer, "Have you eaten a bad bit of beef? Your senses are playing cheats, Son!

' "Why no, father," snapping back out of it, "This is just make-believe. I make-believe to pass the time. To keep my mind from becoming idle."

'I had become visibly shaken, but controlled. "A mind that is in its studies never becomes idle. Bah! Enough of this foolish fancy," I said pausing, "Here." I pulled a letter from my jacket pocket. "A letter from your sister."

' "She has learnt her alphabet? Why Fan, I'm so proud."

'The young Ebenezer hurried over to his small desk, opened the letter and read from it with gladsome smiles.

' "You left before he finished the letter," the Spirit observed.

' "Good-byes are a humbug. His place is at school. He has no place—"

' "In his own family's home on Christmas Day?"

' "Bah—"

' "Yes, a Humbug, quite," the Spirit said lifting his extinguisher cap from the floor beside him. "My time is at an end."

'The flame on the crown of its head, that had produced throughout our journey together the eeriest pleasant light, had melted a pool into its skull around the wick of the Spirit of Christmas Past. The wax had dripped down its strangely youthful face, streaks of wax wrinkling its face into an unmistakably elderly man. As he drew the extinguisher cap over the crown of its head, the flame rebelled against its owner and its own extinguishment, producing a light that must have rivalled nothing else in creation other than the Light called upon by God when He said, "Let there be Light!" I watched in abject horror at the suicide of the first Spirit to visit me, whom lowered the cap over the crown of its head cutting off all that fed the flame, extinguishing the Light of What Was. Now, if only I could prepare myself for What is.'

Stave III
"The Second of the Three Spirits"

'I found myself back my own bedchamber. There was no doubt about that. But it had undergone a surprising transformation. The walls and ceiling were so hung with living green, that it looked a perfect grove; from every part of which, bright gleaming berries glistened. The crisp leaves of holly, mistletoe, and ivy reflected back the light, as if so many little mirrors had been scattered there; and such a mighty blaze went roaring up the chimney, as that dull petrifaction of a hearth had never known in my time, or for many and many a winter season gone. Heaped up on the floor, to form a kind of throne, were turkeys, geese, game, poultry, brawn, great joints of meat, sucking-pigs, long wreaths of sausages, mince-pies, plum-puddings, barrels of oysters, red-hot chestnuts, cherry-cheeked apples, juicy oranges, luscious pears, immense twelfth-cakes, and seething bowls of punch, that made the chamber dim with their delicious steam. In easy state upon this couch, there sat a jolly Giant, glorious to see:, who bore a glowing torch, in shape not unlike Plenty's horn, and held it up, high up, to shed its light on me, as I came peeping through my bedcurtains.

' "Come in! Come in! And know me better, man! I am the Ghost of Christmas Present. Look upon me. Have you never seen the like of me before? Hah! Have you never walked forth with the younger members of my family?"

' "Come you from a great family, Spirit?" I inquired, genuinely.

' "Aye! There are more than seventeen hundred brothers and many, many sisters born to it! Come, walk with me. There is much to show you and very little Time."

' "The time of the last Spirit was very great and seemed to be many years."

' "His province is from Birth until the Present."

' "Whose birth?"

' "Why, your Birth, who else's? But know this, my time upon this earth, from my Birth until my Death, is but a single day."

' "One day?"

' "But what a glorious day it is! Christmas Day! Come! Come! Follow me, man!" A thick London fog rolled into my bedchamber, obscuring the feast of the Ghost of Christmas Past: red berries, ivy, turkeys, geese, game, poultry, brawn, meat, pigs, sausages, oysters, pies, puddings, fruit, and punch, so did the room, the fire, the ruddy glow, the hour of night. And as quickly the fog rolled out, revealing the House of Commons chambers. Flames burst into light from the chandelier, producing a strange ghostly glow. Snow falling from the over-laden overcast sky floated past the three large windows behind the Speaker's Chair. The Members of Parliament were seated, of course they were– why wouldn't they be otherwise?– in rows around the edge of the surprisingly small room used for such grand purposes. A disagreeable fog of discontent filled the room. Nary a Member of Parliament wished to be present in the chamber on a Christmas Day, having been forced to endure the laments of wives and children due to this absence from home all due to an obscure procedural agenda filed by an equally obscure parochial county official.

'The petitioner had been given the floor and addressed the assembled Members of Parliament, "The Poor Laws, as codified in 1597 were administered through parish overseers, who provide relief for the aged, the sick, and the infant poor, as well as for the able-bodied in the Union workhouses. To offer relief to those workers who through their hard labour and consistent work continue to receive wages below what should be considered, in modern society, a level of subsistence. Therefore, Lords, I request an amendment to the system of Poor Laws, to implement a means of providing an allowance to those workers previously mentioned and whose mention must be voiced, heard, and remembered," the petitioner to Parliament said.

'The gentlemen, Charles Dundas, Esq., the most respected representative of Berks who sat in the Chair, continued his argument to the House of Commons, "At a General Meeting of the Justices of the County of Berks, together with several discreet persons assembled by public advertisement on Wednesday the 6th Day of May, 1795, at the Pelican Inn in Speenhamland (in pursuance of an order of the last Court of General Quarter Sessions) for the purpose of rating Husbandry Wages, by the day or week, if then approved of. That the present state of the Poor does require further assistance than has been generally given them.

' "That it is not expedient for the Magistrates to grant that assistance by regulating the Wages of Day Labourers, according to the directions of the Statutes of the 5th Elizabeth and 1st James: But the Magistrates very earnestly recommend to the Farmers and others throughout the county, to increase the pay of their Labourers in proportion to the present price of provisions; and agreeable thereto, the Magistrates now present, have unanimously resolved that they will, in their several divisions, make the following calculations and allowances for relief of all poor and industrious men and their families, who to the satisfaction of the justices of their Parish, shall endeavour (as far as they can) for their own support and maintenance."

' "And what allowance is proposed?" I asked not realizing I was on a journey with a Ghost of Christmas and not in actuality at Parliament at the moment. Yet, the Spirit staid his hand. "This moment, unlike all others, of the Present world requires your presence. Step forward and take your place in it, Man!" And I stepped from that ghostly realm into our certainly more corporeal one as easily as crossing the room.

'Mr. Dundas answered, "That is to say, when the Gallon Loaf of Second Flour, Weighing 8lb. 11ozs. shall cost one shilling, then every poor and industrious man shall have for his own support three shillings weekly, either produced by his own or his family's labour, or an allowance from the poor rates, and for the support of his wife and every other of his family, one shilling sixpence. When the Gallon Loaf shall cost one shilling sixpence, then every poor and industrious man shall have four shillings weekly for his own, and one shilling and tenpence for the support of every other of his family. And so in proportion, as the price of bread rise or falls (that is to say) threepence to the man, and one penny to every other of the family, on every tenpence which the loaf rise above shilling"

' "I must contest your petition, sir. To regard pauperism among the able-bodied workers is a moral failing. There must be provided no relief for the able-bodied poor except the miseries of the workhouse, with the following object: Stimulating the workers to seek regular employment rather than charity."

' "Many cannot secure regular employment. Many are in want of common comforts and necessaries."

' "Are there no prisons?" I asked.

' "Plenty of prisons," said the gentleman.

' "And the Union workhouses?" I demanded. "Are they still in operation?"

' "They are. Still," returned the gentleman, "I wish I could say they were not."

' "The Treadmill and the Poor Law we are debating are still in full vigour, then?" I said.

' "Both very busy, sir."

' "Oh! I was afraid, from what you said at first, that something had occurred to stop them in their useful course. Those who are badly off must go to the Treadmill, to the workhouses."

' "Many can't. Many would rather die!"

' "Well, sir, if they would rather die, they had better do it, and decrease the surplus population forthright."

' "Sir, that is not a Christian sentiment! But permit me to return to the point in question—"

' "Bah!" I argued, "This Speenhamland system encourages the poor in idleness. While it might be hoped that, under such circumstances, a general feeling would have arisen that these abuses are intolerable, and must be put an end to at any risk or at any sacrifice. But many who acknowledge the evil seem to expect the cure of an inveterate disease, without exposing the patient to any suffering or even discomfort. They exclaim against the burden as intolerable. He need not bestir himself to seek work; he need not study to please his master; he need not put any restraint upon his temper; he need not ask relief as a favour. He has all a slave's security for subsistence, without his liability to punishment. As a single man, indeed, his income does not exceed a bare subsistence; but he has only to marry, and it would increase. Even then it is unequal to the support of a family; but it would rise on the birth of every child. If his family is numerous, the parish would become his principal paymaster; for, small as the usual allowance of two shillings a head may be, yet, when there are more than three children, it generally exceeds the average wages given in a pauperized district. A man with a wife and six children, entitled, according to your proposed scale, to have his wages made up to sixteen shillings a week, in a parish where the wages paid by individuals do not exceed ten shillings or twelve, is almost an irresponsible being. All the other classes of society are exposed to the vicissitudes of hope and fear; he alone has nothing to lose or to gain."

'The Ghost of Christmas Past sighed. It was a hearty, jovial sigh, but a sigh nonetheless. How he wished to be anywhere else on a Christmas Day. Why could he not be sprinkling his very uncommon kind of torch upon people who were shovelling away on the housetops chipper and full of glee? Those calling out to one another from the parapets, and now and then exchanging a facetious snowball -- better-natured missile far than many a wordy jest -- laughing heartily if it went right and not less heartily if it went wrong. Why could he not enjoy the smells of great, round, pot-bellied baskets of chestnuts, shaped like the waistcoats of jolly old gentlemen, lolling at the doors, and tumbling out into the street in their apoplectic opulence? Where were the ruddy, brown-faced, broad-girthed Spanish Friars, and winking from their shelves in wanton slyness at the girls as they went by, and glanced demurely at the hung-up mistletoe? Where were pears and apples, clustered high in blooming pyramids; where were the bunches of grapes, made, in the shopkeepers' benevolence to dangle from conspicuous hooks, that people's mouths might water gratis as they passed? Where were piles of filberts, mossy and brown, recalling, in their fragrance, ancient walks among the woods, and pleasant shufflings ankle deep through withered leave? Where were Norfolk Biffins, squab and swarthy, setting off the yellow of the oranges and lemons, and, in the great compactness of their juicy persons, urgently entreating and beseeching to be carried home in paper bags and eaten after dinner? Or the very gold and silver fish, set forth among these choice fruits in a bowl, though members of a dull and stagnant-blooded race, appeared to know that there was something going on; and, to a fish, went gasping round and round their little world in slow and passionless excitement?

'And I continued bloviating, snapping the Spirit back from his Christmas Daydream, "The employers of paupers attached to such a system would enable them to dismiss or resume their labourers according to their daily or even hourly want of them, to reduce wages to the minimum, or even below the minimum of what would support an unmarried man, and throw upon the fund the payment of a part, perhaps even the greater part, and sometimes almost the whole of the wages on the parochial funds. And even if they would pay in rates what they would otherwise pay in wages, they would, not doubt, prefer the payment of rates which recur at intervals, and the payment of which may, from time to time, be put off, to the weekly ready-money expenditure of wages. High rates, too, are a ground for demanding an abatement from rent: high wages are not."

'Where were the Grocers'! oh the Grocers'?!? The Spirit mused. Nearly closed, with perhaps two shutters down, or one; but through those gaps such glimpses. Where were scales descending on the counter making a merry sound, or that the twine and roller parted company so briskly, or that the canisters were rattled up and down like juggling tricks, or even that the blended scents of tea and coffee so grateful to the nose, or even that the raisins so plentiful and rare, the almonds so extremely white, the sticks of cinnamon so long and straight, the other spices so delicious, the candied fruits so caked and spotted with molten sugar as to make the coldest lookers-on feel faint and subsequently bilious? Where were the figs moist and pulpy, or that the French plums blushed in modest tartness from their highly-decorated boxes, or everything that was good to eat and in its Christmas dress? Where were the customers all so hurried and so eager in the hopeful promise of the day, that they tumbled up against each other at the door, clashing their wicker baskets wildly, and leaving their purchases upon the counter, and coming running back to fetch them, and committing hundreds of the like mistakes, in the best humour possible? Where were the Grocer and his people so frank and fresh that the polished hearts with which they fastened their aprons behind might have been their own, worn outside for general inspection, and for Christmas daws to peck at if they chose?

'And I continued oblivious to the consternations of the Spirit, "And the owners of rateable property would enable the proprietor to increase the rent by the amount of rate remitted, and always be the owner of real property and escape the principle burdens to which such property is subjected. This latter practice would give him a solvent tenant, and if he has influence with the vestry, or with the overseer, a liberal one. The welfare of that family naturally depends on his conduct; that he is bound to exercise any sort of prudence or economy; that anything is to be hoped from voluntary charity; are views which many of those who have long resided in pauperized districts seem to reject as too absurd for formal refutation."

'The Spirit pleaded with Christmas day itself, Where were the steeples that called good people all, to church and chapel, and away they must come, flocking through the streets in their best clothes, and with their gayest faces? And at the same time, where were the scores of bye-streets, lanes, and nameless turnings, innumerable people, carrying their dinners to the bakers' shops?

'No! Where! The Spirit was imprisoned on a glorious Christmas Day indoors– in Parliament– listening to pompous windbags pontificate, squabbling over shillings and sixpence. As if there were not more important issues for the good of mankind than Poor Laws! How he wished his very uncommon kind of torch could shed a few drops of water on these Members of Parliament from it, and their good humour would restored directly. For it has been said, it was a shame to quarrel upon Christmas Day. But these men! these men were curiously immune in any sort of Christmas cheer.

' "I cannot foresee any man or men being so covetous as to deprive the poor and destitute of common necessaries," Mr. Dundas protested. "Even in that most festive season of the year, Christmas! when it is more than usually desirable that we should make some slight provision for the Poor and Destitute, who suffer greatly at the present time. Many thousands are in want of common necessaries; hundreds of thousands are in want of common comforts." Ah-ha! The Spirit proudly sprinkled this deviant with his horn to celebrate the season and so the Christmas cheer sounded. God love it, so it sounded. "We are pleasantly under the impression that their means scarcely furnish Christian cheer of mind or body to the multitude, why should not a few of us endeavour to raise a fund to buy the Poor some meat and drink and means of warmth. We choose this time, because it is a time, of all others, when Want is keenly felt, and Abundance rejoices."

' "Why make merry yourself at Christmas?" I asked, to which Mr. Dundas had nary an answer, "Why should we permit idle people to make merry?"

'Again, Mr. Dundas had nary an answer.

' "Let us, sir, return to the point at hand this afternoon," I continued. I was well aware my fellow Members of Parliament would prefer being at home with their families at Christmas, though the superstitious reasonings escaped me. "And too frequently petty thieving, drunkenness or impertinence to a master, throw able-bodied labourers, perhaps with large families, on the parish funds, when relief is demanded as a right, and, if refused, enforced by a magistrate's order, without reference to the cause which has produced his distress, his own misconduct, which remains as a barrier to his obtaining any fresh situation, and leaves him a dead weight upon the honesty and industry of his parish."

' "Sir," Mr. Dundas said interrupting, "I must therefore on the Poor's bequest, not my own, sir, ask that Parliament vote on the petition that stands before you."

'Henry Addington, Speaker of the House, called for a vote: there sounded a Chorus of "Ayes" that came from the depths of darkness and shadow from my fellow Ministers of Parliament, that seemed to echo into eternity.

' "And you, my Lord?" the Petitioner asked with a sly smirk snaking on his lips.

'The "Nay" that escaped my lips sounded thin and hallow.

' "I regret to inform you, sir. The Speenhamland system of allowance is passed."

' "Bah...Humbug!"

'The darkness and shadows crept and clawed as a low fog enveloping me and the Spirit. Flames from the chandelier were snuffed out by an invisible extinguisher, adding to the gloom penetrating the room. And through the three large windows behind the Speaker's Chair, it seemed to an uneducated mind, at the very least, that the sun had burnt out its last.

' "Why are you so adamant against providing charity to those in need of it?" the Spirit asked.

' "Because those in need of it are slothful. The resulting expenditures on public relief will become so great that a new Poor Law will have to be enacted or the whole of the system will become bankrupt. And what then? With no Union workhouses, no Treadmill, the poor will have no other recourse available to them."

' "Except the gladsome charity of their fellowmen."

' "Bare in mind, Spirit, your province is the Present. The Future will bare witness to my good judgment."

' "In this matter, only–"

' "Where do you lead me, Spirit?"

' "To a place where you are needed. A place from which you have strayed–"

'In the Middlesex Infirmary, in one room of but many rooms in the hospital, in one row of but many rows in the room, in but one bed of but many beds in the row lay my wife, Elizabeth Scrooge. The sounds of the coughs, the wheezes, the moans, groans, and the cries of the patients who likewise lay on their death-beds disturbed me immensely. The smell of the primitive antiseptics were an assault on my humanity. If Death were some sort of spectre akin to those that had accompanied me on that Christmas evening, I possessed no doubt that such a spirit made regular appointments on the hospital, walking up and down the rows of beds quite daily.

'Elizabeth had been struck down with Consumption, or Tuberculosis, as it is now known. My most modern mind refused to paint the disease with the rose palette of the White Plague. How dare the romantics sentimentalize this horror as the *mal de vivre*? How could any death be considered a good death, a spiritually pure death, a death affording the wealthy the time to arrange their affairs? How dare the vibrant and youthful women paint their faces with this pallor in their parlours, at Christmas parties and at grand balls? This was a death reserved and deserved for the poor, those whom, unlike mongrels, could not keep their own beds clean. The Blessed Star– Blessed! indeed– led my precious Elizabeth to those districts of poor houses, where filth and disease were harvested in bushels. Where the ways are foul and narrow; the shops and houses wretched; the people half-naked, drunken, slipshod, ugly. Alleys and archways, like so many cesspools, disgorged their offenses of smell, and dirt, and life, upon the straggling streets; and the whole quarter reeked with crime, with filth, and misery. She ignored both the commands of her husband and of the public-health officials. She begged for her alms and then bought the Poor some meat and drink and means of warmth. She always choose this time of year– Bah! out upon Merry Christmas– because it is a time, of all others, when Want is keenly felt, and Abundance rejoices. She was so filled with love for her fellow man that she gladly, with beaming smiles, journeyed to the ramshackle shacks in her labours of love and compassion. And she would die with the love of far more than a single life in her large heart.

'My dear Elizabeth was thin and pale and almost near death, a commonality in that place. Her lips were rosy with blood coughed from lungs drowning in the vital fluid. The Spirit of Christmas Cheer opened her lips, and Elizabeth sang softly and with great pain,

> *On Christmas night all Christians sing,*
> *Of a Blessed Star whose light does lead*
> *Christian hearts to the Poor and Destitute.*
> *With gifts of meat 'n drink to those in need.*
>
> *For the Birth of a Christmas Soul*
> *The Blessed Star led the Magi well,*
> *Upon a lonely Manger of straw and hay*
> *Where God gave the world, Emmanuelle.*
>
> *There a Virgin by a Gift from God,*
> *Gave birth to a child by the morningtide.*

An infant child destined by Heavenly plan.
To grow into manhood and be crucified.

The Birth of this one is the same as all others,
For every Woman who lived upon this Earth.
Whether for a simple life or Son of God born,
Will gladly give up her life, for her child's birth.

Fan, my little Fan, you're such a woman grown,
And swollen with Child, so delicate and mild.
To whom a breathe might have withered,
Is in such great pain, giving life to her child.

Oh, born with Want of common necessaries,
For woman's milk, the infant child cries.
He longs to suckle at her young breast.
My little Fan, a Mother, dies.

' "Elizabeth speaks of our daughter, as if she were a woman," I inquired, quite confused.

' "The veil between this life and the next is thin now," the Spirit ponders. "Elizabeth sees that world which is beyond this one and sees all it's denizens. The air outside in the streets of London, and particularly within the high ceilings of this Infirmary, is filled with phantoms, wandering hither and thither in restless haste, and moaning as they go. Every one of them wear chains; some few (they might be guilty governments) are linked together; none are free. Would you know how many were personally known to you in their lives. There is one old ghost, in a white waistcoat, with a monstrous iron safe attached to its ankle, who cries piteously at being unable to assist your ailing wife. The misery with them all is, clearly, that they seek to interfere, for good, in human matters, and have lost the power for ever.

' "For it is required of every man that the spirit within him should walk abroad among his fellowmen, and travel far and wide; and if that spirit goes not forth in life, it is condemned to do so after death. It is doomed to wander through the world -- oh, woe is me! -- and witness what it cannot share, but might have shared on earth, and turned to happiness!

' "Those whose spirit walked abroad among his fellowmen, and travelled far and wide, following the Blessed Star, that once led the Wise Men to the poor abodes, the aged, the sick, and the infant poor, and worship them, opening the treasures of their hearts: the common welfare, charity, mercy, forbearance, and benevolence, and mankind are their business.

' "And as it is appointed unto men once to die, but after this the judgment: So Christ was once offered to bear the sins of many; and unto them that look for him shall he appear the second time without sin unto salvation. And they who go about in this life can sleep in peace. For if we believe that Jesus died and rose again, even so them also which sleep in Jesus will God bring with him. For this we say unto you by the word of the Lord, that we which are alive and remain unto the coming of the Lord shall not prevent them which are asleep. For the Lord himself shall descend from heaven with a shout, with the voice of the archangel, and with the trump of God: and the dead in Christ shall rise first."

' "I do not understand."

' "You do not," the Spirit said, "Of course, you do not." The Spirit was disheartened by the agnosticism of this modern age.

' "Not that, Spirit, I remember my scriptures well enough– on the occasion– Elizabeth spoke of our daughter, as if she were a woman."

' "But, Jeremiah, be not ignorant of this one thing, that one day is with the Lord as a thousand years, and a thousand years as one day. For a thousand years in His sight are but as yesterday when it is past, and as a watch in the night. The days of your years are threescore years and ten; and if by reason of strength they be fourscore years, yet is their strength labour and sorrow; for it is soon cut off, and ye shall fly away."

' "That is a fascinating debate, one not out of place on the pulpit, my good Spirit, or perhaps even Parliament, but this does not answer the question posed."

' "Elizabeth is shown those whose deaths are in the past, in the present, and in the future by the Holy Ghost. Before the Lord formed Little Fan in Elizabeth's womb, He knew her and seeing her days are determined, the number of her months are with Him, He hast appointed her bounds that she cannot pass."

' "Our daughter, dead? No, no, oh no, kind Spirit. Say she will be spared."

' "If these shadows remain unaltered by the Future, few others of my race," returned the Ghost, "will find her here."

'The Member of Parliament in my heart took the podium to argue, "But if your God has determined the number of her days, the number of her months, and appoint bounds that she cannot pass, how can I yet may affect change on these shadows you have shown me, by an altered life?"

' "Do not dare argue scripture with the Lord your God like a barrister. His ways are Mysterious. Know this, Man, if man you be, forbear that wicked cant. Know that if you honour Christmas in my heart, and try to keep it all the year, living in the Past, the Present; the Future with the Spirits of all Three striving within you, shutting not out the lessons that we teach, you have but a chance and hope of procuring your daughter's life, Jeremiah!"

' "Bah! It's a humbug, I tell you. My daughter shall not die. This is nothing if not a fever-dream upon my wife's pain-idled brain. The Consumption of her lungs has weakened her breath and a lack of breath upon the brain can cause the most horrendous visions. Her fevers, her night sweats, her chills, her fatigue, her lack of a desire for any form of sustenance has brought this nightmare of our daughter's death upon her fevered mind."

' "And if I could show you the death of your daughter, if such a thing were within my purview as the Ghost of Christmas Present, which it is not, would you live by an altered life, Jeremiah Scrooge? What evidence would you have of that cold future, beyond that of your own senses."

' "Bah! Because a little thing affects them. A slight disorder of the stomach makes them cheats. All this journeying with you may be due to an undigested bit of beef, a blot of mustard, a crumb of cheese, a fragment of an underdone potato. There's more of gravy than of grave about you, whatever you are!"

'Though Elizabeth's breath had been stolen from her by the Consumption of her lungs, she miraculously murmured breathlessly and painlessly the Gospel of the Lord, as if she were telling a Christmas story to her two bed-snuggled children on a Christmas Eve, "And there were in the same country shepherds abiding in the field, keeping watch over their flock by night. And, lo, the angel of the Lord came upon them, and the glory of the Lord shone round about them: and they were sore afraid. And the angel said unto them, Fear not: for, behold, I bring you good tidings of great joy, which shall be to all people. For unto you is born this day in the city of David a Saviour, which is Christ the Lord. And this shall be a sign unto you; Ye shall find the babe wrapped in swaddling clothes, lying in a manger. And suddenly there was with the angel a multitude of the heavenly host praising God, and saying (while my poor Elizabeth slipped more and more towards the breathlessness of death),

Glory be to God on high
And in earth peace, goodwill towards men,

We praise thee, we bless thee,
We worship thee, we glorify thee,
We give thanks to thee, for thy great glory
O Lord God, heavenly King,
God the Father Almighty.

O Lord, the only-begotten Son, Jesu Christ;
O Lord God, Lamb of God, Son of the Father,
That takest away the sins of the world,
Have mercy upon us.
Thou that takest away the sins of the world,
Have mercy upon us.
Thou that takest away the sins of the world,
Receive our prayer.
Thou that sittest at the right hand of God the Father,
Have mercy upon us.

For thou only art holy;
Thou only art the Lord;
Thou only, O Christ,

With the Holy Ghost,
Art most high
In the glory of God the Father.
Amen.

' "And it came to pass, as the angels were gone away from them into heaven, the shepherds said one to another, Let us now go even unto Bethlehem, and see this thing which is come to pass, which the Lord hath made known unto us. And they came with haste, and found Mary, and Joseph, and the babe lying in a manger. And when they had seen it, they made known abroad the saying which was told them concerning this child. And all they that heard it wondered at those things which were told them by the shepherds. But Mary kept all these things, and pondered them in her heart. And the shepherds returned, glorifying and praising God for all the things that they had heard and seen, as it was told unto them."

' "She knows how to keep Christmas well, even as the long, dark night falls on her life," the Spirit said. "Lo! the Blessed Star that once led the wise men now stands over the poor homes, the slums, the debtors' prisons, the hospitals, and the asylums. When she saw the Blessed Star, her large heart rejoiced with exceeding great joy. The Devil's Acre? Joy! Whitechapel? Joy! Marshalsea prison? Joy! Middlsex Infirmary? Joy! Bedlam? Joy!"

'I hung my head to hear his wife's own words quoted by the Spirit, and was overcome with penitence and grief.

' "Jeremiah Scrooge! When she came until their houses, she saw the aged, the sick, and the infant poor, and she worshipped them, opening the treasures of her heart: the common welfare, charity, mercy, forbearance, and benevolence, and mankind were her business."

'A seething anger boiled over evaporating the all too brief penitence and grief, "All the good her Christian Spirit did her when she was struck with Consumption. Even a mongrel has the sense to keep his bed clean, yet filth and disease are harvested in bushels throughout those districts of poor houses. Where the ways were foul and narrow; the shops and houses wretched; the people half-naked, drunken, slipshod, ugly. Alleys and archways, like so many cesspools, disgorged their offenses of smell, and dirt, and life, upon the straggling streets; and the whole quarter reeked with crime, with filth, and misery. And my wife, my foolish Elizabeth, spent many a waking hour in that Hell-on-Earth. Now look. Death, if there is such a Spirit akin to yourself, should be walking up that row of beds before long."

' "And when will that Spirit that occupies the flesh of Jeremiah Scrooge's mortal remains come walking up that row?"

' "You, more than any Spirit, should know that I am needed in Parliament to-day, as your last little vision revealed."

' "Jeremiah? Is that you, my husband?"

' "Spirit?" I inquired.

' "Step into the light. Jeremiah?"

'The Spirit said fearfully, "The veil thins—"

' "Jeremiah, step into the light. I can barely see you," Elizabeth pleads to Heaven, "Oh, Lord, please bring me into your Heavenly Kingdom. Please spare me these Ghostly Visions that haunt my eyes." She turned to her husband, "Jeremiah? Can you hear me?"

' "Yes, Elizabeth. I hear you."

' "My time has come to shed this mortal coil. My Spirit will soon walk free among the common throng. I have done my peace during my earthly life," she said turning her eyes towards Heaven, "My grace is sufficient for thee O Lord: for my strength is made perfect in weakness. Most gladly therefore will I rather glory in my infirmities, that the power of Christ may rest upon me. Therefore I take pleasure in infirmities, in reproaches, in necessities, in persecutions, in distresses for Christ's sake: for when I am weak, then am I strong."

' "Strong?" I rebuked, "this Consumption has consumed your vibrancy. Your beauty. Your strength. Where is your Christ during your suffering?"

' "Jeremiah, I know your heart. You are not as agnostic as this masque you choose to wear. You have great Faith, but you stubbornly refuse to believe as a man of the modern world. Since your boyhood, this debate has raged in the Parliament of your mind between the man you perceive Ezekiel Scrooge to be and the man you perceive Jeremiah Scrooge to be: the Man of God and the man of the world. You have kept yourself captive through hollow and deceptive philosophy, which depends on human tradition rather than on Christ. You are darkened in your understanding, alienated from the life of

God because of the ignorance that is in you, due to your hardness of heart. Without the Spirit, my husband, you do not accept the things that come from the Spirit of God but consider them foolishness, and cannot understand them because they are discerned only through the Spirit.

' "Remember, this, my husband, For as the sufferings of Christ abound in us, so our consolation also aboundeth by Christ. And whether we be afflicted, it is for your consolation and salvation, which is effectual in the enduring of the same sufferings which we also suffer: or whether we be comforted, it is for your consolation and salvation.

' "For our light affliction—"

' "Light affliction, Elizabeth? This is no light affliction on your part!"

' "—which is but for a moment, worketh for us a far more exceeding and eternal weight of glory; While we look not at the things which are seen, but at the things which are not seen: for the things which are seen are temporal; but the things which are not seen are eternal. My spirit is now free!" Elizabeth paused, as if her breath as been completely stolen from her. Then she speaks, barely a whisper, "Jeremiah?"

' "Yes, my love."

' "Tell Ebenezer and little Fan, that their mother will forever watch over them. Forever stand by their side, invisible, and unable to do anything more than smile at the lives and loves that they lead." She breathed in deeply, with great pain, with blood suddenly upon her lips. "Spirit?"

' "Yes," answered the Spirit.

' "Please tell Death to come soon. I am so very tired. I cannot bear this pain anymore."

' "Before the clock tolls twelve, your pain will be forever gone."

'I, with tears welling in my eyes, cried, "Take me away from this foolish woman. She has brought this pain and suffering upon herself. She has brought these tears to my eyes, damn her. Please, Spirit, show me no more."

' "Ebenezer? My little, Ebbie. You have grown so, my young man. Oh, how I look forward to standing in the back of the church on your wedding day. You won't see me there, but there I'll stand with a smile upon my face. Belle, oh, Belle, my soon-to-be daughter, cherish your new contract, for you are both poor and content to be so, until, in good season, the two-who-shall-become-one can improve your worldly fortune by your patient industry," then a stark realization shuddered in her dying eyes, "No! My dear, Belle. Another idol has displaced you! Grieve, my dear child, for that idol cannot cheer and comfort my Ebbie in the times to come, as you would have tried to do. Ebbie will come to fear the world too much. No! All his other hopes will have merged into the hope of being beyond the chance of its sordid reproach. I can see his nobler aspirations fall off one by one, until the master-passion, Gain, engrosses him! Spirit, damn you, why show me this Truth like this? Oh can I go to my grave knowing this is the fate of my dear, sweet boy? No! No! No! How strong and irresistible the golden idol will be to him. Ebbie, if you free to-day, to-morrow, yesterday, I cannot bare to think you would spurn this a dowerless girl -- you who, in your very confidence with her, weigh everything by Gain: or, choosing her, if for a moment you were false enough to your one guiding principle to do so, do I not know that your repentance and regret would surely follow? Belle! Don't release him. Your heart is full, for the love of him he once was. Save my boy, Belle. Turn his heart from the golden idol. Please!"

' "Where is Ebenezer?" asked the Spirit, "He would not have forgotten his mother on Christmas Day! Oh, yes. At school, in the country. Forbidden by parental mandate to return."

'A clock in the distance, the darkness, the shadows, begins to toll towards twelve.

' "No, Spirit. Do not let the bell toll for my Elizabeth. She is far too young."

' "Death waits for no man. But–" the Spirit said.

' "But what, Spirit? Confess your secrets to me!"

' "The love of Christmas is a powerful medicine. It cannot cure. But it can and surely does, relieve the pain and suffering of all mankind. If only for a single day."

' "A single day without pain and suffering. Oh, is there such a blessed, blessed thing?" Elizabeth prayed.

'I dropped to my knees beside the bed with my hand in that of my wife's. I was a near to supplication as my harden heart could permit.

' "For in the Father's house are many mansions: if it were not so, the Lord would have told you," the Spirit said, consoling my soulless heart, "And if He goes and prepares a place for you, He will come again, and receive you unto myself; that where He is, there ye may be also. And whither He goes ye know, and the way ye know. He goes to prepare a place for those like Elizabeth"

' "Elizabeth, please do not leave me alone. I cannot bare the pain of this. Not alone. Do not leave your daughter, poor little Fan. Or young Ebenezer, alone at school. News of a Mother's death should not come by post, but be born witness to with his own eyes. Spirit, please, bring my children to this Time and this Place."

' "I cannot," the Spirit said with reluctance. "Did you not send that poor boy away to school when he was still toddling around your writing desk? Have you ever once sent for him to return to his home and to his bed, on holiday or at Christmas time? And as for little Fan? Home is not like Heaven to her. She is afraid to ask you once more if Ebenezer might come home. Would you dare to speak so gently to her one dear night when she is going to bed, that she will not be afraid to ask you once more. Would you say, 'Yes, he should'? Would you send her in a coach to bring him and he is to be a man and he is never to go back there, and be together all the Christmas long, and have the merriest time in all the world?"

' "Please, I beg of you. Please, bring my children to this Time and this Place."

' "This is your journey of reclamation, Jeremiah Scrooge, not theirs. Your children know how to keep Christmas well. You wear your own chain, having made it link by link, and yard by yard, you have girded it of your own free will, and of your own free were you wear it. Your chain, wrought not only in steel, but with the inhumanity of the regulating of common necessaries, common comforts. For every shilling squabbled over in Parliament, a Troy pound of cash-boxes, keys, padlocks, ledgers, deeds, and heavy purses have been added to the length of your chain. It reaches from your own generation to the next, chaining the iniquity of the fathers upon the children unto the third and fourth generation of them, Jeremiah! The spirits of Ebenezer and Fan Scrooge are shackled to desk and bed by the length of your own strong coil! Even if it were within my power to bring your children to this Time and this Place, I could not. I would not!"

' "Good-bye, Jeremiah. My husband. My heart. Good-bye."

'The Phantom, who is the Ghost of Christmas Yet to Come, slowly, gravely, silently approached like a mist along the ground. The dying, whose future Christmases were truly limited, were stirred from their Consumption-idled stupors, to watch the Spirit move towards one bed of but many beds in the row, of one row of many rows in the room, of but one room of but many rooms in the hospital. Gloom and mystery seemed to not only proceed it, but scatter in its wake. It was shrouded in a deep black garment, which concealed its head, its face, its form, and left nothing of it visible save one outstretched (perhaps) skeletal hand, for there was flesh upon it, with a lack of muscle, protruding veins, and shrunken skin, pointing towards Elizabeth and her pleading husband.

' "Hello–" she said to the Phantom, "I dreamt of you–"

'She reached her hand out. The long skeletal fingers of the Phantom extended, almost touching hers. The clock tolled its last. Elizabeth was dead.

' "Take me from this place. Please, I beg of you."

' "Come, Jeremiah," the Spirit of Christmas Present said, suddenly as old and infirm as any inmate of the infirmary, his vibrant fiery curls had turned thin and grey, his genial face ashen, his sparkling eye gloomy, his cheery voice frail, his unconstrained demeanour hampered, his joyful air silenced. "That bells tolls for me as well, my time is come. This Phantom whose shape and form approaches, will host your further journeys." '

Stave IV
"The Last of the Spirits"

' "Phantom, you are to show me Christmases that are yet to come? Events that may happen if my life's course remains unaltered?"

'The Phantom remained as taciturn and inscrutable as a shadow. He betrayed nothing, no emotion, no evidence, only emptiness.

' "I will not be a hypocrite by begging for redemption or pleading for my soul," I countered, undeterred by the silent, seemingly soulless spectre. "I have seen nothing that has occurred during my brief time with Spirits that could not be explained by fanciful dreams or a fever upon the brain."

'The Ghost of Christmas Yet To Come pointed to a counting-house, where a young man was tending its receipts and making this books. The air had a stark chill to it, with only a single, solitary, slight, smouldering coal lit in the hearth. A warm simply could not be had in this counting-house. Dick Wilkins, the once fellow-prentice, sat in the tank copying letters, warming his aching frozen fingers by only candle-light. Alas, the coal-scuttle had been secured with a lock to prevent plightful pilfering.

'Suddenly, another equally young man entered the warehouse

and approached the high-desk so quickly the bell was still ringing when he addressed the owner of the establishment, "Have I the pleasure of addressing Mr. Scrooge?" The young man brushed a light dusting of snow off of his great-coat, pulled his pig-tail out from beneath his collar before straightening his hair. Then he checked his ledger. "A Mister Ebenezer Scrooge?"

' "Aye, you have," said Ebenezer, nary looking up from his books. "Speak your business."

' "My name is Jacob Marley," said the strange, ungracefully thin and tall man, who clasped his hands behind his back and stood quite queerly on the balls of his feet, rocking ever so slightly front and back. Ebenezer momentarily thought of Marley more as a street magician attempting to bamboozle passersby into believing he was levitating through the mastery of dark and arcane arts. In fact, Ebenezer could not remember Jacob Marley walking into his counting-house, and the stubbornly rational man briefly– ever so briefly– truly believed Jacob Marley was a spectre doomed to wander through the world and witness what it cannot share, but might have shared on earth, and turned to happiness. Bah!– Who was this queer, gangling man putting the strangest motions into his head?– Humbug!

'Jacob Marley then continued his rehearsed rhetoric, pulling and stretching Ebenezer suddenly back into the mortal sphere, "My business interests involve locating employment for the poor and destitute members of our society." Ebenezer was bewildered by this almsman, whom seemed to be endeavouring to raise a fund to buy the Poor some meat and drink and means of warmth, and yet, was sinister simultaneously.

' "If you are begging for alms, Mr. Marley, then I suggest you beat a hasty retreat out of my office," said Ebenezer, quietly and stealthily seizing his ruler.

' "Mr. Scrooge, I am not here on behalf of the poor and destitute. I am here on the behalf of businessmen with an eye for profit," said Jacob, with a glint in his eye so unlike the Blessed Star that sparkled in his sister's eyes, but was more akin to the flaming descent of Lucifer, the Morningstar, during the Fall. Was it pride that came before the Fall? Or perhaps it was greed? At that moment, neither Ebenezer nor I could quite remember the Holiest of Scriptures.

' "Profit? What profit can be found in helping those in want? Are there no prisons?"

' "Ah, yes. Plenty of prisons. And the treadmill and Union work-houses are still quite vigorous," Jacob said, grinning like a Cheshire cat. Was this not said of any one who shows his teeth and gums in laughing? The peel of laughter that escaped Jacob's grin echoed around the walls of a counting-house so unfamiliar with the sound.

' "Oh! I was afraid, from what you said at first, that something had occurred to stop them in their useful course," said Ebenezer. "I'm very glad to hear it."

' "This is where our profit lies," again with this laugher. Ebenezer could not justify why did Jacob Marley exert such precious energy in such an unnecessary endeavour.

' "You have my attention, Mr. Marley," said Ebenezer smiling, "But my attention is rather valuable, so speak plain." He retrieved his watch from the pocket of his waistcoat, and clicked open the lid to time Mr. Marley's lecture. He did so rather matter-of-factly, but from an observer's point-of-view it was comically– painfully– dramatic.

'Jacob Marley cleared his throat, and in his own queer way it was comically– painfully– dramatic as well. Cracking his neck with his swift twist of his chin, he readied himself for the performance of a life-time as if he were speaking to the Members of Parliament. He then began his manically memorized monologue, "The current Speenhamland system of charity and aide has a few rather large loop-holes that enterprising young businessmen such as ourselves can exploit to our gain—"

' "Ah yes, the master passion. Go on, go on," said Ebenezer absentmindedly interrupting Mr. Marley.

' "During the course of my enterprise, I locate employment for those poor workers who cannot secure honest employment. Some are burdened with debt, others are burdened with infirmity, but the vast majority are burdened with a wife and an excessive number of children. I hire their services to the treadmill or Union workhouses. These establishments pay their salary to my agency and in turn I pay the workers. Minus the usual fee, of course."

' "Of course," Ebenezer parroted. Just as Ebenezer could not notice the chain he himself had drawn clasped about his middle, long, and wound about him like a tail; and made of cash-boxes, keys, pad-locks, ledgers, deeds, and heavy purses wrought in steel, he failed to realized that Marley was manipulating him as expertly as a puppeteer does a marionette. The strings Marley pulled were just as invisible on account of neither having laboured on theirs for very long.

' "Mr. Scrooge…Ebenezer…," Jacob said practically purring. "These same poor workers who cannot secure loans from the lending institutions, the banks, come to you, whose credit at these institutions is above reproach. And you secure the loan and in return hold the mortgage and deed on the property collecting a rent."

' "Yes, yes this is an interesting course of business, Mr. Marley," said Ebenezer growing increasingly agitated. The hand on his watch had covered too much ground, trying his effortlessly unravelled nerves. "Any man at university knows this. And I have no doubt many a pawnbroker buying the wares of the deceased is aware of our current socioeconomic policies. They are what they are. I help to support the establishments mentioned -- they certainly cost enough. Your point being?"

' "My point, Ebenezer," said Jacob Marley. "Is that if you, as their landlord and title-holder on their property, raise their rents as is your right and if I, as their employer, in as far as I am the agent who have contracted their labour to the debtor's prisons, the treadmills, the union workhouse, lower their salaries," the Cheshire grin curled on his lips.

'The realization that the business plan– the nefarious plot– of Jacob Marley had– at the very least– potential to assist in the pursuit of wealth, which condemns nothings with such severity as poverty. And if the very pursuit of wealth can exploit poverty– dear God– that is practically poetic.

' "Our…depredations," said Jacob, "will be redressed from the public pocket. Combining our business interests, we can make a substantial profit exploiting the very system that means to assist these slothful and idle people who contribute nothing to society."

' "'Scrooge and Marley.' It has a clever ring to it," Ebenezer loudly clasped his watch shut and pocketed it quite quietly. He offered his hand to Jacob Marley, an ancient practice that has survived into the modern era of British society to seal the contract between them.

' "Spirit, surly this is not my son," I said. "Not my Ebenezer. I did not raise a son to love profit. But if you wish to continue with this fanciful game of Charades, then proceed."

'And as silently, as spectre-like, as Jacob Marley entered the counting-house, he left just the same. The door chime rang but a single time, seeing as a impish, dirty gray-haired rascal, a hard, prematurely old thirty-five years of age, sneaked under the arm of Jacob Marley. The old swindler's clothes most unquestionably belied his station in life. Any man may have looked through his shirts till their eyes ached; but they wouldn't find a hole in them, nor a threadbare place. His waistcoat and overcoat were the products the finest bespoke tailors of Savile Row servicing the aristocracy herself. Where they spared no expense in the creation of their finery, he spared no deceit to disburse twopence on the pound for pawnbrokered goods from an assortment of charwomen, laundresses, and undertakers' men, whom shan't hold their hand, when they can get anything in it by reaching it out. And on this day, his client was a businessman who worked upon 'Change, whose name was good upon 'Change. He was certainly moving up in the underworld.

' "Eh, Mr. Ebenezer. I have the figures you requested," he said, pointing to his blackboard with a meagre piece of chalk. The board looked as if it could have been stolen from any child at school. "He-he-he. I do believe you will like the figure. Mind you, it is a generous sum of money and I will pay not a shilling more."

' "Yes, yes, do get on with it, old Joe. Time is a precious commodity."

' "Eh... Mr. Ebenezer?" old Joe asked, unsure of how to broach a very difficult question. His instructions from Mr. Scrooge were quite clear. If the truth be told, the instructions were excruciatingly specific, as if a solicitor had been hired to draw up the contract between the two. But old Joe possessed a knowledge of Mr. Ebenezer Scrooge by his ugly reputation alone, and therefore knew that Mr. Scrooge would not have paid a solicitor a single groat to draw up a proper contract. And who in the right mind would produce a contract between a businessman, whose word was good upon 'Change, and a pawnbroker. Therefore, Mr. Scrooge must have hand-written the contract himself his own self. What a miser.

' "What?" asked Ebenezer, obviously displeased by the continued presence of the pawnbroker.

' "Did you wish me to include everything in the house?" Everything? The contract was quite specific that everything in the house was to be brokered. All the dishes and the silverware in the kitchen, the furniture throughout the whole of the house, the wall-paper, the servant bells, the tiles, the marble, the portraits, the chandeliers, the beds, and— old Joe could not bring himself to even conceive of the thought of brokering the very last item itemized in the contract.

' "Everything," Ebenezer said. Old Joe dealt on the daily basis the most duplicitous of people from every walk of life, but Ebenezer Scrooge wore his heart upon his sleeve, a cold, exact, unfeeling heart as it were.

' "Including the bed-curtains?" Old Joe plainly could not bring himself ask the very question required in this unfortunate situation. He danced around the question as if he were the guest at a quite exquisite Christmas party.

' "Most certainly. I have my own bed-curtains. I have no need for two sets of bed-curtains. Or bed-sheets. Or silverware." Ebenezer was quite correct that he did not require two sets of any thing, he barely required duplicate spoons, forks, knives, or plates or bowls. A single piece of each was all that was required for a man living alone. Could they not be washed easily enough?

'Old Joe could feel that his presence in the counting-house was trying his rather brief employer's very last good nerve by the goose-flesh that crawled upon his own skin. The frog in his throat croaked, "And, uh, what of the pour soul laying dead there upon his bed?"

' "That man was my father," said Ebenezer most matter-of-factly, as if this particular item on the list of possessions to broker were no more important to him than the silverware. He betrayed no emotion, no sorrow, no grief, no any thing.

' "That poor bloke is your father?" old Joe asked, desperately seeking answers to his disbelief at the very nature of this man he had entered into a Devil's bargain with.

'A pale fell upon his weathered and withered old face. And my own as well.

' "I am most certain that a university or some other institute of learning will pay handsomely for a cadaver to experiment upon."

' "You wish me to sell the body?" Never in decades selling honest possessions from honest men or the desperate and dishonest possessions from duplicitous charwomen, laundresses, and undertakers' men, had he encountered a man like Mr. Ebenezer Scrooge. And never had he been asked to broker such a possession as the body of the recently deceased. And particularly the body of a father. Most bereaved family brokering the possessions of their recently deceased are beside themselves with grief, refusing to part for a Sovereign due to the familial memories attached. But in this increasingly uncomfortable situation he unfortunately found himself in, he perceived not a lick of anguish, only the master passion he too worshipped: Gain.

'Could old Joe muster the greed necessary to sell the body of this man's father?

' "Yes," said Ebenezer answering both the spoken and unspoken question, "Take a few moments to recalculate my account."

' "I am not in the business of grave robbing, Mr. Ebenezer," old Joe protested. Would he be willing to further sully his already besmirched reputation in the back alleys of the Devil's Acre? Word of his contract with Mr. Scrooge would, no doubt, spread like the Plague through Whitechapel, Spitalfields, Berthanl Green, and the Old Nichol painting him as a body snatcher. This kind of publicity he could not abide.

' "There is no grave to rob. I shall not waste twopence on a plot of dirt to bury an expensive box that will rot along with its contents. Remove everything in that house or I shall be forced to find another pawnbroker."

' "Aye, Mr. Ebenezer." Old Joe resigned himself to his fate as a grave-robber. How exactly does one broach the selling of my mortal remains to a university? One just does not approach the Headmaster and inquire the wheres and whyfores of cadaver transacting. And how much would– could– the higher institutions of learning be willing to pay for a cadaver? He most assuredly did not know the economics of grave-robbing, and feared to quote too high a price to this miser. And pondering the mathematics in the blackboard of his mind and scratching the calculations of numbers, he took out a filthy handkerchief and wiped the board, then made a few quick marks. "There… I believe you will find this sum acceptable."

' "Yes, yes," said Ebenezer, quite pleased with the figure. "I do believe that we have an agreement. Good afternoon."

' "Aye, good afternoon, Mr. Ebenezer." As old Joe scurried out of the counting-house like a rat fleeing a sinking ship, Ebenezer could hear old Joe murmuring to himself, "Never met a more squeezing, wrenching, grasping, scraping, clutching, covetous old sinner in all your bleeding life, eh, old Joe? He-he-he."

' "Good afternoon!"

'I said, "Phantom, I see the flaw in this little experiment. My Ebenezer is a kind, generous, respectful boy. And nothing so horrid could occur during my rearing of him to result in that creature. Continue, Phantom, I find this as enjoyable as an evening of theater."

'The Phantom led me away from the counting-house and the scene had changed, This new room was bereft of the paper on the walls, bells from their strings, the tiles from the mantle, the marble on the floors, the portraits on their hooks, crystals from the chandelier, and the tools, grates, fireguards, logboxes, pellet baskets, and fire dogs from the hearth, and now I almost touched a bed: a bare, uncurtained bed: on which, beneath a ragged sheet, there lay something covered up, which, though it was dumb, announced itself in awful language.

'The room was very dark, too dark to be observed with any accuracy, though I glanced round it in disobedience to a secret impulse, courageous in the knowing what kind of room it was. A pale light, rising in the outer air, fell straight upon the bed; and on it, plundered and bereft, unwatched, unwept, uncared for, was the body of this man.

'I glanced towards the Phantom. Its steady hand was pointed to the bed. The cover was so carelessly adjusted that the slightest raising of it, the motion of a finger upon my part, would have disclosed the face. I thought of it, felt how easy it would be to do, and longed to do it; and I steeled myself with enough power to withdraw the veil than to dismiss the spectre at my side.

'He lay, in the dark empty house, with not a man, a woman, or a child, to say that he was kind to me in this or that, and for the memory of one kind word I will be kind to him. A cat was tearing at the door, and there was a sound of gnawing rats beneath the hearthstone. What they wanted in the room of death, and why they were so restless and disturbed, I did not dare to think.

' "Is that my body that rests under that cloth, Phantom? I am not so fearful of Death that I'm afraid of witnessing my own burial shroud."

' Then in the library of my memory a book was dislodged from a shelf, which thudded upon the floor under the sheer weight of Truth. It fell open to a particular scripture. I saw myself as a boy sitting in church looking up at my own father standing at the lectern in church with the awe of a child and the reverence of a parishioner. My father read from the Gospel according to John, "Let not your heart be troubled: ye believe in God, believe also in me. In my Father's house are many mansions: if it were not so, I would have told you. I go to prepare a place for you. And if I go and prepare a place for you, I will come again, and receive you unto myself; that where I am, there ye may be also. And whither I go ye know, and the way ye know. Thomas saith unto him, Lord, we know not whither thou goest; and how can we know the way? Jesus saith unto him, I am the way, the truth, and the life: no man cometh unto the Father, but by me."

'I looked around for the Spirit of Christmas Past, but that strange figure with his blazing light were no where to be seen. Curiously, while it seemed like only earlier that same night when I watched in abject horror at the suicide of the Spirit of Christmas Past, whom lowered the cap over the crown of its head cutting off all that fed the flame, extinguishing the Light of What Was, the truth was the light of the Past had been extinguished long, long ago.

'And again, in another memory from another time flooded the darkness with the warm morning Light of Christ. My father strolled leisurely about the aisles of the congregation sternly preaching the Word of God, "But we do not want you to be uninformed, brothers, about those who are asleep, that you may not grieve as others do who have no hope. For since we believe that Jesus died and rose again, even so, through Jesus, God will bring with him those who have fallen asleep. For this we declare to you by a word from the Lord, that we who are alive, who are left until the coming of the Lord, will not precede those who have fallen asleep. For the Lord himself will descend from heaven with a cry of command, with the voice of an archangel, and with the sound of the trumpet of God. And the dead in Christ will rise first. Then we who are alive, who are left, will be caught up together with them in the clouds to meet the Lord in the air, and so we will always be with the Lord."

'Was it the cold heat of an agnostic heart or a budding strange faith in Jesus Christ which steeled my nerves to pull off the bed-sheet to reveal my own corpse laying dead upon the bed? Then a child's cry was heard piercing the darkness and staying my hand.

'And suddenly there was a flash of light and the room was changed. There was pristinely washed paper on the walls, bells rang on their strings, the marble on the floors was polished and washed, the portraits still hung on their hooks, crystals from the chandelier lit like diamonds from the candles, the tools, grates, fireguards, log-boxes, pellet baskets, and fire dogs were warmed from the fire blazing in the hearth, and there were the quaint Dutch tiles, designed to illustrate the Scriptures; the Cains and Abels, Pharaohs' daughters; Queens of Sheba, Angelic messengers descending through the air on clouds like feather-beds, Abrahams, Belshazzars, Apostles putting off to sea in butter-boats, and hundreds of other such figures.

'And a legion of mourners and well-wishers were in the room, comforting the inconsolable Henry Bishop, my son-by-marriage. Oh cold, cold, rigid, dreadful Death, attempted to set up his altar here, and dress it with such terrors as thou hast at thy command: for this is thy dominion. But of the loved, revered, and honoured dead, thou canst not turn one hair to thy dread purposes, or make one feature odious. It is not that the hand is heavy and will fall down when re-leased; it is not that the heart and pulse are still; but that the hand was open, generous, and true; the heart brave, warm, and tender; and the pulse a man's. Strike, Shadow, strike. And see his good deeds springing from the wound, to sow the world with life immortal!

'A wet-nurse exited the bright, dry, gleaming room into the dark-ness of a side-chamber; a plump woman wearing a simple dress and simpler apron, her amble bosom ached with laden milk. She cradled a swaddled babe in his arms.

' "Hush, hush, little one," said the nurse as the child continued to cry. "Hush, now. You must be quiet little one or your mother may linger here too long. Oh poor, poor dear. She was always such a delicate creature, your mother, whom a breathe might have withered." The child quieted for a moment, whimpering softly.

' "Phantom, who is this child's mother?"

'The Nurse said, joyfully, "But Fan, she died a woman!"

' "This child… couldn't be."

'The child's cry grew a little louder.

' "Hush, hush, little one."

' "My grandchild?" I inquired, the stark realization whitening my face. "Fan? My little Fan? No–" I dropped to my knees beside the bed the weight of my sorrow leadening my hand with nary the strength to pull the bed-sheet.

> *Lully lulla, thou little tiny child,*
> *By, by, lully lullay.*
> *Lully lulla, thou little tiny child.*
> *By, by, lully lullay.*
>
> *O sisters too, how may we do,*
> *For to preserve this day?*
> *This poor youngling for whom we sing,*
> *"By, by, lully lullay."*
>
> *Herod the king, in his raging,*
> *Charging he hath this day.*
> *His men of might, in his own sight,*
> *All young children slay.*
>
> *That woe is me, poor child for Thee!*
> *And ever mourn and say,*
> *For thy parting neither say nor sing,*
> *"By, by, lully lullay."*

'And it was a great surprise to my to hear a hearty laugh, because this death instead of infecting the room with disease and sorrow, there is nothing in the world so irresistibly contagious as laughter and good-humour. The husband of my Little Fan laughed in this way: holding his sides, rolling his head, and twisting his face into the most extravagant contortions remembering all the good and wonderful times, the happy and memorable times, the festive and delightful times with his wife. He regaled each of the legion of mourners to laugh, to turn the dark, dreary, gloomy room into a bright, dry, gleaming room.

' "Ha, ha!" laughed my son-by-marriage. "Ha, ha, ha!"

'The Phantom lay his skeletal hand on my shoulder, motioning for us to leave the scene.

' "No, Phantom—please. Fan— my little Fan. She had a large heart! How did I neglect you? How did you become so frail? Answer me. Fan? Please, answer me. Where was this Jesus Christ as my daughter lay at the point of death? Where is He now that she lay dead upon that bed?"

'And then I again heard my father's voice ringing as clear as any church bell on Christmas morning, "And, behold, there cometh one of the rulers of the synagogue, Jairus by name; and when he saw him, he fell at His feet, And besought Him greatly, saying, My little daughter lieth at the point of death: I pray thee, come and lay thy hands on her, that she may be healed; and she shall live. And he cometh to the house of the ruler of the synagogue, and seeth the tumult, and them that wept and wailed greatly. And when he was come in, he saith unto them, Why make ye this ado, and weep? the damsel is not dead, but sleepeth. And they laughed him to scorn. But when He had put them all out, He taketh the father and the mother of the damsel, and them that were with him, and entereth in where the damsel was lying. And He took the damsel by the hand, and said unto her, *Talitha cumi*; which is, being interpreted, Damsel, I say unto thee, arise. And straightway the damsel arose, and walked; for she was of the age of twelve years. And they were astonished with a great astonishment."

'The cold logic of agnosticism rebelled in my heart. The teachings of the three Spirits of Christmases Past, Present, and Yet to Come, were a branch that had begun to bud, soon to flower, and bring forth much fruit, but– but! I was now willing to cast the branch away and such branches are picked up and thrown into a fire and burnt.

'I was ignorant that Jesus alone is the true vine, and His father is the husbandman. Jesus saith, not in the distance of the days of yore, but as the living Word this very day, Every branch in me that beareth not fruit he taketh away: and every branch that beareth fruit, he purgeth it, that it may bring forth more fruit. Now ye are clean through the word which I have spoken unto you. Abide in me, and I in you. As the branch cannot bear fruit of itself, except it abide in the vine; no more can ye, except ye abide in me. I am the vine, ye are the branches: He that abideth in me, and I in him, the same bringeth forth much fruit: for without me ye can do nothing. If a man abide not in me, he is cast forth as a branch, and is withered; and men gather them, and cast them into the fire, and they are burned. If ye abide in me, and my words abide in you, ye shall ask what ye will, and it shall be done unto you. Herein is my Father glorified, that ye bear much fruit; so shall ye be my disciples.

'Why, oh, why was I being assaulted with the purported Holiest of Scriptures? What did the Word of God have to do with my rec-lamation, the grand business of three Spirits of Christmas over the course this fanciful nightmare? Was this not the modern age when men of learning need not concern themselves with the myths and superstitions of the Godfull? While I may not have known the Ho-liest of Scriptures, I most certainly knew my Tacitus. So, therefore if I could work my will, every idiot who goes about with the Word of God on his lips and Jesus Christ nestled in his heart, should be covered with the skins of beasts, to be torn by dogs and perish, or nailed to crosses, or doomed to the flames and burnt, to serve as a nightly illumination, when daylight has expired. How I wished there was some precedent under British jurisprudence to enact similar laws to those of Nero, whom had fastened the guilt for the Great Fire of Rome and inflicted the most exquisite tortures on a class hated for their abominations, called Christians. The Christ, from whom the name had its origin, had suffered the extreme penalty during the reign of Tiberius at the hands of one of the Roman procurators, Pon-tius Pilate, and a most mischievous superstition, thus checked for a moment, again broke out not only in Judaea, the first source of the evil, but spread like the Black Death across the European continent, infecting even London town.

'So, then from the darkness and shadows came a child's cry riding the winds of memory from a long forgotten Christmas Past, "And what of Brother? May I take the carriage and bring him home. It has been so long–"

'The Phantom again lay his skeletal hand on my shoulder, motioning for us to leave. I turned on him.

' "I will not, cannot stand for this anymore!

'I was so weary of my journey with Spirits that Christmas Evening, and so longed for the warm comfort of my bed, the warm comforting glow of my hearth, and had such a desire to dismiss the spectre at my side, to withdraw the veil, a cover so carelessly adjusted that the slightest raising of it, the motion of a finger upon my part, would have disclosed the face of my daughter, that I seized the corner of the bed-sheet. And I ripped it away to reveal—'

Stave V
"The Last of the Spirits - Part the Second"

'The scene was changed once again. Again!

'It was now a morning, a Christmas morning, when dense, low, heavy snow-burdened clouds obscured the light of the sun. On a remarkably small hill beside a remarkably small city church, my son, Ebenezer Scrooge, and a Parson stood at a graveside. If the stone had been engraved at such an early hour after the man's death, the heavy snow that had fallen over the cold Christmas Eve night would have obscured the poor man's name. The undertaker's men lowered the casket into the earth. My son, not unlike myself and quite unlike my father, was as far from being a religious man as the stars are from the dirt, but Ebenezer knew enough of the Holiest of Scriptures to know that "All go unto one place; all are of the dust, and all turn to dust again."

'The Parson read though he knew the words intimately, reverently, "Into your hands, O merciful God, we commend your servant Jacob Marley. Acknowledge, we humbly beseech you, a sheep of your own fold, a lamb of your own flock, a sinner of your own redeeming. Receive Jacob Marley into the arms of your mercy, into the blessed rest of everlasting peace, and into the glorious company of the saints of light. Amen.

' "We lift our eyes up to the hills. From where does our help come? Our help comes from the Unseen One, the Maker of the heavens and the earth, who will not cause our feet to stumble, our protector who never sleeps. The Abundant One preserves us, the Watchful One is our shelter and support. The Vigilant One guards us from evil, and keeps our Life-breath safe. The Shepherd guards our going out and out coming in from now unto eternity.

' "May the road rise to meet you, may the wind be always at your back, may the sun shine warm upon your face, may the rains fall soft upon your fields, and until we meet again, may God hold you in the palm of his hand. Amen."

' "Amen," parroted the clerk and the undertaker's men.

'Under his breath, and breathlessly as he could muster without his breath freezing in the Christmas air, my son said, "Bah! Humbug!"

' "The register of his burial was signed by the clergyman, the clerk, the undertaker, and the chief mourner," the clerk said.

' "I'll sign it," said Ebenezer, "and my name is good upon 'Change for anything I choose to put my hand to."

' "Marley was dead! There is no doubt whatever about that. Old Marley is as dead as a door-nail," mused the undertaker's man, "Mind! I don't mean to say that I know, of my own knowledge, what there is particularly dead about a door-nail. I might have been inclined, myself, to regard a coffin-nail as the deadest piece of ironmongery in the trade. But the wisdom of our ancestors is in the simile; and my unhallowed hands shall not disturb it, or the Country's done for. You will therefore permit me to repeat, emphatically, that Marley is as dead as a door-nail."

'The wit and whimsy of an undertaker's man?'

'My son's neighbours knew him all the well too much, though they wish they did not. Commuters would go out of their way by a league or more to avoid his lane. Children playing in the streets and snow never playfully pelted him with snow. In this merry time of year, the Spirit of Christmas Cheer, like the Muses before her, put her musings as a carol in the air,

Oh, but he was a tight-fisted
Hand at the grindstone,
(A beggar implores him for) A fin? Er-
A squeezing, wrenching, grasping,
Clutching, covetous old sinner.

Hard and sharp as flint, from which
No steel has ever struck generous fire.
Secret and self-contained and solitary
As an oyster, or perhaps town crier.

The cold within him froze his features,
Nipped his point nose, stiffen his gait;
Made his eyes red, his thin lips blue; and
Spoke out shrewdly in a voice that did grate.

He carries his own low temperature
He ices his office in the dog days.
And didn't that it e'en one degree
E'en on merry Christmas day.

External heat and cold on Scrooge
Had little influences night or day.
No warmth can warm him.
Nor winter weather chill, I'll say.

'No wind that blew was bitterer than he, no falling snow was more intent upon its purpose, no pelting rain less open to entreaty. Foul weather didn't know where to have him. The heaviest rain, and snow, and hail, and sleet, could boast of the advantage over him in only one respect. They often "came down" handsomely, and Ebenezer never did.

Nobody ever stops him in the street,
To say, with gladsome charity.
My dear, Scrooge, how are you?
When will you come to see me?

No beggars implore him a trifle.
No children ask him what o'clock it is.
No man or woman inquire where
Such and such a place 'tis.

'Even the blind men's dogs appeared to know him; and when they saw him coming on, would tug their owners into doorways and up courts; and then would wag their tails as though they said, "No eye at all is better than an evil eye, dark master!"

'But what did Ebenezer care? It was the very thing my son seemed now to have liked. To edge his way along the crowded paths of life, warning all human sympathy to keep its distance, was what the knowing ones call "nuts" to Ebenezer. Where did I fail you, my boy?

'Once upon a time -- of all the good days in the year, on Christmas Eve -- the spirit let me to a familiar counting-house, which had became a little darker and more dirty. The panels shrunk, the windows cracked; fragments of plaster fell out of the ceiling, and the naked laths were shown instead; but how all this was brought about, I knew that in the past thirty-five years it had been weathered with age and niggardly disinterest. I could see through the window, my son, now old, sat busy at his desk. It was cold, bleak, biting weather: foggy withal: and I could hear the people in the court outside go wheezing up and down, beating their hands upon their breasts, and stamping their feet upon the pavement stones to warm them. The city clocks had only just gone three, but it was quite dark already -- it had not been light all day: and candles were flaring in the windows of the neighbouring offices, like ruddy smears upon the palpable brown air. The fog came pouring in at every chink and keyhole, and was so dense without, that although the court was of the narrowest, the houses opposite were mere phantoms. To see the dingy cloud come drooping down, obscuring everything, one might have thought that Nature lived hard by, and was brewing on a large scale.

'I made a note that my son never painted out Old Marley's name. There it stood, years afterwards, above the warehouse door: Scrooge and Marley. The firm was known as Scrooge and Marley. Sometimes people new to the business called Scrooge Scrooge, and sometimes

Marley, but he answered to both names: it was all the same to him.

'I entered my son's counting-house by the way of the ice-frosted front window. Crystals formed in the shape of a man before melting into memory. I looked about the counting-house and could see the door was open that Ebenezer might keep his eye upon his clerk, who in a dismal little cell beyond, a sort of tank, was copying letters. Ebenezer had a very small fire, but the clerk's fire was so very much smaller that it looked like one coal. But he couldn't replenish it, for Ebenezer kept the coal-box in his own room; and so surely as the clerk came in with the shovel, the master predicted that it would be necessary for them to part. Wherefore the clerk put on his white comforter, and tried to warm himself at the candle; in which effort, not being a man of a strong imagination, he failed.

'And standing stoically beside my elderly son, near to his high-desk, was a man, if he could be a man, dressed in a usual waistcoat, tights and boots; the tassels on the latter bristling, much like his pig-tail, and his coat-skirts, and the hair upon his head. There was a chain drawn clasped about his middle. It was long, and wound about him like a tail; and it was made of cash-boxes, keys, padlocks, ledgers, deeds, and heavy purses wrought in steel.

' "Spirit," I inquired, "what is that form that stands, bound in chains?"

'And the ghost answered, "In life I was your son's partner, Jacob Marley. This is no light part of my penance. I cannot rest, I cannot stay, I cannot linger anywhere. And weary journeys have lain before me and lie after me!"

'I was astonished. "Seven years dead–"

' "Yet, time and time again my journeys to and fro over this globe God has stretched out the northern skies over empty space and hangs upon nothing! And yet, time and time again I am drawn the narrow limits of our money-changing hole to stand beside Ebenezer Scrooge upon a Christmas day, praying that he may yet a chance and hope of escaping my fate."

' "A merry Christmas, uncle! God save you!" cried a cheerful voice. It was the voice of Ebenezer's nephew, my grandchild, who came upon him so quickly that this was the first intimation he had of his approach.

' "Bah!" said Ebenezer, "Humbug!"

'He had so heated himself with rapid walking in the fog and frost, this nephew of Ebenezer's, that he was all in a glow; his face was ruddy and handsome; his eyes sparkled, and his breath smoked again.

' "Christmas a humbug, uncle!" said my grandchild. "You don't mean that, I am sure."

' "I do," said Ebenezer. "Merry Christmas! What right have you to be merry? What reason have you to be merry? You're poor enough."

' "Come, then," returned my grandchild gaily. "What right have you to be dismal? What reason have you to be morose? You're rich enough."

'Ebenezer having no better answer ready on the spur of the moment, said "Bah!" again; and followed it up with "Humbug."

' "Don't be cross, uncle!" said my grandchild.

' "What else can I be," returned the uncle, "when I live in such a world of fools as this? Merry Christmas! Out upon merry Christmas! What's Christmas time to you but a time for paying bills without money; a time for finding yourself a year older, but not an hour richer; a time for balancing your books and having every item in 'em through a round dozen of months presented dead against you? If I could work my will," said Ebenezer indignantly, "every idiot who goes about with 'Merry Christmas' on his lips, should be boiled with his own pudding, and buried with a stake of holly through his heart. He should!"

' "Uncle!" pleaded my grandchild.

' "Nephew!" returned the uncle, sternly, "keep Christmas in your own way, and let me keep it in mine."

' "Keep it!" repeated my grandchild. "But you don't keep it."

' "Let me leave it alone, then," said Ebenezer. "Much good may it do you! Much good it has ever done you!"

'The gaiety of my grandchild's heart welcomed the Spirit of Christmas Cheer. "There are many things from which I might have derived good, by which I have not profited, I dare say,' returned my grandchild. 'Christmas among the rest. But I am sure I have always thought of Christmas time, when it has come round -- apart from the veneration due to its sacred name and origin, if anything belonging to it can be apart from that -- as a good time: a kind, forgiving, charitable, pleasant time:)

Christmas time is the only time I know of,
In the long calendar of the year.
When men and women seem by one consent
To open their shut-up hearts without fear.

Christmas time, apart from the veneration
Due to its sacred name and origin.
Is a kind, forgiving, pleasant time,
The only time where charity is genuine.

To think of people below them as if
They are fellow-passengers to the grave.
And not another race of creatures
Bound on other journeys like a slave.

And therefore, uncle, though it has never
Put a scrap of gold in my pocket.
I believe that it has done me good.
And will do me good; and I say, "God bless it"

'The clerk in the tank involuntarily applauded: becoming immediately sensible of the impropriety, he poked the fire, and extinguished the last frail spark for ever.

' "Let me hear another sound from you," said my son, "and you'll keep your Christmas by losing your situation. You're quite a powerful speaker, sir," he added, turning to his nephew. "I wonder you don't follow your Grandfather into Parliament."

' "Don't be angry, uncle. Come! Dine with us tomorrow."

'Ebenezer said that he would see him -- yes, indeed he did. He went the whole length of the expression, and said that he would see him in that extremity first.

' "But why?" cried my grandchild. "Why?"

' "Why did you get married?" said Ebenezer.

' "Because I fell in love."

' "Because you fell in love!" growled Ebenezer, as if that were the only one thing in the world more ridiculous than a merry Christmas. "Good afternoon!"

' "Nay, uncle, but you never came to see me before that happened. Why give it as a reason for not coming now?"

' "Good afternoon," said Ebenezer.

' "I want nothing from you; I ask nothing of you; why cannot we be friends?"

' "Good afternoon," said Ebenezer.

' "I am sorry, with all my heart, to find you so resolute. We have never had any quarrel, to which I have been a party. But I have made the trial in homage to Christmas, and I'll keep my Christmas humour to the last. So A Merry Christmas, uncle!"

' "Good afternoon,."

' "And A Happy New Year!"

' "Good afternoon!"

'His nephew, my grandchild, left the room without an angry word, notwithstanding. He stopped at the outer door to bestow the greetings of the season on the clerk, who cold as he was, was warmer than Ebenezer; for he returned them cordially.

' "There's another fellow," muttered Ebenezer; who overheard him: "my clerk, with fifteen shillings a week, and a wife and family, talking about a merry Christmas. I'll retire to Bedlam."

'This lunatic, in letting my grandchild out, had let two other people in. They were portly gentlemen, pleasant to behold, and now stood, with their hats off, in Ebenezer's office. They had books and papers in their hands, and bowed to him.

' "Scrooge and Marley's, I believe," said one of the gentlemen, referring to his list. "Have I the pleasure of addressing Mr. Scrooge, or Mr. Marley?"

' "Mr. Marley has been dead these seven years," Ebenezer replied. "He died seven years ago, this very night."

' "We have no doubt his liberality is well represented by his surviving partner," said the gentleman, presenting his credentials.

'It certainly was; for they had been two kindred spirits. At the ominous word "liberality," Ebenezer frowned, and shook his head, and handed the credentials back.

Mr. Scrooge, if you permit the pleasure.
At this festive season of the year.
It is more than usually desirable
In the pleasant Christmas atmosphere.

That we should make some slight provision
For the poor and destitute in need of support.
Thousands are in want of common necessaries.
Many more are in want of common comforts.

' "Are there no prisons?" asked Ebenezer.

' "Plenty of prisons," said the gentleman, laying down the pen again.

' "And the Union workhouses?" demanded Ebenezer. "Are they still in operation?"

' "They are. Still," returned the gentleman, "I wish I could say they were not."

' "The Treadmill and the Poor Law are in full vigour, then?" said Ebenezer.

' "Both very busy, sir."

' "Oh! I was afraid, from what you said at first, that something had occurred to stop them in their useful course," said Ebenezer. "I'm very glad to hear it."

They scarcely furnish Christian cheer.
Of mind or body to the multitude.
A few of us are raising a fund,
To buy the Poor drink and food.

And some means of warmth
So the infant poor don't chill.
The aged, the sick, and the lame,
Are grateful for our Good Will.

We choose this time, of all others,
When Want is keenly felt.
Where Abundance rejoices.

When cold Neglect melts.

' "What shall I put you down for?"

' "Nothing!" Ebenezer replied.

' "You wish to be anonymous?"

' "I wish to be left alone," said Ebenezer. "Since you ask me what I wish, gentlemen, that is my answer. I don't make merry myself at Christmas and I can't afford to make idle people merry. I help to support the establishments I have mentioned -- they cost enough; and those who are badly off must go there."

' "Many can't go there; and many would rather die."

' "If they would rather die," said Ebenezer, "they had better do it, and decrease the surplus population."

' "My words," I realized hearing my own words spoken on the tongue of my son, and was overcome with penitence and grief. I forbear that wicked cant. I know What the surplus is, and Where it is. I shall not decide what men shall live, what men shall die. Let it not be that in the sight of Heaven, I am more worthless and less fit to live than millions like my own poor child! Little, little Fan.

' "Besides," Ebenezer stammered, continuing his argument with the almsmen, "-- excuse me -- I don't know that."

' "But you might know it," observed the gentleman.

' "It's not my business," Ebenezer returned. "It's enough for a man to understand his own business, and not to interfere with other people's. Mine occupies me constantly. Good afternoon, gentlemen!"

'Seeing clearly that it would be useless to pursue their point, the gentlemen withdrew. Ebenezer returned his labours with an improved opinion of himself, and in a more facetious temper than was usual with him.

'Meanwhile the fog and darkness thickened so, that people ran about with flaring links, proffering their services to go before horses in carriages, and conduct them on their way. The ancient tower of a church, whose gruff old bell was always peeping slyly down at Ebenezer out of a Gothic window in the wall, became invisible, and struck the hours and quarters in the clouds, with tremulous vibrations afterwards as if its teeth were chattering in its frozen head up there. The cold became intense. In the main street at the corner of the court, some labourers were repairing the gas-pipes, and had lighted a great fire in a brazier, round which a party of ragged men and boys were gathered: warming their hands and winking their eyes before the blaze in rapture. The water-plug being left in solitude, its overflowing sullenly congealed, and turned to misanthropic ice. The brightness of the shops where holly sprigs and berries crackled in the lamp heat of the windows, made pale faces ruddy as they passed. Poulterers' and grocers' trades became a splendid joke; a glorious pageant, with which it was next to impossible to believe that such dull principles as bargain and sale had anything to do. The Lord Mayor, in the stronghold of the mighty Mansion House, gave orders to his fifty cooks and butlers to keep Christmas as a Lord Mayor's household should; and even the little tailor, whom he had fined five shillings on the previous Monday for being drunk and bloodthirsty in the streets, stirred up to-morrow's pudding in his garret, while his lean wife and the baby sallied out to buy the beef.

'Foggier yet, and colder! Piercing, searching, biting cold. If the good Saint Dunstan had but nipped the Evil Spirit's nose with a touch of such weather as that, instead of using his familiar weapons, then indeed he would have roared to lusty purpose. The owner of one scant young nose, gnawed and mumbled by the hungry cold as bones are gnawed by dogs, stooped down at Ebenezer's keyhole to regale him with a Christmas carol:

> *God bless you merry, gentlemen,*
> *May nothing you dismay,*
> *Remember Christ our Savior,*
> *Was born on Christmas day,*
> *To save us all from Satan's power.*
> *When we were gone astray.*
>   *O tidings of comfort and joy,*
>   *Comfort and joy*
>   *O tidings of comfort and joy*
>
> *From God our Heavenly Father*
> *A blessed angel came,*
> *And unto certain shepherds*

Broth tidings of the same,
How that in Bethlehem was born
The Son of God by name.
  O tidings of comfort and joy,
  Comfort and joy
  O tidings of comfort and joy

"Fear, not," then said the angel,
"Let nothing you affright,
This day is born a Savior,
Of a pure virgin bright.
To free all those who trust in him
From Satan's power and might."
  O tidings of comfort and joy,
  Comfort and joy
  O tidings of comfort and joy

The shepherds at those tidings
Rejoiced much in mind,
And left their flocks a-feeding
In tempest, storm, and wind,
And went to Bethlehem straightway,
This blessed babe to find.
  O tidings of comfort and joy,
  Comfort and joy
  O tidings of comfort and joy

But when to Bethlehem they came,
Where at this infant lay,
They found him in a manger,
Where oxen feed on hay;
His mother Mary kneeling
Unto the Lord did pray.
  O tidings of comfort and joy,
  Comfort and joy
  O tidings of comfort and joy

Now to the Lord sing praises,
All you within this place,
And with true love and brotherhood
Each other now embrace;
This holy tide of Christmas
All other doth deface.
   O tidings of comfort and joy,
   Comfort and joy
   O tidings of comfort and joy

' "Tuppence, gov'ner," inquired the young man bold enough with Christmas cheer to enter into "Scrooge & Marley's" with his hand outstretched.

'My son sneered, "Tuppence for a song?"

' "It's Christmas time, gov'ner."

' "I ask you, young sir, why should I pay a poor pauper tuppence for a song I did not request nor desire to hear? If I should fancy to hear a Christmas Carol, I could very easily go down to the nearby church and their collection plate would be as empty of my tuppence as your pockets are now."

'The young man stood his ground quite dumbfounded.

' "Good afternoon!"

'And a young lady, just as bold as the boy, smiled with Christmas cheer from ear to ear, "But sir, it is Christmas Eve."

' "Since you, little miss, may not be educated in the laws of gentlemanly society, you are not aware that you are trespassing on my property. Therefore, I will allow you to exit my counting house with your hinds intact. Now get out, or my ruler will be broken across your backsides!"

'My son seized the ruler with such energy of action, that the singers fled in terror, leaving the keyhole to the fog and even more congenial frost.

'At length the hour of shutting up the counting-house arrived. With an ill-will Ebenezer dismounted from his stool, and tacitly admitted the fact to the expectant clerk in the Tank, who instantly snuffed his candle out, and put on his hat.

' "You'll want all day to-morrow, I suppose?" said Ebenezer.

' "If quite convenient, sir."

' "It's not convenient," said Ebenezer, "and it's not fair. If I was to stop half-a-crown for it, you'd think yourself ill-used, I'll be bound?"

'The clerk smiled faintly.

' "And yet," said my son, "you don't think me ill-used, when I pay a day's wages for no work."

'The clerk observed that it was only once a year.

' "A poor excuse for picking a man's pocket every twenty-fifth of December!" said my son, buttoning his great-coat to the chin. "But I suppose you must have the whole day. Be here all the earlier next morning."

'The clerk promised that he would; and my son walked out with a growl. The office was closed in a twinkling, and the clerk, with the long ends of his white comforter dangling below his waist (for he boasted no great-coat). He greeted the children of Cornhill with a "Merry Christmas" and they burst into their caroling,

> *Here we come a sliding,*
> *On down Cornhill Lane.*
> *We must beware the Scrooge.*
> *For he'll likely give us pain.*
>
> *We'll never throw snowballs,*
> *Or ever stand in his way.*
> *We must beware the Scrooge,*
> *We never know what he'll say.*
>
> *Look 'ee there's Bob Cratchit*
> *Who never walks in haste,*
> *The long ends of his comforter*
> *Are dangling below his waist.*
>
> *Hallo there, Mista Bob Cratchit,*
> *Care to join a snowball fight?*
> *Hallo, Halle, watch out there,*
> *Mista Cratchit's snow's in flight!*

Hallo there, Mista Bob Cratchit,
Would you join us in a slide?
Hallo, Halle, down twenty times,
Never once fell on his backside.

Here we come a sliding,
Before the snow it melts.
Mista Bob Cratchit runs
Home as hard as he can pelt.

'A strange warmth came into my son's counting-house, despite of, no!– in spite of, the single, solitary coal in the hearth having breathed out its last, or the candles that had warmed Bob Cratchit's aching, frozen fingers having been snuffed out for the evening. This was all because of the low temperature my poor boy kept about him at all times. But strangely, so very strange, the counting-house began to thaw even by one degree that Christmas, despite, no -- in spite of, his icing it in these dogdays.

'I dropped onto my knees before for ghost of Jacob Marley and grabbed the chains of cash-boxes, keys, padlocks, ledgers, deeds, and heavy purses wrought in steel, and I myself was wrought with sorrow, fear, and shame, and most unawaredly– love.

'And then I stood in the library of my memory frantically scanning the bookshelves for the Holiest of All Scriptures. I was a man of Parliament. Could I not argue for and against any measure brought before the assembly? Was I not considered by many of my fellow Members of Parliament to be an unofficial, unCatholic Devil's Advocate within the members? And if the devil could cite Scripture for his purpose, an evil soul producing holy witness like a villain with a smiling cheek, then by God, so could I. But lo! I could not locate the Scriptures in the rows and rows of books. Of course, I had read the Scriptures, hadn't I? I was educated at university. My father was a Parson, a stern disciplinarian, who never spared the rod nor spoiled his children. Surely, I knew the precedent of the argument I intended to debate.

'And the Ghost of my father, Parson Scrooge echoed, "Jeremiah, remember the LORD, the LORD thy God, is merciful and gracious, longsuffering, and abundant in goodness and truth, keeping mercy for thousands, forgiving iniquity and transgression and sin, and that will by no means clear the guilty; visiting the iniquity of the fathers upon the children, and upon the children's children, unto the third and to the fourth generation."

'I bellowed in sorrow, clutching the chains that Jacob Marley had forged link by link as if they were a lifeline, and prayed in my supplication:

I pray to you Jacob, listen to my plea.
The Christmas Spirits have planted the seed.
Of the Christian Spirit in my cold heart.
I ask you, on my son's behalf intercede.

I'll never forget what is of the Past.
I will forever see what shall be.
Please haunt my son, Jacob.
Please haunt him on this Christmas Eve.

Aah-aah-aah-aah-aah-aah-aah-aah (sang an angelic choir)
My little Fan will bring home my son.
Aah-aah-aah-aah-aah-aah-aah (sang the choir)
We'll be together all Christmas. It's begun!

I will be so much kinder than I used to be.
I'll be a changed man with a changed nature.
I'll be a Christian soul on every calendar day.
My Ebenezer, my Little Fan, I'll nurture.

' "Jeremiah Scrooge. I cannot do as you ask. I pray for nothing more than to effect change in the mortal sphere. But we all must choose the course that our life's path will take. I have chosen mine and I bare these chains as penance. Would you know," pursued the Ghost, "the weight and length of the strong coil Ebenezer bears? It was full as heavy and as long as this, seven Christmas Eves ago. He has laboured on it, since. It is a ponderous chain!"

' "But what if I cannot effect change upon my son?" I pleaded,

"What if the damage is already done? Please, Jacob, please."

' "I cannot," said the ghost of Jacob Marley as he was drawn away from Ebenezer's desk toward the window where he would be doomed to forever wander through the world -- oh, woe is me! -- and witness what he cannot share, but might have shared on earth, and turned to happiness! I clutched at the chains straining like a longshoreman to restrain the ghost, but the chains slipped through my fingers as if they were greased wheels.

'Then the Phantom raised his hand, motioning for the ghost of Jacob Marley to sit, to finally sit, to blessedly rest, upon a stool beside the desk of my son, Ebenezer Scrooge.

' "What? By what miracle–?" the ghost of Jacob Marley said, the weight of his chains noticeably lighter.

'I said, marvelling at the power of prayer, "I pray that this Phantom has answered both our prayers." And I remembered the Word of God which once and always says, Be careful for nothing; but in every thing by prayer and supplication with thanksgiving let your requests be made known unto God. And the peace of God, which passeth all understanding, shall keep your hearts and minds through Christ Jesus.

'And the Phantom lead me back to my own Christmas Present, where I would speak so gently to Little Fan that same dear night after she had gone to bed, that she would not be afraid to ask me once more if Ebenezer might come home so they might visit Mother in the hospital on Christmas Day! And I would say, Yes, you should; and sent her in a coach to bring him home. And he's to be a man! and never to go back there to that school again; and then, Ebenezer and Fan and Father and Mother would be to be together all the Christmas long, and have the merriest time in all the world.'

Stave VI
"Bridge – A Ghastly Interlude"

Jeremiah had endeavoured in this Ghostly little story, to raise the Ghost of an Idea, which shall not put his listeners out of humour with themselves, with each other, with the season, or with him. He hoped may it haunt their houses pleasantly, and no one wish to lay it.

When the ghostly tale was told, Dr. Chattlesworth reached into his waistcoat where any other gentlemen would keep his watch to have impatiently checked the time, and instead withdraw a silver whistle. Upon the sounding the loud, shrill squeal, the front door to the Bishop home was kicked in, its frame and hinges shattered at the onslaught. Four nurses, great barrel-chested, ham-fisted brutes, rushed through like soldiers charging across a battlefield. Some of the house-staff sought to intervene, but were met with blows from billy clubs, while others fled, as if they were rats on a sinking ship, into their own meagre quarters. The guests collapsed to the floor when the door to their room was burst in as if they had as a collective lost the very will to live.

Dr. Chattlesworth bellowed orders to the brutish were-elephants, whom one could quite easily imagine great ivory tusks protruding from their dim grey jowls. They bull-rushed the room, overturning chairs, upending the table. The din of breaking glassware and shattering china mocked the seasonal delights of jingling bells on winter sleighs gliding over snow-shrouded country lanes. The doctor's orders came from the depths of his blackened soul in the iambic pentameter of the most ghastly Christless carol that Christmas Day!

> *He has a religious mania, I am quite sure,*
> *Require he a most vulgar tincture.*
> *He hath worked himself into spark despair.*
> *Sooth his distraught nerves in the calming chair!*
>
> *We shalt extinguish too violent strife*
> *And exorbitant form of fiery life.*
> *Whenst too many fools accidently drown–*
> *Dragg'd out for dead, restor'd to their breath.*
>
> *With full use of their wit is their renown–*
> *Jan Baptista van Helmont doth saith.*
> *Enemas of yogurt art a cure-all.*
> *Leech his arms, his feet. His madness shalt stall*
>
> *Whenst we vomit him strongly. With our help*
> *Cure his head wit' warm lungs of lambs, sheep, whelps.*
> *Prime my (operating) theatre a trephine to trepan.*
> *Rescue his soul from the pressure of madmen.*
>
> *We choose this time of the Christmas season,*
> *When spirits are high; minds out of reason;*
> *Melancholy abounds; reigns the insane.*
> *We can cure them through torture and through pain.*
>
> *Hearts filled with joy, comfort, and glad-tidings,*
> *Turned melancholy and suiciding.*
> *We kind souls at Bethlehem Hospital,*
> *Not-a-thing's too extreme wit' our cure-alls.*

And they, more hoodlum than nurse, seized a frightful and weeping Jeremiah Scrooge and, with the swiftness of a stage-magician and the brutality of a pugilist, dressed him in a straight-waistcoat. The hooligans, they blackened his eyes and broke his teeth with their ham-fists. The ruffians, they kicked him with their leather-booted *Pachydermata*-feet. The thugs, they abandoned him collapsed on the floor in a foetal-position, whimpering like a scolded mongrel, quite briefly before dragging him constrained-flailing from the Bishop home.

Ebenezer said, 'Let my father retire to Bedlam!'

Little Fan cried out for her father, the sorrow, the weeping too much for her large heart. Water and blood cascaded down her legs, staining her yellow Christmas dress crimson, the truest colour of death. Henry Bishop cried out for a doctor, for an ambulance-carriage. The blush of Christmas cheer on her face had decayed into a pallor masque. Little Fan, always a delicate creature, whom a breath might have withered, was in the midst of dying in child-birth.

The seasonal celebration of The Haunting of Ebenezer Scrooge *continues to its conclusion on page **181** after the centre section of the complete score to our* MAGICAL, MYSTICAL, MUSICAL CHRISTMAS MADRIGAL IN PROSE.

The Christmas Carols

Sheet Music

A Merry Christmas, Ebbie (God Save You)

words: Robert Dwight Brown
adapted from Charles Dickens

music: Bette Lunn

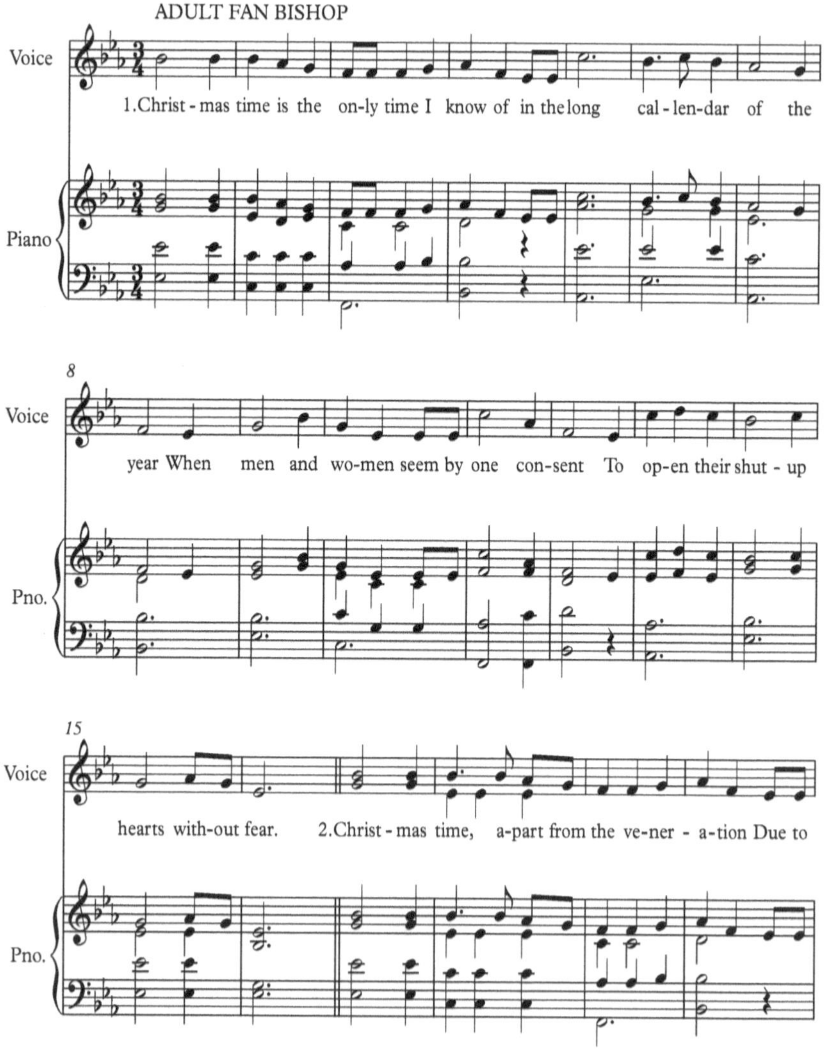
ADULT FAN BISHOP
Voice
Piano
1.Christ - mas time is the on-ly time I know of in the long cal - len-dar of the
8
Voice
year When men and wo-men seem by one con-sent To op-en their shut - up
Pno.
15
Voice
hearts with-out fear. 2.Christ - mas time, a-part from the ve-ner - a-tion Due to
Pno.

2

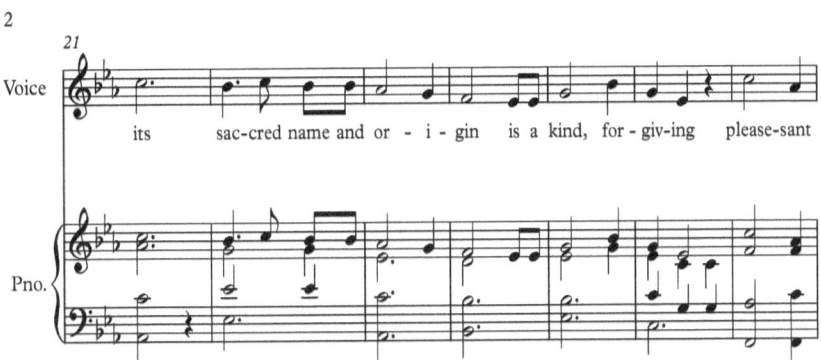

its sac-cred name and or - i - gin is a kind, for-giv-ing please-sant

time, The on - ly time, where char-i-ty is gen-u - ine. 3.To think of

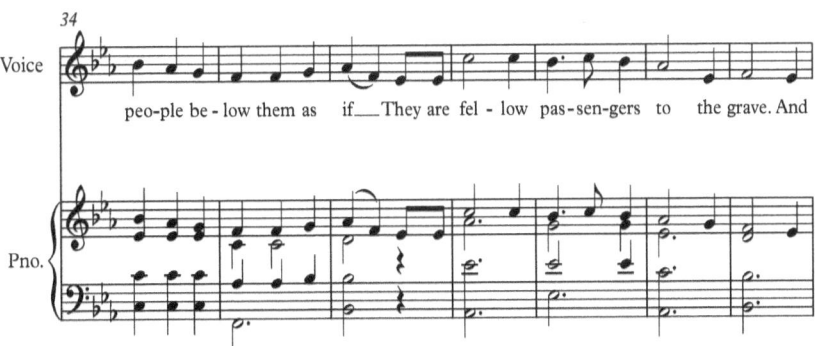

peo-ple be-low them as if___They are fel - low pas-sen-gers to the grave. And

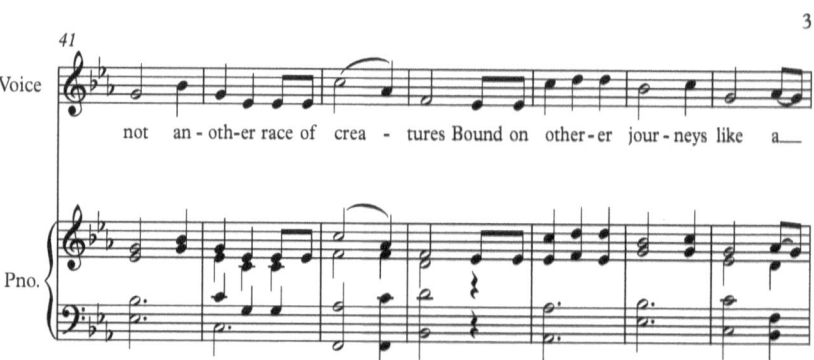

not an-oth-er race of crea - tures Bound on other-er jour-neys like a___

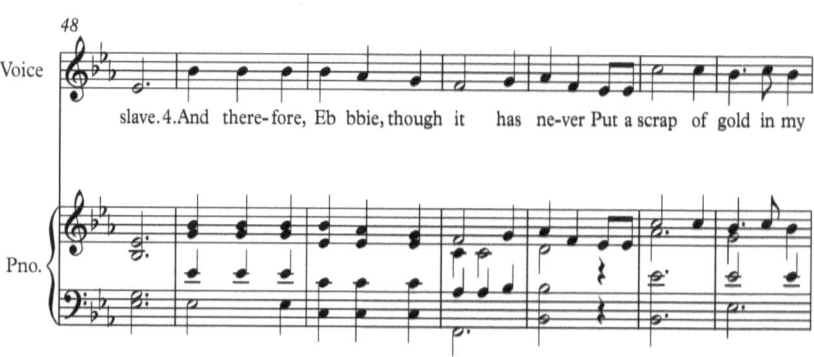

slave. 4.And there-fore, Eb bbie, though it has ne-ver Put a scrap of gold in my

pock - et I be-lieve that it has done me

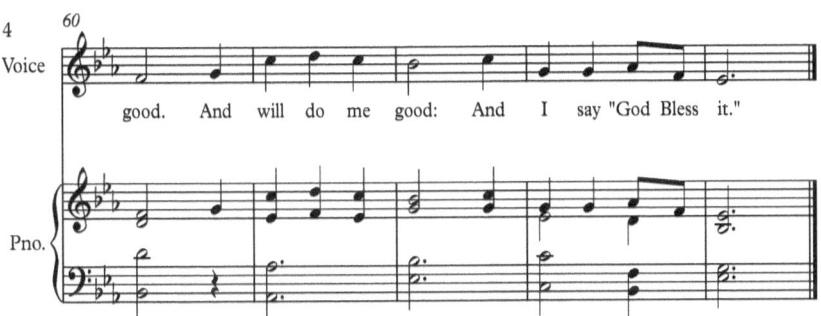

4

Voice

good.   And   will   do   me   good: And   I   say   "God Bless   it."

Pno.

Good King Wenceslas

J.M NEALE

tune: *Tempus Adest Floridum*, 1582

GUESTS AT THE BISHOP HOME

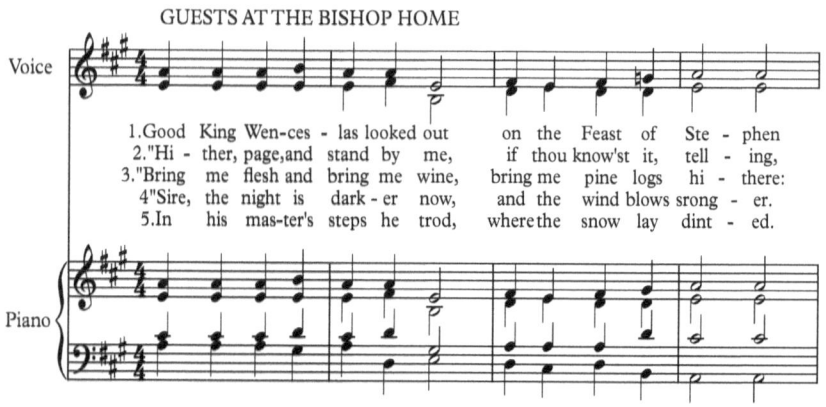

1.Good King Wen-ces - las looked out   on the Feast of Ste - phen
2."Hi - ther, page,and stand by me,   if thou know'st it, tell - ing,
3."Bring me flesh and bring me wine,   bring me pine logs hi - there:
4"Sire, the night is dark - er now,   and the wind blows srong - er.
5.In his mas-ter's steps he trod,   where the snow lay dint - ed.

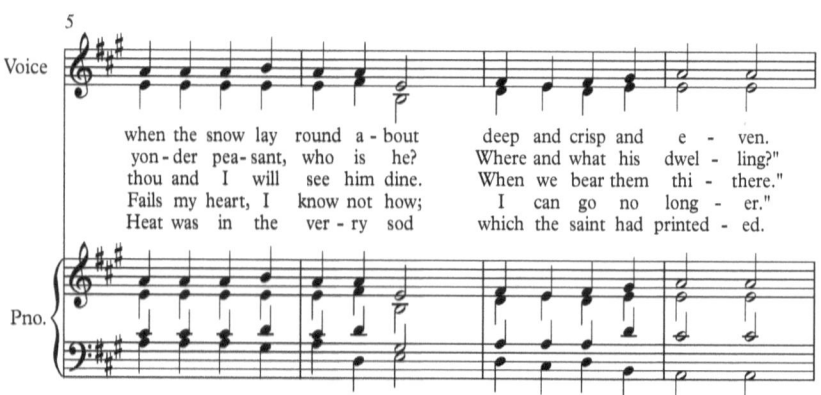

when the snow lay round a - bout   deep and crisp and e - ven.
yon - der pea- sant, who is he?   Where and what his dwel - ling?"
thou and I will see him dine.   When we bear them thi - there."
Fails my heart, I know not how;   I can go no long - er."
Heat was in the ver - ry sod   which the saint had printed - ed.

2

9

Voice

Bright - ly shone the moon that night, though the frost was cru - el,
"Sire, he lives a good league hence, und - der-neath the moun - tain,
Page and mon-arch, forth they went, forth they went to - ge - ther
"Mark my foot-steps, my good page; tread thou in them bold - ly:
There-fore Chris-tian men, be sure, wealth or rank pos - ses - sing,

Pno.

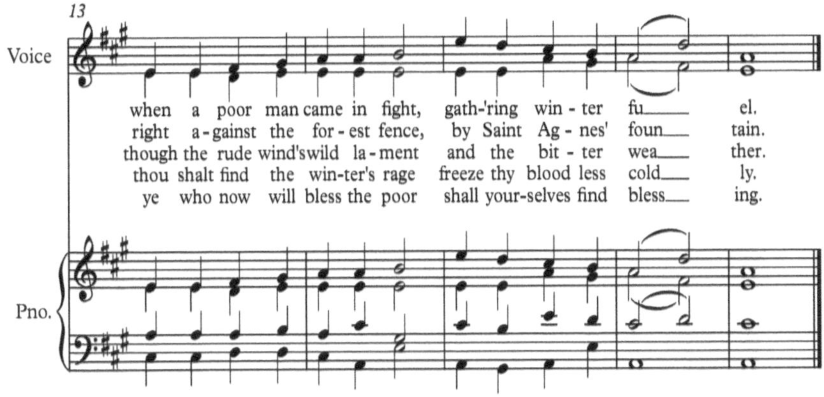

13

Voice

when a poor man came in fight, gath-'ring win - ter fu_____ el.
right a - gainst the for - est fence, by Saint Ag - nes' foun____ tain.
though the rude wind's wild la - ment and the bit - ter wea____ ther.
thou shalt find the win-ter's rage freeze thy blood less cold____ ly.
ye who now will bless the poor shall your-selves find bless____ ing.

Pno.

Joy to the World

ISAAC WATTS

tune: Antioch, George Frederick Handel
adapt. & arr. by Lowell Mason

Voice

Hummed by LITTLE FAN
or sung by CHORUS OF ANGELS

1.Joy   to   the world! The Lord   is   come.   Let   earth   re - ceive   her
2.Joy   to   the earth! The Sav - iour reigns. Let   men   theirsongs   em-
3.No   more let sins   and sor - rows grow   nor   thorns   in - fest   the
4.He   rules the world! with truth and   grace   and   makes   the   na - tions

Piano

Voice

King.   Let ev - 'ry   heart   pre - pare_ Him   room,__ and
ploy   while fields and   floods, rocks, hills_ and_   plains___ re-
ground;   He comes   to   make   his   bless - ing   flow___ Far
prove   the glor - ries   of   his   right-eous ness___ and

Pno.

2

Voice

heav'n and na - ture___ sing, and___ heav'n and na - ture___
peat the sound - ing___ joy, re - peat the sound - ing___
as the curse is___ found. Far___ as the curse is___
wond - ers of His___ love. and___ wond - ers of His___

Pno.

and heave'n and na - ture sing and
re - peat the sound - ing joy re -
and won - ders of His love and

Voice

sing, and hea ven and heav - ven and na - ture sing.
joy, re - peat_ re - peat___ the sound - ing joy.
found. far_ as_ far as___ the curse is found.
love, and won - ders, won - ders of HIis love.

Pno.

heav'n and na - ture sing
peat the sound-ing joy
won - ders of His love

A Christmas Carol

words: Robert Dwight Brown

music: Bette Lunn

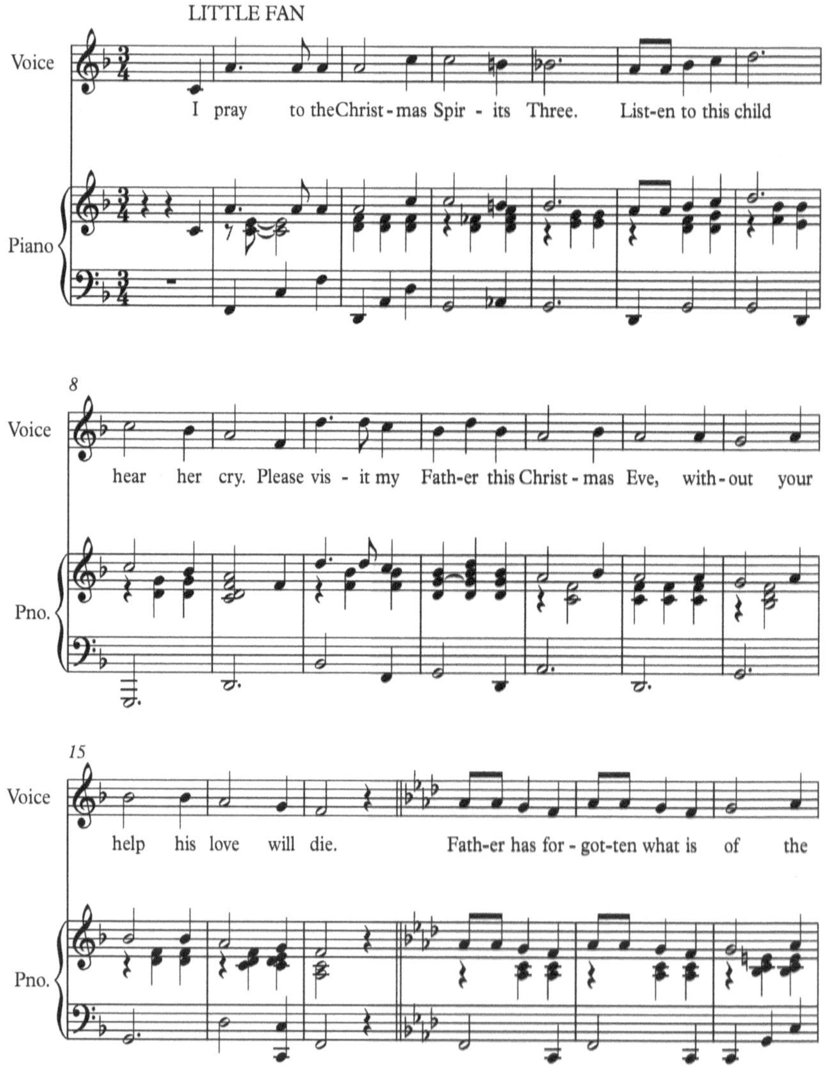

LITTLE FAN

Voice

I pray to the Christ - mas Spir - its Three. List-en to this child

Piano

hear her cry. Please vis - it my Fath-er this Christ - mas Eve, with - out your

Pno.

help his love will die. Fath-er has for - got-ten what is of the

Pno.

2

past Father is blind_____ to what shall be. Please haunt my

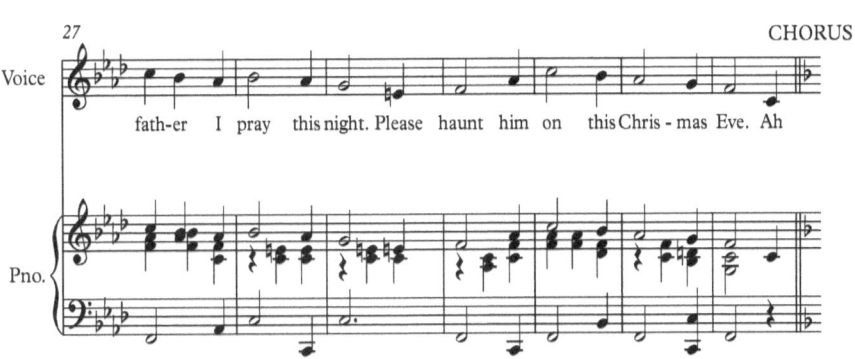

fath-er I pray this night. Please haunt him on this Chris - mas Eve. Ah

OF ANGELS   LITTLE FAN

Ah - ah-ah ah_____ ah_____ ah. Please vis - it my fath-er in this time   of yule.

CHORUS OF ANGELS   LITTLE FAN

Ah - ah-ah   ah_____   ah_____   ah.   And bring   my broth - er   home   from

school.   Fath-er has for - got-ten who his fam'   ly   is.

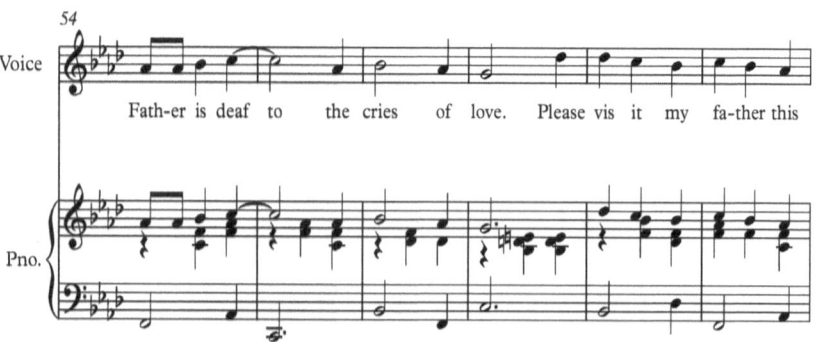

Fath-er is deaf to   the   cries   of   love.   Please vis   it   my   fa-ther this

4

Christ - mas Eve   I   pray   to   Spir   its   up   a - bove.

The First Nowell

traditional English, 18th cent.

traditional English, 17th cent.
harm. John Stainer, alt.

ELIZABETH SCROOGE

1.The first Now well the an-gel did say, was to cer-tain poor
2.They look - ed up and saw a star shin-ing in the
3.And by the light of that same star three wise men
4.This star drew nigh to the north - west o'er Beth - le -
5.Then en - tered in those wise men three, full rev - er - ent -

shep-herds in fields as they lay, in fields where they lay keep-ing their
east be - yond them far, and to the earth it gave great
came from coun - try far, to seek for a king was their in -
hem it took its rest, and there it did both stop and
ly up - on their kness, and of - fered there in His pre -

2

13

Voice

sheep   on   a   cold win-ter's   night   that   was   so   deep.   Now-ell,   Now-
light   and_   so   it   con-tin-ued both   day   and night.
tent,   and to   fol-low   the   star - where-ev - er   it   went.
stay   right   o - ver   the   place   where   Je   -   sus   lay.
sence   their   gold   and   myrhh and   frank -   in-cense.

Pno.

19

Voice

ell.   Now-ell,   Now-ell   Born is   the   King   of   Is   -   ra - el

Pno.

Immaculate Wassail

words: Robert Dwight Brown

music: Bette Lunn

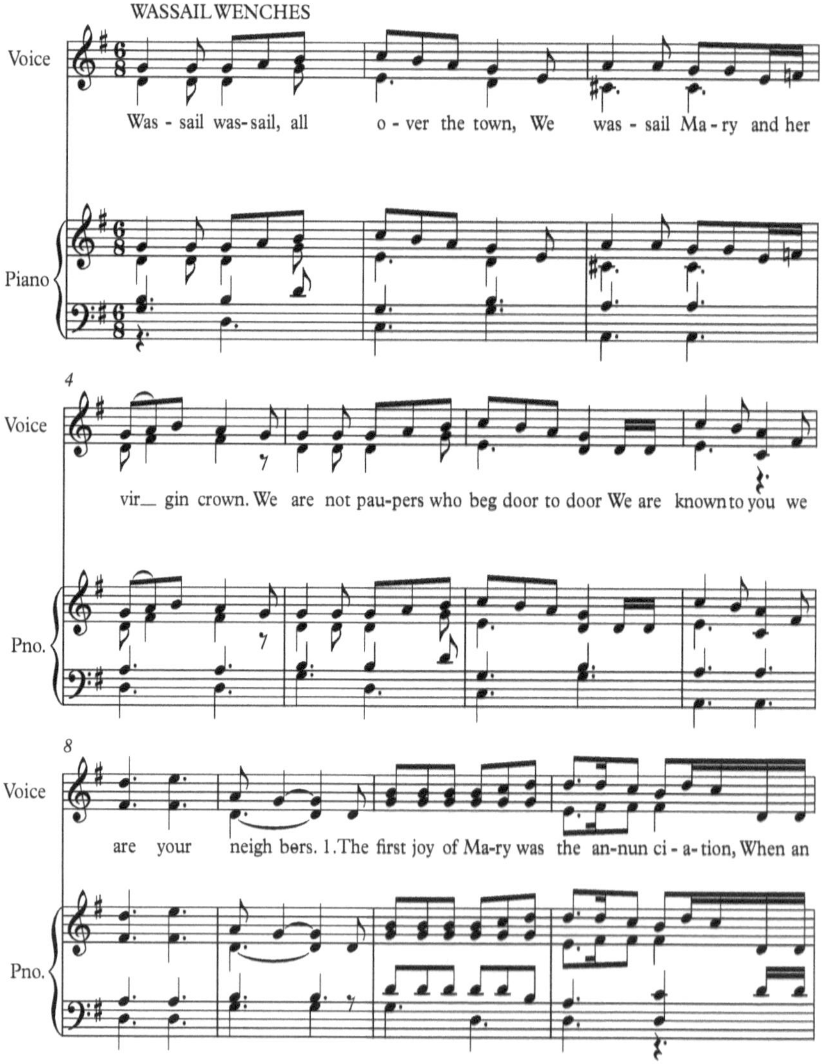
WASSAIL WENCHES
Voice
Piano
Was - sail was- sail, all o - ver the town, We was - sail Ma - ry and her
4
Voice
Pno.
vir_ gin crown. We are not pau-pers who beg door to door We are known to you we
8
Voice
Pno.
are your neigh bers. 1.The first joy of Ma-ry was the an-nun ci - a- tion, When an

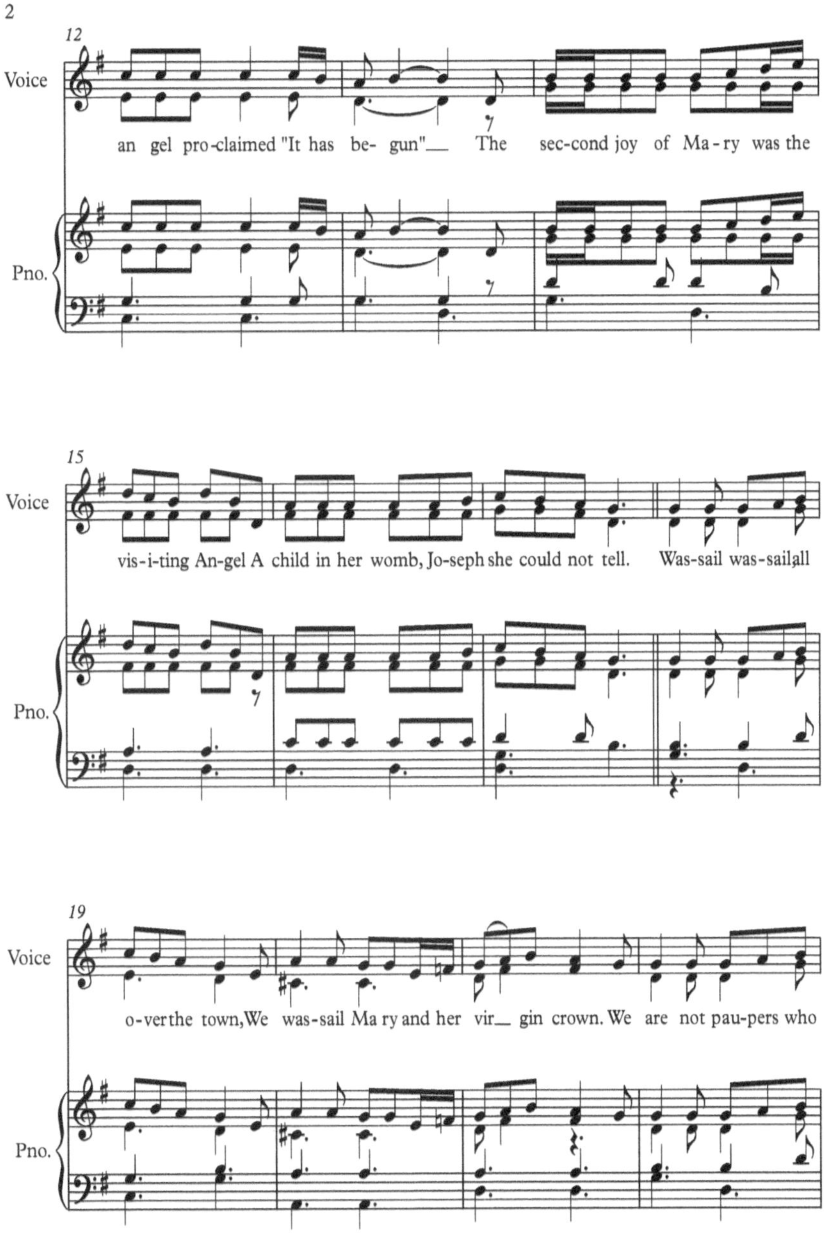

2

Voice: an gel pro-claimed "It has be- gun"__ The sec-cond joy of Ma - ry was the

Voice: vis-i-ting An-gel A child in her womb, Jo-seph she could not tell. Was-sail was-sail all

Voice: o-verthe town, We was-sail Ma ry and her vir__ gin crown. We are not pau-pers who

beg door to door We are known to you we are your neigh bors.__ 2.The

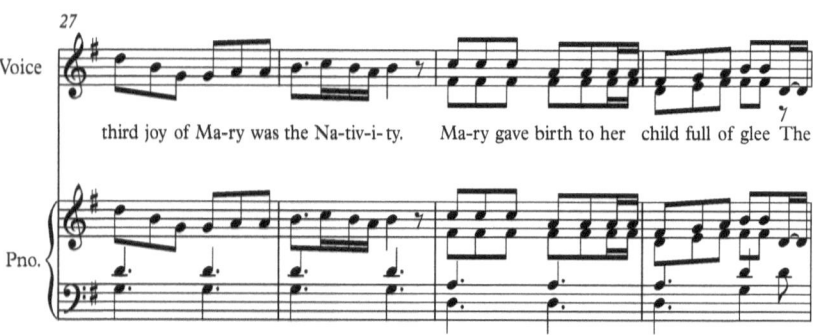

third joy of Ma-ry was the Na-tiv-i-ty. Ma-ry gave birth to her child full of glee The

fourth joy of Ma - ry was the E-pi-pha-ny. The__ Ma-gi came to a-dore the

4

child di-vi-ni-ty. Was-sail was-sail, all o-ver the town, We was-sail Ma ry and her

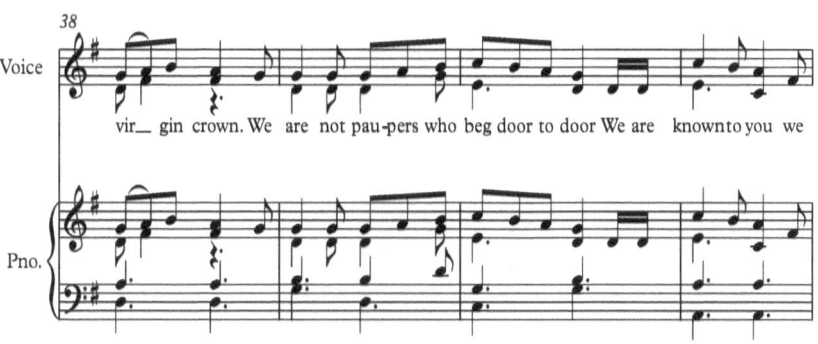

vir_ gin crown. We are not pau-pers who beg door to door We are known to you we

are your neigh bers. 3. The fifth joy of Ma ry was Je - sus in the tem-ple. And a-

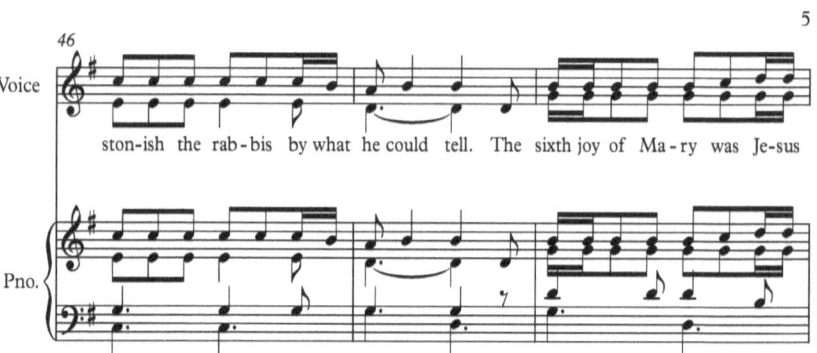

ston-ish the rab-bis by what he could tell. The sixth joy of Ma-ry was Je-sus

res-sur-rec ted.___ Je-sus was a-live af-ter be-ing cru-ci-fied and bled.

Was-sail was-sail, all o-ver the town, We was-sail Ma-ry and her vir___ gin crown. We

6

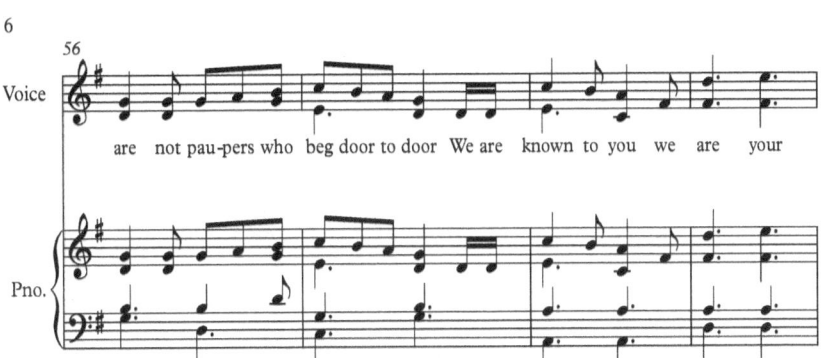

are not pau-pers who beg door to door We are known to you we are your

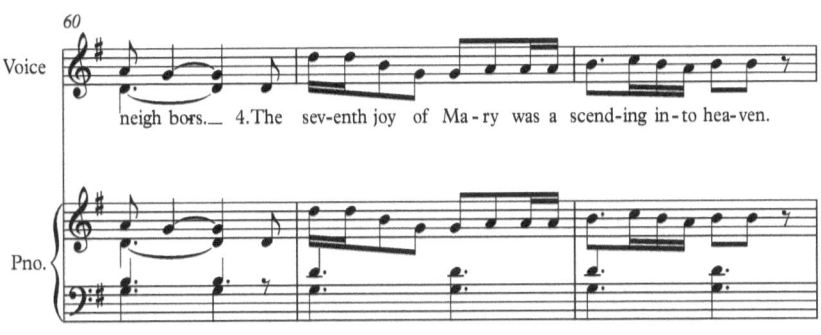

neigh bors.__ 4.The sev-enth joy of Ma - ry was a scend-ing in-to hea-ven.

These are the joys of Ma-ry that num-ber se-ven.We have was-sailed the se-ven joys of

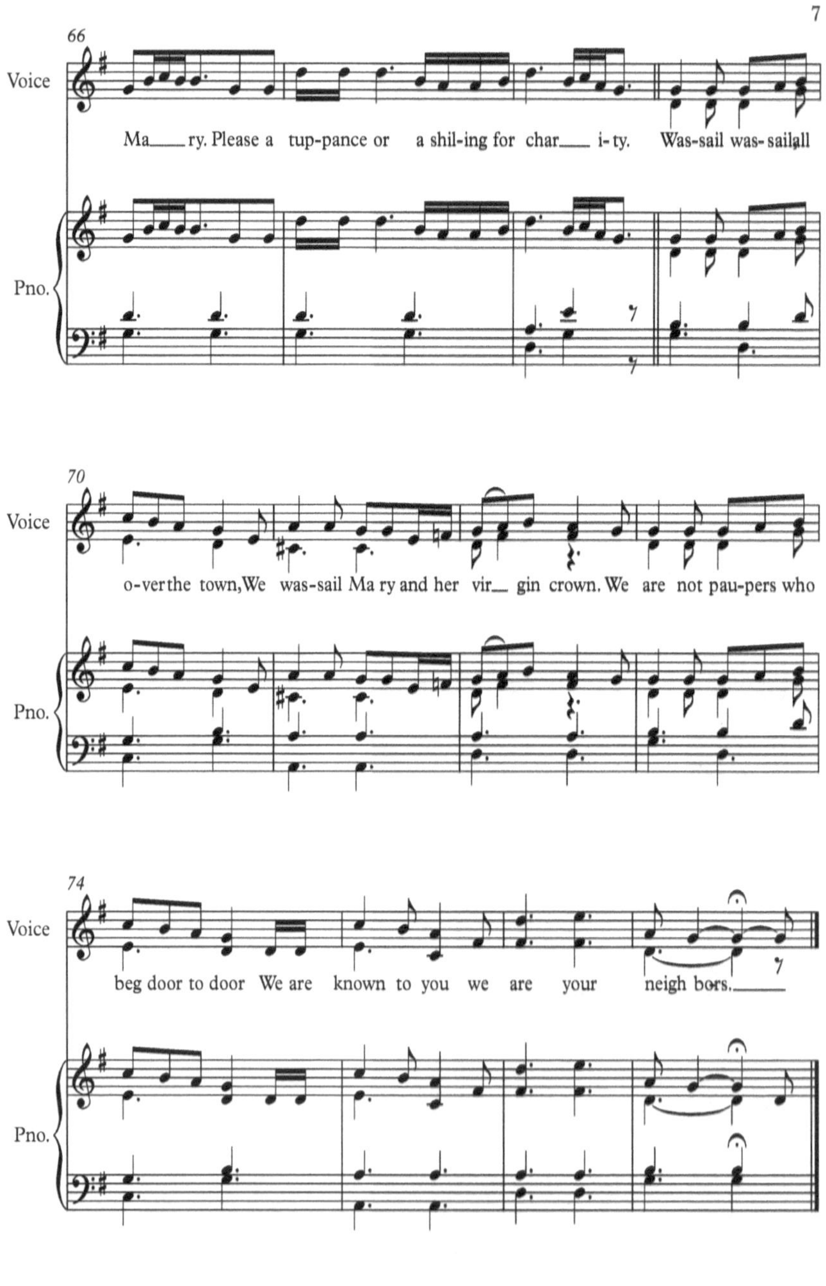

7
66
Voice
Ma___ry. Please a tup-pance or a shil-ing for char___ i-ty. Was-sail was-sail all
Pno.
70
Voice
o-ver the town, We was-sail Ma ry and her vir__ gin crown. We are not pau-pers who
Pno.
74
Voice
beg door to door We are known to you we are your neigh bors.___
Pno.

119

O Come, O Come Emmanuel

words: Latin c. 9th cent.
trans. John M Neale

music: *Veni, veni Emmanuel*
plainsong. 15th cent, alt.

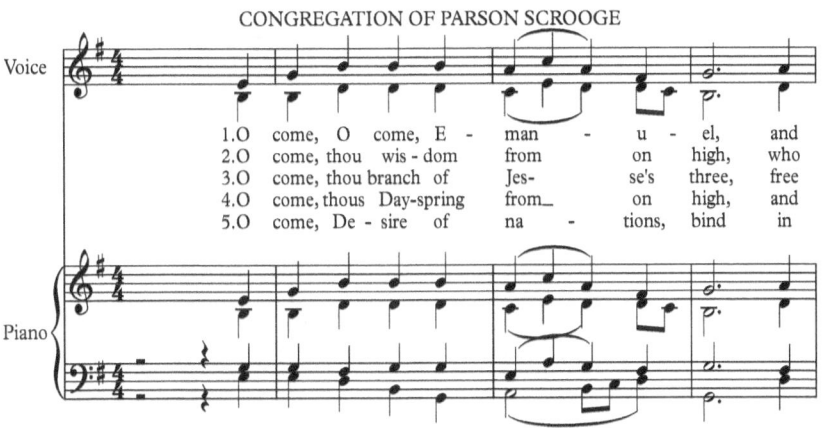

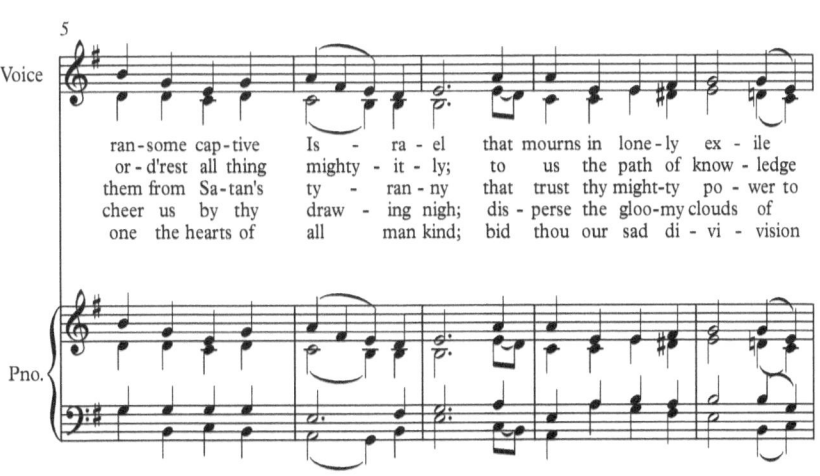

2

Voice

here un - til the Son of God ap - pear. Re - joice! Re -
show, and teach us in her ways to go.
save, and give them vic - t'ry o'er_____ the grave.
night, and death's dark sha-dow put_____ to flight.
cease, and be thy - self our King_____ of Peace.

Pno.

Voice

joice! Em - man - u - el shall come to thee, O Is - ra - el!

Pno.

Adeste Fideles

John F. Wade
trans. Fredrick Oakeley & others

John. F. Wade, 1751

EBENEZER SCROOGE as a Child

1.A - des - te fi - de - les, lae - ti - tri um - phan - tes ve -
2.Can - tet nunc - i - o cho - us an - ge - lo - rum,
3.Er - go qui na - tus di - e ho - de er - na,

ni - te ve - ni - te in Beth - le - hem: na - tum vi - de - te
can - tet nunc au - la cae - les - ti - um: glo - ri - a, glo - ri
Je - su ti - bi sit glor - ri - a: Pa - tris ae - ter - ni

2

re - gem-an-ge - lo - rum: ve - ni - te, a - do - re - mus, ve - ni - te, a - do -
in ex - cel - sis De - o:
ver-bum car - o fac - tum:

re - mus, ve - ni - te, a - do - re - mus, Do - mi - num.

Birth of a Christmas Soul

words: Robert Dwight Brown

music: Bette Lunn

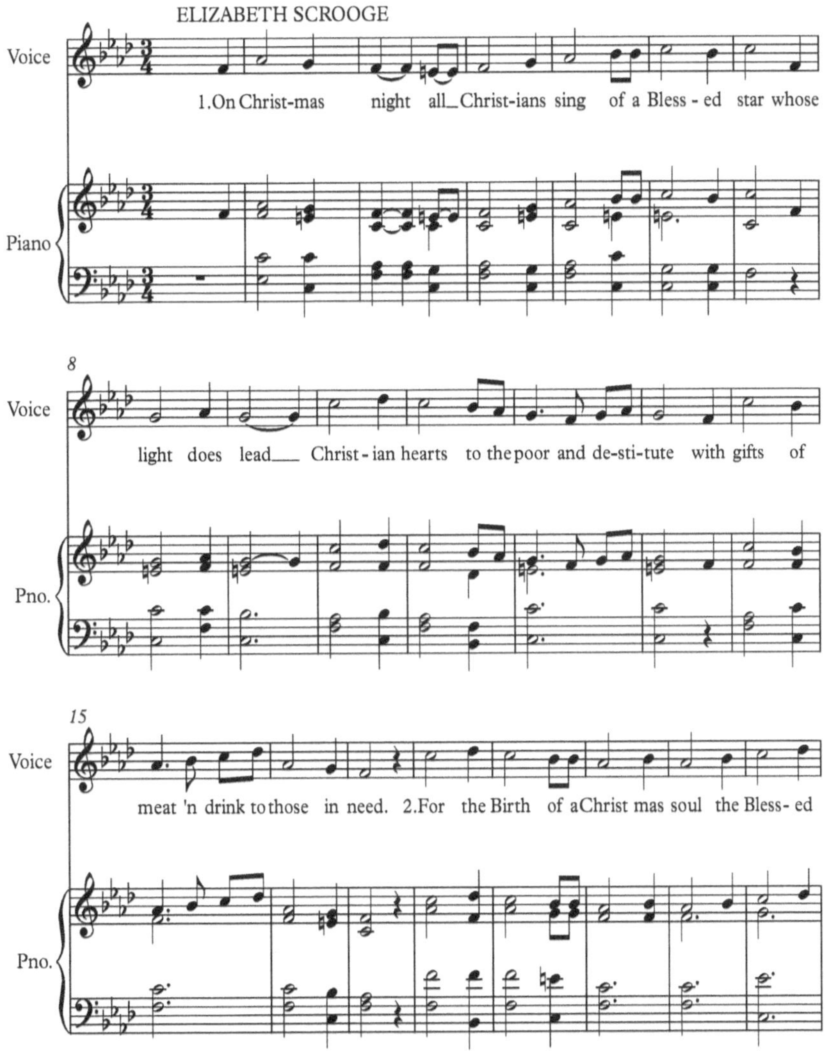
ELIZABETH SCROOGE
Voice
1.On Christ-mas night all_Christ-ians sing of a Bless - ed star whose
Piano
8
Voice
light does lead___ Christ - ian hearts to the poor and de-sti-tute with gifts of
Pno.
15
Voice
meat 'n drink to those in need. 2.For the Birth of a Christ mas soul the Bless- ed
Pno.

124

2

Voice (m. 23): star led the Ma - gi well Up - on a lone - ly man-ger of straw and hay where

Pno.

Voice (m. 30): God gave the world, Em-man - u - elle. 3.There a vir-gin by a gift from

Pno.

Voice (m. 37): God Gave_ birth to a child by the morn - ing tide, An in - fant

Pno.

child des-tined by hea-ven-ly plan to grow in-to man-hood and be cru - ci-

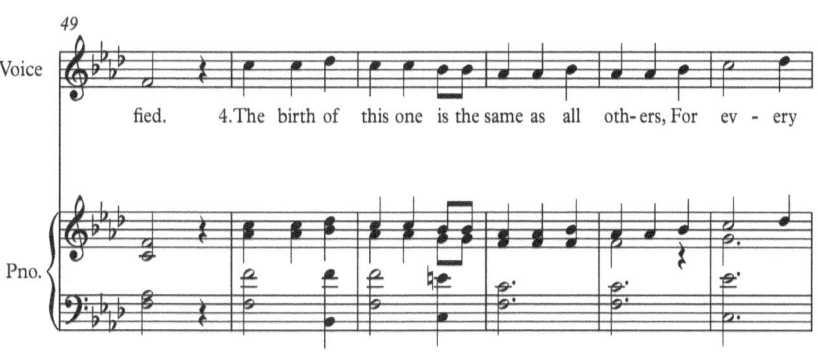

fied. 4.The birth of this one is the same as all oth-ers, For ev - ery

wo-man who has lived up-on this earth, whe-ther for a sim-ple life or Son of God

4

born, will glad-ly give up her life, for her child's birth. 5.Fan, my

lit-tle Fan, you're such a wo-man grown and swol-len with child so

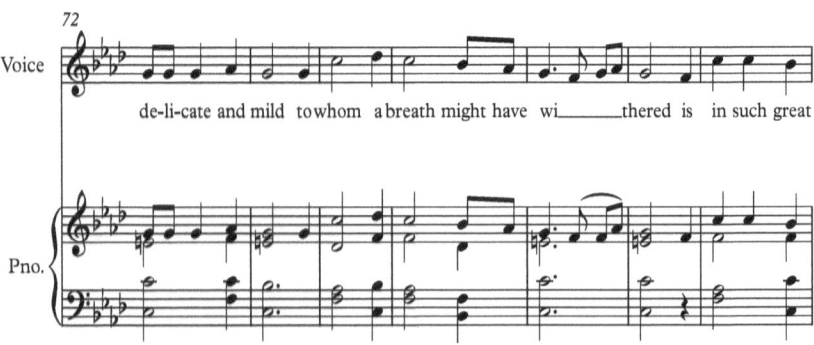

de-li-cate and mild to whom a breath might have wi_____thered is in such great

5

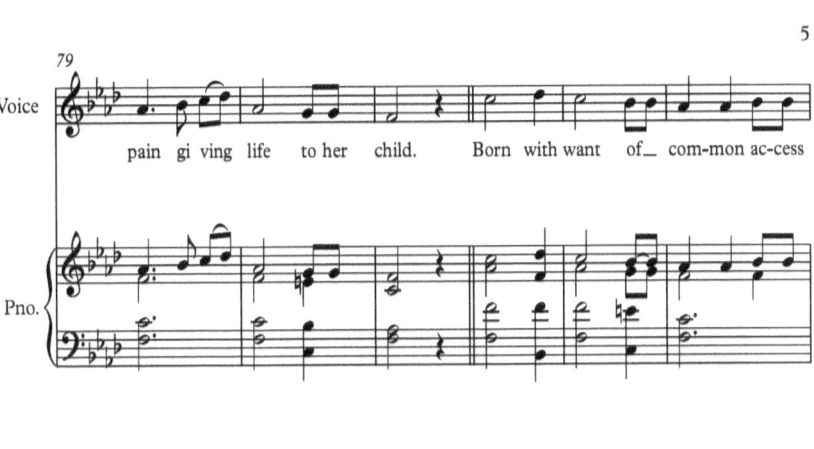

pain gi ving life to her child. Born with want of__ com-mon ac-cess

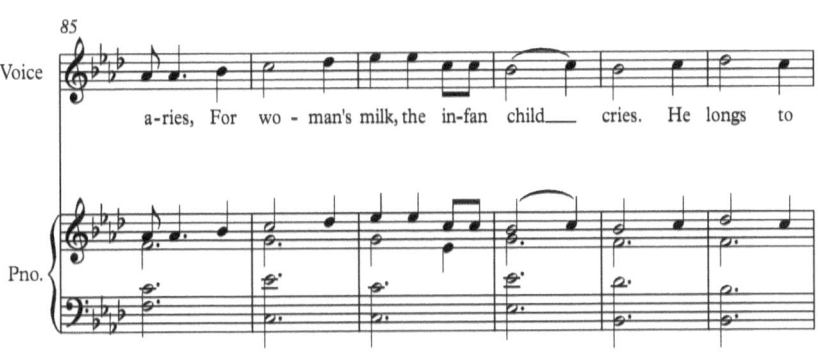

a-ries, For wo - man's milk, the in-fan child___ cries. He longs to

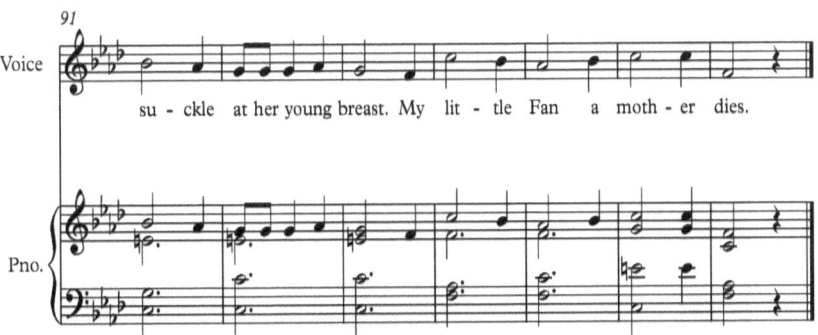

su - ckle at her young breast. My lit - tle Fan a moth - er dies.

The Glory to God

Traditional

Traditional

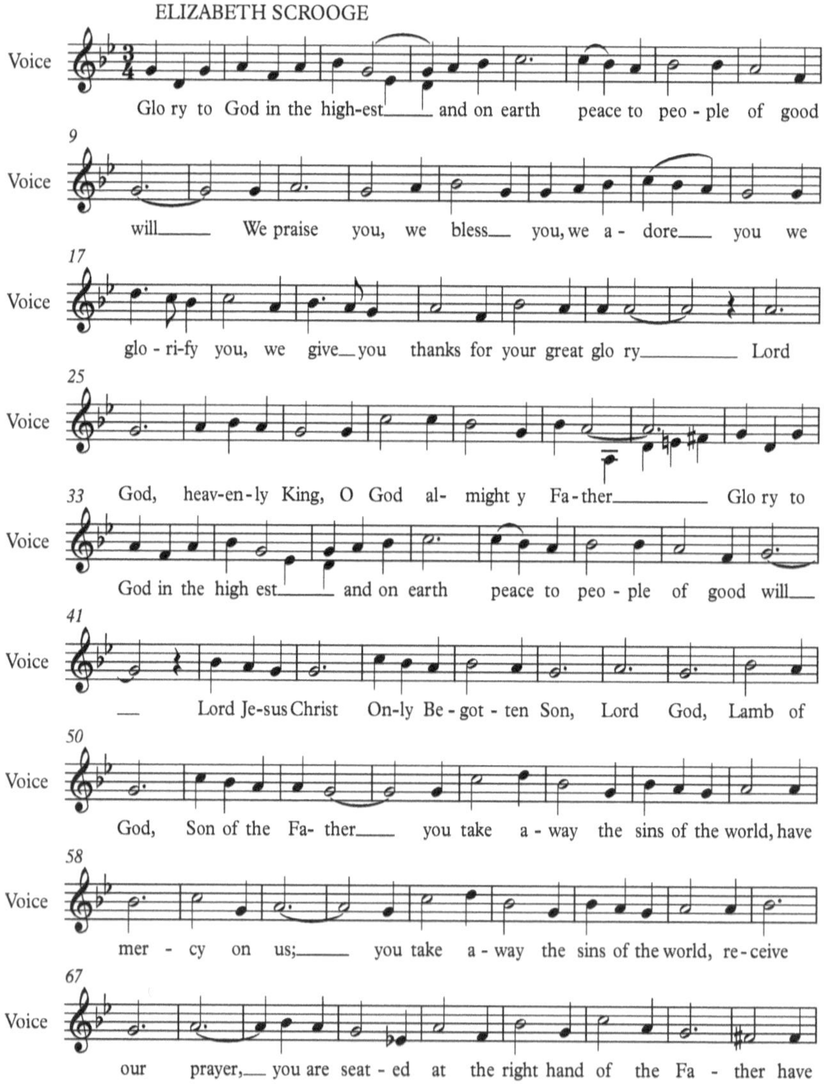
ELIZABETH SCROOGE
Voice
Glo ry to God in the high-est and on earth peace to peo - ple of good
9
Voice
will We praise you, we bless you, we a - dore you we
17
Voice
glo - ri-fy you, we give you thanks for your great glo ry Lord
25
Voice
God, heav-en-ly King, O God al- might y Fa - ther Glo ry to
33
Voice
God in the high est and on earth peace to peo - ple of good will
41
Voice
Lord Je-sus Christ On-ly Be - got - ten Son, Lord God, Lamb of
50
Voice
God, Son of the Fa- ther you take a - way the sins of the world, have
58
Voice
mer - cy on us; you take a - way the sins of the world, re - ceive
67
Voice
our prayer, you are seat - ed at the right hand of the Fa - ther have

2

76 Voice: mer - cy on us._____ Glo-ry to God in the high est_____ and on

84 Voice: earth peace to peo - ple of good will._____ For you a - lone are the

92 Voice: Ho-ly One, you a - lone are the Lord,___ you a - lone are the Most_

101 Voice: High, Je - su Christ___ with the Ho - ly Spir-it_____ in the

110 Voice: glo - ry of God the Fa - ther A - men____ A - men_____

Coventry Carol

15th century

15th century
harm. Martin Fallas Shaw

FRED'S NURSE

Voice

Lul-ly, lul-lay, tho lit-tle ti-ny child, by by, lul-ly, lul-lay

Piano

Voice

1. O sisters too, how many we do for to pre-serve this day this
2. He-od the king, in his rag-ing, char-ged he hath his day his
3. That woe is me, poor child, for thee! And ev-er morn and day, for

Pno.

Voice

poor young-ling for whom we do sing? By by, lul-ly lul-lay.
men of might in his own sight, all young chil-dred to slay.
thy par-ting nei-ther say nor sing by by, lul-ly, lul-lay.

Pno.

A Squeezing, Wrenching, Grasping Clutching, Covetous Old Sinner

words: Robert Dwight Brown
adapted from Charles Dickens

music: Bette Lunn

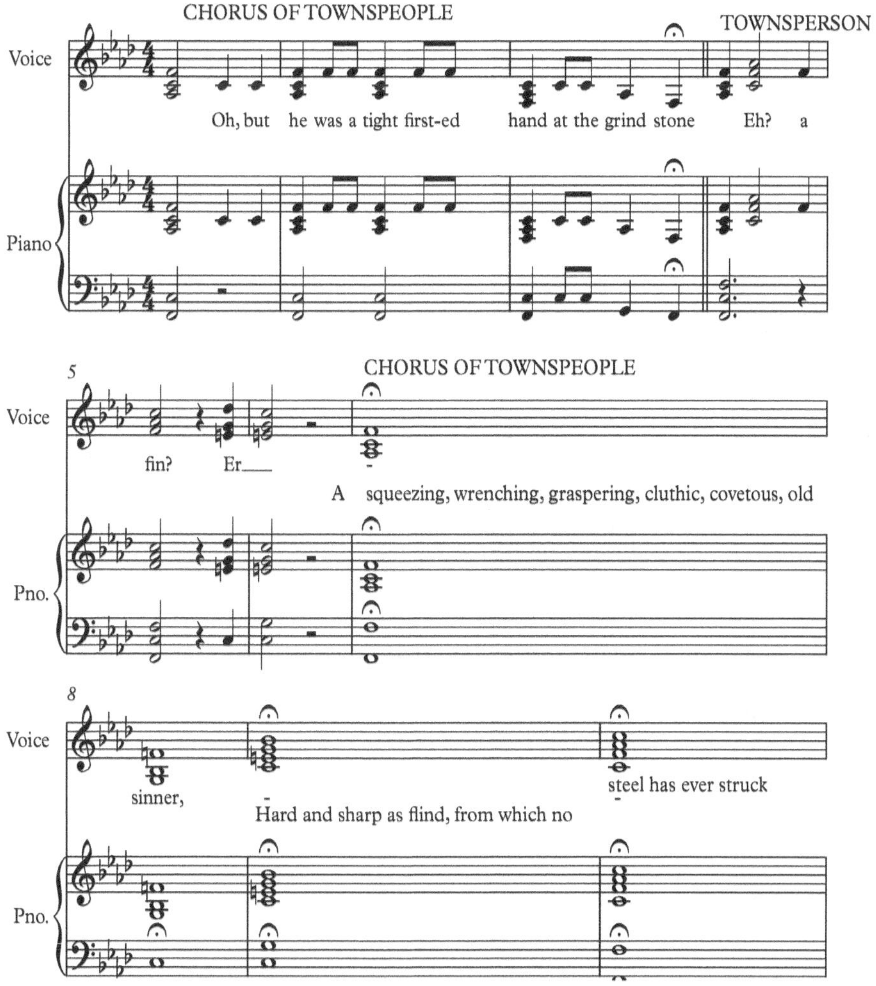
CHORUS OF TOWNSPEOPLE
TOWNSPERSON
Voice
Piano
Oh, but he was a tight first-ed hand at the grind stone Eh? a
5
CHORUS OF TOWNSPEOPLE
Voice
fin? Er
A squeezing, wrenching, graspering, cluthic, covetous, old
Pno.
8
Voice
sinner,
Hard and sharp as flind, from which no
steel has ever struck
Pno.

2

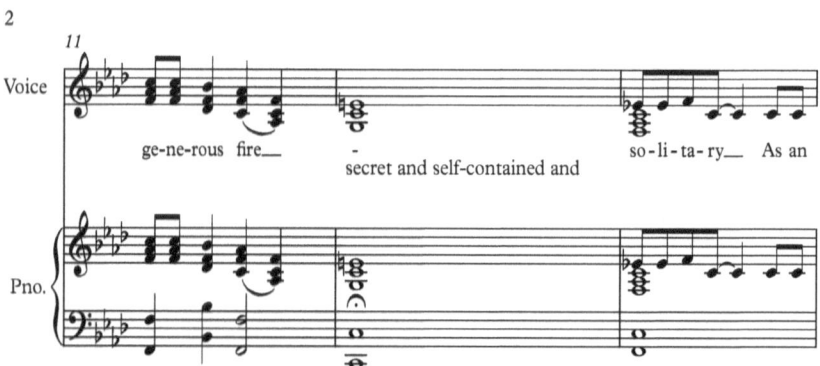

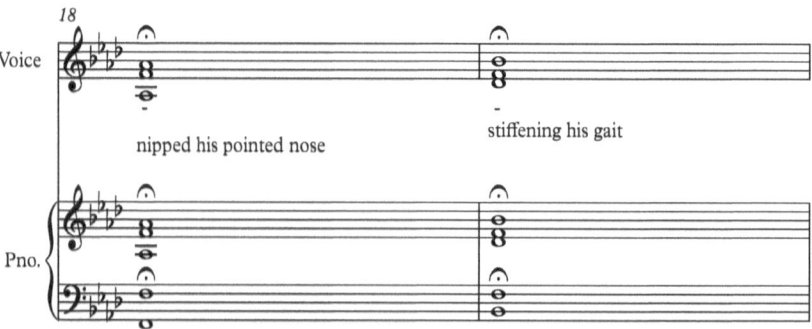

3

20

Voice

made his eyes red, his thin lips blue, and   spoke out shrewdly in a voice that did grate,

Pno.

22

Voice

carrying his own low temperature.   Icing his office in the   dog days

Pno.

25

Voice

No warmth can warm him,   nor winter chill, I'll say

Pno.

27

Voice

-Nobody ever stops him in the street   -to say with gladsome charity.

Pno.

4

My dear, Scrooge, how are you? When will you come to see me?

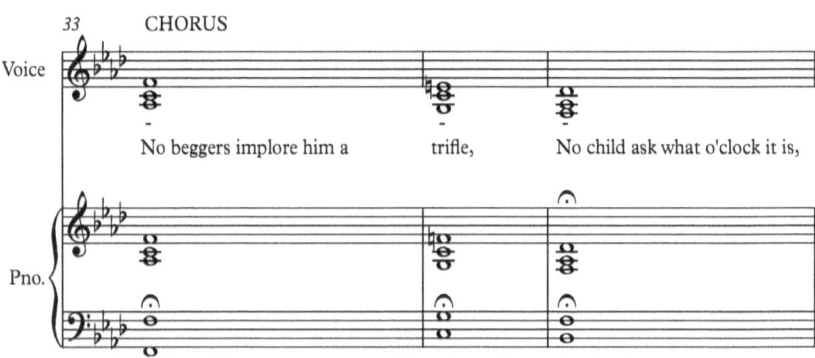

No beggers implore him a trifle, No child ask what o'clock it is,

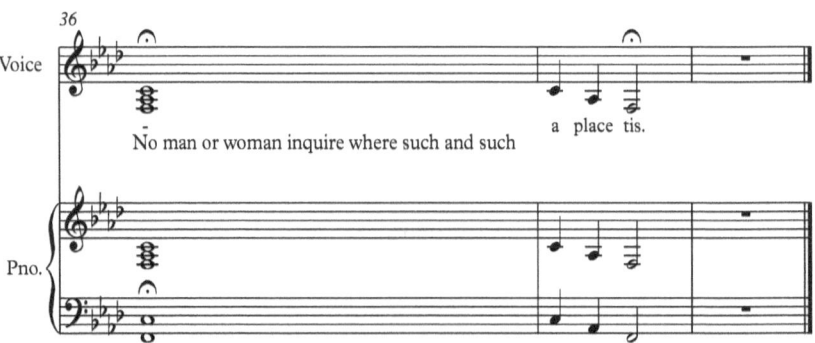

No man or woman inquire where such and such a place tis.

A Merry Christmas, Uncle (God Save You)

words: Robert Dwight Brown
adapted from Charles Dickens

music: Bette Lunn

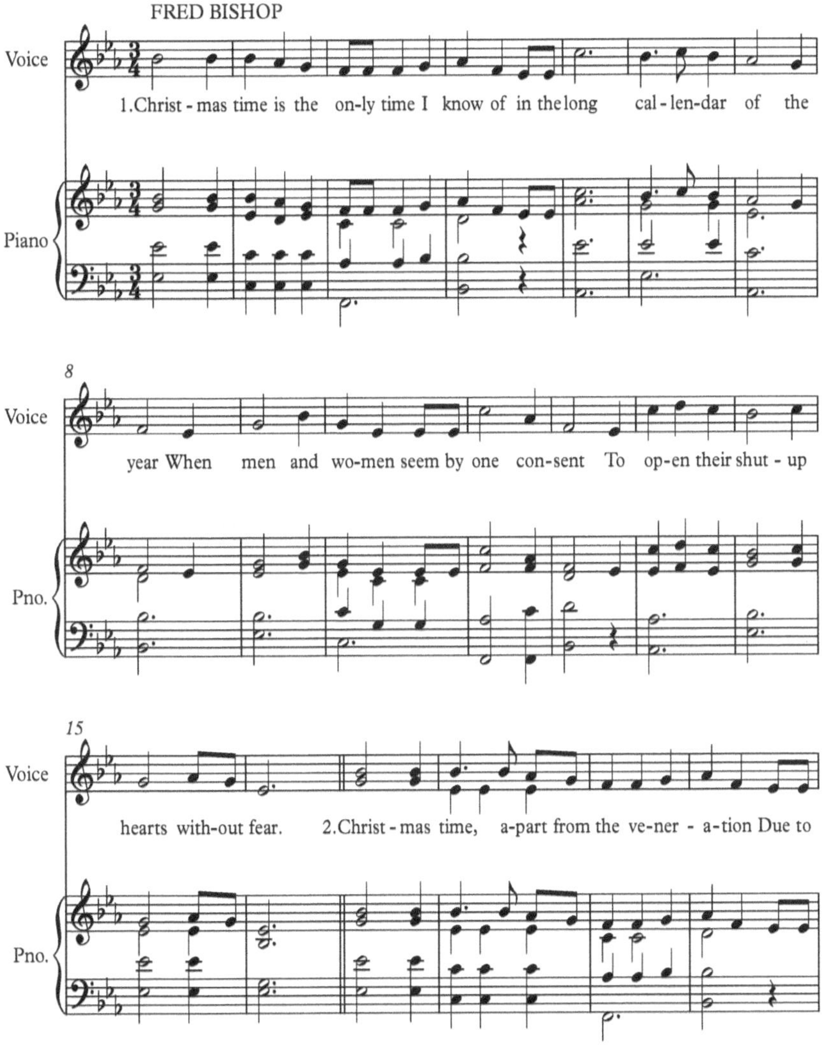
FRED BISHOP
Voice
1.Christ - mas time is the on-ly time I know of in the long cal - len-dar of the
Piano
8
Voice
year When men and wo-men seem by one con-sent To op-en their shut - up
Pno.
15
Voice
hearts with-out fear. 2.Christ - mas time, a-part from the ve-ner - a-tion Due to
Pno.

2

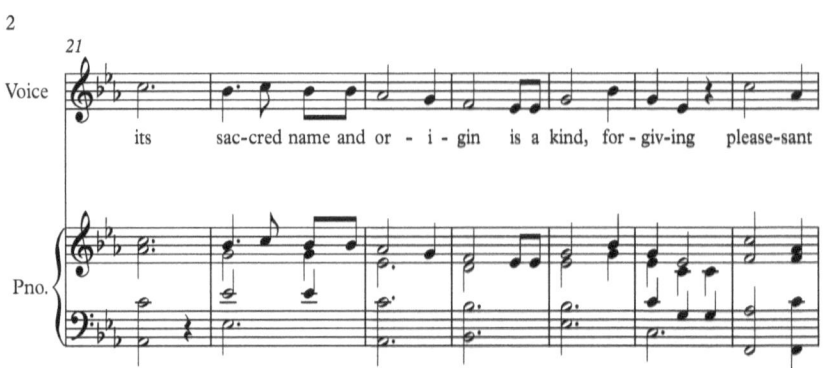

its   sac-cred name and or - i - gin   is a kind, for - giv-ing   please-sant

time, The on - ly time, where   char-i -ty is gen-u - ine.   3.To think of

peo-ple be - low them as   if___They are fel - low pas-sen-gers to   the grave. And

3

Voice 41

not an-oth-er race of crea - tures Bound on oth-er-er jour-neys like a__

Pno.

Voice 48

slave. 4.And there-fore, un-cle, though it has ne-ver Put a scrap of gold in my

Pno.

Voice 55

pock - et I be-lieve that it has done me

Pno.

4

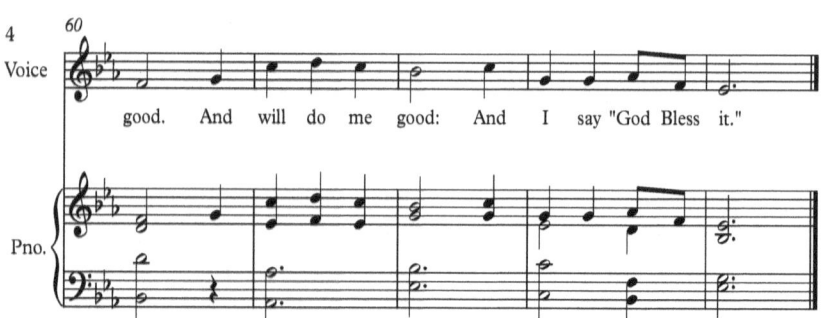

good. And will do me good: And I say "God Bless it."

In Want of Common Comforts

words: Robert Dwight Brown
adapted from Charles Dickens

music: Bette Lunn

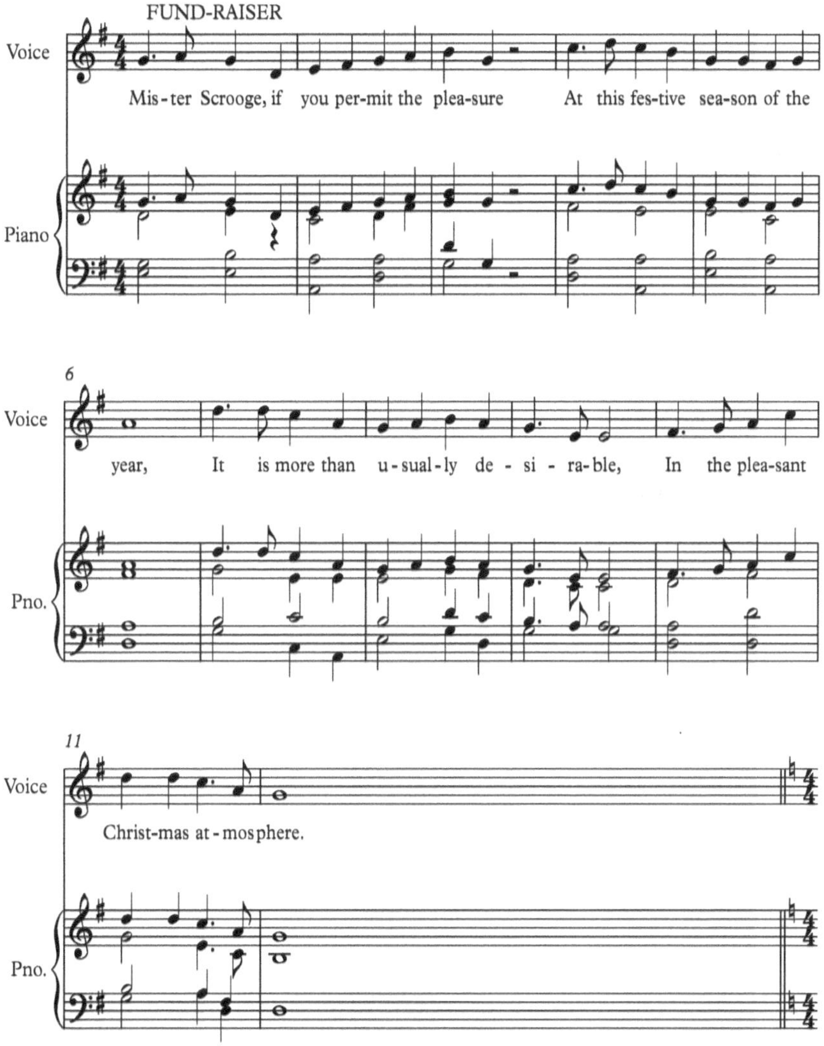
FUND-RAISER
Voice
Piano
Mis-ter Scrooge, if you per-mit the plea-sure At this fes-tive sea-son of the
6
Voice
Pno.
year, It is more than u-sual-ly de - si - ra-ble, In the plea-sant
11
Voice
Pno.
Christ-mas at-mos phere.

140

2

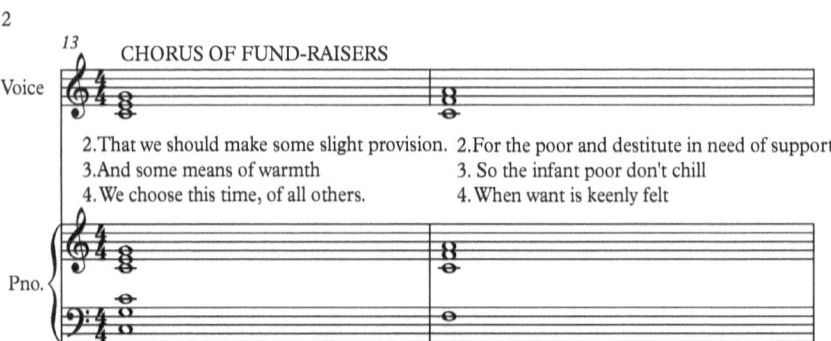

CHORUS OF FUND-RAISERS

2. That we should make some slight provision. 2. For the poor and destitute in need of support
3. And some means of warmth   3. So the infant poor don't chill
4. We choose this time, of all others.   4. When want is keenly felt

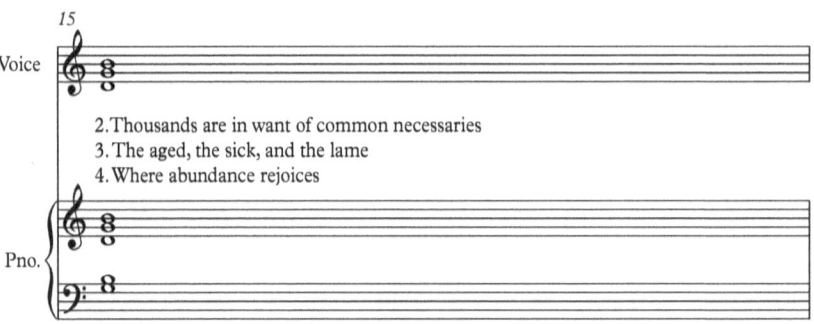

2. Thousands are in want of common necessaries
3. The aged, the sick, and the lame
4. Where abundance rejoices

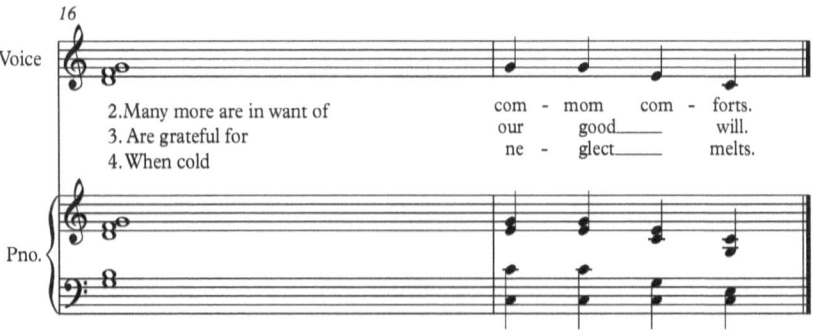

2. Many more are in want of
3. Are grateful for
4. When cold

com - mom com - forts.
our good___ will.
ne - glect___ melts.

God Rest Ye Merry, Gentlemen

words: traditional English

tune: traditional English
harm. by Charles W. Douglass

CHORUS OF YOUNG PAUPERS

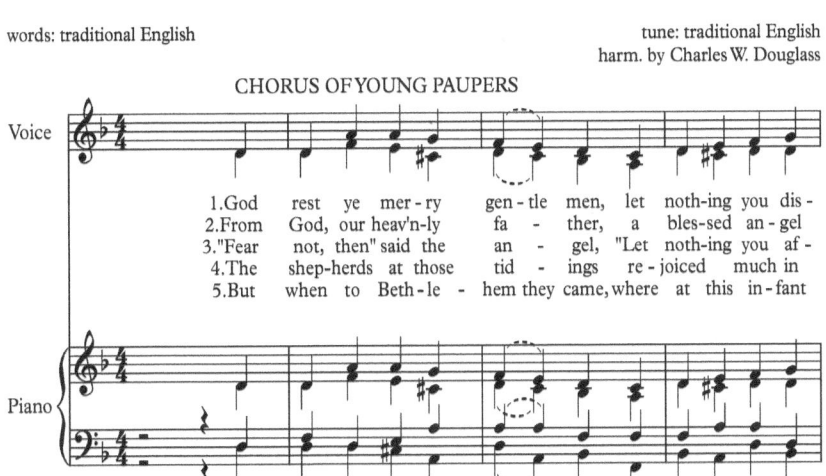

1.God   rest ye mer - ry   gen - tle men, let noth-ing you dis -
2.From   God, our heav'n-ly   fa - ther, a   bles-sed an - gel
3."Fear   not, then" said the   an - gel, "Let noth-ing you af -
4.The   shep-herds at those   tid - ings re - joiced   much in
5.But   when to Beth-le - hem they came, where at this in-fant

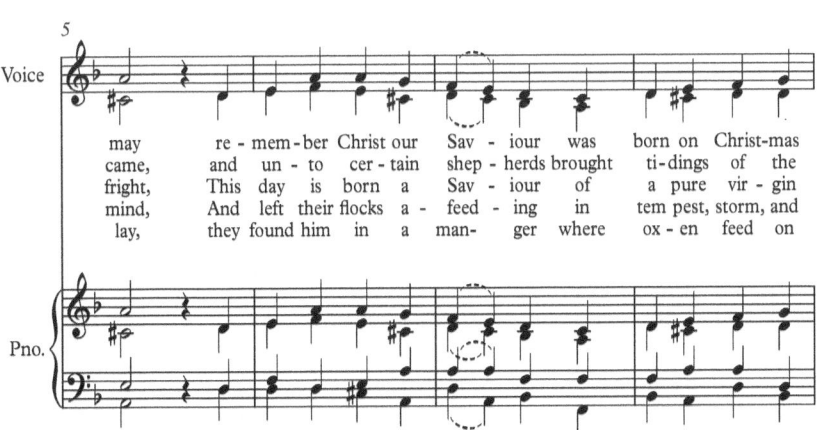

may   re - mem-ber Christ our   Sav - iour was   born on Christ-mas
came,   and un - to cer - tain shep - herds brought ti - dings of   the
fright,   This day is   born   a   Sav - iour of   a pure vir - gin
mind,   And left their flocks a - feed - ing   in   tem pest, storm, and
lay,   they found him in a   man- ger where ox - en feed on

142

2

Voice (m. 9)

day   to save us al from   Sa - tan's power when we were gone a -
same;   how that in Beth - le - hem was born the Son of God by
bright   to free all those who trust in Him from Sa - tan's pow'er and
wind,   and went to Beth - le - hem straight-way, this ble - sed babe to
hay,   His moth-er Mar - ry kneel - ing un - to the___ Lord did

Pno.

Voice (m. 13)

stray. O___ ti - dings of com - fort and joy, com-fort and joy, O___
name.
might.
find.
pray.

Pno.

Voice (m. 18)

ti - dings of com - fort and joy!

Pno.

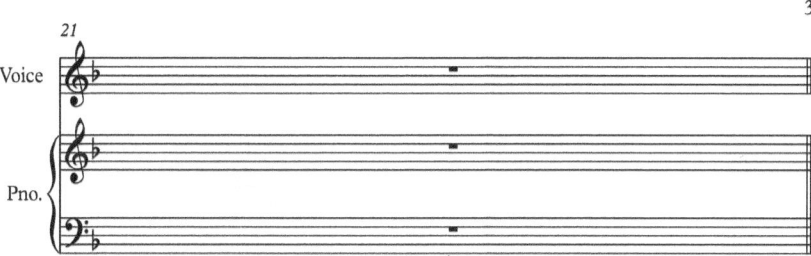

6. Now to the Lord sing praises,
   All you within this place,
   And with true love and brotherhood
   Each other now embrace;
   This holy tide of Christmas
   All other doth deface.
     O tidings of comfort and joy,
     Comfort and joy
     O tidings of comfort and joy

Cornhill Carol

words: Robert Dwight Brown

music: Bette Lunn

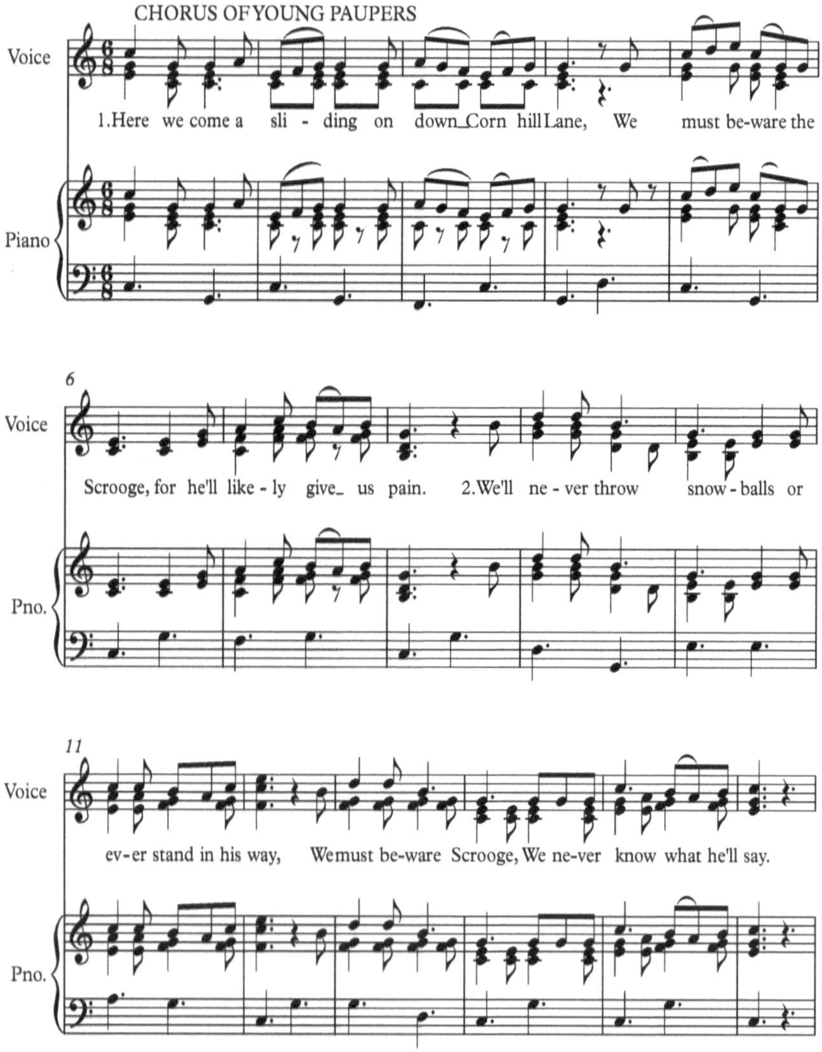
CHORUS OF YOUNG PAUPERS
Voice
1.Here we come a sli - ding on down Corn hill Lane, We must be-ware the
Piano
6
Voice
Scrooge, for he'll like - ly give us pain. 2.We'll ne - ver throw snow - balls or
Pno.
11
Voice
ev - er stand in his way, We must be-ware Scrooge, We ne-ver know what he'll say.
Pno.

2

3.Look 'ee there's Bob Cratch it who nev - er walks in haste.   The long___ends of his

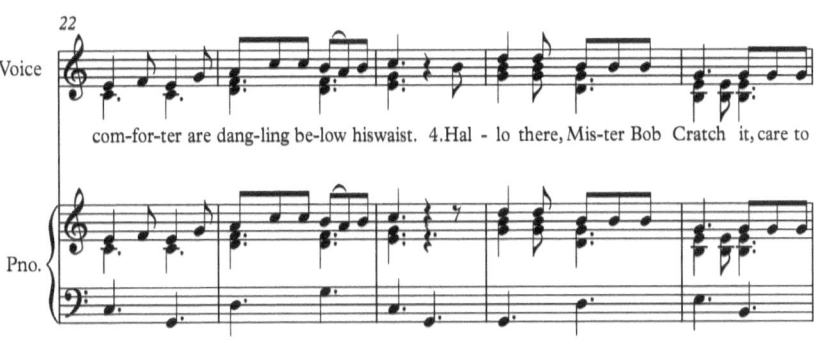

com-for-ter are dang-ling be-low his waist. 4.Hal - lo there, Mis-ter Bob Cratch it, care to

join a   snow ballfight?   Hal - lo, Hal-lo watch out there, Mis-ta Cratch-it'snow's in___

146

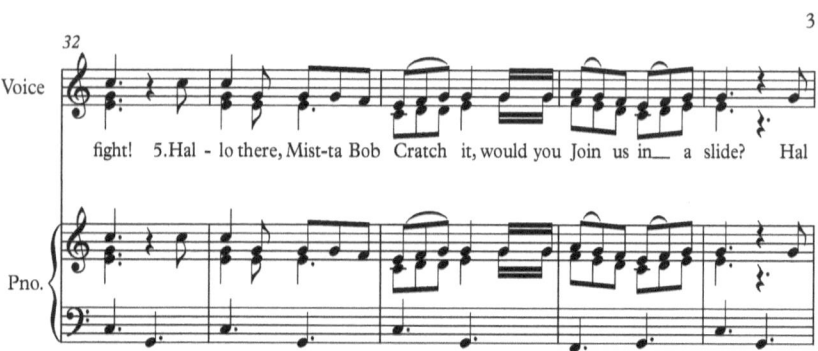

fight! 5. Hal - lo there, Mist-ta Bob Cratch it, would you Join us in__ a slide? Hal

lo, Hal - lo, down twen-ty times, nev-er once fell on his back- side____

6. Here we come a slid - ding be - fore the snow it does melt,

4

Mis-ter Bob Cratch-it runs homes   as   hard   as   he___   can   pelt___

A Father's Christmas Carol

words: Robert Dwight Brown

music: Bette Lunn

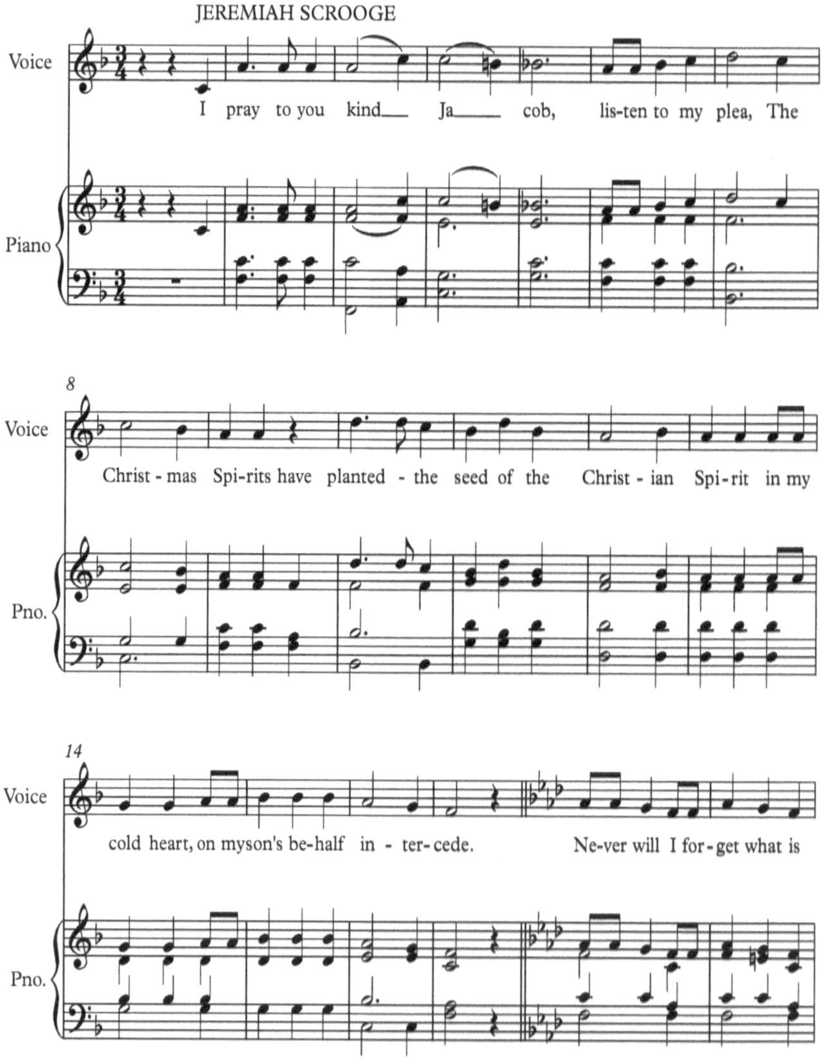
JEREMIAH SCROOGE
Voice
I pray to you kind___ Ja___ cob, lis-ten to my plea, The
Piano
8
Voice
Christ - mas Spi-rits have planted - the seed of the Christ - ian Spi-rit in my
Pno.
14
Voice
cold heart, on myson's be-half in - ter- cede. Ne-ver will I for-get what is
Pno.

2

of the past. I will for-e-ver see___ what shall be. Please haunt my

CHORUS

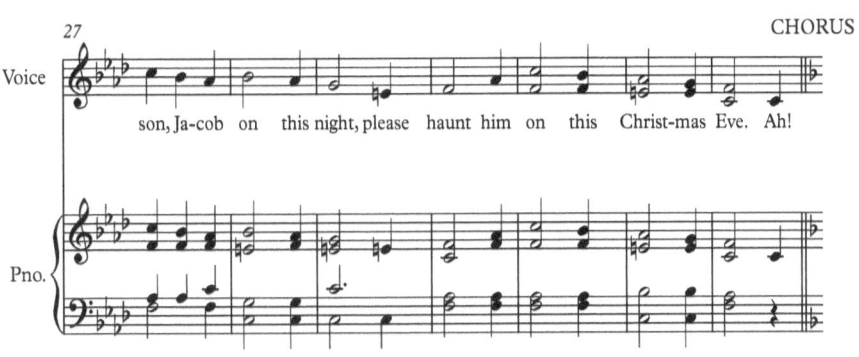

son, Ja-cob on this night, please haunt him on this Christ-mas Eve. Ah!

OF ANGELS

JEREMIAH SCROOGE

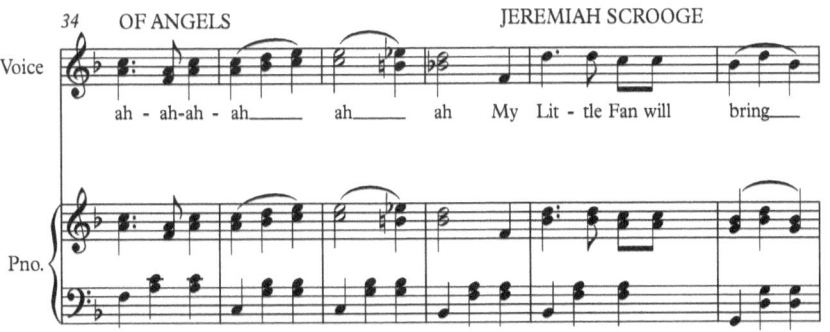

ah - ah-ah - ah_____ ah_____ ah My Lit - tle Fan will bring___

150

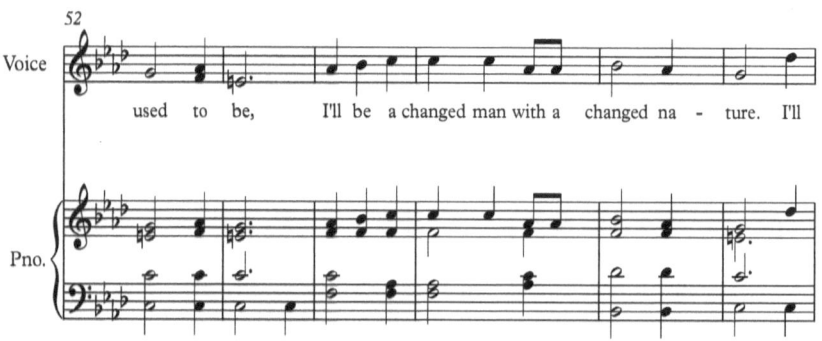

4

be a Christ - ian soul on ev - ery cal - en - dar day, My

Eb - en - e - zer, my Lit - tle Fan, I'll nur_____ ture.

The Bethlehem Carol

words: Robert Dwight Brown

Voice

DR. CHATTLESWORTH (Spoken)

1. He has a religious mania, I am quite sure,
2. We shalt extinguish too violent strife
3. With full use of their wit is their renown-
4. Whenst we vomit him strongly. With our help
5. We choose this time of the Christmas season,
6. Hearts filled with joy, comfort, and glad-tidings,

Voice

1. Require he a most vulgar tincture.
2. And exorbitant form of fiery life.
3. Jan Baptista van Helmont doth saith.,
4. Cure his head wit' warm lungs of lambs, sheep, whelps.
5. When spirits are high; minds out of reason;
6. Turned melancholy and suiciding.

Voice

1. He hath worked himself into spark despair.
2. Whenst too many fools accidently drown-
3. Enemas of yogurt art a cure-all.
4. Prime my (operating) theatre a trephine to trepan.
5. Melancholy abounds; reigns the insane.
6. We kind souls at Bethlehem Hospital,

2

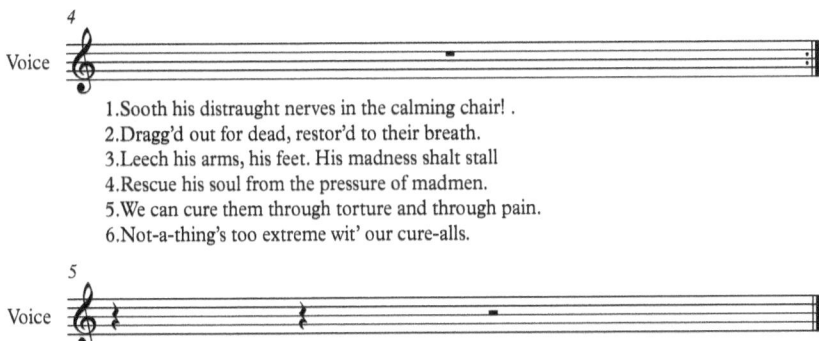

1.Sooth his distraught nerves in the calming chair! .
2.Dragg'd out for dead, restor'd to their breath.
3.Leech his arms, his feet. His madness shalt stall
4.Rescue his soul from the pressure of madmen.
5.We can cure them through torture and through pain.
6.Not-a-thing's too extreme wit' our cure-alls.

Home's Like Heaven (Sussex Carol)

traditional English

traditional English
harm. Ralph Vaughan Williams

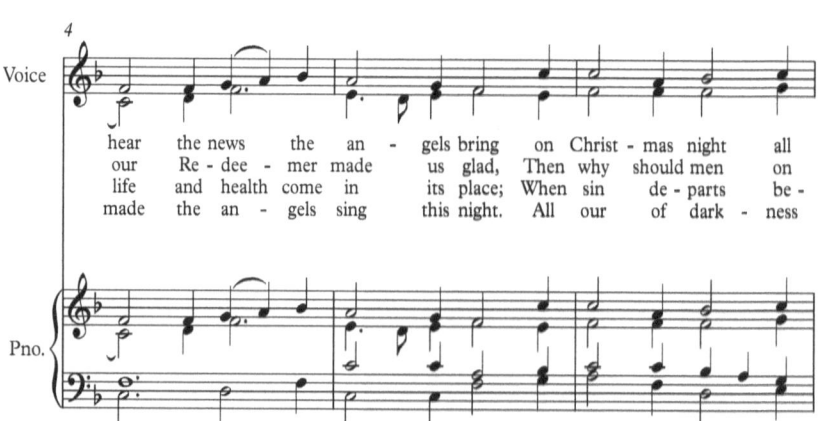

2

7

Voice

Chris - tians sing to here the news_ the an - gels bring;
earth be sad, Since our Re - dee - mer made us glad.
fore his grace, Then life and health come in its place.
we have light, Which made the an - gels sing this night.

Pno.

10

Voice

News of great joy news of great mirth;
When from our sin he set us free,
An - gels and men with joy may sing.
Glo - ry to God and peace to men,

Pno.

13

Voice

News of our mer - ci - ful_ King's birth.
All for to gain our lib - er - ty.
All for to see the new_ born King.
Now and for ev - er more_ A - men.

Pno.

Fezziwig's Wassail

words: Robert Dwight Brown
adapted from Charles Dickens
based on "The Gloucestershire Wassail"

music: Bette Lunn

FEZZIWIG & GUESTS

Voice

1.Was - sail, was - sail_ all o - ver the town - our toast it is white, and our

Piano

Voice

ale_ it_ is brown, Our bowl it____ is__ made of the white ma-ple tree; with the

Pno.

Voice

was - sail-ling bowl we'll drink to thee. 2.So here's to Mis__ sus
4.So here's to the cook, with
6.And here's to the shy_____
8.And at last to the push

Pno.

2

Voice (m. 21)

Fez - zi - wig and___ her sub-stan-tial smile. Pray God send___ some___ guests
her broth-er's par - tic - u - lar friend_____ Pray God send our mas - ter some
and here's to the bold_____ Pray God send our Mas - ter bread
_____ing and here's to the pull____ing! Pray God send our Mas - ter the

Pno.

Voice (m. 26)

up the aisle! Some___ guests up the ai - sle that we all see. With the
whis - key of good blend. And dou - ble malt that we all see; With the
that's not a day old!__ And fresh loaves of bread that we all see; With the
long life of a King! A bowl of strong beer Pray you draw near; And___

Pno.

Voice (m. 31)

was - sai - ling bowl we'll drink___ to thee. 3. And here's to the house-maid
was sai - ling bowl we'll drink___ to thee. 5. And here's to the boy___
was - sail - ing bowl we'll drink___ to thee. 7. And here's to the grace___
our jol - ly was - sail then you shall bare. 9. Come on now, Dick___

Pno.

38

Voice

and— her cou— sin the bak - er—— Pray God send our mas-ter good beef by
who hide be-hind the girl from next door— Pray God send our Mas-ter a good head
— ful— and here's to the awk - ward— Pray God send our Mas-ter pas-tries of
fill us a bowl— of the best; then your soul in Hea - ven— may rest. But

Pno.

44

Voice

the ac - re And an— acre of beef that we all see; With the was - sail-ling
of— boar! And— a good boar's head that we all see; With the was - sail-ling
the best lard! And the— best lard— that we all see; With the was - sai-ling
if you do draw us a bowl of the small— down shall go————

Pno.

49

Voice

bowl we'll drink to thee.
bowl we'll drink to thee.   10. Then here's to the maid in her lily white
bowl we'll drink to thee.
'Prentice bowl and— all.

Pno.

4

smock_ Who trips to the door_ and slips back the lock. Who who trips to_

the door and slips back the pin! For she lets these

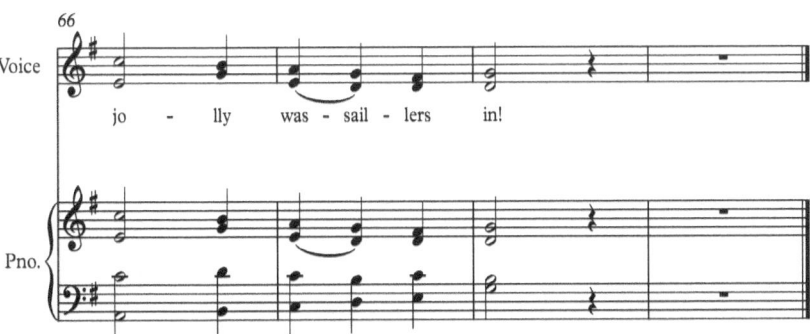

jo - lly was - sail - lers in!

The Boar's Head Carol

words: traditional

tune: traditional

FEZZIWIG

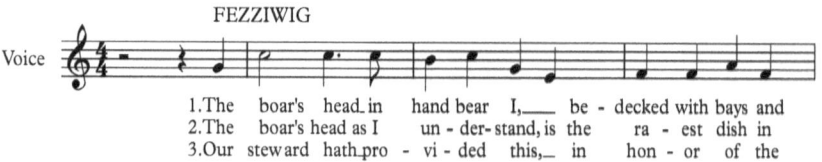

Voice

1.The boar's head_in   hand bear I,____ be - decked with bays and
2.The boar's head as I   un - der-stand, is the   ra - est dish in
3.Our steward hath_pro - vi - ded this,___ in   hon - or of the

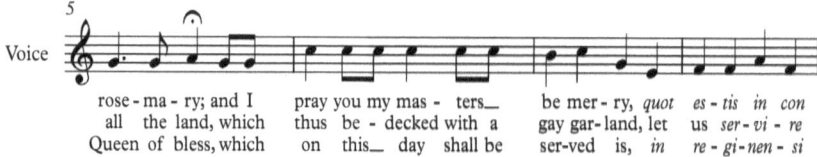

Voice

rose - ma - ry; and I   pray you my mas - ters__   be mer - ry, *quot es - tis in con*
all the land, which   thus be - decked with a   gay gar-land, let us *ser-vi - re*
Queen of bless, which   on this__ day shall be   ser-ved is, *in re - gi-nen - si*

Voice

vi   vi- o.   Ca - put a - pri de - fe - ro,   red-dens lau-des Do - mi - no.
can - ti- co.
a - tri- o.

The Cratchits Wish You A Merry Christmas

traditional English

traditional English
harm. Edward L. Stauff

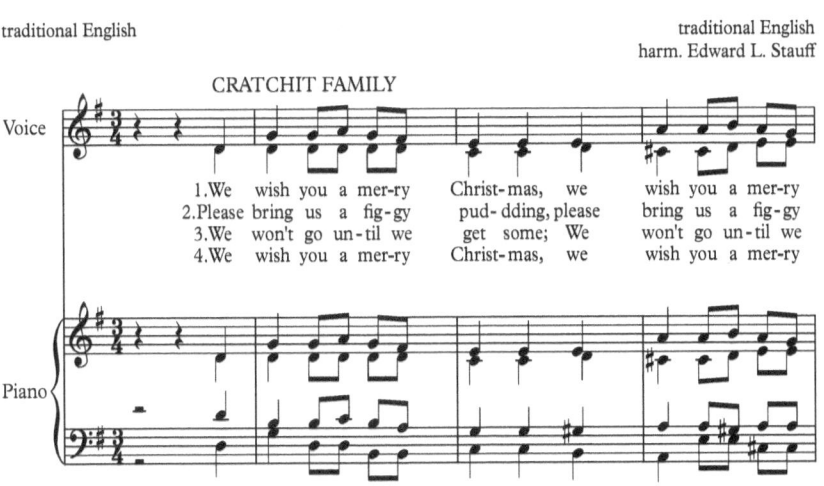

CRATCHIT FAMILY

Voice

1.We wish you a mer-ry Christ-mas, we wish you a mer-ry
2.Please bring us a fig-gy pud-dding, please bring us a fig-gy
3.We won't go un-til we get some; We won't go un-til we
4.We wish you a mer-ry Christ-mas, we wish you a mer-ry

Piano

Voice

Christ-mas, we wish you a mer-ry Christ-mas, and a hap-py new
pud-ding; please bring us a fig-gy pud-ding please bring it right
get some; We won't go un-til we get some, please bring it right
Christ-mas, we wish you a mer-ry Christ-mas, and a hap-py new

Pno.

2

Voice

year.
here.
here.
year.

Good tid - ings we bring   to   you and your   kin,   we

Pno.

Voice

wish you a mer-ry   Christ-mas and a   hap - py new   year.

TINY TIM
4.and God bless us e'ry   one!

Pno.

Silent Night

words: Joseph Mohr
trans. John F. Young

tune: Franz Gruber. Alt.
harm. by Carl. H Reinecke

TINY TIM

Voice

Piano

1.Si - lent night, ho - ly night, all is calm, all is bright.
2.Si - lent night, ho - ly night, shep - herd quake at the sight,
3.Si - lent night, ho - ly night, Son of God, love's pure light

Voice

Pno.

'Round yon vir - gin moth-er and child Ho - ly in-fant so ten-der and mild,
glo - ries stream from heav-en a - far, heav'n-ly hosts sings Al - le - lu - ia.
ra - diant beams from thy ho-ly face with the dawn of re - deem - ing grace,

Voice

Pno.

sleep in heav-en-ly peace___ sleep in heav - en-ly peace.
Christ the Savi-iour is born.___ Christ the Sav - iour is born!
Je - sus, Lord at thy birth,___ Je - sus Lord at thy birth.

4. Stille Nacht, heilige Nacht,
   Alles schläft; einsam wacht
   Nur das traute hochheilige Paar.
   Holder Knabe im lockigen Haar,
   Schlaf in himmlischer Ruh!
   Schlaf in himmlischer Ruh!

5. Stille Nacht, heilige Nacht,
   Hirten erst kundgemacht
   Durch der Engel Halleluja,
   Tönt es laut von fern und nah:
   Christ, der Retter ist da!
   Christ, der Retter ist da!

6. Stille Nacht, heilige Nacht,
   Gottes Sohn, o wie lacht
   Lieb' aus deinem göttlichen Mund,
   Da uns schlägt die rettende Stund'.
   Christ, in deiner Geburt!
   Christ, in deiner Geburt!

7. Glade jul, dejlige jul!
   Engle dale ned i skjul.
   Hid de flyve med paradis-grønt,
   Hvor de se, hvad for Gud er skønt.
   Lønligt iblandt os de gå.

8. Julefryd, evig fryd,
   Hellig sang med himmelsk lyd!
   Det er englene, hyrdene så,
   Dengang Herren i krybben lå.
   Evig er englenes sang.

9. Fred på jord, fryd på jord,
   Jesusbarnet iblandt os bor.
   Engle sjunge om barnet så smukt,
   Han har himmerigs dør oplukt.
   Salig er englenes sang.

10. Salig fred, himmelsk fred,
    Toner julenat herned.
    Engle bringe til store og små
    Bud om ham, som i krybben lå;
    Fryd dig hver sjæl, han har frelst!

11. Noche de paz, noche de amor,
    Todo duerme en derredor.
    Entre sus astros que esparcen su luz
    Bella anunciando al niñito Jesús
    Brilla la estrella de paz
    Brilla la estrella de paz

12. Noche de paz, noche de amor,
    Todo duerme en derredor
    Sólo velan en la oscuridad
    Los pastores que en el campo están;
    Y la estrella de Belén
    Y la estrella de Belén

13. Noche de paz, noche de amor,
    Todo duerme en derredor;
    sobre el santo niño Jesús
    Una estrella esparce su luz,
    Brilla sobre el Rey
    Brilla sobre el Rey.

14. Noche de paz, noche de amor,
    Todo duerme en derredor
    Fieles velando allí en Belén
    Los pastores, la madre también.
    Y la estrella de paz
    Y la estrella de paz

Hark! The Herald Angels Sing

words: Charles Wesley

music: *Mendelssohn*, Felix Mendelssohn
adapt. William H. Cummings

CHORUS OF YOUNG PAUPERS

Voice

1.Hark The her - ald an-gels sing,_ "Glo - ry to the_ new-born King;
2.Christ, by high - est heav'n a - dored; Christ the ev - er - last - ing- Lord;
3.Hail the heav'n born Prince of peace Hail the Son of right-eous- ness!

Piano

5

Voice

peace on earth and mer - cy mild,_ God and sin - ners rec - on - ciled!"
Late in time be-hold him come, off-spring of the Vir-gin's womb.
Light and life to all he brings, ris'n with heal - ing in His wings.

Pno.

9

Voice

Joy - ful all ye na - tions rise,_ join the tri-umph of the skies;_
Veiled in flesh the God-head see;_ hail th'in car-nate dei - i - ty,
Mild he lays his glo - ry by,_ born that man no more may die,_

Pno.

2

with th'an-gel - ic host pro-cliam, "Christ is___ born in Beth-le- hem!"
please as man with men to dwell, Je - sus, our Em-man-u - el.
born to raise the sons of earth, born to___ give them sec - one birth.

Hark! the her - ald an-gels sing, "Glo - ry___ to the new-born King!

O Come, All Ye Faithful

Latin, John F. Wade
trans. by Frederick Oakeley and others

John F. Wade, 1751

1. O Come, all ye faith - ful, joy - ful and tri - um - phant, o
2. God from God, Light from Light e - ter - nal,
3. Sing choirs of an - gels sign in ex - ul - ta - tion
4. Yea, Lord, we greet thee, born this hap - py mor - ning,

come ye, o come ye to Beth - le - hem. Come and be - hold him,
lo! he ab - hors not the Vir - gin's womb. On - ly be - got - ten
sing, all ye ci - ti - zens of heav - ven a - bove. Glo - ry to God, all
Je - sus to thee be all glo - ry giv'n. Word of the Fa - ther

168

2

born the King of an - gels. O come, let us a - dore Him, O come, let us a-
Son__ of the Fa - ther;
glo - ry in the high - est.
now in flesh ap - pear - ing.

dore Him, O come, let us a - dore Him Christ__ the Lord.

The Beggar's Petition

Adapted from THOMAS MOSS

BEGGAR (Spoken)

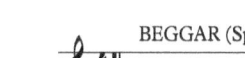

Voice

1.Pity the sorrows of a poor old man!
2.These tattered clothes my poverty bespeak,
3.Yon house, erected on the rising ground,
4.(Hard is the fate of the infirm and poor!)
5.O, take me to your hospitable dome,
6. Should I reveal the source of every grief,
7.Heaven sends misfortunes,—why should we repine?
8.A little farm was my paternal lot,
9.My daughter,—once the comfort of my age!
10.My tender wife,—sweet soother of my care!—
11.Pity the sorrows of a poor old man!

2

Voice

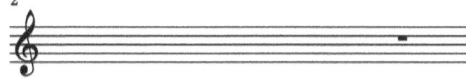

1.Whose trembling limbs have borne him to your door,
2.These hoary locks proclaim my lengthened years;
3.With tempting aspect drew me from my road,
4.Here craving for a morsel of their bread,
5.Keen blows the wind, and piercing is the cold!
6. If soft humanity e'er touched your breast,
7.'T is Heaven has brought me to the state you see:
8.Then, like the lark, I sprightly hailed the morn;
9.Lured by a villain from her native home,
10.Struck with sad anguish at the stern decree,
11.Whose trembling limbs have born him to your door,

3

Voice

2

1.Whose days are dwindled to the shortest span,
2.And many a furrow in my grief-worn cheek
3.For plenty there a residence has found,
4.A pampered menial drove me from the door,
5.Short is my passage to the friendly tomb,
6. Your hands would not withhold the kind relief,
7.And your condition may be soon like mine,
8.But ah! oppression forced me from my cot;
9.Is cast, abandoned, on the world's wild stage,
10.Fell,—lingering fell, a victim to despair,
11.Whose days are dwindled to the shortest span,

Voice

1.O, give relief, and Heaven will bless your store.
2.Has been the channel to a stream of tears.
3.And grandeur a magnificent abode.
4.To seek a shelter in the humble shed.
5.For I am poor and miserably old.
6. Your hands would not withhold the kind relief,
7.The child of sorrow and of misery.
8.My cattle died, and blighted was my corn.
9.And doomed in scanty poverty to roam.
10.And left the world to wretchedness and me.
11.O, give relief, and Heaven will bless your store.

Voice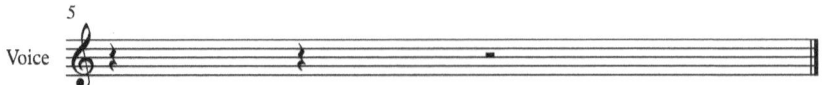

A Christmas Carol (Prayers Answered)

words: Robert Dwight Brown

music: Bette Lunn

ELDERLY FAN

Voice

I prayed to the Christ-mas Spir - its Three. "List-en to this child,"

Piano

I yearned I cried. They vis - it'd my Fath-er that Christ-mas Eve, with-out their

help his love would-'ve died. Fath-er had for-got-ten what is of the

2

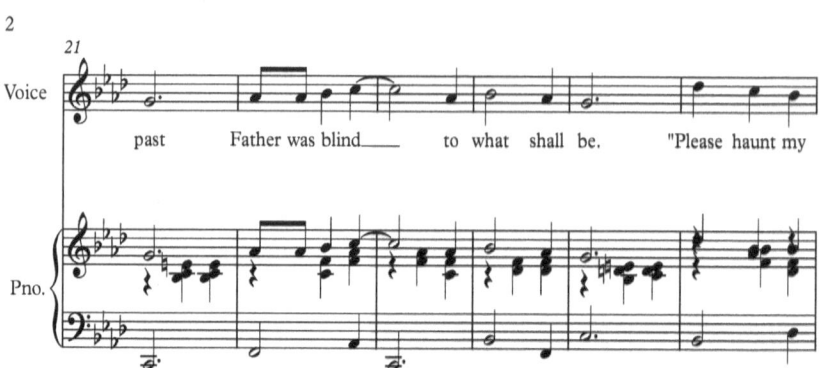

past   Father was blind____   to what   shall   be.   "Please haunt my

CHORUS

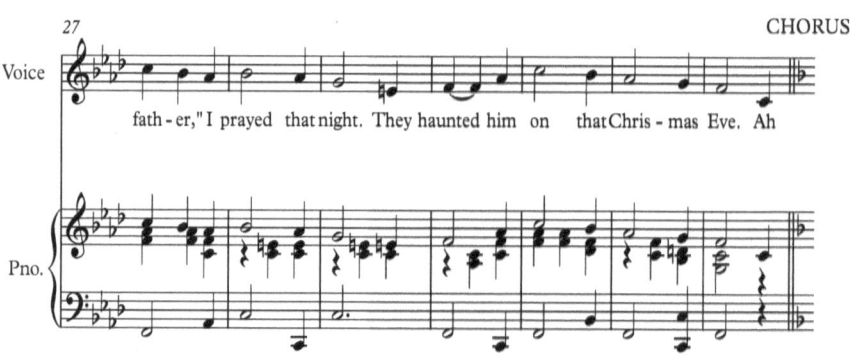

fath - er," I prayed that night. They haunted him on   that Chris - mas Eve. Ah

OF ANGELS   ELDERLY FAN

Ah - ah-ah   ah____   ah____   ah. They vis -it'd my fath-er in that   time   of

CHORUS OF ANGELS   ELDERLY FAN

yule. Ah - ah-ah ah____ ah____ ah. And brought my broth - er home from

school.   Fath-er's so much kind-er than he used   to   be.

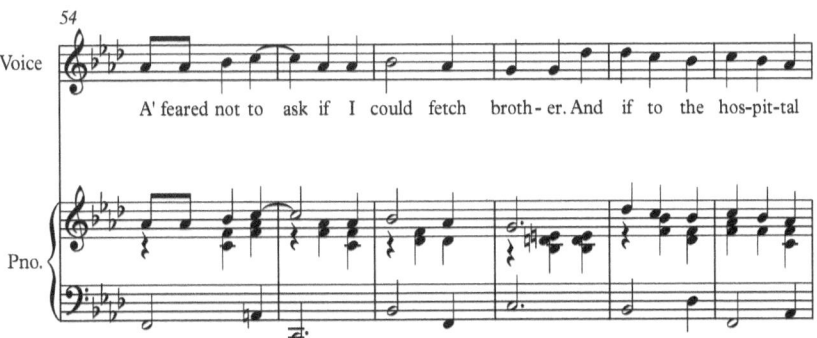

A' feared not to   ask if I could fetch   broth - er. And if to the hos-pit-tal

4

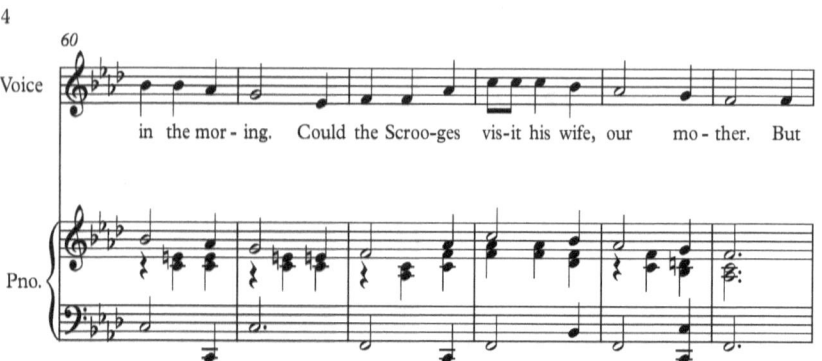

in the mor - ing. Could the Scroo-ges vis-it his wife, our mo - ther. But

Eb-bie soon for got- who his fam' ly is. Eb-bie was deaf to the

cries of love. Eb-bie now vis - its us on this Christ - mas

Eve   I   thank   the   Spir   its   up   a - bove.

God Bless Ye Merry, Gentlemen

words: traditional English
additional: Robert Dwight Brown

tune: traditional English
harm. by Charles W. Douglass

TOPPER

Voice

1.God bless ye mer-ry gen-tle men, let noth-ing you dis-
2.From God, our heav'n-ly fa - ther, Three bles-sed Spir-its
3.God bless ye mer-ry gen-tle men, Your pre-sence is en-

Piano

Voice

may   Un - cle Scro-oge comes to dine with us on this Christ-mas
came,   Brought tid-ings of the Good News of Christ-mas that we pro-
nough, Eb - en - e - ze please join us in a game of Blind-man's

Pno.

Voice

day.   A tight-fist-ed hand at the Grind-stone who'd been led a -
claim. How that in Beth-le - hem born a Man who'd cure the blind/
bluff. Or play at Yes or No, or may - be For - fiets if you're

Pno.

2

13

Voice

stray. O___ ti - dings of com - fort and joy, com-fort and
lame.
tough.

Pno.

17

Voice

joy, O___ ti - dings of com - fort and joy.

Pno.

God Bless Us, Every One!

words: traditional English
additional: Robert Dwight Brown

tune: traditional English
harm. by Charles W. Douglass

EBENEZER SCROOGE (struggling) TINY TIM (helping)

Voice

1.God rest ye mer-ry gen-tle men, let noth-ing you dis-

Piano

EBENEZER SCROOGE (struggling) TINY TIM (helping)

5

Voice

may re-mem-ber Christ our Sav - iour was born on Christ-mas

Pno.

9

EBENEZER SCROOGE

Voice

day to save us all from Sa-tan's power...When I was gone a-

Pno.

2

13
BOTH

Voice

stray. O__ ti - dings of com - fort and goy, com-fort and joy, O__

Pno.

18
CHORUS OF PAUPERS

Voice

ti - dings of com - fort and joy.

From God our ... well

Pno.

23

Voice

we're pick - led. Scrooge? Sing - ing? What a sight! Hal - low there Mis - ta

Pno.

Scrooge, gov' nah care to join us in a snow fight? Watch out there

me lads, the Scroo - ge's snow ball's in flight.

Stave I
"The Ghost of Jacob Marley"

'Marley was dead: to begin with. There is no doubt whatever about that. The register of his burial was signed by the clergyman, the clerk, the undertaker, and the chief mourner. I signed it: and my name was good upon 'Change, for anything I chose to put my hand to. Old Marley was as dead as a door-nail.

'Mind! I don't mean to say that I know, of my own knowledge, what there is particularly dead about a door-nail. I might have been inclined, myself, to regard a coffin-nail as the deadest piece of ironmongery in the trade. But the wisdom of our ancestors is in the simile; and my unhallowed hands shall not disturb it, or the Country's done for. You will therefore permit me to repeat, emphatically, that Marley was as dead as a door-nail.

'Where I had heard this wit and whimsy once before?

'I knew he was dead? Of course I did. How could it be otherwise? He and I were partners for I don't know how many years. I was his sole executor, his sole administrator, his sole assign, his sole residuary legatee, his sole friend and sole mourner. And even I was not so dreadfully cut up by the sad event, but that I was an excellent man of business on the very day of the funeral, and solemnised it with an undoubted bargain.

'There is no doubt that Marley was dead. This must be distinctly understood, or nothing wonderful can come of the story I am going to relate. If we were not perfectly convinced that Hamlet's Father died before the play began, there would be nothing more remarkable in his taking a stroll at night, in an easterly wind, upon his own ramparts, than there would be in any other middle-aged gentleman rashly turning out after dark in a breezy spot -- say Saint Paul's Churchyard for instance -- literally to astonish my weak mind.

'I never painted out Old Marley's name. There it stood, years afterwards, above the warehouse door: Scrooge and Marley. The firm was known as Scrooge and Marley. Sometimes people new to the business called me Scrooge, and sometimes Marley, but I answered to both names: it was all the same to me.

'I took my melancholy dinner in my usual melancholy tavern; and having read all the newspapers, and beguiled the rest of the evening with my banker's-book, went home to bed. I lived in chambers which had once belonged to my deceased partner. They were a gloomy suite of rooms, in a lowering pile of building up a yard, where it had so little business to be, that one could scarcely help fancying it must have run there when it was a young house, playing at hide-and-seek with other houses, and forgotten the way out again. It was old enough now, and dreary enough, for nobody lived in it but me, the other rooms being all let out as offices. The yard was so dark that even I, who knew its every stone, was fain to grope with my hands. The fog and frost so hung about the black old gateway of the house, that it seemed as if the Genius of the Weather sat in mournful meditation on the threshold.

'Now, it is a fact, that there was nothing at all particular about the knocker on the door, except that it was very large. It is also a fact, that I had seen it, night and morning, during my whole residence in that place; also that I had as little of what is called fancy about me as any man in the city of London, even including -- which is a bold word -- the corporation, aldermen, and livery. Let it also be borne in mind that I had not bestowed one thought on Marley, since my last mention of my seven years' dead partner that afternoon. And then let any man explain to me, if he can, how it happened that I, having my key in the lock of the door, saw in the knocker, without its undergo-ing any intermediate process of change -- not a knocker, but Marley's face.

'Marley's face. It was not in impenetrable shadow as the other objects in the yard were, but had a dismal light about it, like a bad lobster in a dark cellar. It was not angry or ferocious, but looked at me as Marley used to look: with ghostly spectacles turned up on its ghostly forehead. The hair was curiously stirred, as if by breath or hot air; and, though the eyes were wide open, they were perfectly motionless. That, and its livid colour, made it horrible; but its horror seemed to be in spite of the face and beyond its control, rather than a part of its own expression.

'As I looked fixedly at this phenomenon, it was a knocker again.

'To say that I was not startled, or that my blood was not con-scious of a terrible sensation to which it had been a stranger from infancy, would be untrue. But I put my hand upon the key I had relinquished, turned it sturdily, walked in, and lighted my candle.

'I did pause, with a moment's irresolution, before I shut the door; and I did look cautiously behind it first, as if I half-expected to be terrified with the sight of Marley's pigtail sticking out into the hall. But there was nothing on the back of the door, except the screws and nuts that held the knocker on, so I said "Pooh, pooh!" and closed it with a bang.

'The sound resounded through the house like thunder. Every room above, and every cask in the wine-merchant's cellars below, appeared to have a separate peal of echoes of its own. I was not a man to be frightened by echoes. I fastened the door, and walked across the hall, and up the stairs; slowly too: trimming my candle as I went.

'You may talk vaguely about driving a coach-and-six up a good old flight of stairs, or through a bad young Act of Parliament; but I mean to say you might have got a hearse up that staircase, and taken it broadwise, with the splinter-bar towards the wall and the door to-wards the balustrades: and done it easy. There was plenty of width for that, and room to spare; which is perhaps the reason why I thought I saw a locomotive hearse going on before me in the gloom. Half a dozen gas-lamps out of the street wouldn't have lighted the entry too well, so you may suppose that it was pretty dark with my dip.

'Up I went, not caring a button for that. Darkness is cheap, and I liked it. But before I shut my heavy door, I walked through my rooms to see that all was right. I had just enough recollection of the face to desire to do that.

'Sitting-room, bedroom, lumber-room. All as they should be. Nobody under the table, nobody under the sofa; a small fire in the grate; spoon and basin ready; and the little saucepan of gruel (I had a cold in my head) upon the hob. Nobody under the bed; nobody in the closet; nobody in my dressing-gown, which was hanging up in a suspicious attitude against the wall. Lumber-room as usual. Old fire-guards, old shoes, two fish-baskets, washing-stand on three legs, and a poker.

'Quite satisfied, I closed my door, and locked myself in; dou-ble-locked myself in, which was not my custom. Thus secured against surprise, I took off my cravat; put on my dressing-gown and slippers, and my nightcap; and sat down before the fire to take my gruel.

'It was a very low fire indeed; nothing on such a bitter night. I was obliged to sit close to it, and brood over it, before I could ex-tract the least sensation of warmth from such a handful of fuel. The fireplace was an old one, built by some Dutch merchant long ago, and paved all round with quaint Dutch tiles, designed to illustrate the Scriptures. There were Cains and Abels, Pharaohs' daughters; Queens of Sheba, Angelic messengers descending through the air on clouds like feather-beds, Abrahams, Belshazzars, Apostles putting off to sea in butter-boats, hundreds of figures to attract my thoughts -- and yet that face of Marley, seven years dead, came like the ancient Prophet's rod, and swallowed up the whole. If each smooth tile had been a blank at first, with power to shape some picture on its sur-face from the disjointed fragments of my thoughts, there would have been a copy of old Marley's head on every one.

' "Humbug!" I said; and walked across the room.

'After several turns, I sat down again. As I threw my head back in the chair, my glance happened to rest upon a bell, a disused bell, that hung in the room, and communicated for some purpose now forgotten with a chamber in the highest story of the building. It was with great astonishment, and with a strange, inexplicable dread, that as I looked, I saw this bell begin to swing. It swung so softly in the outset that it scarcely made a sound; but soon it rang out loudly, and so did every bell in the house.

'This might have lasted half a minute, or a minute, but it seemed an hour. The bells ceased as they had begun, together. They were succeeded by a clanking noise, deep down below; as if some person were dragging a heavy chain over the casks in the wine merchant's cellar. I then remembered to have heard that ghosts in haunted houses were described as dragging chains.

'The cellar-door flew open with a booming sound, and then I heard the noise much louder, on the floors below; then coming up the stairs; then coming straight towards my door.

' "It's humbug still!" I said. "I won't believe it."

'My colour changed though, when, without a pause, it came on through the heavy door, and passed into the room before my eyes. Upon its coming in, the dying flame leaped up, as though it cried, "I know him; Marley's Ghost!" and fell again.

'The same face: the very same. Marley in his pigtail, usual waistcoat, tights and boots; the tassels on the latter bristling, like his pigtail, and his coat-skirts, and the hair upon his head. The chain he drew was clasped about his middle. It was long, and wound about him like a tail; and it was made (for I observed it closely) of cash-boxes, keys, padlocks, ledgers, deeds, and heavy purses wrought in steel. His body was transparent, so that I, observing him, and looking through his waistcoat, could see the two buttons on my coat behind.

'I had often heard it said that Marley had no bowels, but I had never believed it until now.

'No, nor did I believe it even now. Though I looked the phantom through and through, and saw it standing before me; though I felt the chilling influence of its death-cold eyes; and marked the very texture of the folded kerchief bound about its head and chin, which wrapper I had not observed before: I was still incredulous, and fought against my senses.

' "How now!" I said, caustic and cold as ever. "What do you want with me?"

' "Much!" -- Marley's voice, no doubt about it.

' "Who are you?"

' "Ask me who I was."

' "Who were you then?" I said, raising my voice. "You're particular, for a shade." I was going to say "to a shade," but substituted this, as more appropriate.

' "In life I was your partner, Jacob Marley."

' "Can you -- can you sit down?" I asked, looking doubtfully at him.

' "I can."

' "Do it then."

'I asked the question, because I didn't know whether a ghost so transparent might find himself in a condition to take a chair; and felt that in the event of its being impossible, it might involve the necessity of an embarrassing explanation. But the ghost sat down on the opposite side of the fireplace, as if he were quite used to it.

' "You don't believe in me," observed the Ghost.

' "I don't," I said.

' "What evidence would you have of my reality, beyond that of your senses?"

' "I don't know," I said.

' "Why do you doubt your senses?"

' "Because," I said, "a little thing affects them. A slight disorder of the stomach makes them cheats. You may be an undigested bit of beef, a blot of mustard, a crumb of cheese, a fragment of an underdone potato. There's more of gravy than of grave about you, whatever you are!"

'I was not much in the habit of cracking jokes, nor did I feel, in my heart, by any means waggish then. The truth is, that I tried to be smart, as a means of distracting my own attention, and keeping down my terror; for the spectre's voice disturbed the very marrow in my bones.

'To sit, staring at those fixed glazed eyes, in silence for a moment, would play, I felt, the very deuce with him. There was something very awful, too, in the spectre's being provided with an infernal atmosphere of its own. I could not feel it myself, but this was clearly the case; for though the Ghost sat perfectly motionless, its hair, and skirts, and tassels, were still agitated as by the hot vapour from an oven.

' "You see this toothpick?" I said, returning quickly to the charge, for the reason just assigned; and wishing, though it were only for a second, to divert the vision's stony gaze from myself.

' "I do," replied the Ghost.

' "You are not looking at it," I said.

' "But I see it," said the Ghost, "notwithstanding."

' "Well!" I returned, "I have but to swallow this, and be for the rest of my days persecuted by a legion of goblins, all of my own creation. Humbug, I tell you! humbug!"

'At this the spirit raised a frightful cry, and shook its chain with such a dismal and appalling noise, that I held on tight to my chair, to save myself from falling in a swoon. But how much greater was my horror, when the phantom taking off the bandage round its head, as if it were too warm to wear indoors, its lower jaw dropped down upon its breast!

'I fell upon my knees, and clasped my hands before my face.

' "Mercy!" I said. "Dreadful apparition, why do you trouble me?"

' "Man of the worldly mind!" replied the Ghost, "do you believe in me or not?"

' "I do," I said. "I must. But why do spirits walk the earth, and why do they come to me?"

' "It is required of every man," the Ghost returned, "that the spirit within him should walk abroad among his fellowmen, and travel far and wide; and if that spirit goes not forth in life, it is condemned to do so after death. It is doomed to wander through the world -- oh, woe is me! -- and witness what it cannot share, but might have shared on earth, and turned to happiness!"

'Again the spectre raised a cry, and shook its chain and wrung its shadowy hands.

' "You are fettered," I said, trembling. "Tell me why?"

' "I wear the chain I forged in life," replied the Ghost. "I made it link by link, and yard by yard; I girded it on of my own free will, and of my own free will I wore it. Is its pattern strange to you?"

'I trembled more and more.

' "Or would you know," pursued the Ghost, "the weight and length of the strong coil you bear yourself? It was full as heavy and as long as this, seven Christmas Eves ago. You have laboured on it, since. It is a ponderous chain!"

'I glanced about me on the floor, in the expectation of finding myself surrounded by some fifty or sixty fathoms of iron cable: but I could see nothing.

' "Jacob," I said, imploringly. "Old Jacob Marley, tell me more. Speak comfort to me, Jacob!"

' "I have none to give," the Ghost replied. "It comes from other regions, Ebenezer Scrooge, and is conveyed by other ministers, to other kinds of men. Nor can I tell you what I would. A very little more, is all permitted to me. I cannot rest, I cannot stay, I cannot linger anywhere. My spirit never walked beyond our counting-house -- mark me! -- in life my spirit never roved beyond the narrow limits of our money-changing hole; and weary journeys lie before me!"

'It was a habit with me, whenever I became thoughtful, to put my hands in my breeches pockets. Pondering on what the Ghost had said, I did so now, but without lifting up my eyes, or getting off my knees.

' "You must have been very slow about it, Jacob," I observed, in a business-like manner, though with humility and deference.

' "Slow!" the Ghost repeated.

' "Seven years dead," I mused. "And travelling all the time!"

' "The whole time," said the Ghost. "No rest, no peace. Incessant torture of remorse."

' "You travel fast?" I said.

' "On the wings of the wind," replied the Ghost.

' "You might have got over a great quantity of ground in seven years," I said.

'The Ghost, on hearing this, set up another cry, and clanked its chain so hideously in the dead silence of the night, that the Ward would have been justified in indicting it for a nuisance.

' "Oh! captive, bound, and double-ironed," cried the phantom, "not to know, that ages of incessant labour, by immortal creatures, for this earth must pass into eternity before the good of which it is susceptible is all developed. Not to know that any Christian spirit working kindly in its little sphere, whatever it may be, will find its mortal life too short for its vast means of usefulness. Not to know that no space of regret can make amends for one life's opportunity misused! Yet such was I! Oh! such was I!"

' "But you were always a good man of business, Jacob," I faltered, who now began to apply this to myself.

' "Business!" cried the Ghost, wringing its hands again. "Mankind was my business. The common welfare was my business; charity, mercy, forbearance, and benevolence, were, all, my business. The dealings of my trade were but a drop of water in the comprehensive ocean of my business!"

'It held up its chain at arm's length, as if that were the cause of all its unavailing grief, and flung it heavily upon the ground again.

' "At this time of the rolling year," the spectre said "I suffer most. Why did I walk through crowds of fellow-beings with my eyes turned down, and never raise them to that blessed Star which led the Wise Men to a poor abode! Were there no poor homes to which its light would have conducted me!"

'I was very much dismayed to hear the spectre going on at this rate, and began to quake exceedingly.

' "Hear me!" cried the Ghost. "My time is nearly gone."

' "I will," I said. "But don't be hard upon me! Don't be flowery, Jacob! Pray!"

' "How it is that I appear before you in a shape that you can see, I may not tell. I have sat invisible beside you many and many a day."

'It was not an agreeable idea. I shivered, and wiped the perspiration from my brow.

' "That is no light part of my penance," pursued the Ghost. "I am here to-night to warn you, that you have yet a chance and hope of escaping my fate. A chance and hope of my procuring, Ebenezer."

' "You were always a good friend to me," I said. "Thank 'ee!"

' "You will be haunted," resumed the Ghost, "by Three Spirits."

'My countenance fell almost as low as the Ghost's had done.

' "Is that the chance and hope you mentioned, Jacob?" I demanded, in a faltering voice.

' "It is."

' "I -- I think I'd rather not," I said.

' "Without their visits," said the Ghost, "you cannot hope to shun the path I tread. Expect the first tomorrow, when the bell tolls one."

' "Couldn't I take 'em all at once, and have it over, Jacob?" I hinted.

‘ "Expect the second on the next night at the same hour. The third upon the next night when the last stroke of twelve has ceased to vibrate. Look to see me no more; and look that, for your own sake, you remember what has passed between us!"

'When it had said these words, the spectre took its wrapper from the table, and bound it round its head, as before. I knew this, by the smart sound its teeth made, when the jaws were brought together by the bandage. I ventured to raise my eyes again, and found my supernatural visitor confronting me in an erect attitude, with its chain wound over and about its arm.

'The apparition walked backward from me; and at every step it took, the window raised itself a little, so that when the spectre reached it, it was wide open. It beckoned me to approach, which I did. When we were within two paces of each other, Marley's Ghost held up its hand, warning me to come no nearer. I stopped.

'Not so much in obedience, as in surprise and fear: for on the raising of the hand, I became sensible of confused noises in the air; incoherent sounds of lamentation and regret; wailings inexpressibly sorrowful and self-accusatory. The spectre, after listening for a moment, joined in the mournful dirge; and floated out upon the bleak, dark night.

'I followed to the window: desperate in my curiosity. I looked out.

'The air was filled with phantoms, wandering hither and thither in restless haste, and moaning as they went. Every one of them wore chains like Marley's Ghost; some few (they might be guilty governments) were linked together; none were free. Many had been personally known to me in their lives. I had been quite familiar with one old ghost, in a white waistcoat, with a monstrous iron safe attached to its ankle, who cried piteously at being unable to assist a wretched woman with an infant, whom it saw below, upon a door-step. The misery with them all was, clearly, that they sought to interfere, for good, in human matters, and had lost the power for ever.

'Whether these creatures faded into mist, or mist enshrouded them, I could not tell. But they and their spirit voices faded together; and the night became as it had been when I walked home.

'I closed the window, and examined the door by which the Ghost had entered. It was double-locked, as I had locked it with my own hands, and the bolts were undisturbed. I tried to say "Humbug!" but stopped at the first syllable. And being, from the emotion I had undergone, or the fatigues of the day, or my glimpse of the Invisible World, or the dull conversation of the Ghost, or the lateness of the hour, much in need of repose; went straight to bed, without undressing, and fell asleep upon the instant.'

Stave II
"The First of the Three Spirits - Reprise"

'When I awoke, it was so dark, that looking out of bed, I could scarcely distinguish the transparent window from the opaque walls of my chamber. I was endeavouring to pierce the darkness with my ferret eyes, when the chimes of a neighbouring church struck the four quarters. So I listened for the hour.

'To my great astonishment the heavy bell went on from six to seven, and from seven to eight, and regularly up to twelve; then stopped. Twelve. It was past two when I went to bed. The clock was wrong. An icicle must have got into the works. Twelve.

'I touched the spring of my repeater, to correct this most preposterous clock. Its rapid little pulse beat twelve: and stopped.

' "Why, it isn't possible," I said, "that I can have slept through a whole day and far into another night. It isn't possible that anything has happened to the sun, and this is twelve at noon."

'The idea being an alarming one, I scrambled out of bed, and groped my way to the window. I was obliged to rub the frost off with the sleeve of my dressing-gown before I could see anything; and could see very little then. All I could make out was, that it was still very foggy and extremely cold, and that there was no noise of people

194

running to and fro, and making a great stir, as there unquestionably would have been if night had beaten off bright day, and taken possession of the world. This was a great relief, because "three days after sight of this First of Exchange pay to Mr. Ebenezer Scrooge or his order," and so forth, would have become a mere United States' security if there were no days to count by.

'I went to bed again, and thought, and thought, and thought it over and over and over, and could make nothing of it. The more I thought, the more perplexed I was; and the more I endeavoured not to think, the more I thought. Marley's Ghost bothered my exceedingly. Every time I resolved within myself, after mature inquiry, that it was all a dream, my mind flew back again, like a strong spring released, to its first position, and presented the same problem to be worked all through, "Was it a dream or not?"

'I lay in this state until the chimes had gone three quarters more, when I remembered, on a sudden, that the Ghost had warned me of a visitation when the bell tolled one. I resolved to lie awake until the hour was past; and, considering that I could no more go to sleep than go to Heaven, this was perhaps the wisest resolution in my power.

'The quarter was so long, that I was more than once convinced I must have sunk into a doze unconsciously, and missed the clock. At length it broke upon my listening ear.

' "Ding, dong!"

' "A quarter past," I said, counting.

' "Ding dong!"

' "Half past!" I said.

' "Ding dong!"

' "A quarter to it," I said.

' "Ding dong!"

' "The hour itself," I said, triumphantly,

' "And nothing else!"

'I spoke before the hour bell sounded, which it now did with a deep, dull, hollow, melancholy One. Light flashed up in the room upon the instant, and the curtains of my bed were drawn.

'The curtains of my bed were drawn aside, I tell you, by a hand. Not the curtains at my feet, nor the curtains at my back, but those to which my face was addressed. The curtains of my bed were drawn aside; and I, starting up into a half-recumbent attitude, found myself face to face with the unearthly visitor who drew them: as close to it as I am now to you, and I am standing in the spirit at your elbow.

'It was a strange figure -- like a child: yet not so like a child as like an old man, viewed through some supernatural medium, which gave him the appearance of having receded from the view, and being diminished to a child's proportions. Its hair, which hung about its neck and down its back, was white as if with age; and yet the face had not a wrinkle in it, and the tenderest bloom was on the skin. The arms were very long and muscular; the hands the same, as if its hold were of uncommon strength. Its legs and feet, most delicately formed, were, like those upper members, bare. It wore a tunic of the purest white, and round its waist was bound a lustrous belt, the sheen of which was beautiful. It held a branch of fresh green holly in its hand; and, in singular contradiction of that wintry emblem, had its dress trimmed with summer flowers. Its hair was parted down the middle and a strange little cow-lick-- no, it is a wick-- that held a flame that from the crown of its head there sprung a bright clear jet of light, by which all this was visible; and which was doubtless the occasion of its using, in its duller moments, a great extinguisher for a cap, which it now held under its arm.

'Even this, though, when I looked at it with increasing steadiness, was not its strangest quality. For as its belt sparkled and glittered now in one part and now in another, and what was light one instant, at another time was dark, so the figure itself fluctuated in its distinctness: being now a thing with one arm, now with one leg, now with twenty legs, now a pair of legs without a head, now a head without a body: of which dissolving parts, no outline would be visible in the dense gloom wherein they melted away. And in the very wonder of this, it would be itself again; distinct and clear as ever.

' "Are you the Spirit, sir, whose coming was foretold to me?" I asked.

' "I am."

'The voice was soft and gentle. Singularly low, as if instead of being so close beside me, it were at a distance.

' "Who, and what are you?" I demanded.

' "I am the Ghost of Christmas Past."

' "Long Past?" I inquired: observant of its dwarfish stature.

' "No. Your past."

'Perhaps, I could not have told anybody why, if anybody could have asked me; but I had a special desire to see the Spirit in his cap; and begged him to be covered.

' "What!" exclaimed the Ghost, "Would you so soon put out, with worldly hands, the light I give? Is it not enough that you are one of those whose passions made this cap, and force me through whole trains of years to wear it low upon my brow!"

'I reverently disclaimed all intention to offend or any knowledge of having willfully bonneted the Spirit at any period of my life. I then made bold to inquire what business brought him there.

' "Your welfare," said the Ghost.

'I expressed myself much obliged, but could not help thinking that a night of unbroken rest would have been more conducive to that end. The Spirit must have heard me thinking, for it said immediately:

' "Your reclamation, then. Take heed."

'It put out its strong hand as it spoke, and clasped me gently by the arm.

' "Rise. And walk with me."

'It would have been in vain for me to plead that the weather and the hour were not adapted to pedestrian purposes; that bed was warm, and the thermometer a long way below freezing; that I was clad but lightly in my slippers, dressing-gown, and nightcap; and that I had a cold upon me at that time. The grasp, though gentle as a woman's hand, was not to be resisted. I rose: but finding that the Spirit made towards the window, clasped my robe in supplication.

' "I am mortal," I remonstrated, "and liable to fall."

' "Bear but a touch of my hand there," said the Spirit, laying it upon his heart, "and you shall be upheld in more than this."

'As the words were spoken, we passed through the wall, and stood next to the high gates and walls of that rose about the Middlesex Infirmary.

'The Spirit led me into one room of but many room in a hospital, in one row of but many rows in the room, in but one white shrouded bed of but many white shrouded beds in the row lay my mother,

Elizabeth Scrooge and those afflicted by Consumption, or Tuberculosis, as it is now known. The sounds of the coughs, the wheezes, the moans, groans, and the cries of the patients who likewise lay on their death-beds disturbed me immensely. The smell of the primitive antiseptics were an assault on my humanity.

' "Ah, the poor melancholy angels," the Spirit mused.

' "I beg your pardon," I exclaimed.

' "Is it not the White Plague," inquired the Spirit. "Does not consumption bestow the sufferer with the heightened sensitivity of Heaven?"

' "It is not a romantic disease as the poets like to muse. It is a horrid, slow, wasteful death."

' "And how would you know? Your father left you a solitary child neglected at school, far from a mother's death."

' "Fan? Why my little, little Fan," my mother said.

'I whirled around, my nightgown twirling gaily like a dress at the ball. There I saw a spirit as light and as gay as a breeze blow up the aisle of beds. There was my sister, Fan. Oh, little, little Fan.

' "Oh, mother," Fan said embracing her mother about the neck, in an embrace that would smother with love.

' "Where is your father?" Elizabeth inquired.

' "Father is so much kinder than he used to be, home's like Heaven! He spoke so gently to me this morning when I was waking that I was not afraid to ask him once more if we might visit Mother in the hospital. And here we are mother!"

' "Hello, Elizabeth. How are you feeling, my love?"

'I could see the form of my father standing up the aisle dressed as he would for Parliament, but he wasn't at Parliament, was he?

' "I'm sorry, you asked a question, Spirit."

' "Your father wasn't at Parliament, was he?" inquired the Spirit.

' "I'm afraid not. This is not in his nature. This is quite unnatural."

' "I'm feeling like the weight of a thousand lonely nights have been lifted from my heart," my mother said. "Where is Ebbie?"

'Little Fan ran over to me, clasping her now elderly brother by my hand. I was shocked at by light but firm grasp of my little sister.

' "Dear, dear, brother. Come, mother is waiting to see you."

‘ "Spirit," I said, feeling the firm tug of my sister, "I thought that these were but shadows of things that have been? That they would have no consciousness of us?"

‘ "It is required of every man that they relive their past."

‘ "I am permitted the chance to relive this wonderful moment?"

‘ "Yes, you are."

‘ "Here is Ebbie, Mother. He's to be a man and never to go back to that country school," announced Little Fan.

‘ "Is this true, Jeremiah, my love?"

‘ "Ebenezer's place is at home– with his family."

‘ "And we're to be together all the Christmas long, and have the merriest time in all the world!" sang Little Fan.

‘ "You're quite a woman, little Fan!"

'I had stood there remaining silent by the bed with my head hung low with the weight of many, many lonely years. I knelt beside her bed and wept.

‘ "Mother– It has been so very long– I've been so lonely these last years– I've missed the song of your voice– I've missed the touch of your hand– I've been so very alone–"

‘ "I know, my boy, I know," my father said, putting a comforting hand upon my hunched shoulders. "And I am so very sorry. Your place was always at home with your family."

‘ "You have nothing to be sorry for, Father. I've been the one that's been distant. I'm the son who turned my own kin away on Christmas Day," I cried, tears flowing down the frowns which had hardened in my face. I turned my reddened face to my mother, "Please, I need a mother's forgiveness."

‘ "Every child, no matter what his sins, has his mother's forgiveness. It is a mother's nature to be so."

‘ "Spirit, I cannot bear to be here any longer. I buried my family long ago, in both body and mind. I cannot bear to see them so vibrant and alive with spirit. Please, Spirit–"

'And I stood from beside my mother's bed and there knelt the form of my younger self in my stead. The Spirit of Christmas Cheer came upon the Scrooge family:

On Christmas night all Christians sing
To hear the news the angels bring,
On Christmas night all Christians sing
To here the news the angels bring;
News of great joy, news of great mirth,
News of our merciful King's birth.

Then why should men on earth be sad,
Since our Redeemer made us glad,
Then why should men on earth be sad,
Since our Redeemer made us glad.
When from our sins he set us free,
All for to gain our liberty.

When sin departs before his grace,
Then life and health come in its place;
When sin departs before his grace,
Then life and health come in its place;
Angels and men with joy may sing,
All for to see the newborn King.

All out of darkness we have light,
Which made the angels sing this night.
All out of darkness we have light,
Which made the angles sing this night.
"Glory to God and peace to men,
Now and for evermore. Amen"

' "What a moment of happiness was in that room, that Christmas Day."

' "A few fleeting moments, Spirit. She was buried only days later."

' "But happiness, and peace, contented her soul in that time."

'I briefly permitted a reflective pause, then returned, "I buried them long ago."

' "Follow me. We have more to see."

'Although we had but that moment left the hospital behind us, we were now in the busy thoroughfares of a city, where shadowy passengers passed and repassed; where shadowy carts and coaches battle for the way, and all the strife and tumult of a real city were. It was made plain enough, by the dressing of the shops, that here too it was Christmas time again; but it was evening, and the streets were lighted up.

'The Ghost stopped at a certain warehouse door, and asked me if I knew it.

' "Know it!" I said. "Was I apprenticed here?"

'We went in. At sight of an old gentleman in a Welsh wig, sitting behind such a high desk, that if he had been two inches taller he must have knocked his head against the ceiling, I cried in great excitement:

' "Why, it's old Fezziwig! Bless his heart; it's Fezziwig alive again!"

'Old Fezziwig laid down his pen, and looked up at the clock, which pointed to the hour of seven. He rubbed his hands; adjusted his capacious waistcoat; laughed all over himself, from his shoes to his organ of benevolence; and called out in a comfortable, oily, rich, fat, jovial voice:

' "Yo ho, there! Ebenezer! Dick!"

'My former self, now grown a young man, came briskly in, accompanied by our fellow-prentice.

' "Dick Wilkins, to be sure," I said to the Ghost. "Bless me, yes. There he is. He was very much attached to me, was Dick. Poor Dick. Dear, dear."

' "Yo ho, my boys!" said Fezziwig. "No more work to-night. Christmas Eve, Dick. Christmas, Ebenezer. Let's have the shutters up," cried old Fezziwig, with a sharp clap of his hands, "before a man can say Jack Robinson."

'You wouldn't believe how those two fellows went at it. They charged into the street with the shutters -- one, two, three -- had them up in their places -- four, five, six -- barred them and pinned then -- seven, eight, nine -- and came back before you could have got to twelve, panting like race-horses.

' "Hilli-ho!" cried old Fezziwig, skipping down from the high desk, with wonderful agility. "Clear away, my lads, and let's have lots of room here. Hilli-ho, Dick! Chirrup, Ebenezer."

'Clear away! There was nothing we wouldn't have cleared away, or couldn't have cleared away, with old Fezziwig looking on. It was done in a minute. Every movable was packed off, as if it were dismissed from public life for evermore; the floor was swept and watered, the lamps were trimmed, fuel was heaped upon the fire; and the warehouse was as snug, and warm, and dry, and bright a ball-room, as you would desire to see upon a winter's night.

'In came a fiddler with a music-book, and went up to the lofty desk, and made an orchestra of it, and tuned like fifty stomach-aches, and once tuned, Fezziwig, possessed by the Spirit of Christmas Cheer, sang,

> *Wassail, wassail, all over the town!*
> *Our toast it is white and our ale it is brown!*
> *Our bowl it is made of the white maple tree;*
> *With the wassailing bowl, we'll drink to thee.*
>
> *So here is to Mrs. Fezziwig and her substantial smile!*
> *Pray God send our master some guests up the aisle!*
> *Some guests up the aisle that may we all see;*
> *With the wassailing bowl, we'll drink to thee.*
>
> *And here is the housemaid and her cousin the baker!*
> *Pray God send our master good beef by the acre!*
> *And an acre of beef that may we all see;*
> *With the wassailing bowl, we'll drink to thee.*
>
> *So here to the cook, with her brother's particular friend!*
> *Pray God send our master some whiskey of good blend!*
> *And double malt whiskey that may we all see;*
> *With the wassailing bowl, we'll drink to thee.*
>
> *Here to the boy who hid behind the girl from next door!*
> *Pray God send out master a good head of boar!*
> *And a good head of boar that may we all see;*
> *With the wassailing bowl, we'll drink to thee.*
>
> *And here to the shy and here to the bold!*
> *Pray God send our master bread not a day old.*
> *And fresh loaves of bread that may we all see;*

With the wassailing bowl, we'll drink to thee.

And here to the graceful and here to the awkward!
Pray God send our master pastries of the best lard.
And the best lard for our pastries that may we all see;
With the wassailing bowl, we'll drink to thee.

And at last to the pushing and here to the pulling!
Pray God send our master the long life of a King!
A bowl of strong beer! I pray you draw near.
And our jolly wassail' it's then you shall hear.

Come, Dick, fill us a bowl of the best;
Then we hope that your soul in Heaven may rest.
But if you do draw us a bowl of the small.
Then down shall go 'Prentice, bowl and all.

Then here's to the maid in the lily white smock,
Who trips to the door and slips back the lock!
Who trips to the door and pulls back the pin!
For she lets these jolly wassailers in!

'When this result was brought about, old Fezziwig, clapping his hands to stop the dance, cried out, "Well done!" and the fiddler plunged his hot face into a pot of porter, especially provided for that purpose. But scorning rest, upon his reappearance, he instantly began again, though there were no dancers yet, as if the other fiddler had been carried home, exhausted, on a shutter, and he were a brand-new man resolved to beat him out of sight, or perish.

' "Ebenezer, your time it draws near!"

'The Spirit motioned for me to hurry in with the Boar's Head, which I then hurried over to seize with eager, hungry hands. I disappeared into the kitchen and reappeared into the makeshift ballroom, marching like a Field Commander with my knees high, handing the head to old Fezziwig, whom leads a procession of the guests of his Madrigal with Mrs. Fezziwig on his arm. He regally sang and if the King and Queen were in attendance in such a humble ware-house.

The boar's head in hand bear I,
Bedecked with bay and rosemary;
And I pray you, my masters be merry,
Quot estis in convivio
  Caput apri defero
  Redens laudes Domino

The boar's head, as I understand
Is the rarest dish in all this land.
Which thus bedeck with a gay garland
Let us servire cantico
  Caput apri defero
  Redens laudes Domino

Our steward hath provided this
In honor of the King of bliss;
Which on this day to be served is
In Reginensi atrio.
  Caput apri defero
  Redens laudes Domino

'There were more dances, and there were forfeits, and more dances, and there was cake, and there was negus, and there was a great piece of Cold Roast, and there was a great piece of Cold Boiled, and there were mince-pies, and plenty of beer. But the great effect of the evening came after the Roast and Boiled, when the fiddler (an artful dog, mind! The sort of man who knew his business better than you or I could have told it him!) struck up "Sir Roger de Coverley." Then old Fezziwig stood out to dance with Mrs. Fezziwig. Top couple too; with a good stiff piece of work cut out for them; three or four and twenty pair of partners; people who were not to be trifled with; people who would dance, and had no notion of walking.

'But if they had been twice as many -- ah, four times -- old Fezziwig would have been a match for them, and so would Mrs. Fezziwig. As to her, she was worthy to be his partner in every sense of the term. If that's not high praise, tell me higher, and I'll use it. A positive light appeared to issue from Fezziwig's calves. They shone in every part of the dance like moons. You couldn't have predicted, at any given time, what would have become of them next. And when old Fezziwig and Mrs. Fezziwig had gone all through the dance; advance and retire, both hands to your partner, bow and curtsey, corkscrew, thread-the-needle, and back again to your place; Fezziwig cut -- cut so deftly, that he appeared to wink with his legs, and came upon his feet again without a stagger.

'When the clock struck eleven, this domestic ball broke up. Mr. and Mrs. Fezziwig took their stations, one on either side of the door, and shaking hands with every person individually as he or she went out, wished him or her a Merry Christmas. When everybody had retired but the two prentices, they did the same to them; and thus the cheerful voices died away, and the lads were left to their beds; which were under a counter in the back-shop.

'During the whole of this time, I had acted like a man out of my wits. My heart and soul were in the scene, and with my former self. I corroborated everything, remembered everything, enjoyed everything, and underwent the strangest agitation. It was not until now, when the bright faces of my former self and Dick were turned from us, that I remembered the Ghost, and became conscious that it was looking full upon me, while the light upon its head burnt very clear.

' "A small matter," said the Ghost, "to make these silly folks so full of gratitude."

' "Small!" I echoed.

'The Spirit signed to me to listen to the two apprentices, who were pouring out their hearts in praise of Fezziwig: and when he had done so, said,

' "Why! Is it not! He has spent but a few pounds of your mortal money: three or four perhaps. Is that so much that he deserves this praise?"

' "It isn't that," I said, heated by the remark, and speaking unconsciously like my former, not my latter, self. "It isn't that, Spirit. He has the power to render us happy or unhappy; to make our service light or burdensome; a pleasure or a toil. Say that his power lies in words and looks; in things so slight and insignificant that it is impossible to add and count them up: what then? The happiness he gives, is quite as great as if it cost a fortune."

'I felt the Spirit's glance, and stopped.

' "What is the matter?" asked the Ghost.

' "Nothing in particular," I said.

' "Something, I think?" the Ghost insisted.

' "No," I said, "No. I should like to be able to say a word or two to my clerk just now! That's all."

'My former self turned down the lamps as he gave utterance to the wish; and the Ghost and I again stood side by side in the open air.

' "My time grows short," observed the Spirit. "Quick!"

'This was not addressed to me, or to any one whom I could see, but it produced an immediate effect. For there sat alone by the side of a fair young girl in a mourning-dress: in whose eyes there were tears, which sparkled in the light that shone out of the Ghost of Christmas Past.

' "Allow me to repeat: it is required of every man that they relieve their past."

' "I care not to, Spirit. This moment is in the Past."

' "As was the reunion with your mother, as was the Madrigal of old Fezziwig, of which you partook of easily enough."

' "But, Spirit, any other moment but this."

' "Sit!" And I did, reluctantly.

' "It matters little," she said, softly. "To you, very little. Another idol has displaced me; and if it can cheer and comfort you in time to come, as I would have tried to do, I have no just cause to grieve."

' "What Idol has displaced you?" I rejoined.

' "A golden one."

' "This is the even-handed dealing of the world!" I said. "There is nothing on which it is so hard as poverty; and there is nothing it professes to condemn with such severity as the pursuit of wealth!"

' "You fear the world too much," she answered, gently. "All your other hopes have merged into the hope of being beyond the chance of its sordid reproach. I have seen your nobler aspirations fall off one by one, until the master-passion, Gain, engrosses you. Have I not?"

' "What then?" I retorted. "Even if I have grown so much wiser, what then? I am not changed towards you."

'She shook her head.

' "Am I?"

' "Our contract is an old one. It was made when we were both poor and content to be so, until, in good season, we could improve our worldly fortune by our patient industry. You are changed. When it was made, you were another man."

' "I was a boy," I said impatiently.

' "Your own feeling tells you that you were not what you are," she returned. "I am. That which promised happiness when we were one in heart, is fraught with misery now that we are two. How often and how keenly I have thought of this, I will not say. It is enough that I have thought of it, and can release you."

' "Have I ever sought release?"

' "In words? No. Never."

' "In what, then?" I asked, then I implored, "Please, Spirit, remove me from this place. I do not wish to hear those words that are to be spoken."

' "Listen well," the Spirit said.

' "In a changed nature; in an altered spirit; in another atmosphere of life; another Hope as its great end. In everything that made my love of any worth or value in your sight. If this had never been between us," said the girl, looking mildly, but with steadiness, upon me; "tell me, would you seek me out and try to win me now? Ah, no!"

'I seemed to yield to the justice of this supposition, in spite of myself. But I said with a struggle, "You think not?"

' "I would gladly think otherwise if I could," she answered, "Heaven knows. When I have learned a Truth like this, I know how strong and irresistible it must be. But if you were free to-day, to-morrow, yesterday, can even I believe that you would choose a dowerless girl -- you who, in your very confidence with her, weigh everything by Gain: or, choosing her, if for a moment you were false enough to your one guiding principle to do so, do I not know that your repentance and regret would surely follow? I do; and I release you. With a full heart, for the love of him you once were."

'I was about to speak; but with her head turned from me, she resumed.

' "You may -- the memory of what is past half makes me hope

you will -- have pain in this. A very, very brief time, and you will dismiss the recollection of it, gladly, as an unprofitable dream, from which it happened well that you awoke. May you be happy in the life you have chosen."

'She left me, and we parted.

' "Spirit!" I said, "show me no more! Conduct me home. Why do you delight to torture me?"

' "Torture? If man you be, dare speak of torture?" exclaimed the Ghost. "One shadow more!"

' "No more!" I cried! "No more, I don't wish to see it! Show me no more!"

'But the relentless Ghost led me through a collection of chambers of horrors, where lunatics were chained, naked, in rows of cages that flanked a promenade, and were wondered and jeered at through iron bars by London loungers. How in the name of goodness could I, a sane person indeed, seeing, on my entrance into any place, gyves and manacles (however highly polished) yawning for my ankles and wrists; swings dangling in the air, to spin me round like an impaled cockchafer; gags and strait-waistcoats ready at a moment's notice to muzzle and bind me. Have I not always endeavoured to help to support the establishment I have described? Even now, an outside view of Bethlehem Hospital, known to the vulgar as Bedlam, was gloomy enough; and, when on that cold, misty, cheerless afternoon of Christmas Day, I looked up at the high walls, and saw, grimly peering over us, its upper stories and dismal little iron-bound windows. The Spirit did not ring the porter's bell (albeit we were only visitors, and free to go, if we would, without ringing it at all) in the most cheerful frame of mind.

'The Spirit and I walked up a winding staircase into the upper storeys of the asylum. The massive furnaces that made the lower chambers a dreadful hellscape, utterly abandoned the upper storeys to the full wails of the wintry winds through unglazed windows. Of course, the Spirit knew external heat and cold had little influence on his charge. No warmth could warm, no wintry weather chill me. No wind that blew was bitterer than me. And yet the cold reality of memory had put a chill into my breath and I patted my arms to help the course of blood through my veins.

'The Spirit instructed me to proceed through a studded wooden door securing the madness within with massive metal bolts, hinges, and a padlock. The door now appeared to me to be as ghastly and ghostly as the chain the ghost of Jacob Marley bore. My own memories began to fail me. My own sanity had failed me the moment Jacob Marley had entered into my bed-chamber, interrupting my supper. What was real and what was madness?

'I patently refused to obey the instruction of the Spirit. I knew, of course I did, what lessons were going to be taught in that room, and these were lessons I was as unwilling and unable to experience as any other during our brief time together. I was stern in my stubbornness, but a weariness had come upon me walking through Bedlam, and I desired nothing but to return to the soft down and warm of my bed. Acquiescing to the Spirit for what I prayed to be the final time, I passed through the massive wooden door as effortlessly as the ghost of Jacob Marley did my own double-locked bedroom door. In the room, a younger form of myself sat in a chair that belonged elsewhere, anywhere other than this room. In the corner, huddled and bound in a straight-waistcoat, our father. The strangeness of the veil had created a paradox. In that moment of time, Jeremiah Scrooge was both our father, my younger self and the older me accompanied by the Spirit, whom stood not only on the other side of the veil, but in the shadows as well.

'The Spirit knew that this young Ebenezer had been required by his contract with Bedlam to extend the institutionalization of his father before the coming of the New Year. I had once chosen this time of the month, this exact day to sign the papers, due to the shuttering of my counting-house every twenty-fifth of December. Of course, I would have had my counting-house opened for business if I had had my discretion, but none else of the modern world desired to be about for business. And my young clerk, Dick Wilkins wished to make himself merry at Christmas, though I had been at the time temped to dock him half-a-crown for it. Why should I be forced to sit alone at home because the rest of London society chose to celebrate such a foolish little Christian holiday? Bedlam did not stop its business, it continued to operate at full force, and for that I had been most proud. I had not been denied the opportunity to sign these papers, why should I have been likewise denied tending to our books?

'Why my young self sat there with our father was a mystery to us. My younger self felt compelled to visit that afternoon as if guided by an unseen hand. We had no where else to be at the time, so why not spend a moment of it with family. It was, after all, Christmas Day. Why did this thought suddenly cross my mind? I did not know. Bah! Humbug!

'My younger self had sat in a chair brought in by a nurse and felt the sudden shock of imprisonment as the door clanged shut and was bolted from the outside. Our counting-house was small, the hole of our own clerk, Dick Wilkins for him and Bob Cratchit for me, was not much larger than this cell. Though it was a confined space with only himself and our clerk, nary once did my younger self feel claustrophobic in the confines of our counting-house. But here, in Bedlam, panic seized his heart, which pounded all the harder and louder, the *rum-tum-tum* of a drum.

'Jeremiah, his blackened eyes brightened seeing a recognizable face. He had been discarded into the corner of the room by the nurses whom had blackened his eyes, his price for his struggling to accept the gift of a strait-waistcoat. Was he a threat to his own flesh-and-blood? Had he, during the entirety of his incarceration in Bedlam, ever not turned his other cheek? Yet, the mad-doctors sicced upon him those devils masquerading as nurses. In his mind, society should account no man a lunatic whom it requires a mad-doctor to prove insanity.

' "Son, have you come to take me home for Christmas?"

'After a pregnant pause, "Not this year, Father. I was nearby on business and I just came to–"

' "To what, Son?"

' "To sign contracts continuing for institutionalization for another year," my younger self said. I was never one to mince words either then or now. The honesty assaulted our father, who winced in pain.

' "I do not understand why I am imprisoned here. What have I done wrong? Nothing that I can see. Once I was as hard and sharp as flint, from which no steel had ever struck out generous fire; secret, and self-contained, and solitary as an oyster. But then your sister, Little Fan, she prayed for me. She saved me. I became so much kinder than I used to be."

' "I remember," my younger self said.

' "I became as good a friend, as good a master, and as good a man, as the good old city knew, or any other good old city, town, or borough, in the good old world. Some people laughed to see the alteration in me, but I let them laugh, and little heeded them; for I was wise enough to know that nothing ever happened on this globe, for good, at which some people did not have their fill of laughter in the outset; and knowing that such as these would be blind anyway, I thought it quite as well that they should wrinkle up their eyes in grins, as have the malady in less attractive forms. My own heart laughed: and that was quite enough for me.

' "It was always said of me, that I knew how to keep Christmas well, if any man alive possessed the knowledge. I had no further intercourse with Spirits. Have I not lived upon the Total Abstinence Principle, ever afterwards?"

' "The Total Abstinence Principle? How could you abstain from alcohol if you never touched a drop of drink in the entirety of your life, Father?" my younger self said confused by our father's choice of words. "And you never abstained from intercourse. I and my sister are proof of your fertility." Could this be a symptom of his madness?

' "It is a pun, my son. I no longer have intercourse with Spirits. Intercourse. Spirits," our father said, suddenly tickled by his own poetic pun. The sound of his pleasant giggling was foreign to the present atmosphere, but he continued chuckling, "I speak of neither sexual relations with your mother nor alcohol, save for the briefest taste of wine during Communion!"

' "Spirits? Aye, there's the rub, Father. These Spirits you have spoken of– continue to speak of. They are a foolish fantasy. I support institutions like these," my younger self said, indicating Bedlam. "And I cannot afford your fancies, Father, they cost enough."

' "No. No. No!" our father said agitated. "I have failed you as a father. You have become a tight-fisted hand at the grind-stone, my son! You are still the squeezing, wrenching, grasping, scraping, clutching, covetous sinner I was shown during my journey with Spirits! I did not rear a child to worship gain as his master-passion. The cold within you has begun to freeze your youthful features, nipping your pointed nose, shrivelling your cheek, stiffening your gait; making your eyes red, your thin lips blue and you speak shrewdly in a grating voice. A frosty rime is upon your head, and on your eyebrows, and your wiry chin. You carry your own low temperature always about with you; I have no doubt you ice your office in the dogdays; and don't thaw it one degree this Christmas Day. "

' "And what of it?" my younger self said, genuinely inquiring of our father's rationale.

' "What of it? What of it!

' "I honoured Christmas in my heart, and tried to keep it all the year. I lived in the Past, the Present, and the Future. The Spirits of all Three strived within me. I shut not out the lessons that they taught."

' "You were not visited by the Spirits of Christmases Past, Present or Yet To Come. It a humour of the brain, the very reason you are hospitalized here."

'Our father suddenly noticed a bright clear jet of light appearing out of the shadows in the corner of his cell. The strangest thing about it was how could he not have seen it was visible? Then the strange figure he has seen once before when he went on compulsion -- still like a child: yet not so like a child as like an old man. The Spirit of Christmas Present aged from his birth to his death in but one single day! Did Spirits of Christmases Past not age? This was not the question our father wished to ponder at this particular moment in time.

' "Hear me!" our father said pleading with the Spirit. "I am not the man I was. I was not be the man I would have been but for that intercourse. Men's courses will foreshadow certain ends, to which, if persevered in, they must lead," said Jeremiah falling awkwardly onto his knees. He briefly lost his equilibrium due to the constraint of the straight-waistcoat. "But the courses were departed from, Spirit. The ends should have changed. But the ends did not change. Despite my changed nature interceding for me, and piting me. You assured me, Spirit, that I could change those shadows you all had shown me, by an altered life, and change my own son!"

'My younger self no longer felt as if he was the one being addressed. To whom was his father arguing?

' "These were but shadows of the things that have been," said the Ghost to our father. "And could yet be. They had no consciousness of us then, or now."

' "Why show me any of it, if my son is past all hope?"

' "The soul that sinneth, it shall die. The son shall not bear the iniquity of the father, neither shall the father bear the iniquity of the son: the righteousness of the righteous shall be upon him, and the wickedness of the wicked shall be upon him," the Spirit said, quoting the Holiest of Scriptures.

' "Do not dare quote scripture to me. The devil can cite Scripture for his purpose. I know. But I once did and can still, exceedingly well. A foolish son is a grief to his father, and bitterness to her that bare him. And I bearing the iniquity of my son through my unjust imprisonment at his hands!

' "Your nature interceded for me, and pitied me. Ye three Spirits of Christmases Past, Present, and Yet to Come assured me that I yet could change these shadows you had shown me, by an altered life. But my son did not live by an altered life, he still choose the master-passion: gain, despite, or in spite of, the intercession due to my intercourse with you."

' "For this cause shall a man leave his father and mother, and shall be joined unto his wife, and they two shall be one flesh," the Spirit said, trying to bring reason, "Jeremiah, Ebenezer must leave his father and his mother, and cleave unto his wife."

' "But he didn't cleave unto a wife. Oh, how I wish he would have chosen that dowerless girl -- through her would he have learned a Truth like–"

' "Belle?" my younger self asked unable to comprehend his conversation with his obviously mad father. Our father appeared to be arguing with no one and yet arguing with his son, all being equal. "A dowerless girl, Father? This is the even-handed dealing of the world! There is nothing on which it is so hard as poverty; and there is nothing it professes to condemn with such severity as the pursuit of wealth!" he said, all this seeming very familiar– somehow, somewhere? somewhen?

' "Why should you not marry a dowerless girl -- in you very confidence with her, weigh nothing by Gain: and, choosing her, not for a moment would you never be false enough to your one guiding principle to do so, do I know that happiness and contentment would surely follow?" my father pleaded.

'Our father then continued addressing the Spirit, bringing further confusions to his son. "Again. Again! Spirit. Ebenezer chose the master passion: gain! Despite my efforts of affecting change upon my son, because of your intercession, he still hastens to be rich with an evil eye, and he considers not the poverty of spirit that shall come upon him."

' "But every one shall die for his own iniquity: every man that eateth the sour grape, his teeth shall be set on edge," said the Spirit.

' "Father," my younger self said, only hearing Jeremiah's words and not those of the Spirit. "I have the right to chose my own path in this life. So what if I have grown so much wiser."

'Our father answered, "Wiser!" He turned his eyes to Heaven in supplication, peering through the unglazed windows towards the Blessed Star, "He that loveth silver shall not be satisfied with silver; nor he that loveth abundance with increase: this is also vanity. When goods increase, they are increased that eat them: and what good is there to the owners thereof, saving the beholding of them with their eyes? The sleep of a labouring man is sweet, whether he eat little or much: but the abundance of the rich will not suffer him to sleep. There is a sore evil which I have seen under the sun, namely, riches kept for the owners thereof to their hurt. But those riches perish by evil travail: and he begetteth a son, and there is nothing in his hand. As he came forth of his mother's womb, naked shall he return to go as he came, and shall take nothing of his labour, which he may carry away in his hand. And this also is a sore evil, that in all points as he came, so shall he go: and what profit hath he that hath laboured for the wind. All his days also he eateth in darkness, and he hath much sorrow and wrath with his sickness."

' "Now who is quoting scripture, Father? You are quite the powerful preacher, sir, Why did you become a Parson like Grandfather?"

' "It is because of the intercession with the Spirits of Christmases Past, Present, and Yet To Come that I came to read the Holiest of Scripture, embracing the Word of God, and accepting the Word as my Lord and Personal Saviour!"

' "Bah!" my younger self said.

' "Feed the flock of God which is among you, taking the over-

sight thereof, not by constraint, but willingly; not for the filthy master-passion: gain, but of a ready mind; neither as being lords over
God's heritage, but being examples to the flock."

‘ "Humbug!"

‘ "Yes, a humbug, quite," said our father, "I put the most foolish notions into your head, Son. A humbug? Of all you could have
gleamed from me, you chose humbugs? Do not believe that your
Father or your Father in Heaven will ever be deceptive, wilfully false
talking to you. God is whom your name should be good upon, not
'Change."

‘ "You are quite mad!"

‘ "Is it madness to believe in God? To accept Jesus Christ as Lord
and Saviour? In this godless modern age, the preaching of the cross
is foolishness to you that perish; but unto us which are saved it is the
power of God. Where is the wise? where is the scribe? where is the
disputer of this world? hath not God made foolish the wisdom of
this world? For after that in the wisdom of God the world by wisdom
knew not God, it pleased God by the foolishness of preaching to
save them that believe. For the godless require a sign, and the men of
science seek after wisdom: But we preach Christ crucified, unto the
godless a stumblingblock, and unto the scientists foolishness; But
unto them which are called, both godless and men of science, Christ
the power of God, and the wisdom of God. Because the foolishness
of God is wiser than men; and the weakness of God is stronger than
men.

‘ "For ye see your calling, brethren, how that not many wise men
after the flesh, not many mighty, not many noble, are called: But God
hath chosen the foolish things of the world to confound the wise; and
God hath chosen the weak things of the world to confound the things
which are mighty; And base things of the world, and things which are
despised, hath God chosen, yea, and things which are not, to bring to
nought things that are: That no flesh should glory in his presence. But
of him are ye in Christ Jesus, who of God is made unto us wisdom,
and righteousness, and sanctification, and redemption: That, according as it is written, He that boasts, let him boast in the Lord."

'A part of my older self's spirit felt that arguments with our father
were once as common as drawing breath, but strangely, my younger

self only knew of a father full of glad-tiding, comfort, and joy! "Why did you ever endeavour in that Ghostly little tale to me and Little Fan as children that Christmas evening? To raise the Ghost of an Idea? It most certainly put me out of humour with myself, with each other, with the season, or with you. It has haunted my home bitterly. The knowing with each and every Christmas recitation of the ghastly tale in the warm company of family and friends, that as I grew so much wiser, my father grew so much more mad."

' "My purpose was, in a whimsical kind of masque, which the good humour of the season justified, to awaken some loving and forbearing thoughts, never out of season in a Christian land," our father said, "I dared not be the man I was. I would not be the man I would have been but for that intercourse with Spirits. Why would they show me that, if I was past all hope? Mark my words, my son, and remember them well, for you too must have an intercourse with Spirits if my prayers are answered. Men's courses will foreshadow certain ends, to which, if persevered in, they must lead. But if the courses be departed from, the ends will change."

' "Change? Why should I change, Father? This day, my name is good upon 'Change, for anything I chose to put my hand to."

' "But you do not chose to put your hand to any thing! At this festive season of the year, my son," our father pleaded, "it is more than usually desirable that you should make some slight provision for the Poor and Destitute, who suffer greatly at the present time. Many thousands are in want of common necessaries; hundreds of thousands are in want of common comforts. You should put your hand to raising a fund to buy the Poor some meat and drink and means of warmth. Choose this time, Son, because it is a time, of all others, when Want is keenly felt, and Abundance rejoices."

'Again and again, somewhere– somewhen– both of our spirits felt they had had this argument before.

'And I stepped from the shadows into the light cast by the strange figure of the Spirit of Christmas Past, "Don't be grieved, Father. Jacob Marley, in his pigtail, usual waistcoat, tights and boots, the tassels on the latter bristling, like his pigtail, and his coat-skirts, and the hair upon his head, visited me this night."

' "You encountered your old partner Jacob Marley, my son?" our father asked dumbfounded.

' "Yes! Yes! The chain he drew had been clasped about his middle. It was long, and wound about him like a tail; and it was made of cash-boxes, keys, padlocks, ledgers, deeds, and heavy purses wrought in steel. His body was transparent! I looked through his waistcoat, could see the two buttons on my coat behind," I said, the peel of laughter from me was so bright that our father shielded his eyes from its brilliance.

' "He came upon me to-night to warn me, that I have yet a chance and hope of escaping his fate. A chance and hope of his procuring, Father. I am being haunted by Three Spirits. This is but the first. I am going forth this night on compulsion and learning a lesson, which is working now."

' "Spirit, where is Jacob Marley, I wish to thank him, Spirit," our father said, a torrent of tears welling up and overflowing his eyes.

' "That was no light part of his penance," the Spirit said, "He cannot rest, he cannot stay, he cannot linger anywhere. He sought to interfere, for good, in human matters, and the power was granted to him– albeit briefly. But lost is the power for ever."

' "Oh, Jacob Marley, poor, poor soul," our father said weeping, incoherent sounds of lamentation and regret; wailings inexpressibly sorrowful and self-accusatory issued from him.

' "But the length of that chain he bears is now lighter with the very light of the infant Christ!"

' "Thank 'ee, Spirit!" said two of the three Scrooges in the room, father and one of the sons.

'This sudden weeping and wailing concerned the heart and the pocketbook of my younger, far more material self standing in the cell. How long until these medical shysters cured our father of his ills? Or did not they seek a cure, only to prolong the madness at the suffering his pocketbook? What sort of madness was he witnessing with his own eyes, yet being sane cannot truly comprehend.

' "Oh, foolish, foolish man ye be Ebenezer," I said, the laughter aching my sides, "Indeed, Father, you too were haunted by these Spirits. The very same Spirits! Indeed. Indeed. Your yearly Christmas recitations return to haunt my memories! Indeed, they do. Indeed, they do!"

'My younger self, distraught for our father's sanity and with great concern for his own safety, banged on the cell's door hoping the pounding would penetrate the studded wooden doors secured most expertly with massive metal bolts, hinges, and a padlock, and sound down the hallway.

'Three asylum nurses, barrel-chested and ham-fisted were-elephants as insane as any of the inmates in Bedlam, burst into the cell and began an onslaught on Jeremiah with billy clubs across his shoulders and his back and striking blunt blows to his skull. Our father wept and wailed with each blow, unable to fend off any of the blows from the terrible truncheons with his forearms, or put any type of fight, due to the contracts of the straight-waistcoat. Our father curled into the foetal-position, whimpering like a scolded mongrel. The late-in-life abortionists continued their procedure, with the surgical precision of a madman. My younger self cowered in a corner.

'My older ghostly self cried out for our father. I sought to intervene on our father's behalf by seizing the nurses and manhandling them off our father, but as the Spirit reminded me, "These are but shadows of the things that have been. They have no consciousness of us." My hands were, in fact, as immaterial to the nurses as a shadow. Not only had the nurses no consciousness of us, I could not affect any change upon the scene. The Spirit may have been right, but it was not right!

' "But they're killing him! Don't you see! They're killing him!"

' "That they are what they are," said the Ghost, "do not blame me!"

' "But Father caught a swelling on the brain from the thrashing and died on this very Christmas Day!" I cried.

'The Spirit once, and once again, reminded me, "These were shadows of the things that have been, that they are what they are, do not blame me!"

' "Remove me!" I exclaimed, "I cannot bear it!"

'I turned upon the Ghost, and seeing that it looked upon me with a face, in which in some strange way there were fragments of all the faces it had shown me, wrestled with it.

' "Leave me! Take me back. Haunt me no longer!"

'In the struggle, if that can be called a struggle in which the

Ghost with no visible resistance on its own part was undisturbed by any effort of its adversary, I observed that its light was burning high and bright; and dimly connecting that with its influence over me, I seized the extinguisher-cap and by a sudden action pressed it down upon its head.

' "No! No, my son!" my father cried in spite of his continued and continuous beating, "you require his light! This is the light of infant Christ! Don't put out, with worldly hands, the light he gives! You are one of those whose passions made this cap, and force him through whole trains of years to wear it low upon his brow!" His own brow burst open from a forceful blow, blood obscuring his vision of the comforting light of the Spirit, "If you extinguish the light he gives, remembrance of me, remembrance of that Ghost of an Idea, will likewise be extinguished! Forever!" One of the nurse's blows shattered his jaw, but could not shutter his plea, "Don't put yourself out of humour with yourself or with me!"

'The Spirit dropped beneath it, so that the extinguisher covered its whole form; but though I pressed it down with all my force, I could not hide the light, which streamed from under it, in an unbroken flood upon the ground.

'I was conscious of being exhausted, and overcome by an irresistible drowsiness; and, further, of being in my own bedroom. I gave the cap a parting squeeze, in which my hand relaxed; and had barely time to reel to bed, before I sank into a heavy sleep.'

Stave III
"The Second of the Three Spirits - Reprise"

'Awaking in the middle of a prodigiously tough snore, and sitting up in bed to get my thoughts together, I had no occasion to be told that the bell was again upon the stroke of One. I felt that I was restored to consciousness in the right nick of time, for the especial purpose of holding a conference with the second messenger dispatched to me through Jacob Marley's intervention. But, finding that I turned uncomfortably cold when I began to wonder which of my curtains this new spectre would draw back, I put them every one aside with my own hands, and lying down again, established a sharp look-out all round the bed. For, I wished to challenge the Spirit on the moment of its appearance, and did not wish to be taken by surprise, and made nervous.

'Gentlemen of the free-and-easy sort, who plume themselves on being acquainted with a move or two, and being usually equal to the time-of-day, express the wide range of their capacity for adventure by observing that they are good for anything from pitch-and-toss to manslaughter; between which opposite extremes, no doubt, there lies a tolerably wide and comprehensive range of subjects. Without venturing for I was quite as hardily as this, I don't mind calling on

you to believe that I was ready for a good broad field of strange appearances, and that nothing between a baby and rhinoceros would
have astonished me very much.

'Now, being prepared for almost anything, I was not by any
means prepared for nothing; and, consequently, when the Bell struck
One, and no shape appeared, I was taken with a violent fit of trembling. Five minutes, ten minutes, a quarter of an hour went by, yet
nothing came. All this time, I lay upon my bed, the very core and
centre of a blaze of ruddy light, which streamed upon it when the
clock proclaimed the hour; and which, being only light, was more
alarming than a dozen ghosts, as I was powerless to make out what
it meant, or would be at; and was sometimes apprehensive that I
might be at that very moment an interesting case of spontaneous
combustion, without having the consolation of knowing it. At last,
however, I began to think -- as you or I would have thought at first;
for it is always the person not in the predicament who knows what
ought to have been done in it, and would unquestionably have done
it too -- at last, I say, I began to think that the source and secret of
this ghostly light might be in the adjoining room, from whence, on
further tracing it, it seemed to shine. This idea taking full possession
of my mind, I got up softly and shuffled in my slippers to the door.

'The moment my hand was on the lock, a strange voice called me
by me name, and bade me enter. I obeyed.

'It was my own room. There was no doubt about that. But it had
undergone a surprising transformation. The walls and ceiling were so
hung with living green, that it looked a perfect grove; from every part
of which, bright gleaming berries glistened. The crisp leaves of holly,
mistletoe, and ivy reflected back the light, as if so many little mirrors
had been scattered there; and such a mighty blaze went roaring up
the chimney, as that dull petrifaction of a hearth had never known in
my time, or Marley's, or for many and many a winter season gone.
Heaped up on the floor, to form a kind of throne, were turkeys,
geese, game, poultry, brawn, great joints of meat, sucking-pigs, long
wreaths of sausages, mince-pies, plum-puddings, barrels of oysters,
red-hot chestnuts, cherry-cheeked apples, juicy oranges, luscious
pears, immense twelfth-cakes, and seething bowls of punch, that
made the chamber dim with their delicious steam. In easy state upon

this couch, there sat a jolly Giant, glorious to see:, who bore a glowing torch, in shape not unlike Plenty's horn, and held it up, high up, to shed its light on me, as I came peeping round the door.

' "Come in!" exclaimed the Ghost. "Come in, and know me better, man."

'I entered timidly, and hung my head before this Spirit. I was not the dogged Ebenezer I had been; and though the Spirit's eyes were clear and kind, I did not like to meet them.

' "I am the Ghost of Christmas Present," said the Spirit. "Look upon me."

'I reverently did so. It was clothed in one simple green robe, or mantle, bordered with white fur. This garment hung so loosely on the figure, that its capacious breast was bare, as if disdaining to be warded or concealed by any artifice. Its feet, observable beneath the ample folds of the garment, were also bare; and on its head it wore no other covering than a holly wreath, set here and there with shining icicles. Its dark reddish curls were long and free; free as its genial face, its sparkling eye, its open hand, its cheery voice, its unconstrained demeanour, and its joyful air. Girded round its middle was an antique scabbard; but no sword was in it, and the ancient sheath was eaten up with rust.

' "You have never seen the like of me before!" exclaimed the Spirit.

' "Never," I made answer to it.

' "Have never walked forth with the younger members of my family; meaning (for I am very young) my elder brothers born in these later years?" pursued the Phantom.

' "I don't think I have," I said. "I am afraid I have not. Have you had many brothers, Spirit?"

' "More than eighteen hundred," said the Ghost.

' "A tremendous family to provide for," I muttered.

'The Ghost of Christmas Present rose.

' "Spirit," I said submissively, "conduct me where you will. I went forth last night on compulsion, and I learnt a lesson which is working now. To-night, if you have aught to teach me, let me profit by it."

' "Touch my robe."

'I did as I was told, and held it fast.

'Holly, mistletoe, red berries, ivy, turkeys, geese, game, poultry, brawn, meat, pigs, sausages, oysters, pies, puddings, fruit, and punch, all vanished instantly. So did the room, the fire, the ruddy glow, the hour of night, and we stood in the city streets on Christmas morning, where (for the weather was severe) the people made a rough, but brisk and not unpleasant kind of music, in scraping the snow from the pavement in front of their dwellings, and from the tops of their houses, whence it was mad delight to the boys to see it come plumping down into the road below, and splitting into artificial little snow-storms.

'The house fronts looked black enough, and the windows blacker, contrasting with the smooth white sheet of snow upon the roofs, and with the dirtier snow upon the ground; which last deposit had been ploughed up in deep furrows by the heavy wheels of carts and wagons; furrows that crossed and recrossed each other hundreds of times where the great streets branched off, and made intricate channels, hard to trace in the thick yellow mud and icy water. The sky was gloomy, and the shortest streets were choked up with a dingy mist, half thawed, half frozen, whose heavier particles descended in shower of sooty atoms, as if all the chimneys in Great Britain had, by one consent, caught fire, and were blazing away to their dear hearts' content. There was nothing very cheerful in the climate or the town, and yet was there an air of cheerfulness abroad that the clearest summer air and brightest summer sun might have endeavoured to diffuse in vain.

'For, the people who were shovelling away on the housetops were jovial and full of glee; calling out to one another from the parapets, and now and then exchanging a facetious snowball -- better-natured missile far than many a wordy jest -- laughing heartily if it went right and not less heartily if it went wrong. The poulterers' shops were still half open, and the fruiterers' were radiant in their glory. There were great, round, pot-bellied baskets of chestnuts, shaped like the waistcoats of jolly old gentlemen, lolling at the doors, and tumbling out into the street in their apoplectic opulence. There were ruddy, brown-faced, broad-girthed Spanish Friars, and winking from their shelves in wanton slyness at the girls as they went by, and glanced demurely at the hung-up mistletoe. There were pears and apples, clustered high in blooming pyramids; there were bunches of grapes, made, in the shopkeepers' benevolence to dangle from conspicuous hooks, that people's mouths might water gratis as they passed; there were piles of filberts, mossy and brown, recalling, in their fragrance, ancient walks among the woods, and pleasant shufflings ankle deep through withered leaves; there were Norfolk Biffins, squab and swarthy, setting off the yellow of the oranges and lemons, and, in the great compactness of their juicy persons, urgently entreating and beseeching to be carried home in paper bags and eaten after dinner. The very gold and silver fish, set forth among these choice fruits in a bowl, though members of a dull and stagnant-blooded race, appeared to know that there was something going on; and, to a fish, went gasping round and round their little world in slow and passionless excitement.

'The Grocers'! oh the Grocers'! Nearly closed, with perhaps two shutters down, or one; but through those gaps such glimpses. It was not alone that the scales descending on the counter made a merry sound, or that the twine and roller parted company so briskly, or that the canisters were rattled up and down like juggling tricks, or even that the blended scents of tea and coffee were so grateful to the nose, or even that the raisins were so plentiful and rare, the almonds so extremely white, the sticks of cinnamon so long and straight, the other spices so delicious, the candied fruits so caked and spotted with molten sugar as to make the coldest lookers-on feel faint and subsequently bilious. Nor was it that the figs were moist and pulpy, or that the French plums blushed in modest tartness from their highly-decorated boxes, or that everything was good to eat and in its Christmas dress; but the customers were all so hurried and so eager in the hopeful promise of the day, that they tumbled up against each other at the door, clashing their wicker baskets wildly, and left their purchases upon the counter, and came running back to fetch them, and committed hundreds of the like mistakes, in the best humour possible; while the Grocer and his people were so frank and fresh that the polished hearts with which they fastened their aprons behind might have been their own, worn outside for general inspection, and for Christmas daws to peck at if they chose.

'Then the queerest of sights, during my unimaginable phantamiscal journey with Spirits, emerged from the crowd. An Ebenezer

Scrooge, dressed all in his best, came up to me and it was a mercy he didn't shake my arm off. The queer, quite curious man, so much like myself, but also so very alien, (and as strange and wondrous as this many read) he wished myself a "Merry Christmas, Mr. Scrooge, how are you? You are going forth on compulsion, and you did, in fact, learn a lesson which has worked and continues to work! Bear them company, my good man, and do it with a thankful heart. The night you walk is waning fast, and it is precious time to us. You must and will honour Christmas in your heart, and try to keep it all the year. We will live in the Past, the Present, and the Future. The Spirits of all Three shall strive within us. We will not shut out the lessons that they teach!" And with a whoop and a hallo, his strange, foreign, giddy, drunken, and ever-so slightly older self disappeared into the throng of common people.

'And then the steeples called good people all, to church and chapel, and away they came, flocking through the streets in their best clothes, and with their gayest faces. And at the same time there emerged from scores of bye-streets, lanes, and nameless turnings, in-numerable people, carrying their dinners to the bakers' shops. The sight of these poor revellers appeared to interest the Spirit very much, for he stood with me beside him in a baker's doorway, and taking off the covers as their bearers passed, sprinkled incense on their dinners from his torch. And it was a very uncommon kind of torch, for once or twice when there were angry words between some dinner-carriers who had jostled each other, he shed a few drops of water on them from it, and their good humour was restored directly. For they said, it was a shame to quarrel upon Christmas Day. And so it was. God love it, so it was.

'In time the bells ceased, and the bakers were shut up; and yet there was a genial shadowing forth of all these dinners and the pro-gress of their cooking, in the thawed blotch of wet above each baker's oven; where the pavement smoked as if its stones were cooking too.

' "Is there a peculiar flavour in what you sprinkle from your torch?" I asked.

' "There is. My own."

' "Would it apply to any kind of dinner on this day?" I asked.

' "To any kindly given. To a poor one most."

' "Why to a poor one most?" I asked.

' "Because it needs it most."

' "Spirit," I said, after a moment's thought, "I wonder you, of all the beings in the many worlds about us, should desire to cramp these people's opportunities of innocent enjoyment."

' "I!" cried the Spirit.

' "You would deprive them of their means of dining every seventh day, often the only day on which they can be said to dine at all," I said. "Wouldn't you?"

' "I!" cried the Spirit.

' "You seek to close these places on the Seventh Day," I said. "And it comes to the same thing."

' "I seek!" exclaimed the Spirit.

' "Forgive me if I am wrong. It has been done in your name, or at least in that of your family," I said.

' "There are some upon this earth of yours," returned the Spirit, "who lay claim to know us, and who do their deeds of passion, pride, ill-will, hatred, envy, bigotry, and selfishness in our name, who are as strange to us and all our kith and kin, as if they had never lived. Remember that, and charge their doings on themselves, not us."

'I promised that I would; and we went on, invisible, as we had been before, into the suburbs of the town. It was a remarkable quality of the Ghost (which I had observed at the baker's), that notwithstanding his gigantic size, he could accommodate himself to any place with ease; and that he stood beneath a low roof quite as gracefully and like a supernatural creature, as it was possible he could have done in any lofty hall.

'And perhaps it was the pleasure the good Spirit had in showing off this power of his, or else it was his own kind, generous, hearty nature, and his sympathy with all poor men, that led him straight to my clerk's; for there he went, and took me with him, holding to his robe; and on the threshold of the door the Spirit smiled, and stopped to bless Bob Cratchit's dwelling with the sprinkling of his torch.

' "Think of that. Bob had but fifteen bob a-week himself; he pocketed on Saturdays but fifteen copies of his Christian name; and yet I bless his four-roomed house. Ha!"

'Then up rose Mrs. Cratchit, Bob's wife, dressed out but poorly in a twice-turned gown, but brave in ribbons, which are cheap and make a goodly show for sixpence; and she laid the cloth, assisted by Belinda Cratchit, second of her daughters, also brave in ribbons; while Master Peter Cratchit plunged a fork into the saucepan of potatoes, and getting the corners of his monstrous shirt collar (Bob's private property, conferred upon his son and heir in honour of the day) into his mouth, rejoiced to find himself so gallantly attired, and yearned to show his linen in the fashionable Parks. And now two smaller Cratchits, boy and girl, came tearing in, screaming that outside the baker's they had smelt the goose, and known it for their own; and basking in luxurious thoughts of sage and onion, these young Cratchits danced about the table, and exalted Master Peter Cratchit to the skies, while he (not proud, although his collars nearly choked him) blew the fire, until the slow potatoes bubbling up, knocked loudly at the saucepan-lid to be let out and peeled.

' "What has ever got your precious father then?" said Mrs. Cratchit. "And your brother, Tiny Tim; And Martha warn't as late last Christmas Day by half-an-hour."

' "Here's Martha, mother," said a girl, appearing as she spoke.

' "Here's Martha, mother!" cried the two young Cratchits. "Hurrah! There's such a goose, Martha!"

' "Why, bless your heart alive, my dear, how late you are!" said Mrs. Cratchit, kissing her a dozen times, and taking off her shawl and bonnet for her with officious zeal.

' "We'd a deal of work to finish up last night," replied the girl, "and had to clear away this morning, mother."

' "Well. Never mind so long as you are come," said Mrs. Cratchit. "Sit ye down before the fire, my dear, and have a warm, Lord bless ye."

' "No, no. There's father coming," cried the two young Cratchits, who were everywhere at once. "Hide, Martha, hide!"

'So Martha hid herself, and in came little Bob, the father, with at least three feet of comforter exclusive of the fringe, hanging down before him; and his threadbare clothes darned up and brushed, to look seasonable; and Tiny Tim upon his shoulder. Alas for Tiny Tim, he bore a little crutch, and had his limbs supported by an iron frame.

' "Why, where's our Martha?" cried Bob Cratchit, looking round.

' "Not coming," said Mrs. Cratchit.

' "Not coming!" said Bob, with a sudden declension in his high spirits; for he had been Tim's blood horse all the way from church, and had come home rampant. "Not coming upon Christmas Day?"

'Martha didn't like to see him disappointed, if it were only in joke; so she came out prematurely from behind the closet door, and ran into his arms, while the two young Cratchits hustled Tiny Tim, and bore him off into the wash-house, that he might hear the pudding singing in the copper.

' "And how did little Tim behave?" asked Mrs. Cratchit, when she had rallied Bob on his credulity, and Bob had hugged his daughter to his heart's content.

' "As good as gold," said Bob, "and better. Somehow he gets thoughtful sitting by himself so much, and thinks the strangest things you ever heard. He told me, coming home, that he hoped the people saw him in the church, because he was a cripple, and it might be pleasant to them to remember upon Christmas Day, who made lame beggars walk, and blind men see."

'Bob's voice was tremulous when he told them this, and trembled more when he said that Tiny Tim was growing strong and hearty.

'His active little crutch was heard upon the floor, and back came Tiny Tim before another word was spoken, escorted by his brother and sister to his stool before the fire; and while Bob, turning up his cuffs -- as if, poor fellow, they were capable of being made more shabby -- compounded some hot mixture in a jug with gin and lemons, and stirred it round and round and put it on the hob to simmer; Master Peter, and the two ubiquitous young Cratchits went to fetch the goose, with which they soon returned in high procession.

'Such a bustle ensued that you might have thought a goose the rarest of all birds; a feathered phenomenon, to which a black swan was a matter of course -- and in truth it was something very like it in that house. Mrs. Cratchit made the gravy (ready beforehand in a little saucepan) hissing hot; Master Peter mashed the potatoes with incredible vigour; Miss Belinda sweetened up the apple-sauce; Martha dusted the hot plates; Bob took Tiny Tim beside him in a tiny corner at the table; the two young Cratchits set chairs for everybody, not forgetting themselves, and mounting guard upon their posts, crammed spoons into their mouths, lest they should shriek for goose before their turn came to be helped. At last the dishes were set on, and grace was about to be said:

' "Bless us, oh Lord, and these thy gifts which we are about to receive from thy bounty through Christ our Lord. Amen" prayed their father. Bob knew in his heart that the food they were about to eat; and they prayed to You, O God, that it may be good for their body and soul; and if there be any poor creature hungry or thirsty walking along the road, send them into the Cratchits that they could share the food with them, just as You share your gifts with the Cratchit family all.

This was be succeeded by a breathless pause, as Mrs. Cratchit, looking slowly all along the carving-knife, prepared to plunge it in the breast; but when she did, and when the long expected gush of stuffing issued forth, one murmur of delight arose all round the board, and even Tiny Tim, excited by the two young Cratchits, beat on the table with the handle of his knife, and feebly cried Hurrah!

'O! There never was such a goose. Bob said he didn't believe there ever was such a goose cooked. Its tenderness and flavour, size and cheapness, were the themes of universal admiration. Eked out by apple-sauce and mashed potatoes, it was a sufficient dinner for the whole family; indeed, as Mrs. Cratchit said with great delight (surveying one small atom of a bone upon the dish), they hadn't ate it all at last. Yet every one had had enough, and the youngest Cratchits in particular, were steeped in sage and onion to the eyebrows.

' "We give Thee thanks for all Thy benefits, O Almighty God, who livest and reignest world without end. Amen. May the souls of the faithful departed, through the mercy of God, rest in peace. Amen," said Bob, concluding the grace.

'But now, the plates being changed by Miss Belinda, Mrs. Cratchit left the room alone -- too nervous to bear witnesses -- "I should go take up the pudding."

' "Suppose it should not be done enough? Suppose it should break in turning out?" Martha teased the two younger Cratchits.

' "Suppose somebody should have got over the wall of the back-yard, and stolen it, while we were merry with the goose" -- a supposition at which the two young Cratchits became livid? All sorts of horrors were supposed.

'And the Spirit of Christmas Cheer swept into the Cratchit home and they all burst out in song,

We wish you a Merry Christmas!
We wish you a Merry Christmas!
We wish you a Merry Christmas!
And a happy New Year!
  Glad tidings we bring
  To you and your kin,
  Glad tidings for Christmas
  And a happy New Year!

Please bring us some figgy pudding.
Please bring us some figgy pudding.
Please bring us some figgy pudding.
Please bring it right here!
  Glad tidings we bring
  To you and your kin,
  Glad tidings for Christmas
  And a happy New Year!

We won't go until we get some
We won't go until we get some.
We won't go until we get some.
Please bring it right here!
  Glad tidings we bring
  To you and your kin,
  Glad tidings for Christmas
  And a happy New Year!

We wish you a merry Christmas!
We wish you a merry Christmas!
We wish you a merry Christmas!
  Glad tidings we bring
  To you and your kin,
  Glad tidings for Christmas
  And God bless us - every one! sang little Tiny Tim.

'Hallo! A great deal of steam! The pudding was out of the copper. A smell like a washing-day. That was the cloth. A smell like an eating-house and a pastrycook's next door to each other, with a laundress's next door to that. That was the pudding. In half a minute Mrs. Cratchit entered -- flushed, but smiling proudly -- with the pudding, like a speckled cannon-ball, so hard and firm, blazing in half of half-a-quartern of ignited brandy, and bedight with Christmas holly stuck into the top.

' "Oh, a wonderful pudding!" Bob Cratchit said, and calmly too, "This is the greatest success achieved by Mrs. Cratchit since our wedding day."

'Mrs. Cratchit said that now the weight was off her mind, "I should confess, I had had my doubts about the quantity of flour."

'Everybody had something to say about it. And the Spirit mused, "It is a rather small pudding for a large family."

' "I heard no complaints," I said.

' "It would have been flat heresy to do so. Any Cratchit would have blushed to hint at such a thing."

' "Dig in!" said Bob, "Dig in!"

'At last the dinner was all done, the cloth was cleared, the hearth swept, and the fire made up. The compound in the jug being tasted, and considered perfect, apples and oranges were put upon the table, and a shovel-full of chestnuts on the fire. Then all the Cratchit family drew round the hearth, in what Bob Cratchit called a circle, meaning half a one; and at Bob Cratchit's elbow stood the family display of glass. Two tumblers, and a custard-cup without a handle.

'These held the hot stuff from the jug, however, as well as golden goblets would have done; and Bob served it out with beaming looks, while the chestnuts on the fire sputtered and cracked noisily. Then Bob proposed:

' "A Merry Christmas to us all, my dears. God bless us."

'Which all the family re-echoed.

' "God bless us every one!" said Tiny Tim, the last of all.

'He sat very close to his father's side upon his little stool. Bob held his withered little hand in his, as if he loved the child, and wished to keep him by his side, and dreaded that he might be taken from him.

' "Spirit," I said, with an interest I had never felt before, "tell me if Tiny Tim will live."

' "I see a vacant seat," replied the Ghost, "in the poor chimney-corner, and a crutch without an owner, carefully preserved. If these shadows remain unaltered by the Future, the child will die."

' "No, no," I said. "Oh, no, kind Spirit. Say he will be spared."

' "If these shadows remain unaltered by the Future, none other of my race," returned the Ghost, "will find him here. What then? If he be like to die, he had better do it, and decrease the surplus population."

'I hung my head to hear my own words quoted by the Spirit, and was overcome with penitence and grief.

' "Man," said the Ghost, "if man you be in heart, not adamant, forbear that wicked cant until you have discovered What the surplus is, and Where it is. Will you decide what men shall live, what men shall die? It may be, that in the sight of Heaven, you are more worthless and less fit to live than millions like this poor man's child. Oh God! To hear the Insect on the leaf pronouncing on the too much life among his hungry brothers in the dust."

'I bent before the Ghost's rebuke, and trembling cast my eyes upon the ground.

'After it had passed away, Bob Cratchit told them how he had a situation in his eye for Master Peter, which would bring in, if obtained, full five-and-sixpence weekly. The two young Cratchits laughed tremendously at the idea of Peter's being a man of business; and Peter himself looked thoughtfully at the fire from between his collars, as if he were deliberating what particular investments he should favour when he came into the receipt of that bewildering income. Martha, who was a poor apprentice at a milliner's, then told them what kind of work she had to do, and how many hours she worked at a stretch, and how she meant to lie abed to-morrow morning for a good long rest; to-morrow being a holiday she passed at home. Also how she had seen a countess and a lord some days before, and how the lord was much about as tall as Peter; at which Peter pulled up his collars so high that you couldn't have seen his head if you had been there. All this time the chestnuts and the jug went round and round; and by-and-bye they had a song, about a lost child travelling in the snow, from Tiny Tim, who had a plaintive little voice, and sang it very well indeed.

'There was nothing of high mark in this. They were not a handsome family; they were not well dressed; their shoes were far from being water-proof; their clothes were scanty; and Peter might have known, and very likely did, the inside of a pawnbroker's. But, they were happy, grateful, pleased with one another, and contented with the time; and when they faded, and looked happier yet in the bright sprinklings of the Spirit's torch at parting, I had my eye upon them, and especially on Tiny Tim, until the last.

'And the Spirit of Christmas Cheer lifted Tiny Tim weak little voice to song,

Silent night, holy night!
All is calm, all is bright.
'Round yon Virgin Mother and Child
Holy Infant, so tender and mild.
Sleep in heavenly peace!
Sleep in heavenly peace!

Silent night, holy night,
Shepherds quake at the sight;
Glories stream from heaven afar,
Heavenly hosts sing Alleluia!
Christ the Savior is born,
Christ the Savior is born!

Silent night, holy night,
Son of God, love's pure light;
Radiant beams from thy holy face
With the dawn of redeeming grace,
Jesus, Lord, at thy birth,
Jesus, Lord, at thy birth.

'By this time it was getting dark, and snowing pretty heavily; and as the Spirit and I went along the streets, the brightness of the roaring fires in kitchens, parlours, and all sorts of rooms, was wonderful. Here, the flickering of the blaze showed preparations for a cosy dinner, with hot plates baking through and through before the fire, and deep red curtains, ready to be drawn to shut out cold and darkness. There all the children of the house were running out into the snow to meet their married sisters, brothers, cousins, uncles, aunts, and be the first to greet them. Here, again, were shadows on the window-blind of guests assembling; and there a group of handsome girls, all hooded and fur-booted, and all chattering at once, tripped lightly off to some near neighbour's house; where, woe upon the single man who saw them enter -- artful witches, well they knew it -- in a glow.

'But, if you had judged from the numbers of people on their way to friendly gatherings, you might have thought that no one was at home to give them welcome when they got there, instead of every house expecting company, and piling up its fires half-chimney high. Blessings on it, how the Ghost exulted. How it bared its breadth of breast, and opened its capacious palm, and floated on, outpouring, with a generous hand, its bright and harmless mirth on everything within its reach. The very lamplighter, who ran on before dotting the dusky street with specks of light, and who was dressed to spend the evening somewhere, laughed out loudly as the Spirit passed, though little kenned the lamplighter that he had any company but Christmas.

'And now, without a word of warning from the Ghost, we stood upon a bleak and desert moor, where monstrous masses of rude stone were cast about, as though it were the burial-place of giants; and water spread itself wheresoever it listed -- or would have done so, but for the frost that held it prisoner; and nothing grew but moss and furze, and coarse rank grass. Down in the west the setting sun had left a streak of fiery red, which glared upon the desolation for an instant, like a sullen eye, and frowning lower, lower, lower yet, was lost in the thick gloom of darkest night.

' "What place is this?" I asked.

' "A place where Miners live, who labour in the bowels of the earth," returned the Spirit. "But they know me. See."

'A light shone from the window of a hut, and swiftly they advanced towards it. Passing through the wall of mud and stone, we found a cheerful company assembled round a glowing fire. An old, old man and woman, with their children and their children's children, and another generation beyond that, all decked out gaily in their holiday attire. The old man, in a voice that seldom rose above the howling of the wind upon the barren waste, was singing them a Christmas song -- So surely as they raised their voices, the old man got quite blithe and loud.

Stille Nacht, heilige Nacht,
Alles schläft; einsam wacht
Nur das traute hochheilige Paar.
Holder Knabe im lockigen Haar,
Schlaf in himmlischer Ruh!
Schlaf in himmlischer Ruh!

Stille Nacht, heilige Nacht,
Hirten erst kundgemacht
Durch der Engel Halleluja,
Tönt es laut von fern und nah:
Christ, der Retter ist da!
Christ, der Retter ist da!

Stille Nacht, heilige Nacht,
Gottes Sohn, o wie lacht
Lieb' aus deinem göttlichen Mund,
Da uns schlägt die rettende Stund'.
Christ, in deiner Geburt!
Christ, in deiner Geburt!

'And so surely as they stopped, his vigour sank again.

'The Spirit did not tarry here, but bade me hold his robe, and passing on above the moor, sped -- whither. Not to sea? To sea. To my horror, looking back, I saw the last of the land, a frightful range of rocks, behind them; and his ears were deafened by the thundering of water, as it rolled and roared, and raged among the dreadful caverns it had worn, and fiercely tried to undermine the earth.

'Built upon a dismal reef of sunken rocks, some league or so from shore, on which the waters chafed and dashed, the wild year through, there stood a solitary lighthouse. Great heaps of sea-weed clung to its base, and storm-birds -- born of the wind one might suppose, as sea-weed of the water -- rose and fell about it, like the waves they skimmed.

'But even here, two men who watched the light had made a fire, that through the loophole in the thick stone wall shed out a ray of brightness on the awful sea. Joining their horny hands over the rough table at which they sat, they wished each other Merry Christmas in their can of grog; and one of them: the elder, too, with his face all damaged and scarred with hard weather, as the figure-head of an old ship might be: struck up a sturdy song that was like a Gale in itself.

Glade jul, dejlige jul!
Engle dale ned i skjul.
Hid de flyve med paradis-grønt,
Hvor de se, hvad for Gud er skønt.
Lønligt iblandt os de gå.

Julefryd, evig fryd,
Hellig sang med himmelsk lyd!
Det er englene, hyrdene så,
Dengang Herren i krybben lå.
Evig er englenes sang.

Fred på jord, fryd på jord,
Jesusbarnet iblandt os bor.
Engle sjunge om barnet så smukt,
Han har himmerigs dør oplukt.
Salig er englenes sang.

Salig fred, himmelsk fred,
Toner julenat herned.
Engle bringe til store og små
Bud om ham, som i krybben lå;
Fryd dig hver sjæl, han har frelst!

'Again the Ghost sped on, above the black and heaving sea -- on, on -- until, being far away, as he told me, from any shore, we lighted on a ship. We stood beside the helmsman at the wheel, the look-out in the bow, the officers who had the watch; dark, ghostly figures in their several stations; but every man among them hummed a Christmas tune,

Noche de paz, noche de amor,
Todo duerme en derredor.
Entre sus astros que esparcen su luz
Bella anunciando al niñito Jesús
Brilla la estrella de paz
Brilla la estrella de paz

Noche de paz, noche de amor,
Todo duerme en derredor
Sólo velan en la oscuridad
Los pastores que en el campo están;
Y la estrella de Belén
Y la estrella de Belén

Noche de paz, noche de amor,
Todo duerme en derredor;
sobre el santo niño Jesús
Una estrella esparce su luz,
Brilla sobre el Rey
Brilla sobre el Rey.

Noche de paz, noche de amor,
Todo duerme en derredor
Fieles velando allí en Belén
Los pastores, la madre también.
Y la estrella de paz
Y la estrella de paz

'Or had a Christmas thought, or spoke below his breath to his companion of some bygone Christmas Day, with homeward hopes belonging to it. And every man on board, waking or sleeping, good or bad, had had a kinder word for another on that day than on any day in the year; and had shared to some extent in its festivities; and had remembered those he cared for at a distance, and had known that they delighted to remember him.

'It was a great surprise to me, while listening to the moaning of the wind, and thinking what a solemn thing it was to move on through the lonely darkness over an unknown abyss, whose depths were secrets as profound as Death: it was a great surprise to me, while thus engaged, to hear a hearty laugh. It was a much greater surprise to me to recognise it as my own nephew's and to find myself in a bright, dry, gleaming room, with the Spirit standing smiling by my side, and looking at that same nephew with approving affability.

' "Ha, ha!" laughed my nephew. "Ha, ha, ha!"

'If you should happen, by any unlikely chance, to know a man more blest in a laugh than my nephew, all I can say is, I should like to know him too. Introduce him to me, and I'll cultivate his acquaintance.

'It is a fair, even-handed, noble adjustment of things, that while there is infection in disease and sorrow, there is nothing in the world so irresistibly contagious as laughter and good-humour. When my nephew laughed in this way: holding his sides, rolling his head, and twisting his face into the most extravagant contortions: my niece, by marriage, laughed as heartily as he. And their assembled friends being not a bit behindhand, roared out lustily.

' "Ha, ha! Ha, ha, ha, ha!"

' "He said that Christmas was a humbug, as I live!" cried my nephew. "He believed it too."

' "More shame for him, Fred." said my niece, indignantly. Bless those women; they never do anything by halves. They are always in earnest.

'She was very pretty: exceedingly pretty. With a dimpled, surprised-looking, capital face; a ripe little mouth, that seemed made to be kissed -- as no doubt it was; all kinds of good little dots about her chin, that melted into one another when she laughed; and the sunniest pair of eyes you ever saw in any little creature's head. Altogether she was what you would have called provoking, you know; but satisfactory, too. Oh perfectly satisfactory!

' "He's a comical old fellow," said my nephew, "that's the truth:

and not so pleasant as he might be. However, his offenses carry their own punishment, and I have nothing to say against him."

' "I'm sure he is very rich, Fred," hinted my niece. "At least you always tell me so."

' "What of that, my dear?" said my nephew. "His wealth is of no use to him. He don't do any good with it. He don't make himself comfortable with it. He hasn't the satisfaction of thinking -- ha, ha, ha! -- that he is ever going to benefit us with it."

' "I have no patience with him," observed my niece. My niece's sisters, and all the other ladies, expressed the same opinion.

' "Oh, I have," said my nephew. "I am sorry for him; I couldn't be angry with him if I tried. Who suffers by his ill whims? Himself, always. Here, he takes it into his head to dislike us, and he won't come and dine with us. What's the consequence? He don't lose much of a dinner."

' "Indeed, I think he loses a very good dinner," interrupted my niece. Everybody else said the same, and they must be allowed to have been competent judges, because they had just had dinner; and, with the dessert upon the table, were clustered round the fire, by lamplight.

' "Well. I'm very glad to hear it," said my nephew, "because I haven't great faith in these young housekeepers. What do you say, Topper?"

'Topper had clearly got his eye upon one of my niece's sisters, for he answered that a bachelor was a wretched outcast, who had no right to express an opinion on the subject. Whereat my niece's sister -- the plump one with the lace tucker: not the one with the roses -- blushed.

' "Do go on, Fred," said my niece, clapping her hands. "He never finishes what he begins to say. He is such a ridiculous fellow."

'My nephew revelled in another laugh, and as it was impossible to keep the infection off; though the plump sister tried hard to do it with aromatic vinegar; his example was unanimously followed.

' "I was only going to say," said my nephew, "that the consequence of his taking a dislike to us, and not making merry with us, is, as I think, that he loses some pleasant moments, which could do him no harm. I am sure he loses pleasanter companions than he can find in his own thoughts, either in his mouldy old office, or his dusty chambers. I mean to give him the same chance every year, whether he likes it or not, for I pity him. He may rail at Christmas till he dies, but he can't help thinking better of it -- I defy him -- if he finds me going there, in good temper, year after year, and saying Uncle Ebenezer, how are you. If it only puts him in the vein to leave his poor clerk fifty pounds, that's something; and I think I shook him yesterday."

'It was their turn to laugh now at the notion of his shaking me. But being thoroughly good-natured, and not much caring what they laughed at, so that they laughed at any rate, he encouraged them in their merriment, and passed the bottle joyously.

'After tea they had some music. For they were a musical family, and knew what they were about, when they sung a Glee or Catch, I can assure you: especially Topper, who could growl away in the bass like a good one, and never swell the large veins in his forehead, or get red in the face over it. My niece played well upon the harp; and played among other tunes a simple little air (a mere nothing: you might learn to whistle it in two minutes), which had been familiar to the child who fetched me from the boarding-school, as I had been reminded by Father's yearly recitations of his Ghostly little tale. When this strain of music sounded, all the things that Ghost had shown me, came upon me mind; I softened more and more; and thought that if I could have listened to it often, years ago, I might have cultivated the kindnesses of life for my own happiness with my own hands, without resorting to the sexton's spade that buried Jacob Marley.

'But they didn't devote the whole evening to music. After a while they played at forfeits; for it is good to be children sometimes, and never better than at Christmas, when its mighty Founder was a child himself. Stop. There was first a game at blind-man's buff. Of course there was. And I no more believe Topper was really blind than I believe he had eyes in his boots. My opinion is, that it was a done thing between him and my nephew; and that the Ghost of Christmas Present knew it. The way he went after that plump sister in the lace tucker, was an outrage on the credulity of human nature. Knocking down the fire-irons, tumbling over the chairs, bumping against the piano, smothering himself among the curtains, wherever she went, there went he. He always knew where the plump sister was. He wouldn't catch anybody else. If you had fallen up against him (as some of them did), on purpose, he would have made a feint of endeavouring to seize you, which would have been an affront to your understanding, and would instantly have sidled off in the direction of the plump sister. She often cried out that it wasn't fair; and it really was not. But when at last, he caught her; when, in spite of all her silken rustlings, and her rapid flutterings past him, he got her into a corner whence there was no escape; then his conduct was the most execrable. For his pretending not to know her; his pretending that it was necessary to touch her head-dress, and further to assure himself of her identity by pressing a certain ring upon her finger, and a certain chain about her neck; was vile, monstrous. No doubt she told him her opinion of it, when, another blind-man being in office, they were so very confidential together, behind the curtains.

'My niece was not one of the blind-man's buff party, but was made comfortable with a large chair and a footstool, in a snug corner, where the Ghost and I were close behind her. But she joined in the forfeits, and loved her love to admiration with all the letters of the alphabet. Likewise at the game of How, When, and Where, she was very great, and to the secret joy of my nephew, beat her sisters hollow: though they were sharp girls too, as could have told you. There might have been twenty people there, young and old, but they all played, and so did I, for, wholly forgetting the interest I had in what was going on, that my voice made no sound in their ears, I sometimes came out with my guess quite loud, and very often guessed quite right, too; for the sharpest needle, best Whitechapel, warranted not to cut in the eye, was not sharper than me; blunt as I took it in my head to be.

'The Ghost was greatly pleased to find me in this mood, and looked upon me with such favour, that I begged like a boy to be allowed to stay until the guests departed. But this the Spirit said could not be done.

' "I'm thinking of something and the rest of you must find out what, I'll only answer your question with a yes or no as the case may be," said Fred.

' "Here's a new game," I said. "One half hour, Spirit, only one."

' "Is it an animal?" asked my niece.

' "Yes," confirmed Fred.

' "Is it a live animal?" asked my niece's sister.

' "Yes."

' "Is it a pleasant animal?" asked my niece.

' "No."

' "Is it a rather disagreeable animal?" asked Topper.

' "Yes."

' "Is it a savage animal?" asked my niece's sister.

' "Yes.

' "Is it an animal that growls?" asked Topper as growled at the plump sister, whom giggled.

' "Yes."

' "Does it grunt?" asked my niece.

' "Yes, and it ta -- oops!"

' "Oh, oh, does it talk?" asked my niece's sister.

' "Yes."

' "Where does it live?" asked Topper.

' "In London." He caught himself answering a non-question. "Topper! No tricks."

' "Then you should be a pinch more clever, my friend", Topper teased.

' "Look upon your nephew, Ebenezer," said the Spirit. "At every fresh question that is put to him, this nephew bursts into a fresh roar of laughter; and is so expressibly tickled, that he is obliged to get up off the sofa and stamp."

' "He has his mother's gay spirit," I said smiling.

' "So, it lives in London. Then it must be in a menagerie," asked Topper.

' "Is that a question? The answer is 'No.'"

' "Is it killed in the market?" asked my niece.

' "No."

' "Is it led about by anybody?" asked my niece's sister.

' "No.

' "Is it a horse, an ass, a cow, or a bull, or a tiger, or a dog, or a pig, or a cat, or a bear?" asked Topper, who was quickly out of breath.

' "No, no, no, no, no, no, no, no, and no."

' "I have found it out! I know what it is, Fred! I know what it is!"

' "What is it?" cried Fred.

' "It's your Uncle Scro-o-o-o-oge!"

' "It most certainly is."

' "When I inquired if it was a bear, your answer should have been 'yes!'", Topper corrected.

'And they all burst out in the most uncontrollable bails of laughters, including Scro-o-o-o-oge myself.

' "Mr. Scrooge!" said Bob; "I'll give you Mr. Scrooge, the Founder of the Feast!"

'The toast came from afar on the wings of the wind. I could almost see across both time and space. The Cratchit hovel blending with Fred's apartment like ingredients in a pudding.

' "The Founder of the Feast indeed!" cried Mrs. Cratchit, reddening. "I wish I had him here. I'd give him a piece of my mind to feast upon, and I hope he'd have a good appetite for it."

' "My dear," said Bob, "the children. Christmas Day."

' "He has given us plenty of merriment, I am sure," said Fred, "and it would be ungrateful not to drink his health. "

' "It should be Christmas Day, I am sure," said she, "on which one drinks the health of such an odious, stingy, hard, unfeeling man as Mr. Scrooge. You know he is, Robert. Nobody knows it better than you do, poor fellow."

' "My dear," was Bob's mild answer, "Christmas Day."

' "Here is a glass of mulled wine ready to our hand at the moment; and I say, 'Uncle Scrooge!'"

' "I'll drink his health for your sake and the Day's," said Mrs. Cratchit, "not for his. Long life to him. A merry Christmas and a happy new year! -- he'll be very merry and very happy, I have no doubt!"

' "A Merry Christmas and a Happy New Year to the old man, whatever he is," said my nephew. "He wouldn't take it from me, but may he have it, nevertheless. Uncle Scrooge!"

'An "Uncle Scrooge" and a "Mr. Scrooge", they all toasted.

'The children drank the toast after her. It was the first of their proceedings which had no heartiness. Tiny Tim drank it last of all, but he didn't care twopence for it. I was the Ogre of the family. The mention of my name cast a dark shadow on the party, which was not dispelled for full five minutes.

'But I had imperceptibly become so gay and light of heart, that I would have pledged the unconscious company in return, and thanked them in an inaudible speech, if the Ghost had given me time. But the whole scene passed off in the breath of the last word spoken by my nephew; and the Spirit and I were again upon our travels.

'Much we saw, and far we went, and many homes we visited, but always with a happy end. The Spirit stood beside sick beds, and they were cheerful; on foreign lands, and they were close at home; by struggling men, and they were patient in their greater hope; by poverty, and it was rich. In almshouse, hospital, and jail, in misery's every refuge, where vain man in his little brief authority had not made fast the door and barred the Spirit out, he left his blessing, and taught me his precepts.

'It was a long night, if it were only a night; but I had my doubts of this, because the Christmas Holidays appeared to be condensed into the space of time we passed together. It was strange, too, that while I remained unaltered in my outward form, the Ghost grew older, clearly older. I had observed this change, but never spoke of it, until we left a children's Twelfth Night party, when, looking at the Spirit as we stood together in an open place, I noticed that its hair was grey.

' "Are spirits' lives so short?" I asked.

' "My life upon this globe, is very brief," replied the Ghost. "It ends to-night."

' "To-night!" I cried.

' "To-night at midnight. Hark! The time is drawing near."

'The chimes were ringing the three quarters past eleven at that moment.

' "Forgive me if I am not justified in what I ask," I said, looking intently at the Spirit's robe, "but I see something strange, and not belonging to yourself, protruding from your skirts. Is it a foot or a claw?"

' "It might be a claw, for the flesh there is upon it," was the Spirit's sorrowful reply. "Look here."

'From the foldings of its robe, it brought two children; wretched, abject, frightful, hideous, miserable. They knelt down at its feet, and clung upon the outside of its garment.

' "Oh, Man, look here! Look, look, down here!" exclaimed the Ghost.

'They were a boy and a girl. Yellow, meagre, ragged, scowling, wolfish; but prostrate, too, in their humility. Where graceful youth should have filled their features out, and touched them with its freshest tints, a stale and shrivelled hand, like that of age, had pinched, and twisted them, and pulled them into shreds. Where angels might have sat enthroned, devils lurked, and glared out menacing. No change, no degradation, no perversion of humanity, in any grade, through all the mysteries of wonderful creation, has monsters half so horrible and dread.

'I started back, appalled. Having them shown to me in this way, I tried to say they were fine children, but the words choked themselves, rather than be parties to a lie of such enormous magnitude.

' "Spirit, are they yours?" I could say no more.

' "They are Man's," said the Spirit, looking down upon them. "And they cling to me, appealing from their fathers. This boy is Ignorance. This girl is Want. Beware them both, and all of their degree, but most of all beware this boy, for on his brow I see that written which is Doom, unless the writing be erased. Deny it!" cried the Spirit, stretching out its hand towards the city. "Slander those who tell it ye. Admit it for your factious purposes, and make it worse. And abide the end."

' "Have they no refuge or resource?" I cried.

' "Are there no prisons?" said the Spirit, turning on him for the last time with his own words. "Are there no workhouses?"

'The bell struck twelve.

'I looked about myself for the Ghost, and saw it not. As the last stroke ceased to vibrate, I remembered the prediction of old Jacob Marley, and lifting up my eyes, beheld a solemn Phantom, draped and hooded, coming, like a mist along the ground, towards me.'

Stave IV
"The Last of the Spirits = Reprise"

'The Phantom slowly, gravely, silently approached. When it came, I bent down upon my knee; for in the very air through which this Spirit moved it seemed to scatter gloom and mystery.

'It was shrouded in a deep black garment, which concealed its head, its face, its form, and left nothing of it visible save one outstretched hand. But for this it would have been difficult to detach its figure from the night, and separate it from the darkness by which it was surrounded.

'I felt that it was tall and stately when it came beside me, and that its mysterious presence filled me with a solemn dread. I knew no more, for the Spirit neither spoke nor moved.

' "I am in the presence of the Ghost of Christmas Yet To Come?" I asked.

'The Spirit answered not, but pointed downward with its hand.

' "You are about to show me shadows of the things that have not happened, but will happen in the time before us," I pursued. "Is that so, Spirit?"

'The upper portion of the garment was contracted for an instant in its folds, as if the Spirit had inclined its head. That was the only answer I received.

'Although well used to ghostly company by this time, I feared the silent shape so much that my legs trembled beneath me, and I found that I could hardly stand when I prepared to follow it. The Spirit paused a moment, as observing my condition, and giving me time to recover.

'But I was all the worse for this. It thrilled me with a vague uncertain horror, to know that behind the dusky shroud there were ghostly eyes intently fixed upon me, while I, though I stretched my own to the utmost, could see nothing but a spectral hand and one great heap of black.

' "Ghost of the Future!" I exclaimed, "I fear you more than any spectre I have seen. But as I know your purpose is to do me good, and as I hope to live to be another man from what I was, I am prepared to bear you company, and do it with a thankful heart. Will you not speak to me?"

'It gave me no reply. The hand was pointed straight before us.

' "Lead on," I said. "Lead on. The night is waning fast, and it is precious time to me, I know. Lead on, Spirit."

'The Phantom moved away as it had come towards me. I followed in the shadow of its dress, which bore me up, I thought, and carried me along.

'We scarcely seemed to enter the city; for the city rather seemed to spring up about us, and encompass us of its own act. But there we were, in the heart of it; on 'Change, amongst the merchants; who hurried up and down, and chinked the money in their pockets, and conversed in groups, and looked at their watches, and trifled thoughtfully with their great gold seals; and so forth, as I had seen them often.

'The Spirit stopped beside one little knot of business men. Observing that the hand was pointed to them, I advanced to listen to their talk.

' "No," said a great fat man with a monstrous chin," I don't know much about it, either way. I only know he's dead."

' "When did he die?" inquired another.

' "Last night, I believe."

' "Why, what was the matter with him?" asked a third, taking a vast quantity of snuff out of a very large snuff-box. "I thought he'd never die."

' "God knows," said the first, with a yawn.

' "What has he done with his money?" asked a red-faced gentleman with a pendulous excrescence on the end of his nose, that shook like the gills of a turkey-cock.

' "I haven't heard," said the man with the large chin, yawning again. "Left it to his company, perhaps. He hasn't left it to me. That's all I know."

'This pleasantry was received with a general laugh.

' "It's likely to be a very cheap funeral," said the same speaker; "for upon my life I don't know of anybody to go to it. Suppose we make up a party and volunteer?"

' "I don't mind going if a lunch is provided," observed the gentleman with the excrescence on his nose. "But I must be fed, if I make one."

'Another laugh.

' "Well, I am the most disinterested among you, after all," said the first speaker, "for I never wear black gloves, and I never eat lunch. But I'll offer to go, if anybody else will. When I come to think of it, I'm not at all sure that I wasn't his most particular friend; for we used to stop and speak whenever we met. Bye, bye."

'Speakers and listeners strolled away, and mixed with other groups. I knew the men, and looked towards the Spirit for an explanation.

'The Phantom glided on into a street. Its finger pointed to two persons meeting. I listened again, thinking that the explanation might lie here.

'I knew these men, also, perfectly. They were men of business: very wealthy, and of great importance. I had made a point always of standing well in their esteem: in a business point of view, that is; strictly in a business point of view.

' "How are you?" said one.

' "How are you?" returned the other.

' "Well!" said the first. "Old Scratch has got his own at last, hey."

' "So I am told," returned the second. "Cold, isn't it."

' "Seasonable for Christmas time. You're not a skater, I suppose?"

' "No. No. Something else to think of. Good morning."

'Not another word. That was their meeting, their conversation, and their parting.

'I was at first inclined to be surprised that the Spirit should attach importance to conversations apparently so trivial; but feeling assured that they must have some hidden purpose, I set myself to consider what it was likely to be. They could scarcely be supposed to have any bearing on the death of Jacob, his old partner, for that was Past, and this Ghost's province was the Future. Nor could I think of any one immediately connected with myself, to whom I could apply them. But nothing doubting that to whomsoever they applied they had some latent moral for my own improvement, I resolved to treasure up every word I heard, and everything I saw; and especially to observe the shadow of myself when it appeared. For I had an expectation that the conduct of my future self would give me the clue I missed, and would render the solution of these riddles easy.

'I looked about in that very place for my own image; but another man stood in my accustomed corner, and though the clock pointed to my usual time of day for being there, I saw no likeness of myself among the multitudes that poured in through the Porch. It gave me little surprise, however; for I had been revolving in my mind a change of life, and thought and hoped I saw my new-born resolutions carried out in this.

'Quiet and dark, beside me stood the Phantom, with its outstretched hand. When I roused myself from my thoughtful quest, I fancied from the turn of the hand, and its situation in reference to myself, that the Unseen Eyes were looking at me keenly. It made me shudder, and feel very cold.

'We left the busy scene, and went into an obscure part of the town, where I had never penetrated before, although I recognised its situation, and its bad repute. The ways were foul and narrow; the shops and houses wretched; the people half-naked, drunken, slipshod, ugly. Alleys and archways, like so many cesspools, disgorged their offenses of smell, and dirt, and life, upon the straggling streets; and the whole quarter reeked with crime, with filth, and misery.

'Far in this den of infamous resort, there was a low-browed, beetling shop, below a pent-house roof, where iron, old rags, bottles, bones, and greasy offal, were bought. Upon the floor within, were piled up heaps of rusty keys, nails, chains, hinges, files, scales, weights, and refuse iron of all kinds. Secrets that few would like to scrutinise were bred and hidden in mountains of unseemly rags, masses of corrupted fat, and sepulchres of bones. Sitting in among the wares he dealt in, by a charcoal stove, made of old bricks, was a grey-haired rascal, nearly seventy years of age; who had screened himself from the cold air without, by a frowsy curtaining of miscellaneous tatters, hung upon a line; and smoked his pipe in all the luxury of calm retirement.

'The Phantom and I came into the presence of this man, just as a woman with a heavy bundle slunk into the shop. But she had scarcely entered, when another woman, similarly laden, came in too; and she was closely followed by a man in faded black, who was no less startled by the sight of them, than they had been upon the recognition of each other. After a short period of blank astonishment, in which the old man with the pipe had joined them, they all three burst into a laugh.

' "Let the charwoman alone to be the first!" cried she who had entered first. "Let the laundress alone to be the second; and let the undertaker's man alone to be the third. Look here, old Joe, here's a chance. If we haven't all three met here without meaning it!"

' "You couldn't have met in a better place," said old Joe, removing his pipe from his mouth. "Come into the parlour. You were made free of it long ago, you know; and the other two an't strangers. Stop till I shut the door of the shop. Ah. How it skreeks. There an't such a rusty bit of metal in the place as its own hinges, I believe; and I'm sure there's no such old bones here, as mine. Ha, ha! We're all suitable to our calling, we're well matched. Come into the parlour. Come into the parlour."

'The parlour was the space behind the screen of rags. The old man raked the fire together with an old stair-rod, and having trimmed his smoky lamp (for it was night), with the stem of his pipe, put it in his mouth again.

'While he did this, the woman who had already spoken threw her bundle on the floor, and sat down in a flaunting manner on a stool; crossing her elbows on her knees, and looking with a bold defiance at the other two.

' "What odds then. What odds, Mrs. Dilber." said the woman. "Every person has a right to take care of themselves. He always did."

' "That's true, indeed," said the laundress. "No man more so."

' "Why then, don't stand staring as if you was afraid, woman; who's the wiser? We're not going to pick holes in each other's coats, I suppose?"

' "No, indeed," said Mrs. Dilber and the man together. "We should hope not."

' "Very well, then!" cried the woman. "That's enough. Who's the worse for the loss of a few things like these? Not a dead man, I suppose."

' "No, indeed," said Mrs. Dilber, laughing.

' "If he wanted to keep them after he was dead, a wicked old screw," pursued the woman, "why wasn't he natural in his lifetime? If he had been, he'd have had somebody to look after him when he was struck with Death, instead of lying gasping out his last there, alone by himself."

' "It's the truest word that ever was spoke," said Mrs. Dilber. "It's a judgment on him."

' "I wish it was a little heavier judgment," replied the woman; "and it should have been, you may depend upon it, if I could have laid my hands on anything else. Open that bundle, old Joe, and let me know the value of it. Speak out plain. I'm not afraid to be the first, nor afraid for them to see it. We know pretty well that we were helping ourselves, before we met here, I believe. It's no sin. Open the bundle, Joe."

'But the gallantry of her friends would not allow of this; and the man in faded black, mounting the breach first, produced his plunder. It was not extensive. A seal or two, a pencil-case, a pair of sleeve-buttons, and a brooch of no great value, were all. They were severally examined and appraised by old Joe, who chalked the sums he was disposed to give for each upon the wall, and added them up into a total when he found there was nothing more to come.

' "That's your account," said Joe, "and I wouldn't give another sixpence, if I was to be boiled for not doing it. Who's next?"

'Mrs. Dilber was next. Sheets and towels, a little wearing apparel, two old-fashioned silver teaspoons, a pair of sugar-tongs, and a few boots. Her account was stated on the wall in the same manner.

' "I always give too much to ladies. It's a weakness of mine, and that's the way I ruin myself," said old Joe. "That's your account. If you asked me for another penny, and made it an open question, I'd repent of being so liberal and knock off half-a-crown."

' "And now undo my bundle, Joe," said the first woman.

'Joe went down on his knees for the greater convenience of opening it, and having unfastened a great many knots, dragged out a large and heavy roll of some dark stuff.

' "What do you call this?" said Joe. "Bed-curtains?"

' "Ah!" returned the woman, laughing and leaning forward on her crossed arms. "Bed-curtains."

' "You don't mean to say you took them down, rings and all, with him lying there?" said Joe.

' "Yes I do," replied the woman. "Why not?"

' "You were born to make your fortune," said Joe," and you'll certainly do it."

' "I certainly shan't hold my hand, when I can get anything in it by reaching it out, for the sake of such a man as he was, I promise you, Joe," returned the woman coolly. "Don't drop that oil upon the blankets, now."

' "His blankets?" asked Joe.

' "Whose else's do you think?" replied the woman. "He isn't likely to take cold without them, I dare say."

' "I hope he didn't die of any thing catching. Eh?" said old Joe, stopping in his work, and looking up.

' "Don't you be afraid of that," returned the woman. "I an't so fond of his company that I'd loiter about him for such things, if he did. Ah. you may look through that shirt till your eyes ache; but you won't find a hole in it, nor a threadbare place. It's the best he had, and a fine one too. They'd have wasted it, if it hadn't been for me."

' "What do you call wasting of it?" asked old Joe.

' "Putting it on him to be buried in, to be sure," replied the woman with a laugh. "Somebody was fool enough to do it, but I took it off again. If calico an't good enough for such a purpose, it isn't good enough for anything. It's quite as becoming to the body. He can't look uglier than he did in that one."

'I listened to this dialogue in horror. As they sat grouped about their spoil, in the scanty light afforded by the old man's lamp, I viewed them with a detestation and disgust, which could hardly have been greater, though they demons, marketing the corpse itself.

' "Ha, ha!" laughed the same woman, when old Joe, producing a flannel bag with money in it, told out their several gains upon the ground. "This is the end of it, you see. He frightened every one away from him when he was alive, to profit us when he was dead. Ha, ha, ha!"

' "Spirit," I said, shuddering from head to foot. "I see, I see. The case of this unhappy man might be my own. My life tends that way, now. Merciful Heaven, what is this?"

'I recoiled in terror, for the scene had changed, and now I almost touched a bed: a bare, uncurtained bed: on which, beneath a ragged sheet, there lay a something covered up, which, though it was dumb, announced itself in awful language.

'The room was very dark, too dark to be observed with any accuracy, though I glanced round it in obedience to a secret impulse, anxious to know what kind of room it was. A pale light, rising in the outer air, fell straight upon the bed; and on it, plundered and bereft, unwatched, unwept, uncared for, was the body of this man.

'I glanced towards the Phantom. Its steady hand was pointed to the head. The cover was so carelessly adjusted that the slightest raising of it, the motion of a finger upon my part, would have disclosed the face. I thought of it, felt how easy it would be to do, and longed to do it; but had no more power to withdraw the veil than to dismiss the spectre at my side.

'Oh cold, cold, rigid, dreadful Death, set up thine altar here, and dress it with such terrors as thou hast at thy command: for this is thy dominion. But of the loved, revered, and honoured head, thou canst not turn one hair to thy dread purposes, or make one feature odious. It is not that the hand is heavy and will fall down when released; it is not that the heart and pulse are still; but that the hand was open, generous, and true; the heart brave, warm, and tender; and the pulse a man's. Strike, Shadow, strike. And see his good deeds springing from the wound, to sow the world with life immortal!

'No voice pronounced these words in my ears, and yet I heard them when I looked upon the bed. I thought, if this man could be raised up now, what would be his foremost thoughts. Avarice, hard-dealing, griping cares. They have brought this man to a rich end, truly.

'He lay, in the dark empty house, with not a man, a woman, or a child, to say that he was kind to me in this or that, and for the memory of one kind word I will be kind to him. A cat was tearing at the door, and there was a sound of gnawing rats beneath the hearth-stone. What they wanted in the room of death, and why they were so restless and disturbed, I did not dare to think.

' "Spirit," I said, "this is a fearful place. In leaving it, I shall not leave its lesson, trust me. Let us go."

'Still the Ghost pointed with an unmoved finger to the head.

' "I understand you," I returned, "and I would do it, if I could. But I have not the power, Spirit. I have not the power."

'Again it seemed to look upon me.

' "If there is any person in the town, who feels emotion caused by this man's death," I said quite agonised, "show that person to me, Spirit, I beseech you."

'The Phantom spread its dark robe before me for a moment, like a wing; and withdrawing it, revealed a room by daylight, where a mother and her children were.

'She was expecting some one, and with anxious eagerness; for she walked up and down the room; started at every sound; looked out from the window; glanced at the clock; tried, but in vain, to work with her needle; and could hardly bear the voices of the children in their play.

'At length the long-expected knock was heard. She hurried to the door, and met her husband; a man whose face was careworn and de-pressed, though he was young. There was a remarkable expression in it now; a kind of serious delight of which he felt ashamed, and which he struggled to repress.

'He sat down to the dinner that had been boarding for him by the fire; and when she asked him faintly what news (which was not until after a long silence), he appeared embarrassed how to answer.

' "Is it good." she said, "or bad?" -- to help him.

' "Bad," he answered.

' "We are quite ruined."

' "No. There is hope yet, Caroline."

' "If he relents," she said, amazed, "there is. Nothing is past hope, if such a miracle has happened."

' "He is past relenting," said her husband. "He is dead."

'She was a mild and patient creature if her face spoke truth; but she was thankful in her soul to hear it, and she said so, with clasped hands. She prayed forgiveness the next moment, and was sorry; but the first was the emotion of her heart.

' "What the half-drunken woman whom I told you of last night, said to me, when I tried to see him and obtain a week's delay; and what I thought was a mere excuse to avoid me; turns out to have been quite true. He was not only very ill, but dying, then."

' "To whom will our debt be transferred?"

' "I don't know. But before that time we shall be ready with the money; and even though we were not, it would be a bad fortune indeed to find so merciless a creditor in his successor. We may sleep to-night with light hearts, Caroline."

'Yes. Soften it as they would, their hearts were lighter. The children's faces hushed, and clustered round to hear what they so little understood, were brighter; and it was a happier house for this man's death. The only emotion that the Ghost could show me, caused by the event, was one of pleasure.

' "Let me see some tenderness connected with a death," I said; "or that dark chamber, Spirit, which we left just now, will be for ever present to me."

'The Ghost conducted me through several streets familiar to my feet; and as we went along, I looked here and there to find myself, but nowhere was I to be seen. We entered poor Bob Cratchit's house; the dwelling I had visited before; and found the mother and the children seated round the fire.

'Quiet. Very quiet. The noisy little Cratchits were as still as statues in one corner, and sat looking up at Peter, who had a book before him. The mother and her daughters were engaged in sewing. But surely they were very quiet.

' "At the same time came the disciples unto Jesus, saying, Who is the greatest in the kingdom of heaven? And Jesus called a little child unto Him, and set Him in the midst of them, And said, Verily I say unto you, Except ye be converted, and become as little children, ye shall not enter into the kingdom of heaven. Whosoever therefore shall humble Himself as this little child, the same is greatest in the kingdom of heaven. And whoso shall receive one such little child in my name receiveth me. But whoso shall offend one of these little ones which believe in me, it were better for him that a millstone were hanged about his neck, and that he were drowned in the depth of the sea."

'Where had I heard those words? I had not dreamed them. The boy must have read them out, as the Spirit and I crossed the threshold. Why did he not go on?

'The mother laid her work upon the table, and put her hand up to her face.

' "The colour hurts my eyes," she said.

'The colour? Ah, poor Tiny Tim.

' "They're better now again," said Cratchit's wife. "It makes them weak by candle-light; and I wouldn't show weak eyes to your father when he comes home, for the world. It must be near his time."

' "Past it rather," Peter answered, shutting up his book. "But I think he's walked a little slower than he used, these few last evenings, mother."

'They were very quiet again. At last she said, and in a steady, cheerful voice, that only faltered once:

' "I have known him walk with -- I have known him walk with Tiny Tim upon his shoulder, very fast indeed."

' "And so have I," cried Peter. "Often."

' "And so have I," exclaimed another. So had all.

' "But he was very light to carry," she resumed, intent upon her work, "and his father loved him so, that it was no trouble -- no trouble. And there is your father at the door!"

'She hurried out to meet him; and little Bob in his comforter -- he had need of it, poor fellow -- came in. His tea was ready for him on the hob, and they all tried who should help him to it most. Then the two young Cratchits got upon his knees and laid, each child a little cheek, against his face, as if they said, "Don't mind it, father.

Don't be grieved."

'Bob was very cheerful with them, and spoke pleasantly to all the family. He looked at the work upon the table, and praised the industry and speed of Mrs. Cratchit and the girls. They would be done long before Sunday, he said.

' "Sunday. You went to-day, then, Robert?" said his wife.

' "Yes, my dear," returned Bob. "I wish you could have gone. It would have done you good to see how green a place it is. But you'll see it often. I promised him that I would walk there on a Sunday. My little, little child!" cried Bob. "My little child!"

Silent night, holy night!
All is calm, all is bright.
'Round yon Virgin Mother and Child
Holy Infant, so tender and mild.
Sleep in heavenly peace!
Sleep in heavenly peace!–

'He broke down all at once. He couldn't help it. If he could have helped it, he and his child would have been farther apart perhaps than they were.

'He left the room, and went up-stairs into the room above, which was lighted cheerfully, and hung with Christmas. There was a chair set close beside the child, and there were signs of some one having been there, lately. Poor Bob sat down in it, and when he had thought a little and composed himself, he kissed the little face. He was reconciled to what had happened, and went down again quite happy.

'They drew about the fire, and talked; the girls and mother working still. Bob told them of the extraordinary kindness of Mr. Scrooge's nephew, whom he had scarcely seen but once, and who, meeting him in the street that day, and seeing that he looked a little -- "just a little down you know," said Bob, inquired what had happened to distress him. "On which," said Bob, "for he is the pleasantest-spoken gentleman you ever heard, I told him. 'I am heartily sorry for it, Mr. Cratchit,' he said, 'and heartily sorry for your good wife.' By the bye, how he ever knew that, I don't know."

' "Knew what, my dear?"

' "Why, that you were a good wife," replied Bob.

' "Everybody knows that," said Peter.

' "Very well observed, my boy!" cried Bob. "I hope they do. 'Heartily sorry,' he said, 'for your good wife. If I can be of service to you in any way,' he said, giving me his card, 'that's where I live. Pray come to me.' Now, it wasn't," cried Bob," for the sake of anything he might be able to do for us, so much as for his kind way, that this was quite delightful. It really seemed as if he had known our Tiny Tim, and felt with us."

' "I'm sure he's a good soul," said Mrs. Cratchit.

' "You would be surer of it, my dear," returned Bob, "if you saw and spoke to him. I shouldn't be at all surprised mark what I say, if he got Peter a better situation."

' "Only hear that, Peter," said Mrs. Cratchit.

' "And then," cried one of the girls, "Peter will be keeping company with some one, and setting up for himself."

' "Get along with you!" retorted Peter, grinning.

' "It's just as likely as not," said Bob, "one of these days; though there's plenty of time for that, my dear. But however and when ever we part from one another, I am sure we shall none of us forget poor Tiny Tim -- shall we -- or this first parting that there was among us."

' "Never, father!" cried they all.

' "And I know," said Bob, "I know, my dears, that when we recollect how patient and how mild he was; although he was a little, little child; we shall not quarrel easily among ourselves, and forget poor Tiny Tim in doing it."

' "No, never, father!" they all cried again.

' "I am very happy," said little Bob, "I am very happy!"

'Mrs. Cratchit kissed him, his daughters kissed him, the two young Cratchits kissed him, and Peter and himself shook hands. Spirit of Tiny Tim, thy childish essence was from God.

' "Spectre," I said, "something informs me that our parting moment is at hand. I know it, but I know not how. Tell me what man that was whom we saw lying dead."

'The Ghost of Christmas Yet To Come conveyed me, as before -- though at a different time, I thought: indeed, there seemed no order in these latter visions, save that we were in the Future -- into the resorts of business men, but showed me not myself. Indeed, the Spirit did not stay for anything, but went straight on, as to the end just now desired, until besought by me to tarry for a moment.

' "This courts," I said, "through which we hurry now, is where my place of occupation is, and has been for a length of time. I see the house. Let me behold what I shall be, in days to come."

'The Spirit stopped; the hand was pointed elsewhere.

' "The house is yonder," I exclaimed. "Why do you point away?"

'The inexorable finger underwent no change.

'I hastened to the window of my office, and looked in. It was an office still, but not mine. The furniture was not the same, and the figure in the chair was not myself. The Phantom pointed as before.

'I joined it once again, and wondering why and whither we had gone, accompanied it until we reached an iron gate. I paused to look round before entering.

'A churchyard. Here, then, the wretched man whose name I was now to learn, lay underneath the ground. It was a worthy place. Walled in by houses; overrun by grass and weeds, the growth of vegetation's death, not life; choked up with too much burying; fat with repleted appetite. A worthy place!

'The Spirit stood among the graves, and pointed down to One. I advanced towards it trembling. The Phantom was exactly as it had been, but I dreaded that I saw new meaning in its solemn shape.

' "Before I draw nearer to that stone to which you point," I said, "answer me one question. Are these the shadows of the things that Will be, or are they shadows of things that May be, only?"

'Still the Ghost pointed downward to the grave by which it stood.

' "Men's courses will foreshadow certain ends, to which, if persevered in, they must lead," I said. "But if the courses be departed from, the ends will change. Say it is thus with what you show me."

'The Spirit was immovable as ever.

'I crept towards it, trembling as I went; and following the finger, read upon the stone of the neglected grave my own name, EBENEZER SCROOGE.

' "Am I that man who lay upon the bed?" I cried, upon my knees.

'The finger pointed from the grave to me, and back again.

' "No, Spirit! Oh no, no!"

'The finger still was there.

' "Spirit!" I cried, tight clutching at its robe, "hear me. I am not the man I was. I will not be the man I must have been but for this intercourse. Why show me this, if I am past all hope?"

'For the first time the hand appeared to shake.

' "Good Spirit," I pursued, as down upon the ground I fell before it: "Your nature intercedes for me, and pities me. Assure me that I yet may change these shadows you have shown me, by an altered life."

'The kind hand trembled.

' "I will honour Christmas in my heart, and try to keep it all the year. I will live in the Past, the Present, and the Future. The Spirits of all Three shall strive within me. I will not shut out the lessons that they teach. Oh, tell me I may sponge away the writing on this stone!"

'In my agony, I caught the spectral hand. It sought to free itself, but I was strong in my entreaty, and detained it. The Spirit, stronger yet, repulsed me.

'Holding up my hands in a last prayer to have my fate reversed, I saw an alteration in the Phantom's hood and dress. It shrunk, collapsed, and dwindled down into a bedpost.'

Stave V
"Coda - The Spirit of Christmas Cheer"

'Yes! and the bedpost was my own. The bed was my own, the room was my own. Best and happiest of all, the Time before me was my own, to make amends in!

' "I will live in the Past, the Present, and the Future!" I repeated, as I scrambled out of bed. "The Spirits of all Three shall strive within me. Oh Jacob Marley! Little Fan and Father! Heaven, and the Christmas Time be praised for this. I say it on my knees, old Jacob, on my knees!"

'I was so fluttered and so glowing with my good intentions, that my broken voice would scarcely answer to my call. I had been sobbing violently in my conflict with the Spirit, and my face was wet with tears.

' "They are not torn down!" I cried, folding one of my bed-curtains in my arms, "they are not torn down, rings and all. They are here -- I am here -- the shadows of the things that would have been, may be dispelled. They will be! I know they will."

'My hands were busy with my garments all this time; turning them inside out, putting them on upside down, tearing them, mislaying them, making them parties to every kind of extravagance.

' "I don't know what to do!" I cried, laughing and crying in the same breath; and making a perfect Laocoön of myself with my stockings. "I am as light as a feather, I am as happy as an angel, I am as merry as a schoolboy. I am as giddy as a drunken man. A merry Christmas to everybody! A happy New Year to all the world! Hallo here! Whoop! Hallo!"

'I had frisked into the sitting-room, and was now standing there: perfectly winded.

' "There's the saucepan that the gruel was in!" I cried, starting off again, and frisking round the fireplace. "There's the door, by which the Ghost of Jacob Marley entered. There's the corner where the Ghost of Christmas Present, sat. There's the window where I saw the wandering Spirits. It's all right, it's all true, it all happened. Ha ha ha!"

'Really, for a man who had been out of practice for so many years, it was a splendid laugh, a most illustrious laugh. The father of a long, long line of brilliant laughs.

' "I don't know what day of the month it is," I said. "I don't know how long I've been among the Spirits. I don't know anything. I'm quite a baby. Never mind. I don't care. I'd rather be a baby. Hallo! Whoop! Hallo here!"

'I was checked in my transports by the churches ringing out the lustiest peals I had ever heard. Clash, clang, hammer; ding, dong, bell! Bell, dong, ding; hammer, clang, clash! Oh, glorious, glorious!

'Running to the window, I opened it, and put out my head. No fog, no mist; clear, bright, jovial, stirring, cold; cold, piping for the blood to dance to; Golden sunlight; Heavenly sky; sweet fresh air; merry bells. Oh, glorious. Glorious!

' "What's to-day?" I cried, calling downward to a boy in Sunday clothes, who perhaps had loitered in to look about him.

' "Eh?" returned the boy, with all his might of wonder.

' "What's to-day, my fine fellow?" I said.

' "To-day?" replied the boy. "Why, Christmas Day."

' "It's Christmas Day!" I said to myself. "I haven't missed it. The Spirits have done it all in one night. They can do anything they like. Of course they can. Of course they can. Hallo, my fine fellow!"

' "Hallo!" returned the boy.

‘ "Do you know the Poulterer's, in the next street but one, at the corner?" I inquired.

‘ "I should hope I did," replied the lad.

‘ "An intelligent boy!" I said. "A remarkable boy! Do you know whether they"ve sold the prize Turkey that was hanging up there -- Not the little prize Turkey: the big one?"

‘ "What, the one as big as me?" returned the boy.

‘ "What a delightful boy!" I said. It's a pleasure to talk to him. "Yes, my buck."

‘ "It's hanging there now," replied the boy.

‘ "Is it?" I said. "Go and buy it."

‘ "Walk-er!" exclaimed the boy.

‘ "No, no," I said, "I am in earnest. Go and buy it, and tell them to bring it here, that I may give them the direction where to take it. Come back with the man, and I'll give you a shilling. Come back with him in less than five minutes and I'll give you half-a-crown."

‘The boy was off like a shot. He must have had a steady hand at a trigger who could have got a shot off half so fast.

‘ "I'll send it to Bob Cratchit's!" I whispered, rubbing my hands, and splitting with a laugh. "He shan't know who sends it. It's twice the size of Tiny Tim. Joe Miller never made such a joke as sending it to Bob's will be!"

‘The hand in which I wrote the address was not a steady one, but write it I did, somehow, and went down-stairs to open the street door, ready for the coming of the poulterer's man. As I stood there, waiting his arrival, the knocker caught my eye.

‘ "I shall love it, as long as I live!" I cried, patting it with my hand. "I scarcely ever looked at it before. What an honest expression it has in its face. It's a wonderful knocker. -- Here's the Turkey. Hallo! Whoop! How are you? Merry Christmas!"

‘It was a Turkey! He never could have stood upon his legs, that bird. He would have snapped them short off in a minute, like sticks of sealing-wax.

‘ "Why, it's impossible to carry that to Camden Town," I said. "You must have a cab."

‘The chuckle with which I said this, and the chuckle with which I paid for the Turkey, and the chuckle with which I paid for the cab, and the chuckle with which I recompensed the boy, were only to be exceeded by the chuckle with which I sat down breathless in my chair again, and chuckled till I cried.

'Shaving was not an easy task, for my hand continued to shake very much; and shaving requires attention, even when you don't dance while you are at it. But if I had cut the end of my nose off, I would have put a piece of sticking-plaister over it, and been quite satisfied.

'I dressed myself all in my best, and at last got out into the streets. The people were by this time pouring forth, as I had seen them with the Ghost of Christmas Present; and walking with my hands behind me, I regarded every one with a delighted smile. I looked so irresistibly pleasant, in a word, that three or four good-humoured fellows said, "Good morning, sir. A merry Christmas to you." And I said often afterwards, that of all the blithe sounds I had ever heard, those were the blithest in my ears.

'I had not gone far, when coming on towards me I beheld the portly gentleman, who had walked into my counting-house the day before, and said, "Scrooge and Marley's, I believe." It sent a pang across my heart to think how this old gentleman would look upon me when we met; but I knew what path lay straight before him, and I took it.

' "My dear sir," I said, quickening my pace, and taking the old gentleman by both my hands. "How do you do. I hope you succeeded yesterday. It was very kind of you. A merry Christmas to you, sir!"

' "Mr. Scrooge?"

' "Yes," I said. "That is my name, and I fear it may not be pleasant to you. Allow me to ask your pardon. And will you have the goodness" -- here I whispered in his ear.

' "Lord bless me!" cried the gentleman, as if his breath were taken away. "My dear Mr. Scrooge, are you serious?"

' "If you please," I said. "Not a farthing less. A great many back-payments are included in it, I assure you. Will you do me that favour?"

' "My dear sir," said the other, shaking hands with me. "I don't know what to say to such munificence."

' "Don't say anything please," I retorted. "Come and see me. Will you come and see me?"

' "I will!" cried the old gentleman. And it was clear he meant to do it.

' "Thank you," I said. "I am much obliged to you. I thank you fifty times. Bless you!"

'And a choir of young paupers, including the two whom were threatened with a ruler across their backsides, sang on the corner of a street, the street having been packed with both days-old and new-fallen snow, the snow having fallen from the low-hanging, heavy-laden clouds, the clouds obscuring the bright light of the Blessed Star, a Blessed Star that still could direct the journey of Ebenezer Scrooge to the poor homes, to the aged, the sick, and the infant poor.

HARK! the Herald Angels sing
Glory to the new-born King!
Peace on Earth, and Mercy mild,
God and Sinners reconcil'd.

Joyful all ye Nations rise,
Join the Triumphs of the Skies;
Nature rise and worship him,
Who is born at Bethlehem.

Christ by highest Heav'n ador'd,
Christ the everlasting Lord;
Late in Time behold-him come,
Offspring of the Virgin's Womb.

Veil'd in Flesh the Godhead see,
Hail th' incarnate Deity!
Pleas'd as Man with Men t'appear,
Jesus our Emmanuel here.

Hail the Heav'n-born Prince of Peace
Hail the Son of Righteousness!
Light and Life around he brings,
Ris'n with Healing in his Wings.

Mild he lays his Glory by,
Born that Men no more may die;
Born to raise the Sons of Earth,
Born to give them second Birth.

Come, Desire of Nations, come,
Fix in us thy heav'nly Home;
Rise the Woman's conqu'ring Seed,
Bruise in us the Serpent's Head.

Adam's Likeness now efface,
Stamp thy Image in its Place;
Second Adam from above,
Work it in us by thy Love.

'I plunked down, quite loudly to the dismay of my newfound humility, several coins into the young man's bent tin cup. "Half a crown for a song, gov'na!" I said, patting the children on the head. I then tipped my hat and to their astonishment, I clicked my heels. And the children of Cornhill town were amazed at the transformation of the squeezing, wrenching, grasping, scraping, clutching, covetous, old sinner (they feared the very sight of) into a sliding, carolling, snow-flinging, generous new saint.

'The Scrooge greeted each and every passersby on the street with a "Merry Christmas" on my lips, singing like a boiling pudding in the copper; my heart was a speckled cannon-ball, so hard and firm, blazing in half of half-a-quartern of ignited brandy, and bedight with Christmas holly stuck into the top, made, no doubt, this Christmas morning with the correct quantity of flour.

'I was delighted when I observed the people who were shovelling away on the housetops jovial and full of glee; calling out to one another from the parapets, and now and then exchanging a facetious snowball -- better-natured missile far than many a wordy jest -- laughing heartily if it went right and not less heartily if it went wrong. The second Spirit's vision was truly more than a dream. The journey I had taken the night before was real, I squealed. Where was the Spirit? Why could I no longer see that jovial face. Oh! There was the

Spirit for he stood in a baker's doorway and the ghostly shade of my ever so slightly younger former self stood beside him. I ran up upon the shade, whom was still in his dressing gown and slippers, and his nightcap, and it was a mercy I didn't shake his arm off. I (as strange and wondrous as this may read) wished myself a "Merry Christmas, Mr. Scrooge, how are you? You are going forth on compulsion, and you did, in fact, learn a lesson which has worked and continues to work! Bear them company, my good man, and do it with a thankful heart. The night you walk is waning fast, and it is precious time to us. You must and will honour Christmas in your heart, and try to keep it all the year. We will live in the Past, the Present, and the Future. The Spirits of all Three shall strive within us. We will not shut out the lessons that they teach!"

'The reality of my senses pulled me from my brief Christmas Daydream. Oh, dear! I exclaimed disappearing into the common throng, pelting down the lane. There were the poulterers' shops still half open, I pointed, and the fruiterers' were radiant in their glory. There were the great, round, pot-bellied baskets of chestnuts, shaped like the waistcoats of jolly old gentlemen, lolling at the doors, and tumbling out into the street in their apoplectic opulence. There were the ruddy, brown-faced, broad-girthed Spanish Friars, and winking from their shelves in wanton slyness at the girls as they went by, and glanced demurely at the hung-up mistletoe. There were the pears and apples, clustered high in blooming pyramids; There were the bunches of grapes, made, in the shopkeepers' benevolence to dangle from conspicuous hooks, that people's mouths might water gratis as they passed; There were the piles of filberts, mossy and brown, recalling, in their fragrance, ancient walks among the woods, and pleasant shufflings ankle deep through withered leaves; There were the Norfolk Biffins, squab and swarthy, setting off the yellow of the oranges and lemons, and, in the great compactness of their juicy persons, urgently entreating and beseeching to be carried home in paper bags and eaten after dinner. The very gold and silver fish, set forth among these choice fruits in a bowl, though members of a dull and stagnant-blooded race, appeared to know that there was something going on; and, to a fish, went gasping round and round their little world in slow and passionless excitement.

'The Grocers'! oh the Grocers'! I giggled, as merry as a schoolboy. Nearly closed, with perhaps two shutters down, or one; but through those gaps such glimpses. It was not alone that the scales descending on the counter made a merry sound, or that the twine and roller parted company so briskly, or that the canisters were rattled up and down like juggling tricks, or even that the blended scents of tea and coffee were so grateful to the nose, or even that the raisins were so plentiful and rare, the almonds so extremely white, the sticks of cinnamon so long and straight, the other spices so delicious, the candied fruits so caked and spotted with molten sugar as to make the coldest lookers-on feel faint and subsequently bilious. Nor was it that the figs were moist and pulpy, or that the French plums blushed in modest tartness from their highly-decorated boxes, or that everything was good to eat and in its Christmas dress; but the customers were all so hurried and so eager in the hopeful promise of the day, that they tumbled up against each other at the door, clashing their wicker baskets wildly, and left their purchases upon the counter, and came running back to fetch them, and committed hundreds of the like mistakes, in the best humour possible; while the Grocer and his people were so frank and fresh that the polished hearts with which they fastened their aprons behind might have been their own, worn outside for general inspection, and for Christmas daws to peck at if they chose.

'And soon the steeples called good people all, to church and chapel, and away they came, flocking through the streets in their best clothes, and with their gayest faces. I was led not only the ringing of the steeples, but by that Blessed Star, shining through the bright, grey Christmas sky to church, any good old church of which I had passed by each and every day with my nose buried in my collar. So nervous was this old sinner that I forgot to take off my silk hat. I gleefully emptied my purse into the collection plate with nary any hesitation. Would good come of the money, I wondered, like buying the Poor meat and drink and means of warmth? Bah! of course, good would come of it! It would be a Humbug to think otherwise. Charity is their business! I stood not in the avaricious halls of the 'Change, but in a charitable House of God! But as a plate was being passed from parishioner to parishioner, I saw a poor widow put in a mere tuppence. Such a small sum of money, I blushed to think. Then the Word of

Jesus Christ the Saviour whispered to my soul, "Verily I say unto you, That this poor widow hath cast more in, than all they which have cast into the treasury: For all they did cast in of their abundance; but she of her want did cast in all that she had, even all her living." The rebuke saddened and yet enlightened me all in the same moment. What a queer paradox this was, wasn't it? If a soul desires the world to see their generosity, then this charity is vainglory and is the same as greed. Woe unto me, I thought, if I seek to tithe mint and anise and cummin, and omit the weightier matters of the law, judgment, mercy, and faith. Where were these thoughts coming from?

'And although I knew not the words to any hymn sung that Christmas day, my heart still sang louder than all of the rest,

O come, all ye faithful, joyful and triumphant!
O come ye, O come ye to Bethlehem;
Come and behold him
Born the King of Angels:
O come, let us adore Him,
  O come, let us adore Him,
    O come, let us adore Him,
Christ the Lord.

God of God, light of light,
Lo, he abhors not the Virgin's womb;
Very God, begotten, not created:
O come, let us adore Him,
  O come, let us adore Him,
    O come, let us adore Him,
Christ the Lord.

Sing, choirs of angels, sing in exultation,
Sing, all ye citizens of Heaven above!
Glory to God, glory in the highest:
O come, let us adore Him,
  O come, let us adore Him,
    O come, let us adore Him,
Christ the Lord.

Yea, Lord, we greet thee, born this happy morning;
Jesus, to thee be glory given!
Word of the Father, now in flesh appearing!
O come, let us adore Him,
  O come, let us adore Him,
    O come, let us adore Him,
Christ the Lord.

'And at the same time I walked out of the church, there emerged from scores of bye-streets, lanes, and nameless turnings, innumerable people, carrying their dinners to the bakers' shops. I upon seeing the sight of these poor revellers that briefly saw the Spirit sprinkle incense on their dinners from his torch. For once or twice when there were angry words between some dinner-carriers who had jostled each other, the Spirit shed a few drops of water on them from it, and their good humour was restored directly, I knew it was said, it was a shame to quarrel upon Christmas Day. And so it was. God love it, so it was.

'And I questioned the beggars. I now knew, I told them, what was said of Jesus the Christ our Lord and Saviour: that the blind received their sight, and the lame could walk, the lepers are cleansed, and the deaf could hear, the dead were raised up, and the poor had the gospel preached to them. But what could a mere man do in the sight of such suffering? A beggar pulled a tattered poem in printed calico from his equally tattered pocket. Inspired by the Spirit of Christmas Cheer, he sang extemporaneous to me,

Pity the sorrows of a poor old man!
Whose trembling limbs have borne him to your door,
Whose days are dwindled to the shortest span,
O, give relief, and Heaven will bless your store.

These tattered clothes my poverty bespeak,
These hoary locks proclaim my lengthened years;
And many a furrow in my grief-worn cheek
Has been the channel to a stream of tears.

Yon house, erected on the rising ground,

With tempting aspect drew me from my road,
For plenty there a residence has found,
And grandeur a magnificent abode.

(Hard is the fate of the infirm and poor!)
Here craving for a morsel of their bread,
A pampered menial drove me from the door,
To seek a shelter in the humble shed.

O, take me to your hospitable dome,
Keen blows the wind, and piercing is the cold!
Short is my passage to the friendly tomb,
For I am poor and miserably old.

Should I reveal the source of every grief,
If soft humanity e'er touched your breast,
Your hands would not withhold the kind relief,
And tears of pity could not be repressed.

Heaven sends misfortunes,—why should we repine?
'T is Heaven has brought me to the state you see:
And your condition may be soon like mine,
The child of sorrow and of misery.

A little farm was my paternal lot,
Then, like the lark, I sprightly hailed the morn;
But ah! oppression forced me from my cot;
My cattle died, and blighted was my corn.

My daughter,—once the comfort of my age!
Lured by a villain from her native home,
Is cast, abandoned, on the world's wild stage,
And doomed in scanty poverty to roam.

My tender wife,—sweet soother of my care!—
Struck with sad anguish at the stern decree,
Fell,—lingering fell, a victim to despair,

And left the world to wretchedness and me.

Pity the sorrows of a poor old man!
Whose trembling limbs have born him to your door,
Whose days are dwindled to the shortest span,
O, give relief, and Heaven will bless your store.

'In time the bells ceased, and the bakers were shut up; and yet there was a genial shadowing forth of all these dinners and the progress of their cooking, in the thawed blotch of wet above each baker's oven; where the pavement smoked as if its stones were cooking too.

'In the afternoon, I turned my steps towards my nephew's house. I passed the door a dozen times, before I had the courage to go up and knock. But I made a dash, and did it:

' "Is your master at home, my dear?" I said her. Nice girl. Very.

' "Yes, sir."

' "Where is he, my love?" I said.

' "He's in the dining-room, sir, along with mistress. I'll show you up-stairs, if you please."

' "Thank you. He knows me," I said, with my hand already on the dining-room lock. "I'll go in here, my dear."

'I turned it gently, and sidled my face in, round the door. They were looking at the table (which was spread out in great array); for these young housekeepers are always nervous on such points, and like to see that everything is right.

' "Fred!" I said.

'Dear heart alive, how my niece-by-marriage started. I had forgotten, for the moment, about her sitting in the corner with the footstool, or I wouldn't have done it, on any account.

' "Why bless my soul!" cried Fred," who's that?"

' "It's I. Your uncle Scrooge. I have come to dinner. Will you let me in, Fred?"

' "Let you in? Let you in?" Fred said and it was a mercy he didn't shake my arm off. "Let you in! My wife."

' "My dear, I hope you'll forgive a stubborn old man," I apologized.

' "Her sister."

' "Miss," I said, tipping my hat.

' "Our mutual friend, Topper."

' "I'd watch this one, Miss. That I'll warrant," said I playfully elbowing my niece's sister.

' "And last but certainly not least. Mother!"

'Fan came hurrying in, with an apron all covered in flour.

' "What is it, Fred, darling. The pudding is not yet ready," said Little Fan, howbeit not so little -- quite elderly in fact.

' "Fan. My little Little Fan. Alive?"

' "Ebby? Home at last? Home at last!"

Then the Spirit of Christmas Cheer entered her large heart,

I prayed to the Christmas Spirits Three.
"Listen to this child," I yearned, I cried.
They visit'd my Father that Christmas Eve,
Without their help his love would've died.

Father had forgotten what is of the Past.
Father was blind to what shall be,
"Please haunt my father," I prayed that night,
They haunted him on that Christmas Eve.

Aah-aah-aah-aah-aah-aah-aah-aah (sang a choir of angels)
They visit'd our Father in that time of Yule,
Aah-aah-aah-aah-aah-aah-aah (sang the choir)
And brought my brother home from school.

Father was so much kinder than he used to be,
Afeared not to ask if I could fetch Brother,
And if, to the hospital in the morning
Could the Scrooges visit his wife, our Mother.

But Ebbie soon forgot who his family was,
Ebbie was deaf to the cries of love.
Ebbie now visits us on this Christmas Eve,
I thank the Spirits up above.'

And I then regaled them all, my Little Fan, my nephew, Fred, all of the guests at their Christmas dinner with this very Ghostly little story, to raise the Ghost of an Idea first raised by my Father during his annual recitations of his own Ghostly journey with Spirit. I had hoped I would not put my listeners out of humour with themselves, with each other, with the season, or with me. I hoped it may haunt their houses pleasantly, and no one wish to lay in it.

My little Little Fan clapped her hands at the telling of the story and laughed, and tried to touch my head; but being too short, laughed again, and stood on tiptoe to embrace me as if we hadn't in thirty years. And we hadn't.

And Topper then took centre stage for himself as blocked by the Spirit of Christmas Cheer, and he sang,

God bless you merry, gentleman,
May nothing you dismay,
Uncle Scrooge comes to dine
With us, on this Christmas Day.
A tight-fisted hand at the Grindstone
Who'd once been led astray.
  O tidings of comfort and joy,
  Comfort and joy
  O tidings of comfort and joy

From God our Heavenly Father
Three blessed Spirits came,
Brought tidings of the Good News
Of Christmas Day that we proclaim!
How that in Bethlehem was born
A man who cured the blind and lame.
  O tidings of comfort and joy,
  Comfort and joy
  O tidings of comfort and joy

God bless you merry, gentleman,
Your presence is enough,
Ebenezer, please join with us,
In a game of Blindman's Bluff.

Perhaps we'll play at Yes or No,
Or maybe Forfeits, if you're tough.
  O tidings of comfort and joy,
  Comfort and joy
  O tidings of comfort and joy

God bless you merry, Gentleman—

But I was early at the office next morning. Oh I was early there. If I could only be there first, and catch Bob Cratchit coming late! That was the thing I had set my heart upon.

And I did it; yes, I did. The clock struck nine. No Bob. A quarter past. No Bob. He was full eighteen minutes and a half behind his time. I sat with my door wide open, that I might see him come into the Tank.

His hat was off, before he opened the door; his comforter too. He was on his stool in a jiffy; driving away with his pen, as if he were trying to overtake nine o'clock.

'Hallo,' I growled, in my accustomed voice, as near as I could feign it. 'What do you mean by coming here at this time of day?'

'I'm very sorry, sir,' said Bob. 'I am behind my time.'

'You are?' I repeated. 'Yes. I think you are. Step this way, if you please.' The chuckle started deep within my bowels, rumbling upwards, a laugh I desperately wanted to stifle.

'It's only once a year, sir,' pleaded Bob, appearing from the Tank. 'It shall not be repeated. I was making rather merry yesterday, sir.'

'Now, I'll tell you what, my friend,' I said, 'I am not going to stand this sort of thing any longer. And therefore,' I continued, leaping from my stool, and giving Bob such a dig in the waistcoat that he staggered back into the Tank again; 'and therefore I am about to raise your salary.' The laughter that escaped my lips was infectious, there is truly nothing in the world so irresistibly contagious as laughter and good-humoured.

'Bob trembled, and got a little nearer to the ruler. He had a momentary idea of knocking me down with it, holding me, and calling to the people in the court for help and a strait-waistcot.

'A merry Christmas, Bob,' I chuckled, with an earnestness that could not be mistaken, as I clapped him on the back. Then I laughed in the manner of my dear nephew: holding my sides, rolling my head, and twisting my face into the most extravagant contortions: 'A merrier Christmas, Bob, my good fellow, than I have given you for many a year. I'll raise your salary, and endeavour to assist your struggling family, and we will discuss your affairs this very afternoon, over a Christmas bowl of smoking bishop, Bob. Make up the fires, and buy another coal-scuttle before you dot another i, Bob Cratchit!'

And the Spirit of Christmas Cheer would enter into me while visiting the Cratchit's poor four-roomed house and a song appeared from the dark depths of my bowels and sang, but I did not know the words, so poor Tiny Tim sang in duet, helping me remember the words (Lord bless the child) across the gulf of a lifetime to my own childhood,

> *God rest you merry, gentlemen,*
> *Let nothing you dismay,*
> *For Jesus Christ our Saviour*
> *Was born upon this day,*
> *To save us all from Satan's power*
>   *When I was gone astray:*
>   *O tidings of comfort and joy,*
>   *Comfort and joy*
>   *O tidings of comfort and joy*

And the children of Cornhill town, they too sang,

> *From God Our– well we'll be pickled.*
> *The Scrooge is singing, what a sight!*
> *Hallo, there Mista Scrooge, gov'ner,*
> *Care to join in a snowball fight?*
> *Hallo, Halle, watch out there me lads*
> *Mista Scrooge's snowball's in flight!'*

And my little Little Fan would entertain her friends in person and in letters and in this, her very own collection of Ghostly little tales of the Hauntings of her father and her brother. In this, here epilogue she writes, 'Our father, due to the intercession with Spirits, walked freely among his fellowmen, and travelled far and wide, a spirit that went forth in life, being at peace having shared on earth and turned to happiness. He was so much kinder than he used to be, that home was like Heaven! He had spoken so gently to me after his journey with Spirits, when I was waking up that blessed Christmas morning, that I was not afraid to ask him once more if Ebenezer might come home so that we could visit Mother in the hospital; and he said Yes, he should; and sent me in a coach to bring him. And he was to be a man and are never to come back here; but first, we were all, Mother, Father, Sister, Brother, to be together all the Christmas long, and have the merriest time in all the world.

'My dear sweet brother was better than his word. He did it all, and infinitely more; and to Tiny Tim, who did not die, he was a second father. He became as good a friend, as good a master, and as good a man, as the good old city knew, or any other good old city, town, or borough, in the good old world. Some people laughed to see the alteration in him, but he let them laugh, and little heeded them; for he was wise enough to know that nothing ever happened on this globe, for good, at which some people did not have their fill of laughter in the outset; and knowing that such as these would be blind anyway, he thought it quite as well that they should wrinkle up their eyes in grins, as have the malady in less attractive forms. His own heart laughed: and that was quite enough for him.

'He had no further intercourse with Spirits, but lived upon the Total Abstinence Principle, ever afterwards; and it was always said of him, that he knew how to keep Christmas well, if any man alive possessed the knowledge. May that be truly said of us, and all of us! And so, as Tiny Tim observed, "God bless Us, Every One!"'

Source Materials:

A Christmas Carol by Charles Dickens

The Holy Bible - King James Authorized Translation

Annals by Tacitus, translated by Alfred John Church & William Jackson Brodribb

Exposition of the Old and New Testaments by Matthew Henry

Poor Laws Commissioners' Report of 1834 by Nassau William Senior

First Annual Report of the Poor Law Commissioners for England and Wales

"A Curious Dance Round a Curious Tree" by Charles Dickens

"Sunday Under Three Heads" by Charles Dickens

Christmas Carols:

"Good King Wenceslas" by John Mason Neale

"The First Noel", a traditional English carol

"Here We Come A-wassailing", a traditional English carol

"Joy to the World" by Isaac Watts

"Adeste Fideles" by John Francis Wade

"The Gloria" a traditional Christian hymn

"O Come O Come Emmanuel" by John Mason Neale

"The Coventry Carol", a traditional English carol

"God Rest You Merry, Gentleman", a traditional English carol

"The Boar's Head Carol", first published by Wynkyn de Worde

"We Wish You a Merry Christmas", a traditional West Country carol

"Silent Night" by Franz Xaver Gruber

"Hark! The Herald Angels Sing" by Charles Wesley

"O Come, All Ye Faithful", English translation by Frederick Oakeley

"The Beggar's Petition", a poem by Thomas Moss.

Additional Materials:

The Sacred Wood: Essays On Poetry and Criticism by T. S. Eliot,

"What does a conductor actually do?" by Clemency Burton-Hill, BBC. com

—**Note on using *A Christmas Carol*:** Many authors have taken *A Christmas Carol* and used it as the source for their own novels, plays, and motion pictures, this is a tradition with a long and storied history. How many cartoons or sitcoms have had *A Christmas Carol*-style episode for Christmas? As early as 1917, Dale Powell wrote a sequel *Timothy Cractchit's Christmas Carol* with Tiny Tim as a wealthy, elderly immigrant living in America, requiring the intercession of the Spirits. And in 2017, *The Afterlife of Holly*

Chase, by Cynthia Hand, is young adult modern re-imagining of *A Christmas Carol* about an unrepentant teenager forced to become a Ghost of Christmas Past. *The Man Who Invented Christmas* motion picture weaves *A Christmas Carol* into the own very writing of *A Christmas Carol*. So, I had no intention of writing a prequel novel starring Jeremiah Scrooge. Jeremiah's haunting requires Ebenezer's own haunting to fully tell the story. The story conceived by Charles Dickens was going to be completed by myself. This meant weaving my story of Jeremiah into *A Christmas Carol*, while also weaving the entire text of the source material completely and repeatedly and irrevocably in and out of the Jeremiah storyline, creating an entirely new tapestry. If I tried to pull the thread of Jeremiah's plot out of the tapestry to be its own prequel, the entire story would unravel.

—**Note on using the Holy Bible:** To too many Christians and non-Christians, *A Christmas Carol* is a quaint little secular story that happens to take place during the Christmas season. Charles Dickens wrote of *A Christmas Carol*, "My purpose was, in a whimsical kind of masque, which the good humour of the season justified, to awaken some loving and forbearing thoughts, never out of season in a Christian land." My own desire was to sprinkle as much scripture into the story as possible, seasoning the novel with the spice of the Word of God. While Dickens also layered the ingredients of the Holy Bible into *A Christmas Carol*, not enough Christians, and certainly too few secularists, have caught the surprisingly subtle scriptural sources. It is time to finally celebrate the Christ in *A Christmas Carol*.

—**Note on using Matthew Henry Commentary:** Ezekiel Scrooge has two soliloquies that are drawn from the commentaries on the Bible by Matthew Henry. Henry, a Nonconformist minister, along with Charles Spurgeon, a Particular Baptist preacher, and John Wesley, an Anglican cleric, helped define English Protestant thought in the 18th and 19th centuries. I put Henry's esteemed words on the lips of Ezekiel to give his voice a respected and revered quality of sound theology.

—**Note on using the Commissions' Report:** Every adaptation of *A Christmas Carol* tries to define Scrooge's business. Does his business concern loans, mortgages, property management? Charles Dickens never specifies. I had located, thanks to the wondrous Internet, a resolution by magistrates of Speenhamland, Berkshire, that helped institute a wide-ranging Poor Law that led to the creation of "Scrooge & Marley" business in my own adaptation. In order to counter the implementation of the Speenhamland system, Jeremiah needed a rebuttal to the petition before the House of Commons. I found his rebuttal in the *Poor Laws Commissioner's Report of 1834* that amended and criticized the Speenhamland system. Though the scene between Jeremiah Scrooge and Charles Dundas takes place in 1795, I put the words of the Commissioner's Report on the lips of Jeremiah, assuming that Dickens, writing in 1843, could have had access to said report.

—Note on using Charles Dickens' short stories: For the description of the Bedlam Asylum, I drew from a paragraph in Dickens' "A Curious Dance Round a Curious Tree". And I also quoted his "Sunday Under Three Heads a couple of times, including the description of Parson Scrooge's church service.

—Note on using Christmas Carols: Charles Dickens called his novel on the title-page, *A Christmas Carol* IN PROSE. When Little Fan's single, solitary line struck up a ghost of an idea, I thought of the story as a novel, the very same kind of novel you hold in your hands. But since I was knee deep into theatre at the time, *The Hauntings* was born as a play, and soon grew into a musical. I didn't want my *Haunting* to be a traditional musical, where characters break out into song for "no apparent reason". I wanted my characters to sing Christmas carols, both traditional carols and those adapted from the Dickensian lyrical prose. No film adaptation fails to include a Christmas carol or several in the background, so I wanted to bring Christmas carols to the foreground in what I considered a musical novel.

—Note on "A Squeezing, Wrenching, Grasping, Clutching, Covetous Old Sinner", "A Merry Christmas (God Save You), "In Want of Common Comforts", "Fezziwig's Wassail", and "Cornhill Carol": These Christmas carols are original with me, in as far as they are paraphrases of the beautiful lyrical Dickensian narration found in the original *A Christmas Carol*. In the original conceptualizing of the madrigal dinner, I wanted to turn the poetic turns of phrase made famous by Charles Dickens and immortalize them in Christmas carols. Unlike many musicals, where characters break out into singing at the most seemingly inopportune times, these Christmas carols seemed most appropriate in the context of the scene.

The music for *The Haunting of Jeremiah & Ebenezer Scrooge* was beautifully composed and arranged by Bette Lunn, a long-time music teacher at a local high-school, and the resident musical director at Damon Runyon Repertory Theatre Company. The company finally brought our musical to life during the Christmas season of the year of our Lord, two-thousand-and-fifteen. I was pleased that she was finally able to music-direct her own music, and I was proud to have been cast as the a squeezing, wrenching, grasping, scraping, clutching, covetous, old sinner himself, Ebenezer Scrooge.

—Note on using "Here We Come A-wassailing": While I didn't actually use this Christmas carol, it was the inspiration for "The Wassail Wenches", an original carol in the style of the former. My carol was also inspired by the Seven Joys of the Virgin, a popular devotion dating back to at least the 14th century, as the source of Gawain's strength.

—Note on using "Adeste Fideles" and "O Come, All Ye Faithful": This carol, presented first in Latin, seemed perfect for the single solitary child neglected by his friends. And it is repeated in the church service after Ebenezer's journey with the Spirits and his reclamation, completing a circular story arc where the seed of being a squeezing, wrenching, grasping, scraping, clutching, covetous, old sinner was planted and where he was reborn as good a friend, as good a master, and as good a man, as the good old city knew.

—Note on using "O Come O Come Emmanuel": Charles Dickens made Ebenezer a miser. This was his sin. I needed another sin for Jeremiah, so I chose agnosticism. While this may have been unheard of for a Member of Parliament in the 19th century, he kept his agnosticism quietly in his heart. And when Jeremiah's own father, Ezekiel, entered the story, I knew there needed to be a break between father and son. Making Ezekiel a Parson and his son an agnostic, played like a fiddle. Jeremiah was kicked out of the seminary for questioning Messianic prophesies, just I did during my own rebellious religious teenage-years. I too did not understand why Jesus Christ was named "Jesus" when it violated prophesy, so here the argument is again all these years later and a carol to go with it.

—Note on using "The Gloria": This is less a Christmas carol and more an integral part of the liturgy. When Elizabeth is reciting the nativity story found in Luke 2, the angels recite the first words of this *psalmi idiotici* ("private psalms"). The Gloria is found in the Byzantine and Roman Rites and in the Church of England's *Book of Common Prayer*. It made sense to expand upon the angels words by having Elizabeth sing entire *Gloria in excelsis Deo* in her delirious recitation of the nativity story to her children.

—Note on using "The Coventry Carol" & "The Boar's Head Carol": These carols I first heard while running lights and sound for a Madrigal dinner at a prestigious restaurant. "The Boar's Head Carol" with its pomp and procession made it perfect for Fezziwig's own Christmas Madrigal dinner, while "The Coventry Carol" was so beautiful and heart-wrenching that it had to be sung after Fan had died in child-birth.

—Note on using "God Rest Ye Merry, Gentlemen": I believe this is the only actual Christmas carol actually quoted in *A Christmas Carol*. The young urchin stooping down at Scrooge's keyhole to regale him with a Christmas carol: but at the first sound of --"God bless you, merry gentleman! May nothing you dismay!" Scrooge seized the ruler with such energy of action, that the singer fled in terror. I needed to include the entire song, along with some imploring for alms.

—Note on using "We Wish You a Merry Christmas": While the rest of the Christmas carols are from the 18th and 19th centuries, this is the lone 20th century carol (that could be much, much older, no one knows), but it fit the story of the Cratchit's enjoyment of a Christmas pudding so perfectly, that I had to break my own self-imposed rule to only use material that Charles Dickens would have had access to during his whole lifetime.

—Note on using "Silent Night": This Christmas carol has been translated into many languages around the world. I felt it was the perfect carol for people to sing while Ebenezer is on his journey with the Spirit of Christmas Present. During a performance of *The Hauntings* in the Christmas season of 2015, while the cast was singing "A Silent Night" in many different languages, a lone audience member moved up towards the stage and sang in each and every language as we were. It was the most moving experience in all my years of doing theatre to have moved her so.

—Note on using "The Beggar's Petition": This poem as well known to Charles Dickens. In *Nicholas Nickleby*, while having his ears boxed by the schoolmaster Mr. Squeers, a little boy sobbed, rubbing his face very hard with the "Beggar's Petition" in printed calico. Jane Austin, also, wrote in *Northanger Abbey* that Catherine Morland is taught by her mother to only repeat the "Beggar's Petition". This poem was the only contemporary source I could find for Ebenezer's questioning of beggars, and thankfully it fits too well not to be included.

—Note on using "God Bless Us, Every One": This final original Christmas carol, though both a direct quoting of the first stanza from "God Rest Ye Merry, Gentleman" and a new paraphrase was an instant crowd-pleaser when I and the rest of the cast appeared on stage and Ebenezer Scrooge attempts to sing, with the assistance of Tiny Tim, a classic Christmas Carol.

www.ingramcontent.com/pod-product-compliance
Lightning Source LLC
Chambersburg PA
CBHW031338020726
47499CB00005B/1312